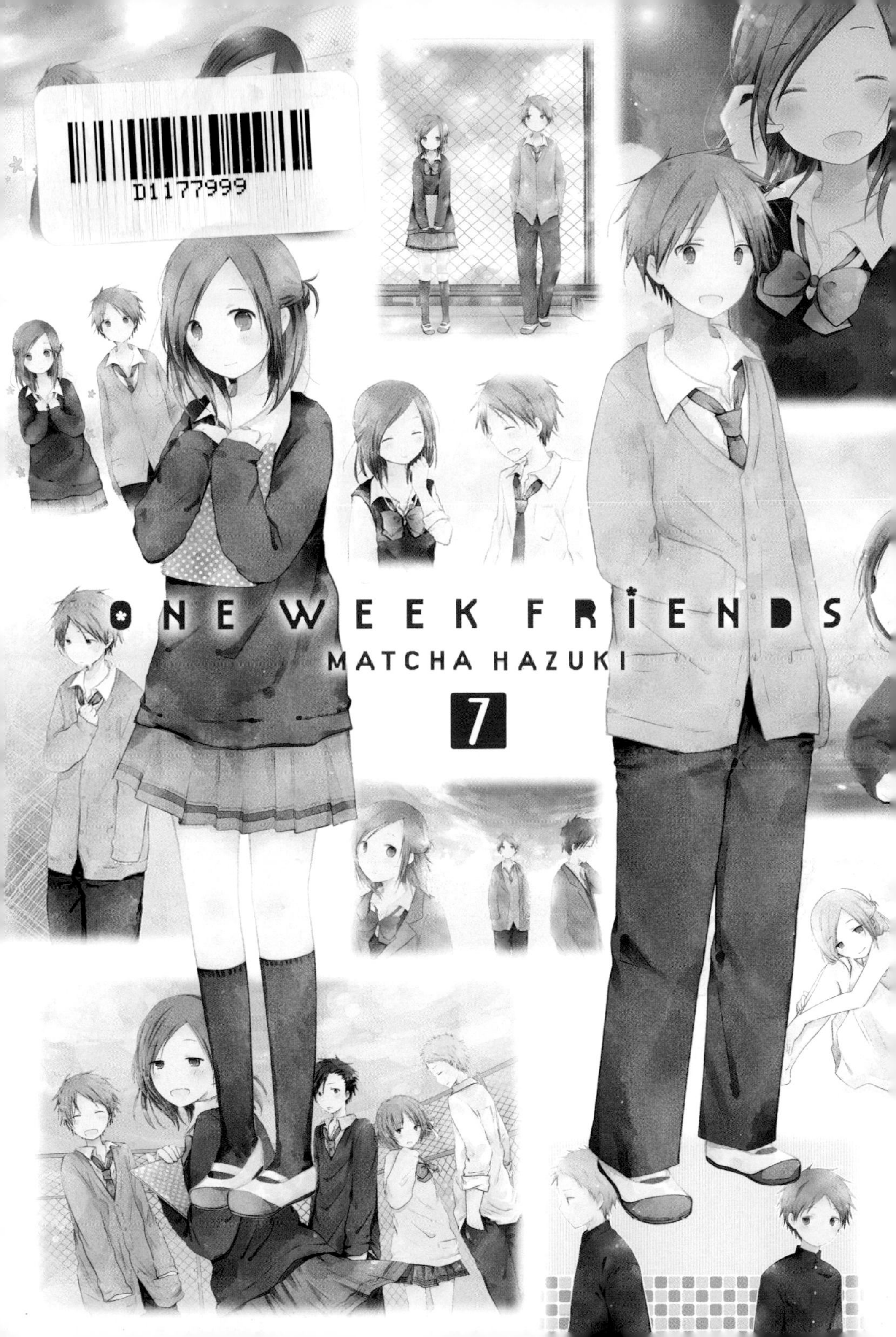

D1177999
ONE WEEK FRIENDS
MATCHA HAZUKI
7

ONE WEEK FRIENDS 7

Contents

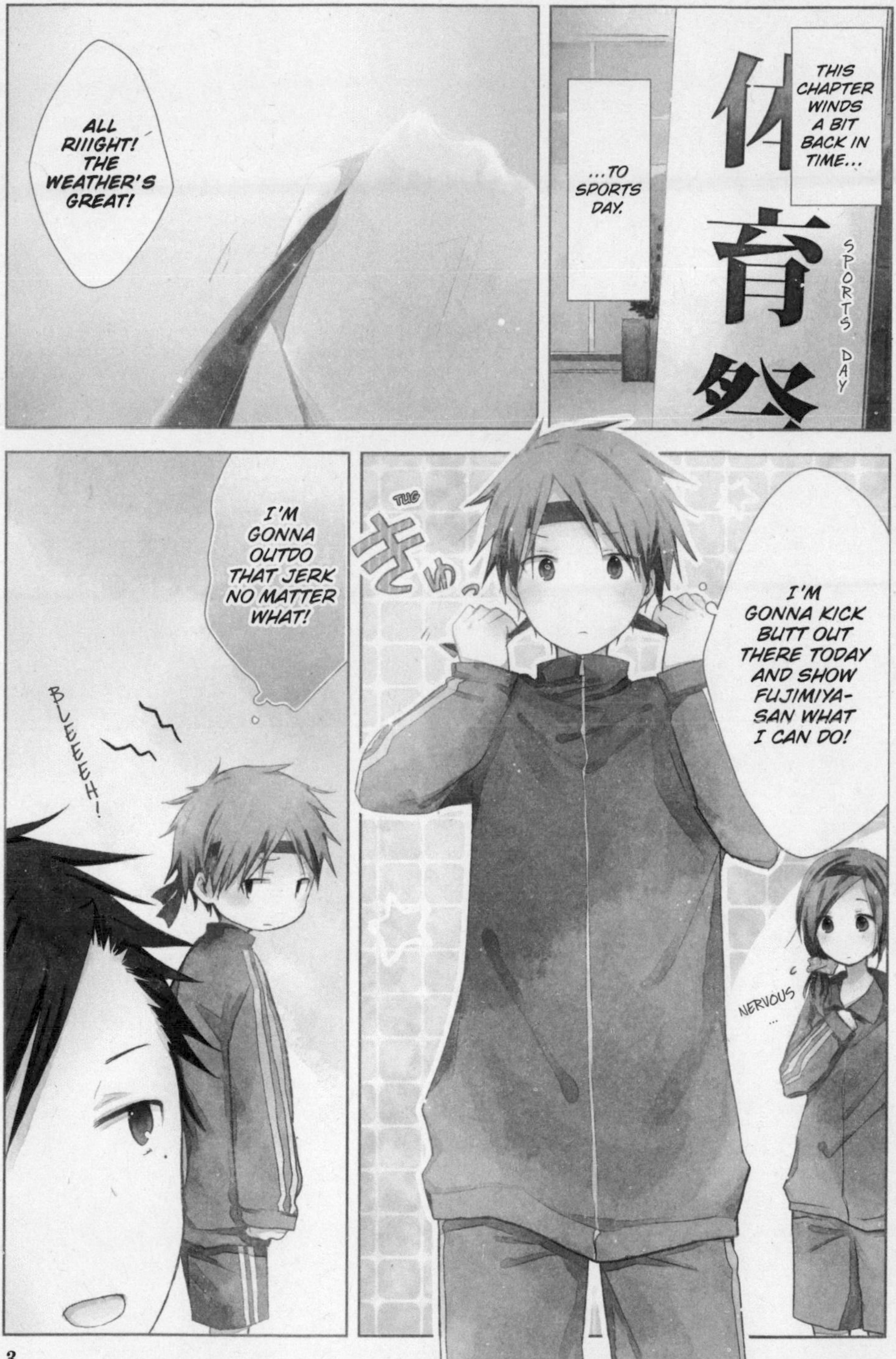
体育祭
SPORTS DAY
THIS CHAPTER WINDS A BIT BACK IN TIME...
...TO SPORTS DAY.
ALL RIIIGHT! THE WEATHER'S GREAT!
I'M GONNA KICK BUTT OUT THERE TODAY AND SHOW FUJIMIYA-SAN WHAT I CAN DO!
TUG
きゅっ
NERVOUS ...
I'M GONNA OUTDO THAT JERK NO MATTER WHAT!
BLEEEH!

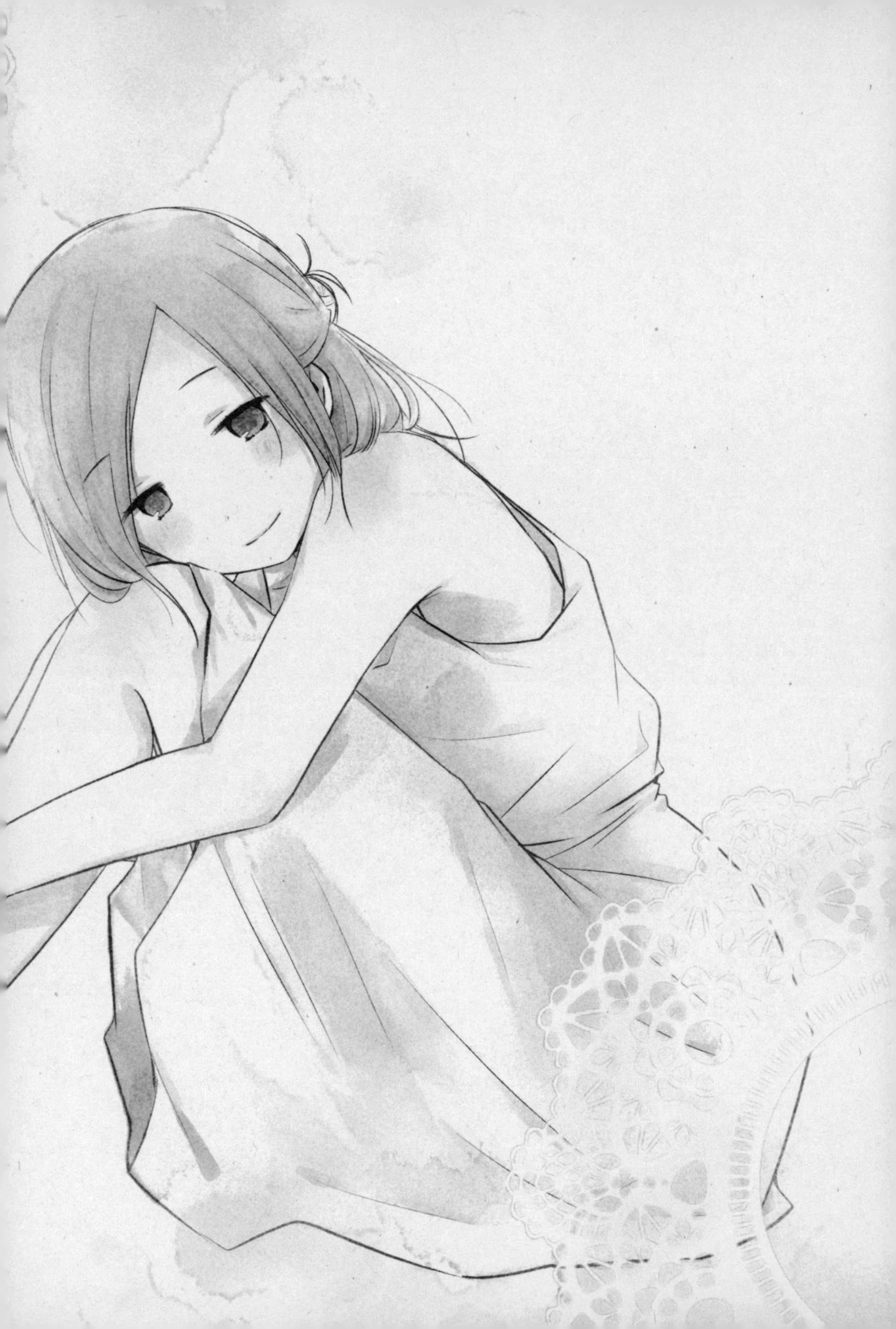

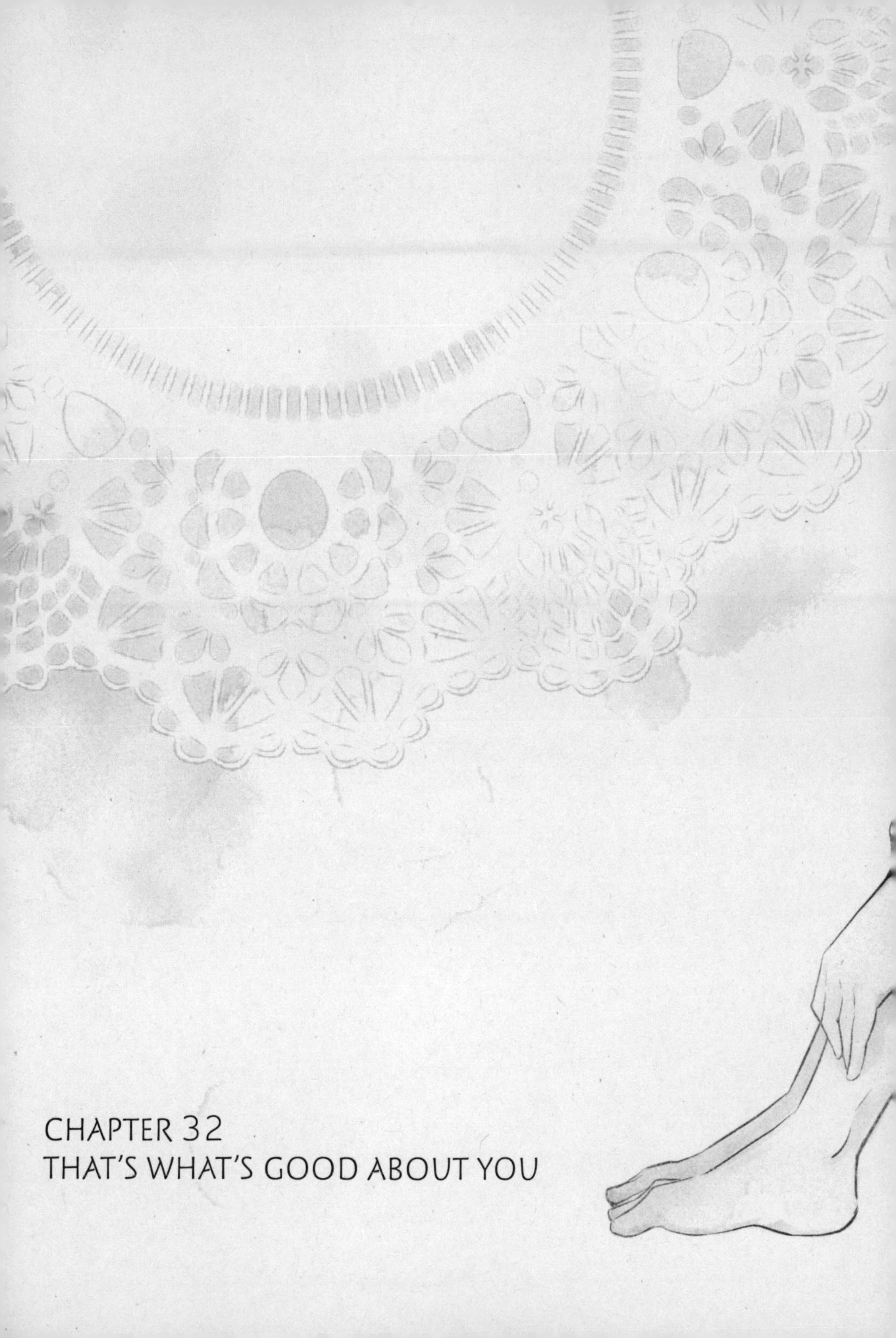

CHAPTER 32
THAT'S WHAT'S GOOD ABOUT YOU

ONE
WEEK
FRIENDS

SPORTS DAY

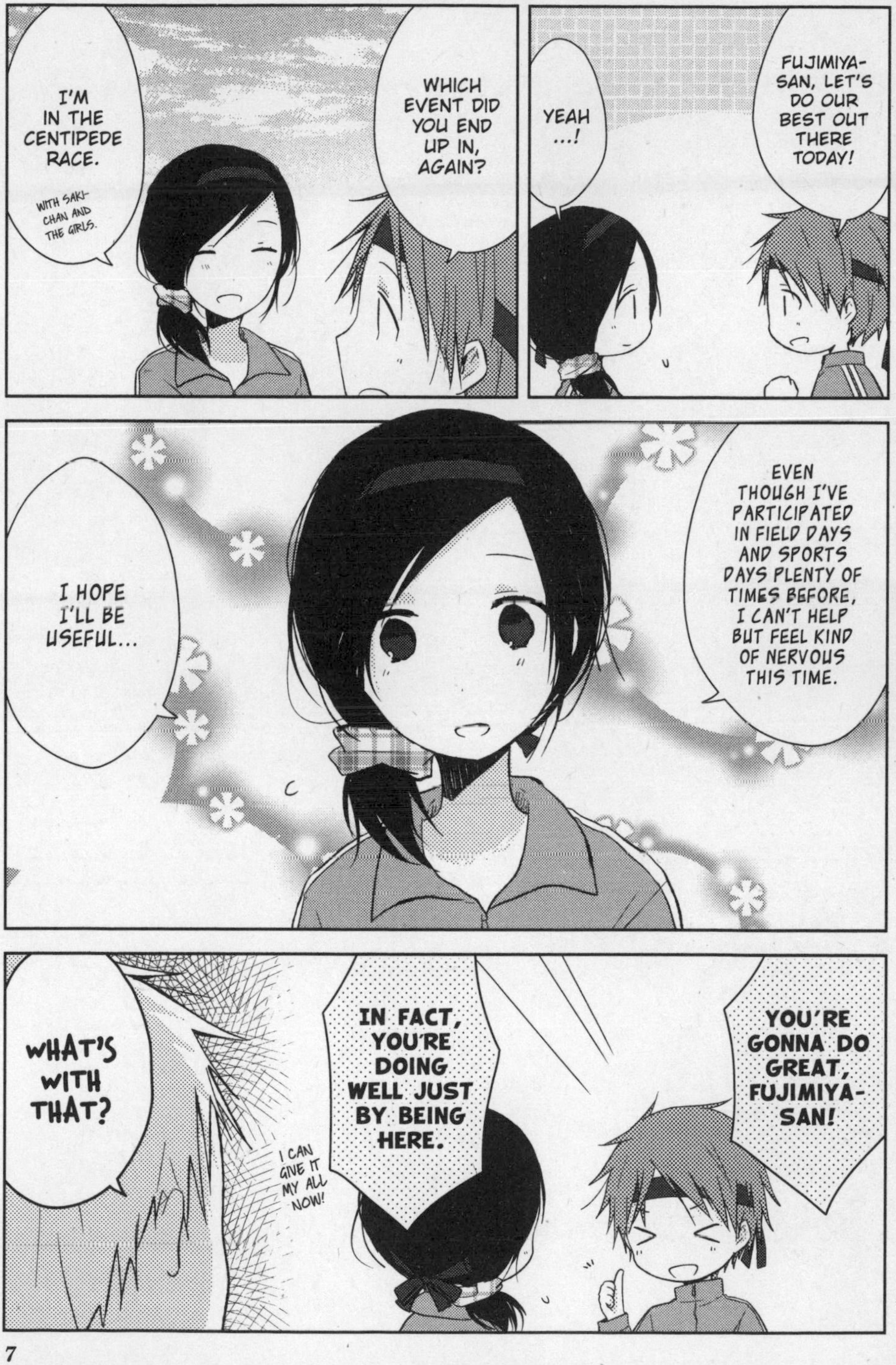
FUJIMIYA-SAN, LET'S DO OUR BEST OUT THERE TODAY!
YEAH ...!
WHICH EVENT DID YOU END UP IN, AGAIN?
I'M IN THE CENTIPEDE RACE.
WITH SAKI-CHAN AND THE GIRLS.
EVEN THOUGH I'VE PARTICIPATED IN FIELD DAYS AND SPORTS DAYS PLENTY OF TIMES BEFORE, I CAN'T HELP BUT FEEL KIND OF NERVOUS THIS TIME.
I HOPE I'LL BE USEFUL...
YOU'RE GONNA DO GREAT, FUJIMIYA-SAN!
IN FACT, YOU'RE DOING WELL JUST BY BEING HERE.
I CAN GIVE IT MY ALL NOW!
WHAT'S WITH THAT?

THE COMPETITION THAT SUITS YOU

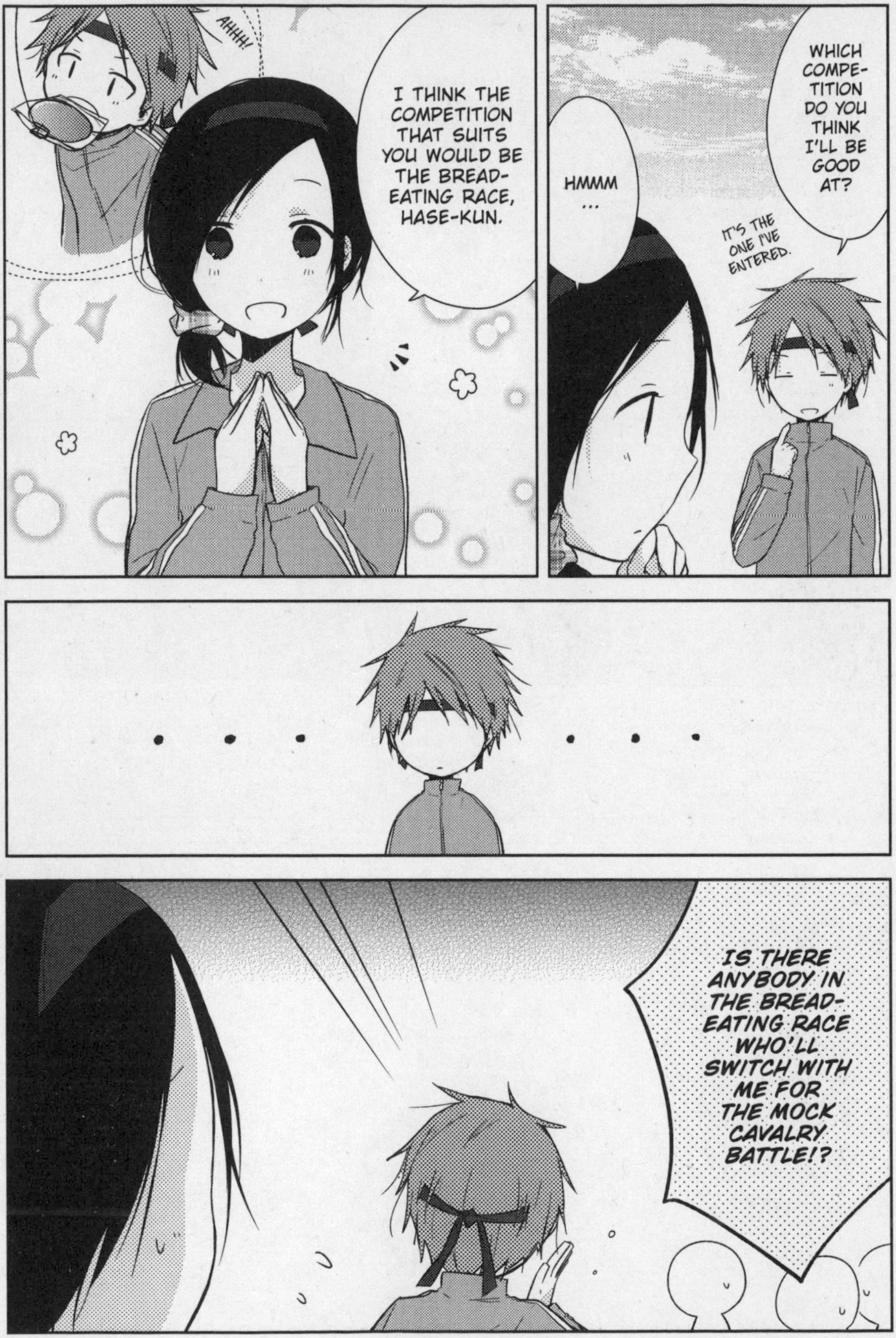
WHICH COMPETITION DO YOU THINK I'LL BE GOOD AT?
IT'S THE ONE I'VE ENTERED.
HMMM ...
I THINK THE COMPETITION THAT SUITS YOU WOULD BE THE BREAD-EATING RACE, HASE-KUN.
AHHH!
. . . . . .
IS THERE ANYBODY IN THE BREAD-EATING RACE WHO'LL SWITCH WITH ME FOR THE MOCK CAVALRY BATTLE!?

MOCK CAVALRY BATTLE

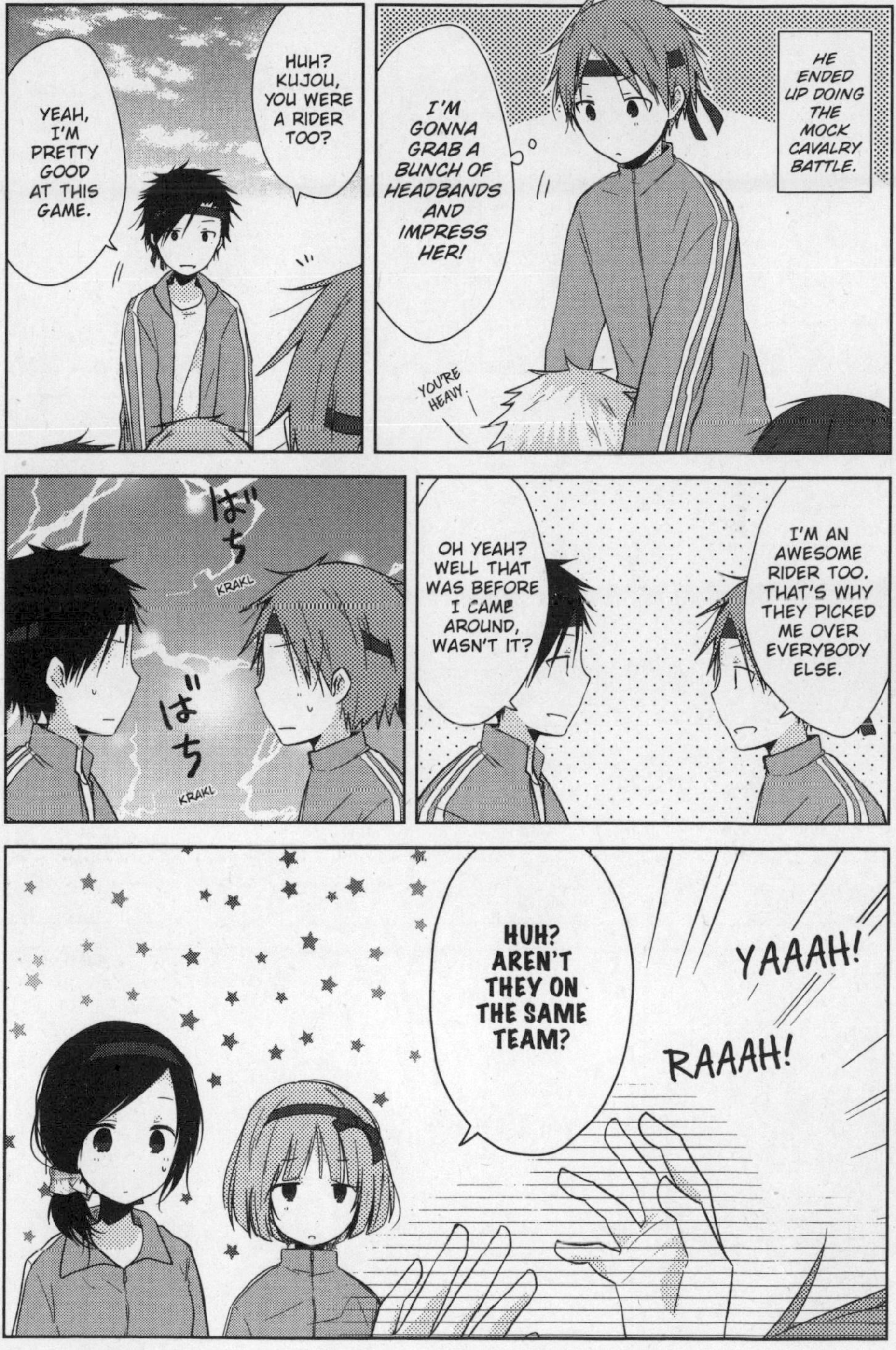
HE ENDED UP DOING THE MOCK CAVALRY BATTLE.
I'M GONNA GRAB A BUNCH OF HEADBANDS AND IMPRESS HER!
YOU'RE HEAVY.
HUH? KUJOU, YOU WERE A RIDER TOO?
YEAH, I'M PRETTY GOOD AT THIS GAME.
I'M AN AWESOME RIDER TOO. THAT'S WHY THEY PICKED ME OVER EVERYBODY ELSE.
OH YEAH? WELL THAT WAS BEFORE I CAME AROUND, WASN'T IT?
ばち
KRAKL
ばち
KRAKL
YAAAH!
RAAAH!
HUH? AREN'T THEY ON THE SAME TEAM?

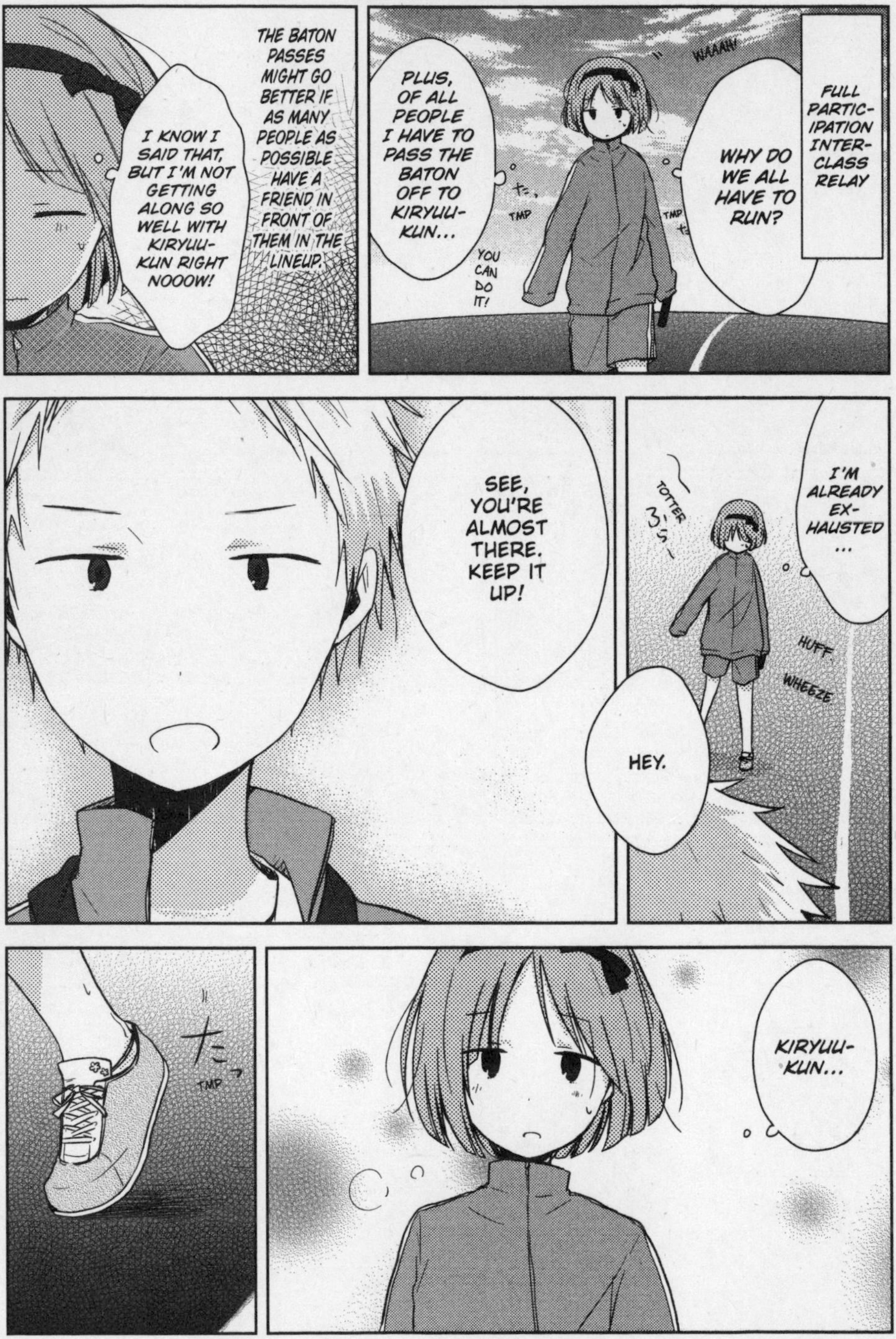
FULL PARTICIPATION INTER-CLASS RELAY
WAAAH
WHY DO WE ALL HAVE TO RUN?
TMP
PLUS, OF ALL PEOPLE I HAVE TO PASS THE BATON OFF TO KIRYUU-KUN...
TMP
YOU CAN DO IT!
THE BATON PASSES MIGHT GO BETTER IF AS MANY PEOPLE AS POSSIBLE HAVE A FRIEND IN FRONT OF THEM IN THE LINEUP.
I KNOW I SAID THAT, BUT I'M NOT GETTING ALONG SO WELL WITH KIRYUU-KUN RIGHT NOOOW!
I'M ALREADY EX-HAUSTED...
TOTTER
HUFF
WHEEZE
HEY.
SEE, YOU'RE ALMOST THERE. KEEP IT UP!
KIRYUU-KUN...
TMP

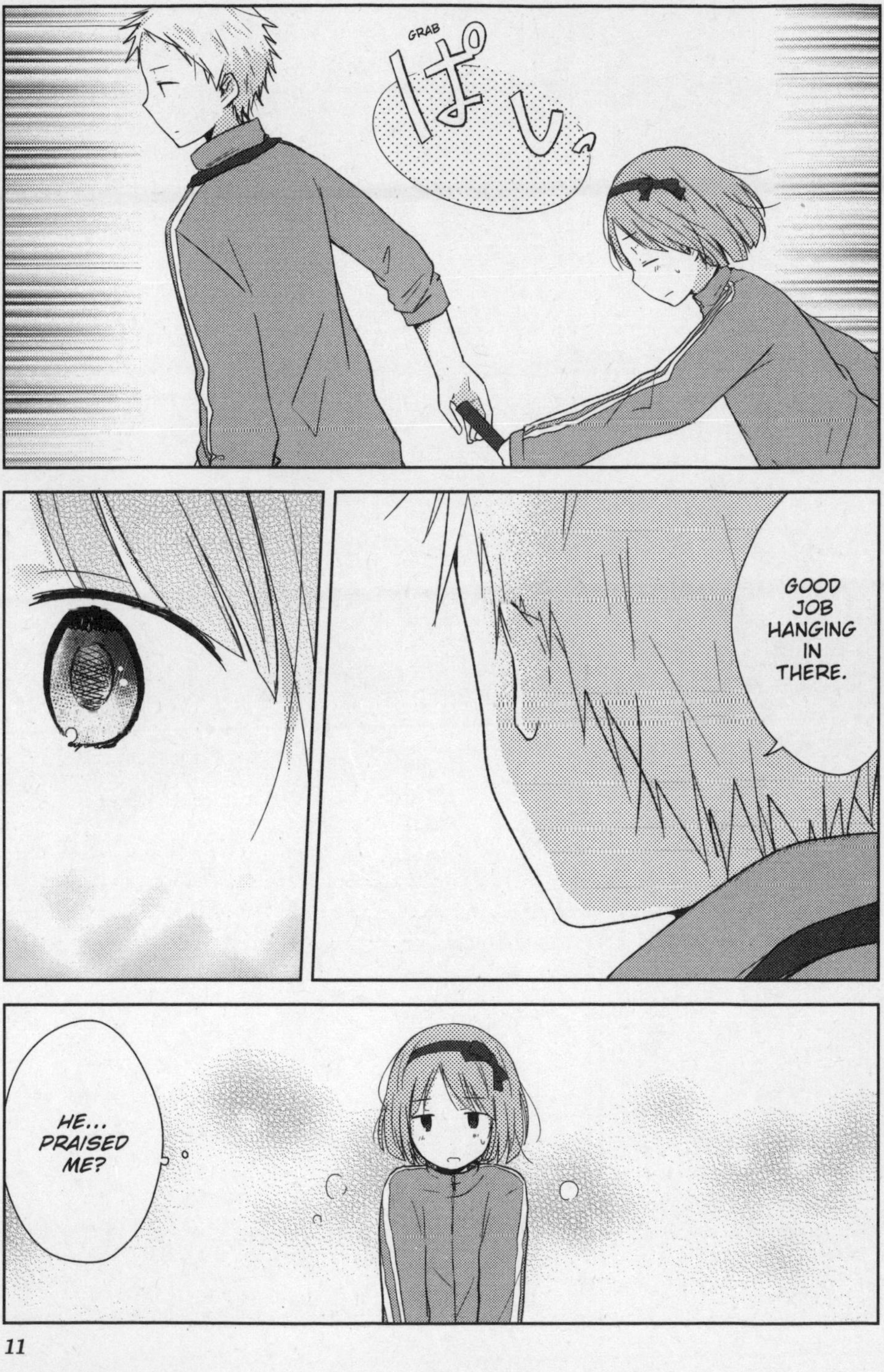
GRAB
ぱし
GOOD JOB HANGING IN THERE.
HE... PRAISED ME?

SHOWING HIS STUFF

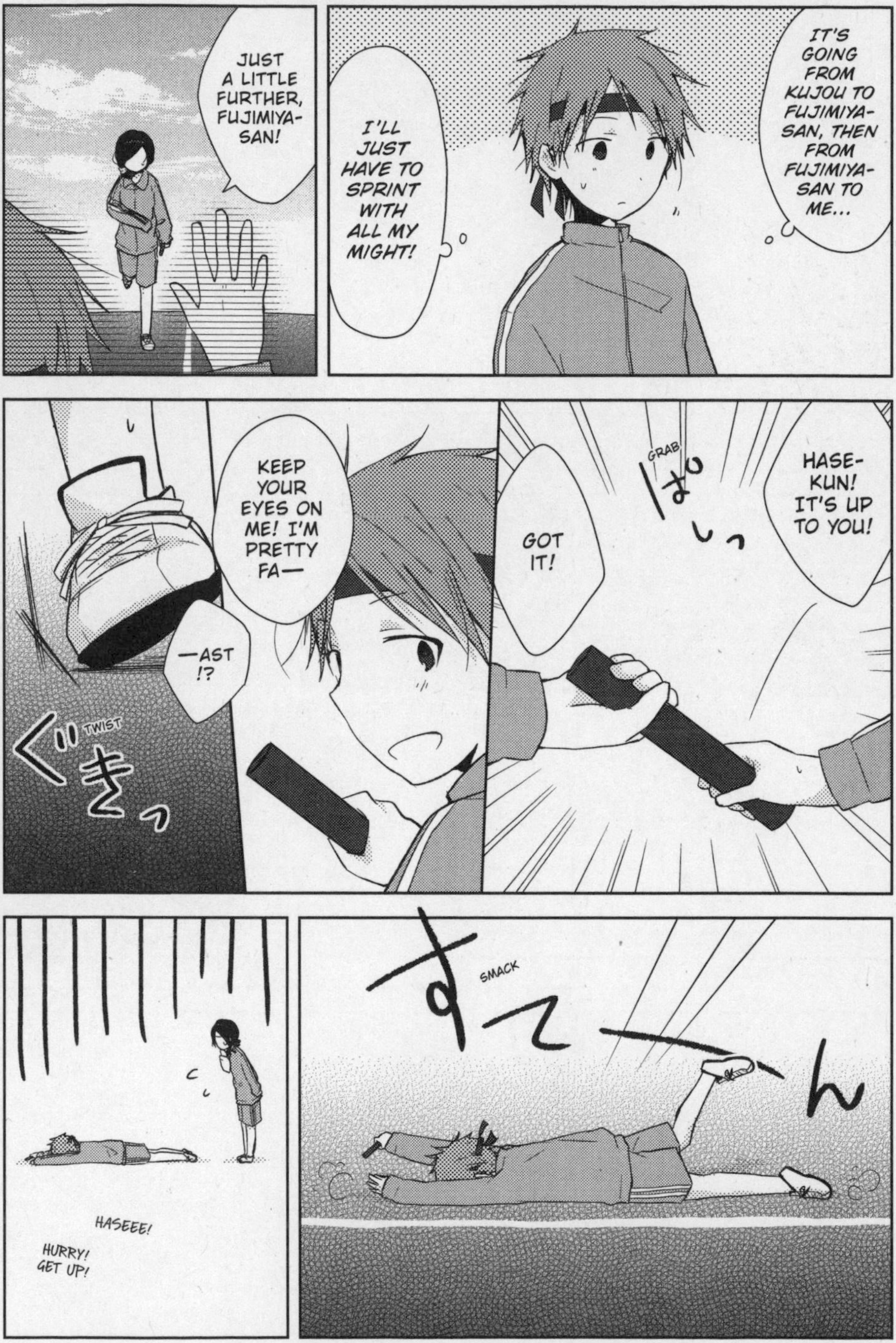
IT'S GOING FROM KUJOU TO FUJIMIYA-SAN, THEN FROM FUJIMIYA-SAN TO ME...
I'LL JUST HAVE TO SPRINT WITH ALL MY MIGHT!
JUST A LITTLE FURTHER, FUJIMIYA-SAN!
HASE-KUN! IT'S UP TO YOU!
GRAB
GOT IT!
KEEP YOUR EYES ON ME! I'M PRETTY FA—
—AST !?
TWIST
SMACK
HASEEE!
HURRY! GET UP!

HASE-KUN!

RATS. I ENDED UP LOOKING JUST AS LAME AS USUAL.

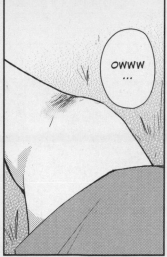

OWWW...

HOW'S YOUR SCRAPE?

AH, OKAY...

IT'S FINE. I WASHED IT WITH WATER A MINUTE AGO.

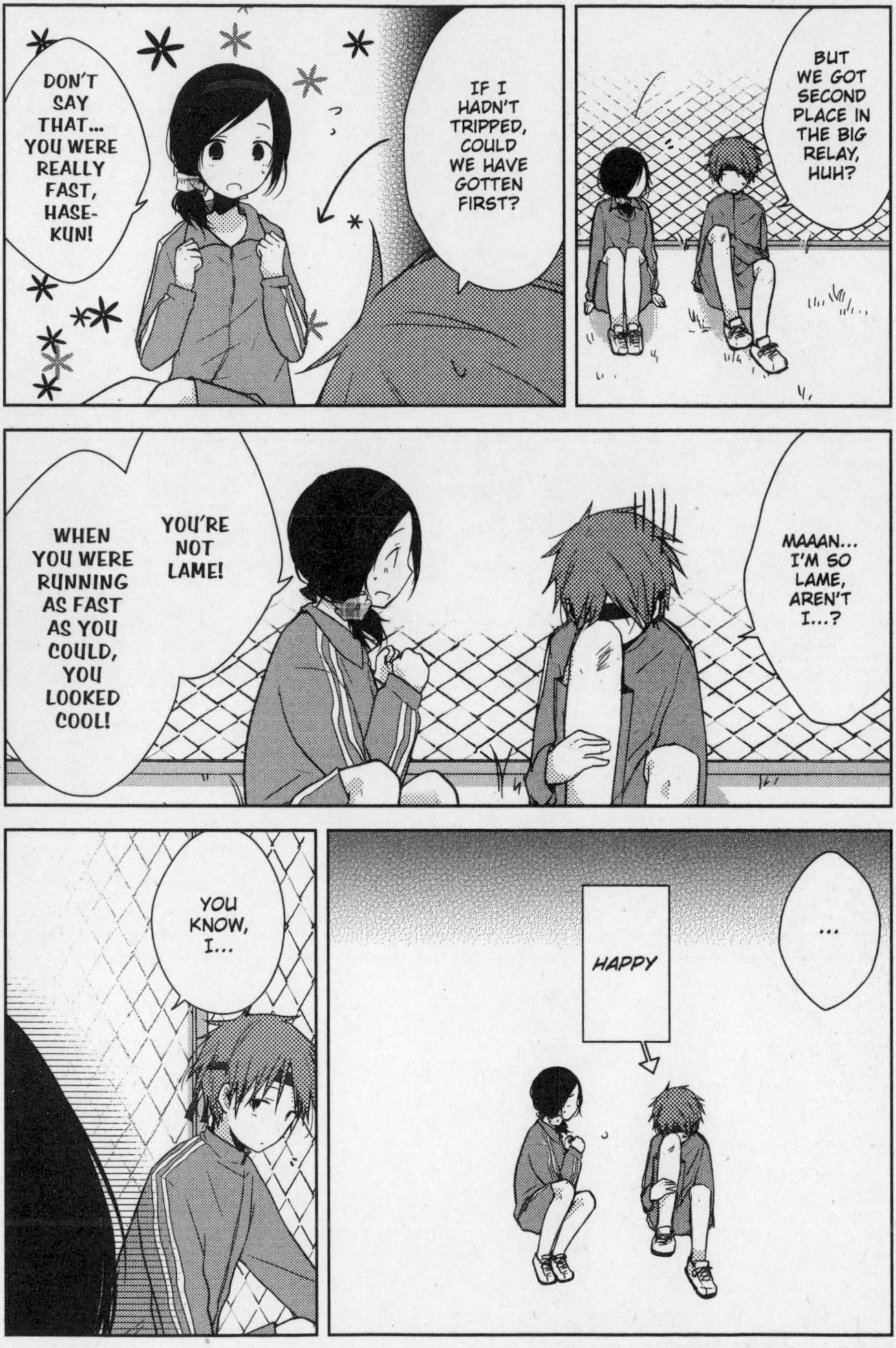
BUT WE GOT SECOND PLACE IN THE BIG RELAY, HUH?
IF I HADN'T TRIPPED, COULD WE HAVE GOTTEN FIRST?
DON'T SAY THAT... YOU WERE REALLY FAST, HASE-KUN!
MAAAN... I'M SO LAME, AREN'T I...?
YOU'RE NOT LAME!
WHEN YOU WERE RUNNING AS FAST AS YOU COULD, YOU LOOKED COOL!
...
HAPPY
YOU KNOW, I...

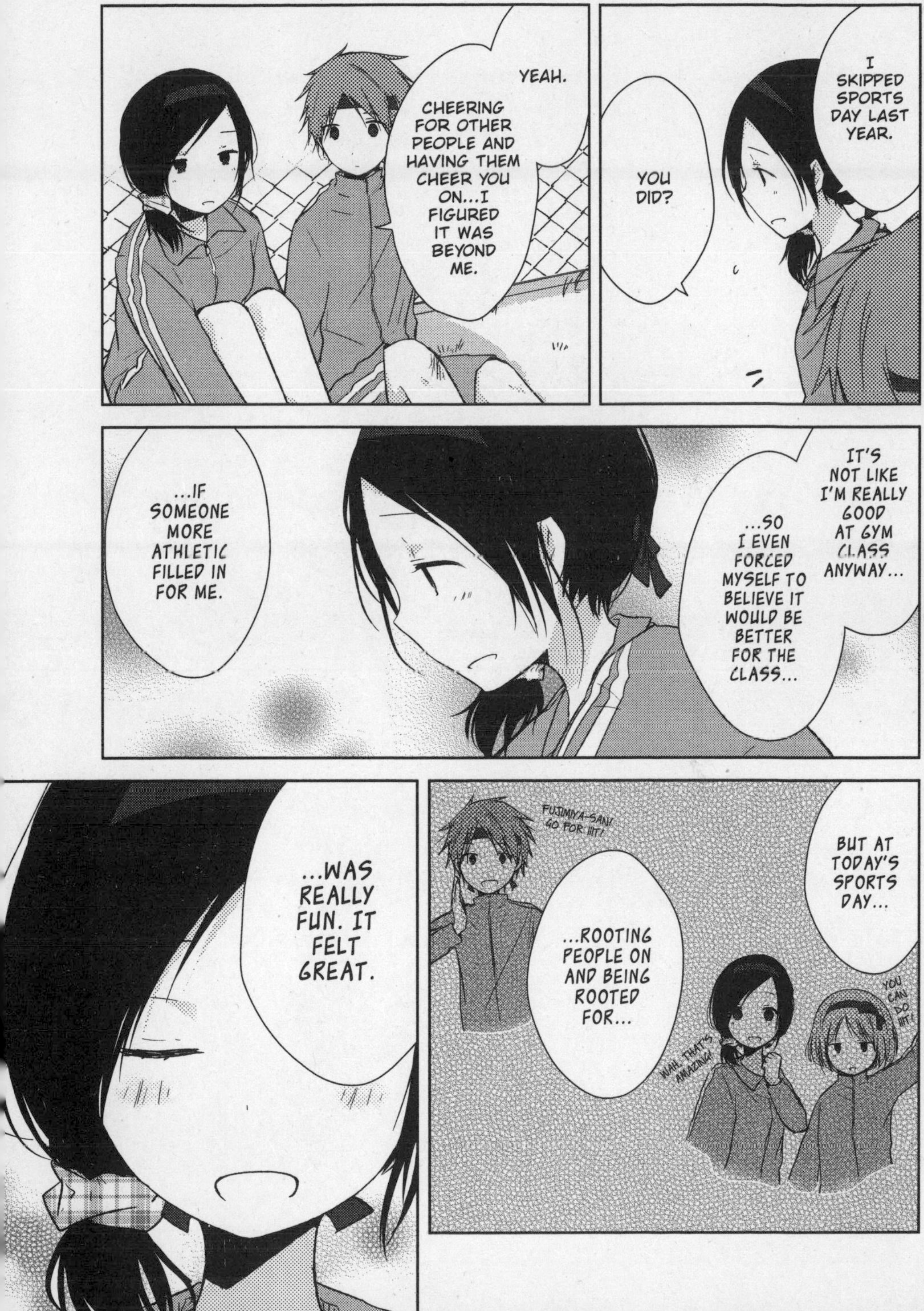
I SKIPPED SPORTS DAY LAST YEAR.
YOU DID?
YEAH.
CHEERING FOR OTHER PEOPLE AND HAVING THEM CHEER YOU ON...I FIGURED IT WAS BEYOND ME.
IT'S NOT LIKE I'M REALLY GOOD AT GYM CLASS ANYWAY...
...SO I EVEN FORCED MYSELF TO BELIEVE IT WOULD BE BETTER FOR THE CLASS...
...IF SOMEONE MORE ATHLETIC FILLED IN FOR ME.
BUT AT TODAY'S SPORTS DAY...
YOU CAN DO IIIT!
FUJIMIYA-SAN! GO FOR IIIT!
...ROOTING PEOPLE ON AND BEING ROOTED FOR...
WAH, THAT'S AMAZING!
...WAS REALLY FUN. IT FELT GREAT.

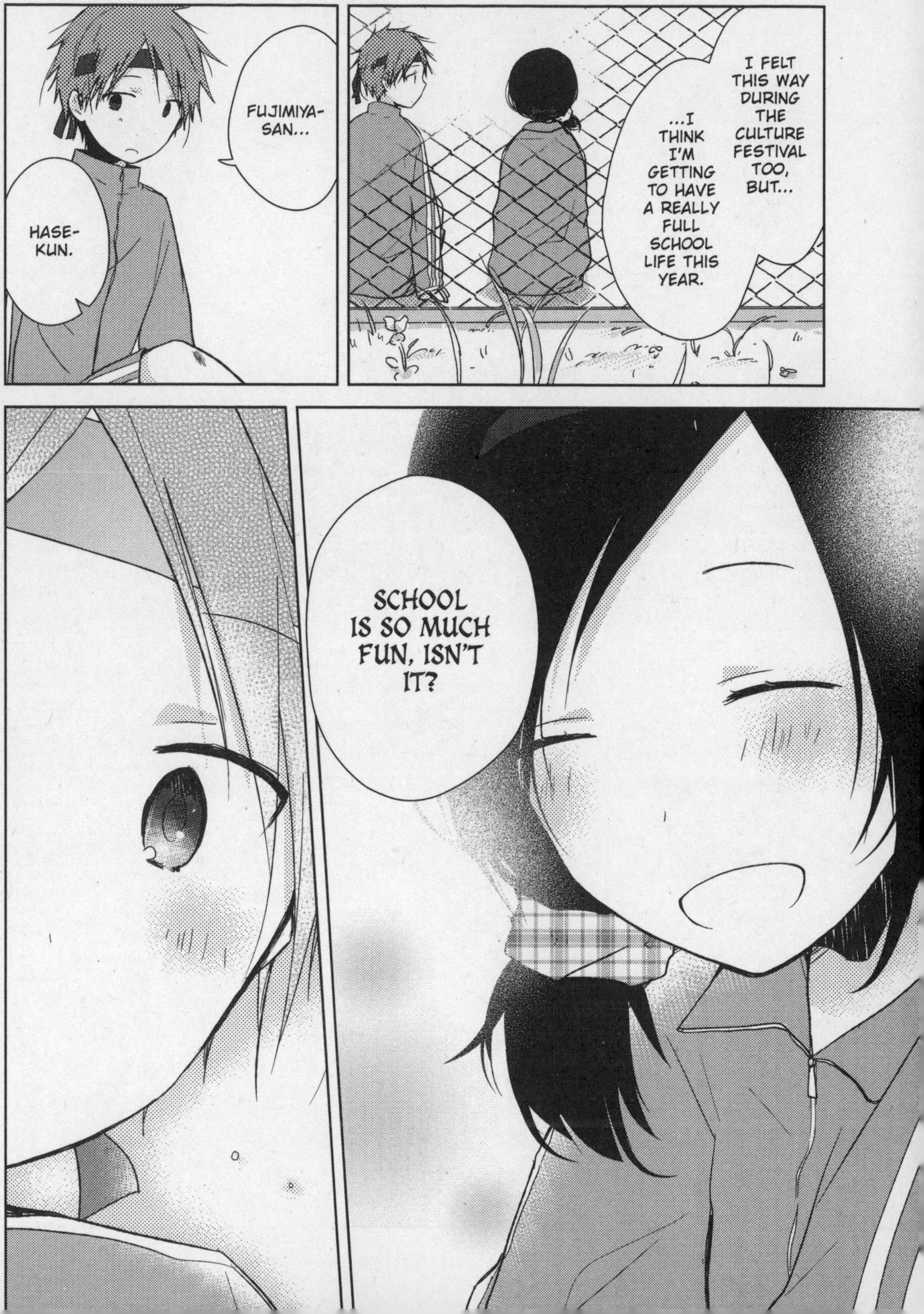
I FELT THIS WAY DURING THE CULTURE FESTIVAL TOO, BUT...
...I THINK I'M GETTING TO HAVE A REALLY FULL SCHOOL LIFE THIS YEAR.
FUJIMIYA-SAN...
HASE-KUN.
SCHOOL IS SO MUCH FUN, ISN'T IT?

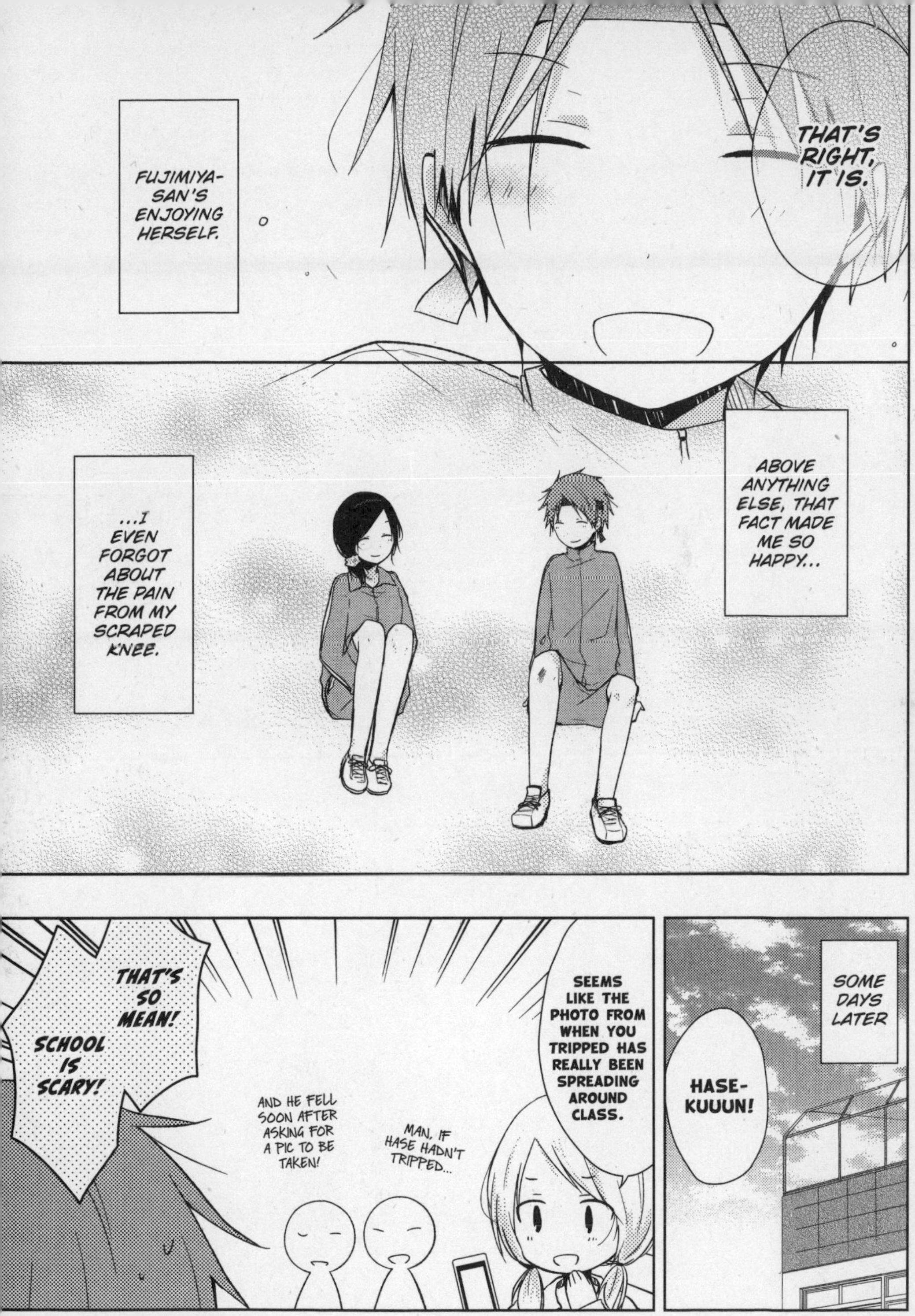
THAT'S RIGHT, IT IS.
FUJIMIYA-SAN'S ENJOYING HERSELF.
ABOVE ANYTHING ELSE, THAT FACT MADE ME SO HAPPY...
...I EVEN FORGOT ABOUT THE PAIN FROM MY SCRAPED KNEE.
SOME DAYS LATER
HASE-KUUUN!
SEEMS LIKE THE PHOTO FROM WHEN YOU TRIPPED HAS REALLY BEEN SPREADING AROUND CLASS.
MAN, IF HASE HADN'T TRIPPED...
AND HE FELL SOON AFTER ASKING FOR A PIC TO BE TAKEN!
THAT'S SO MEAN!
SCHOOL IS SCARY!

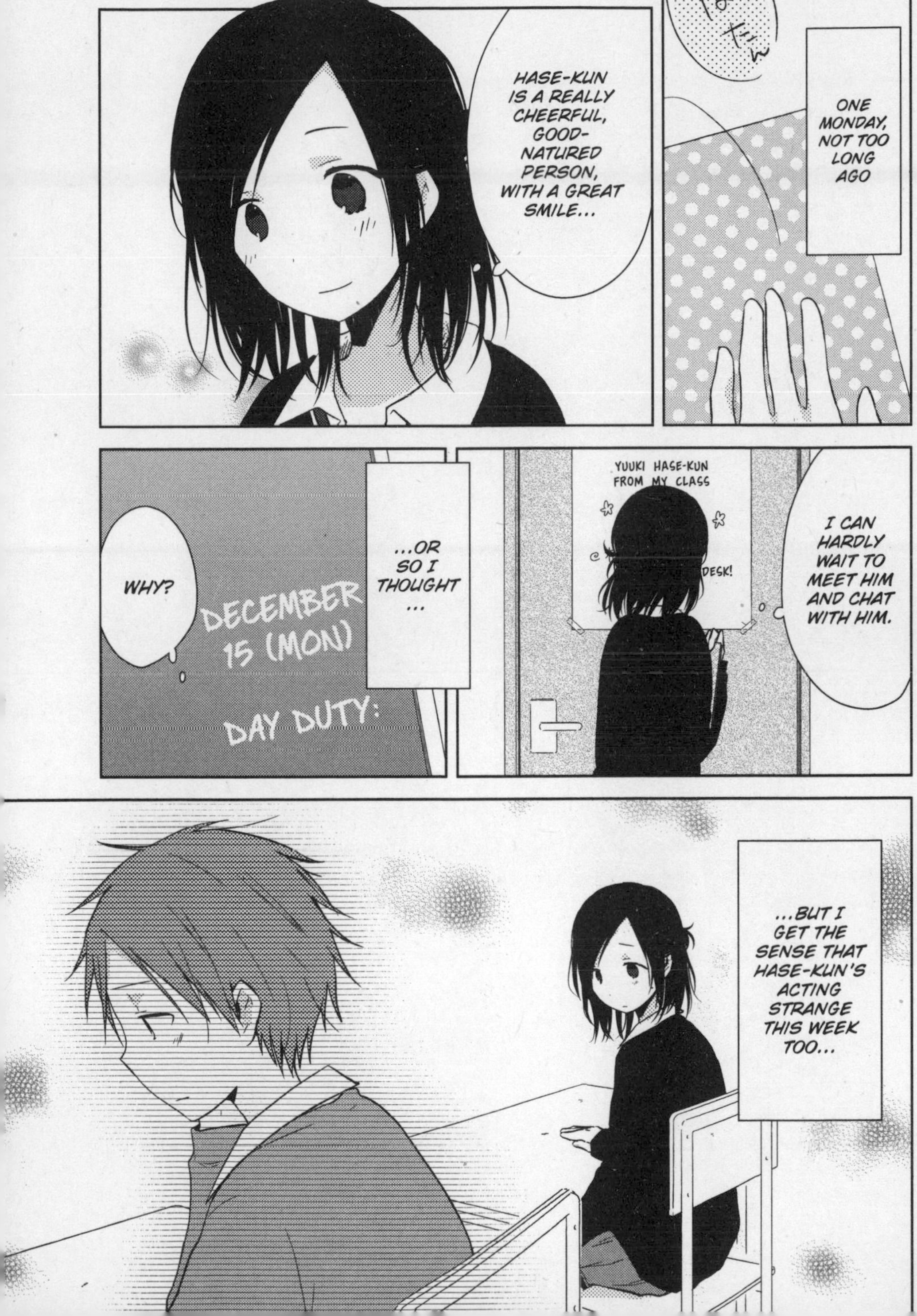
SHUT
ONE MONDAY, NOT TOO LONG AGO
HASE-KUN IS A REALLY CHEERFUL, GOOD-NATURED PERSON, WITH A GREAT SMILE...
YUUKI HASE-KUN FROM MY CLASS
DESK!
I CAN HARDLY WAIT TO MEET HIM AND CHAT WITH HIM.
...OR SO I THOUGHT...
WHY?
DECEMBER 15 (MON)
DAY DUTY:
...BUT I GET THE SENSE THAT HASE-KUN'S ACTING STRANGE THIS WEEK TOO...

CHAPTER 33 TAKEOFF FROM THE ESCAPE ROUTE

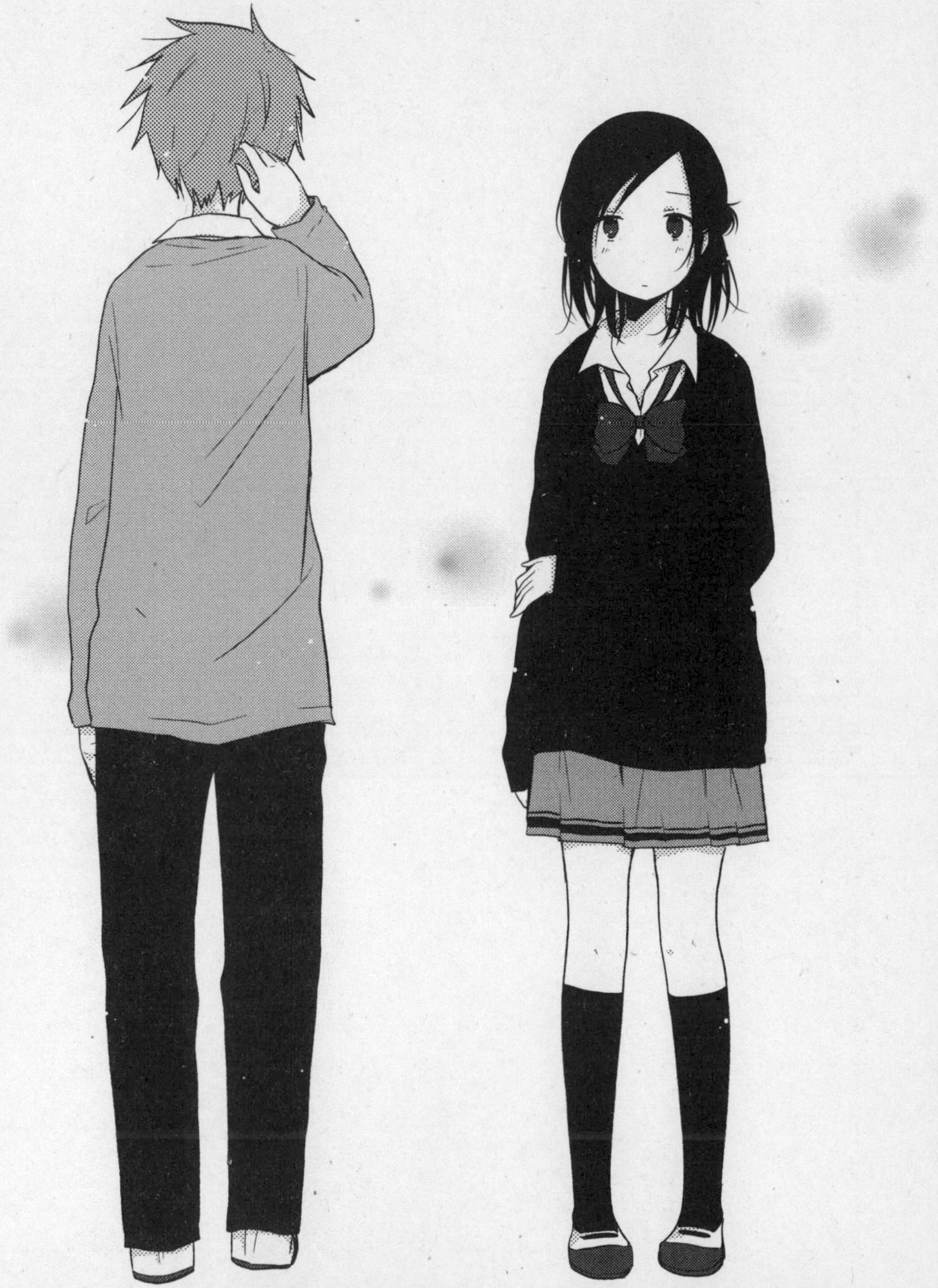

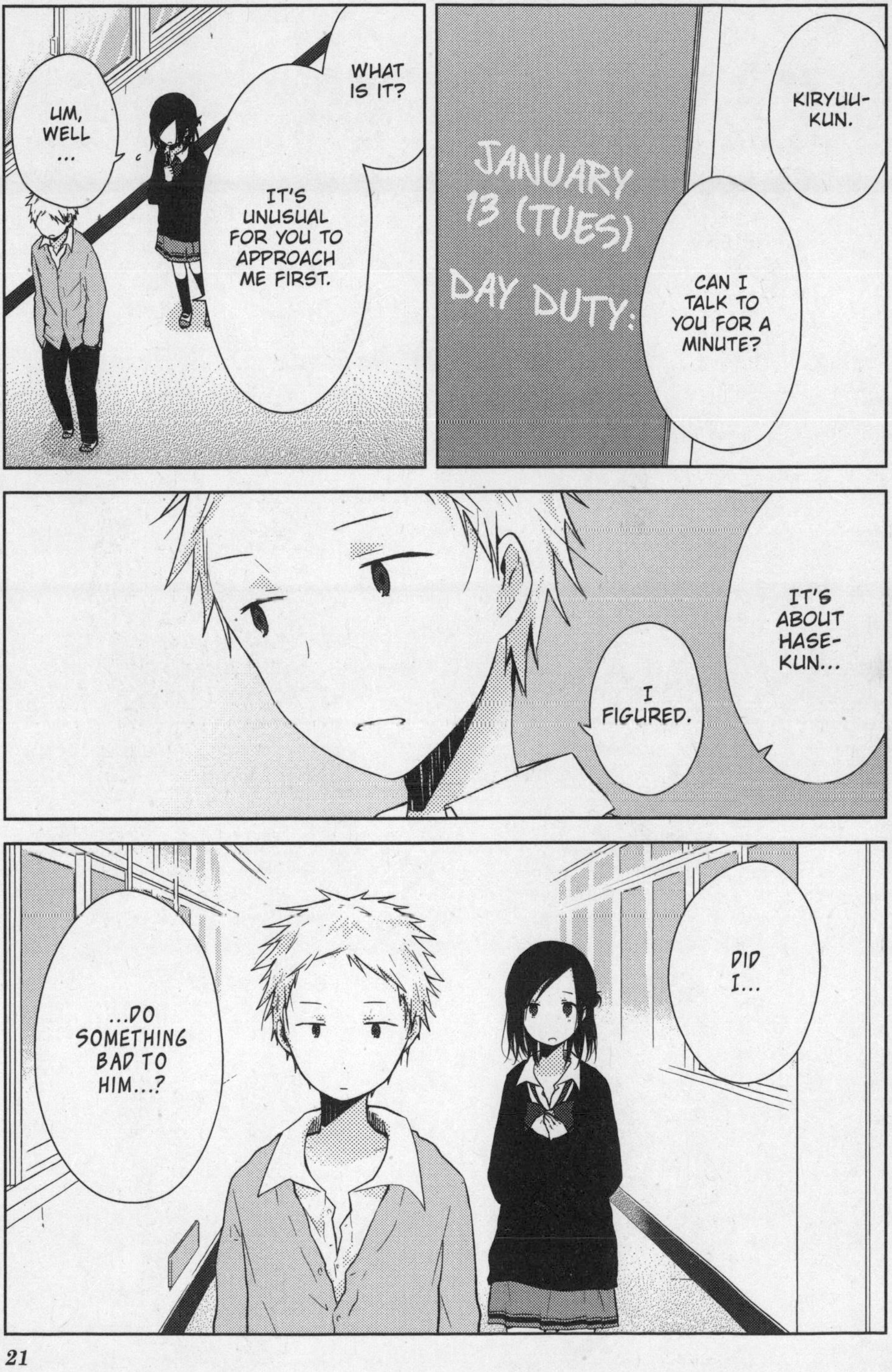
KIRYUU-KUN.
CAN I TALK TO YOU FOR A MINUTE?
JANUARY 13 (TUES)
DAY DUTY:
WHAT IS IT?
IT'S UNUSUAL FOR YOU TO APPROACH ME FIRST.
UM, WELL ...
IT'S ABOUT HASE-KUN...
I FIGURED.
DID I...
...DO SOMETHING BAD TO HIM...?

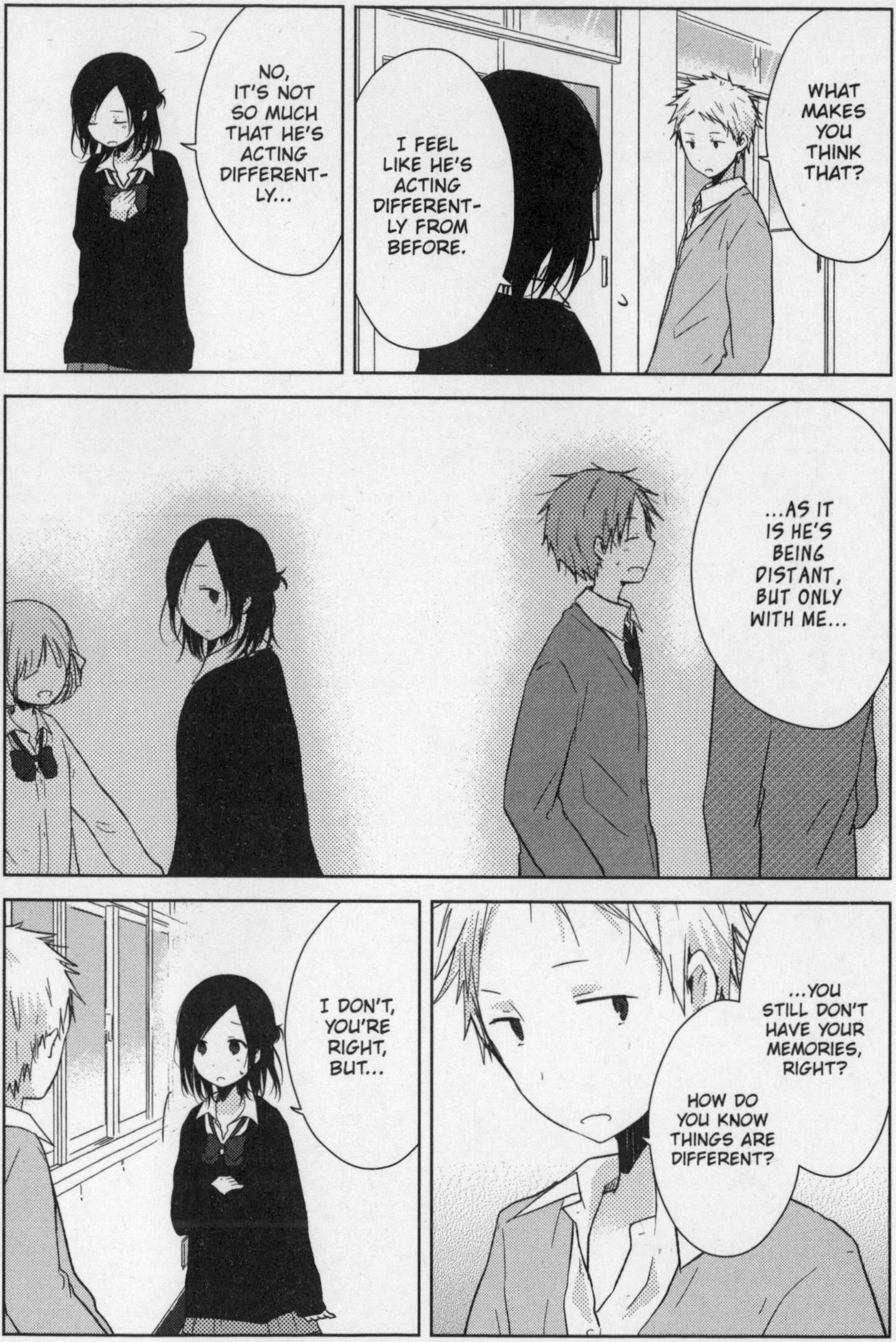
WHAT MAKES YOU THINK THAT?
I FEEL LIKE HE'S ACTING DIFFERENTLY FROM BEFORE.
NO, IT'S NOT SO MUCH THAT HE'S ACTING DIFFERENTLY...
...AS IT IS HE'S BEING DISTANT, BUT ONLY WITH ME...
...YOU STILL DON'T HAVE YOUR MEMORIES, RIGHT?
HOW DO YOU KNOW THINGS ARE DIFFERENT?
I DON'T, YOU'RE RIGHT, BUT...

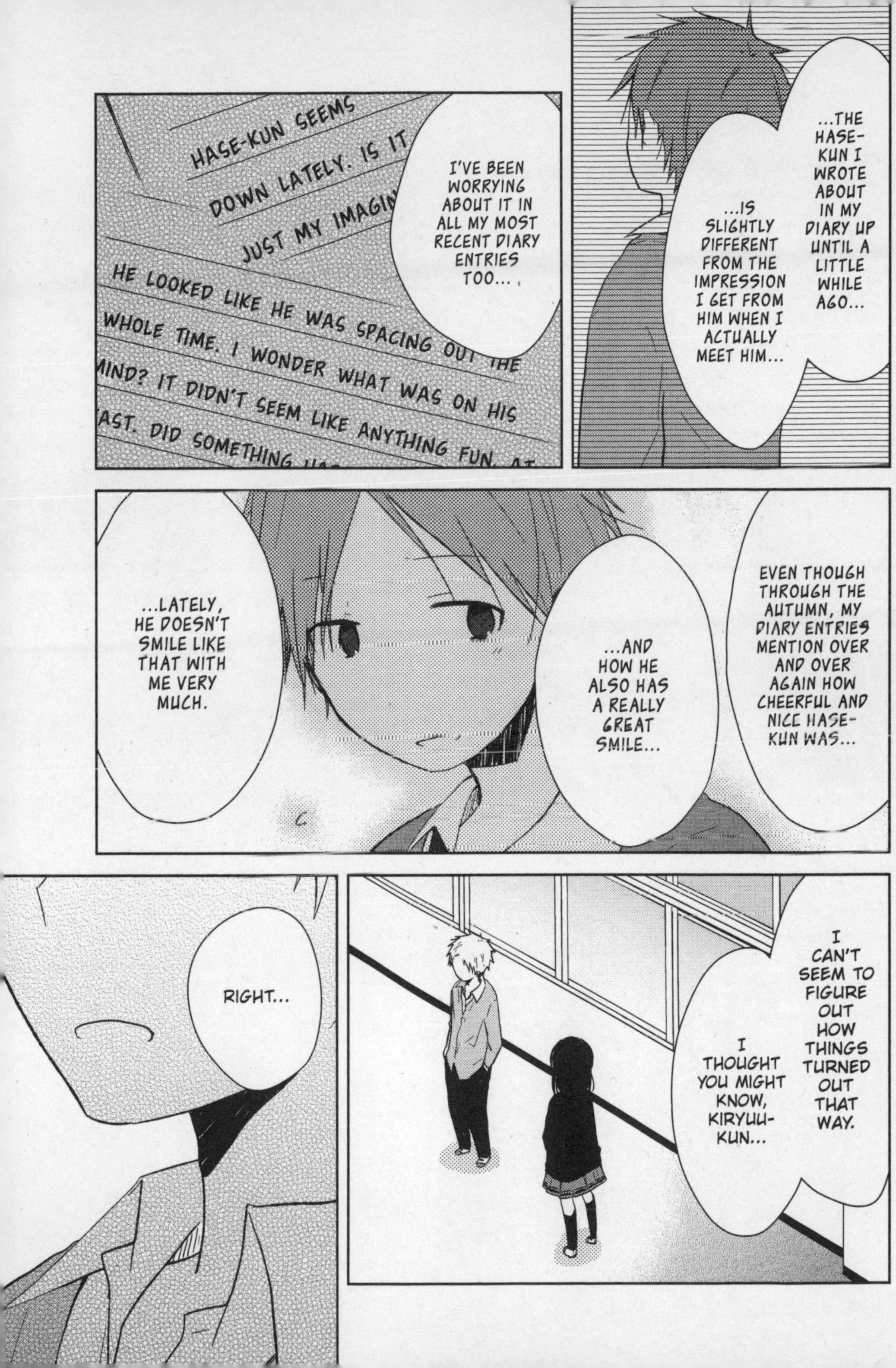
...THE HASE-KUN I WROTE ABOUT IN MY DIARY UP UNTIL A LITTLE WHILE AGO...
...IS SLIGHTLY DIFFERENT FROM THE IMPRESSION I GET FROM HIM WHEN I ACTUALLY MEET HIM...
I'VE BEEN WORRYING ABOUT IT IN ALL MY MOST RECENT DIARY ENTRIES TOO...
HASE-KUN SEEMS DOWN LATELY. IS IT JUST MY IMAGIN
HE LOOKED LIKE HE WAS SPACING OUT THE WHOLE TIME. I WONDER WHAT WAS ON HIS MIND? IT DIDN'T SEEM LIKE ANYTHING FUN. AT
AST. DID SOMETHING
EVEN THOUGH THROUGH THE AUTUMN, MY DIARY ENTRIES MENTION OVER AND OVER AGAIN HOW CHEERFUL AND NICE HASE-KUN WAS...
...AND HOW HE ALSO HAS A REALLY GREAT SMILE...
...LATELY, HE DOESN'T SMILE LIKE THAT WITH ME VERY MUCH.
I CAN'T SEEM TO FIGURE OUT HOW THINGS TURNED OUT THAT WAY.
I THOUGHT YOU MIGHT KNOW, KIRYUU-KUN...
RIGHT...

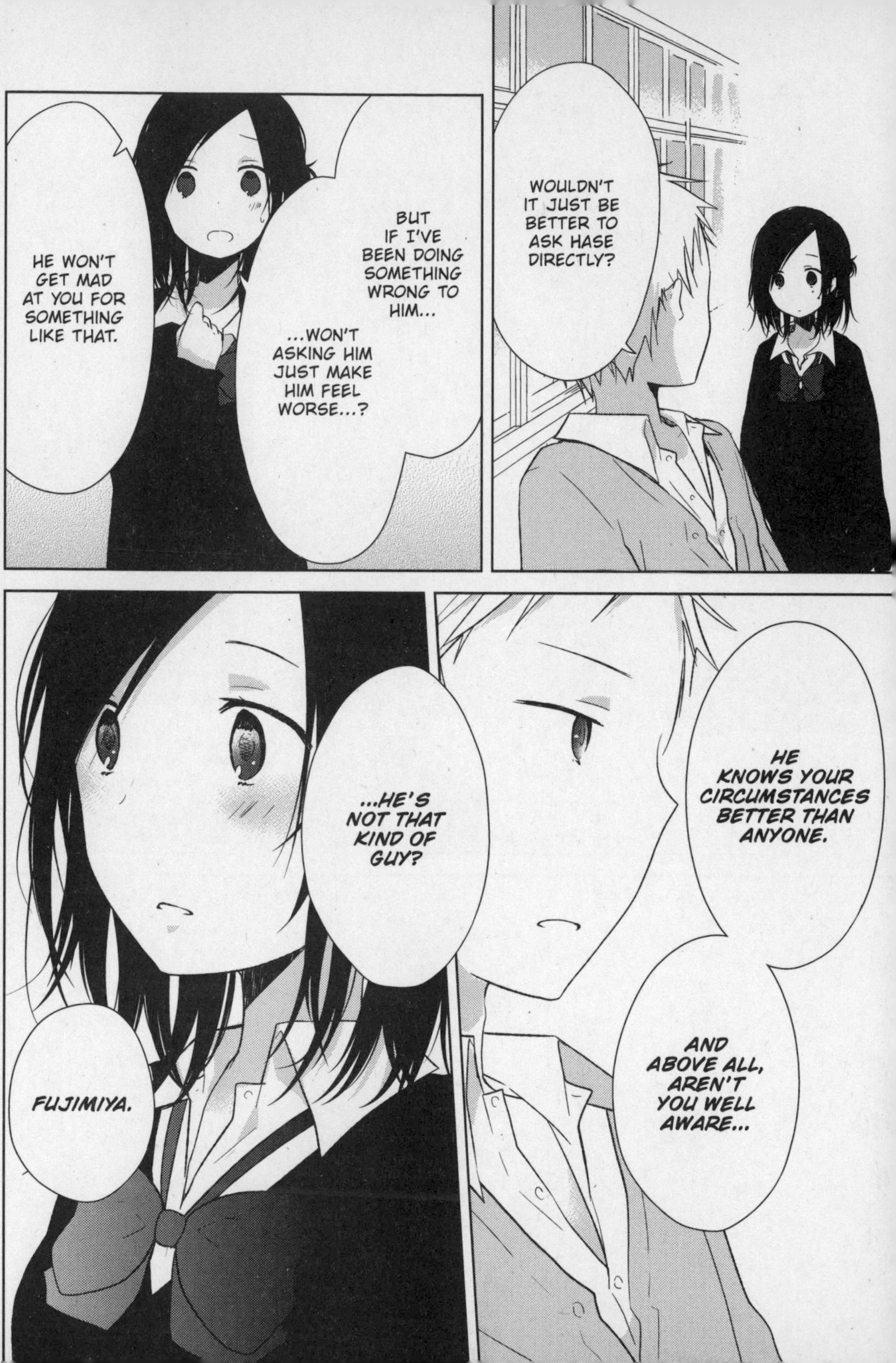
WOULDN'T IT JUST BE BETTER TO ASK HASE DIRECTLY?
BUT IF I'VE BEEN DOING SOMETHING WRONG TO HIM...
...WON'T ASKING HIM JUST MAKE HIM FEEL WORSE...?
HE WON'T GET MAD AT YOU FOR SOMETHING LIKE THAT.
HE KNOWS YOUR CIRCUMSTANCES BETTER THAN ANYONE.
AND ABOVE ALL, AREN'T YOU WELL AWARE...
...HE'S NOT THAT KIND OF GUY?
FUJIMIYA.

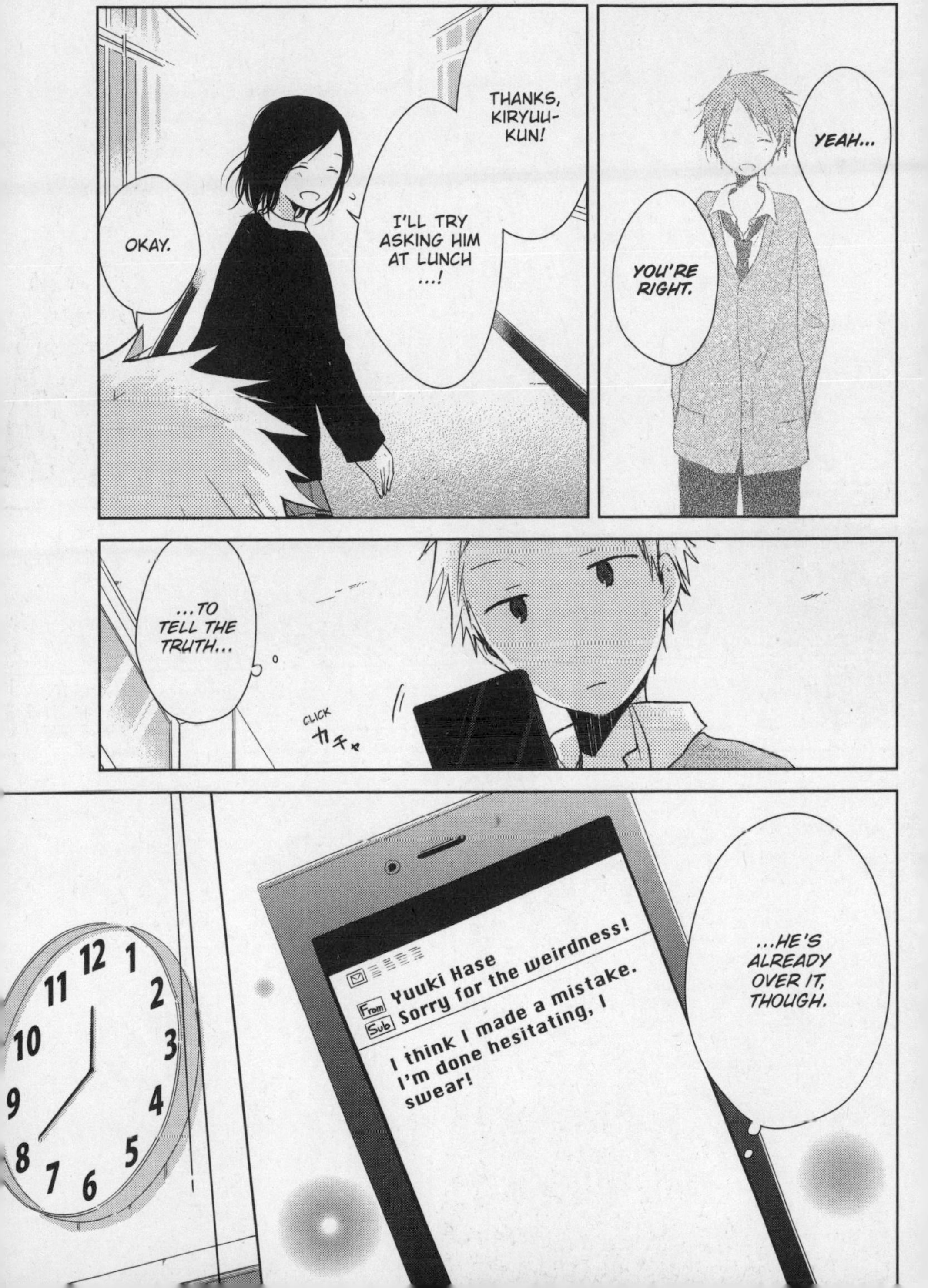
YEAH...
YOU'RE RIGHT.
THANKS, KIRYUU-KUN!
I'LL TRY ASKING HIM AT LUNCH ...!
OKAY.
...TO TELL THE TRUTH...
CLICK
カチャ
...HE'S ALREADY OVER IT, THOUGH.
From Yuuki Hase
Sub Sorry for the weirdness!
I think I made a mistake. I'm done hesitating, I swear!

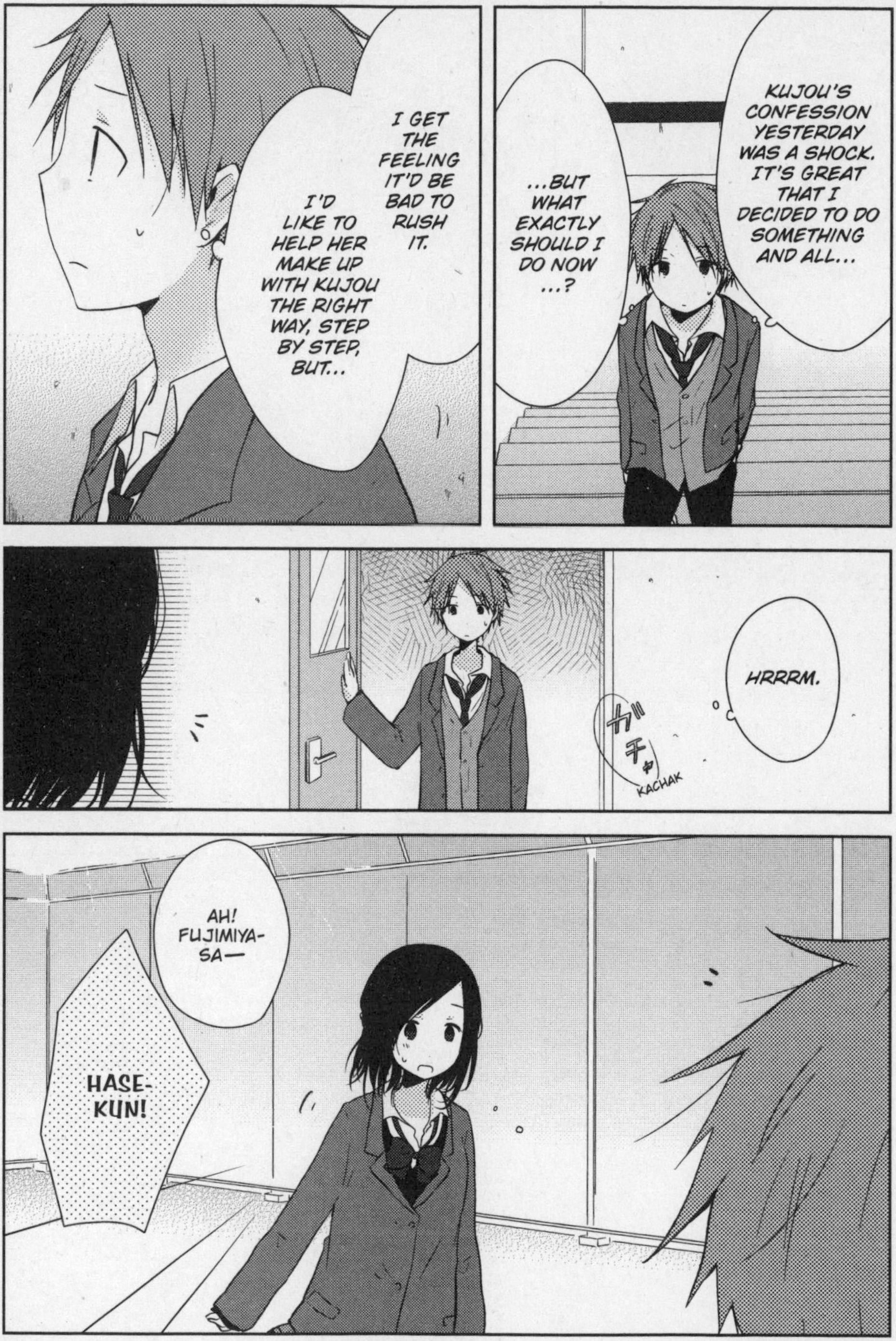
KUJOU'S CONFESSION YESTERDAY WAS A SHOCK. IT'S GREAT THAT I DECIDED TO DO SOMETHING AND ALL...
...BUT WHAT EXACTLY SHOULD I DO NOW ...?
I GET THE FEELING IT'D BE BAD TO RUSH IT.
I'D LIKE TO HELP HER MAKE UP WITH KUJOU THE RIGHT WAY, STEP BY STEP, BUT...
HRRRM.
ガチャ
KACHAK
AH! FUJIMIYA-SA—
HASE-KUN!

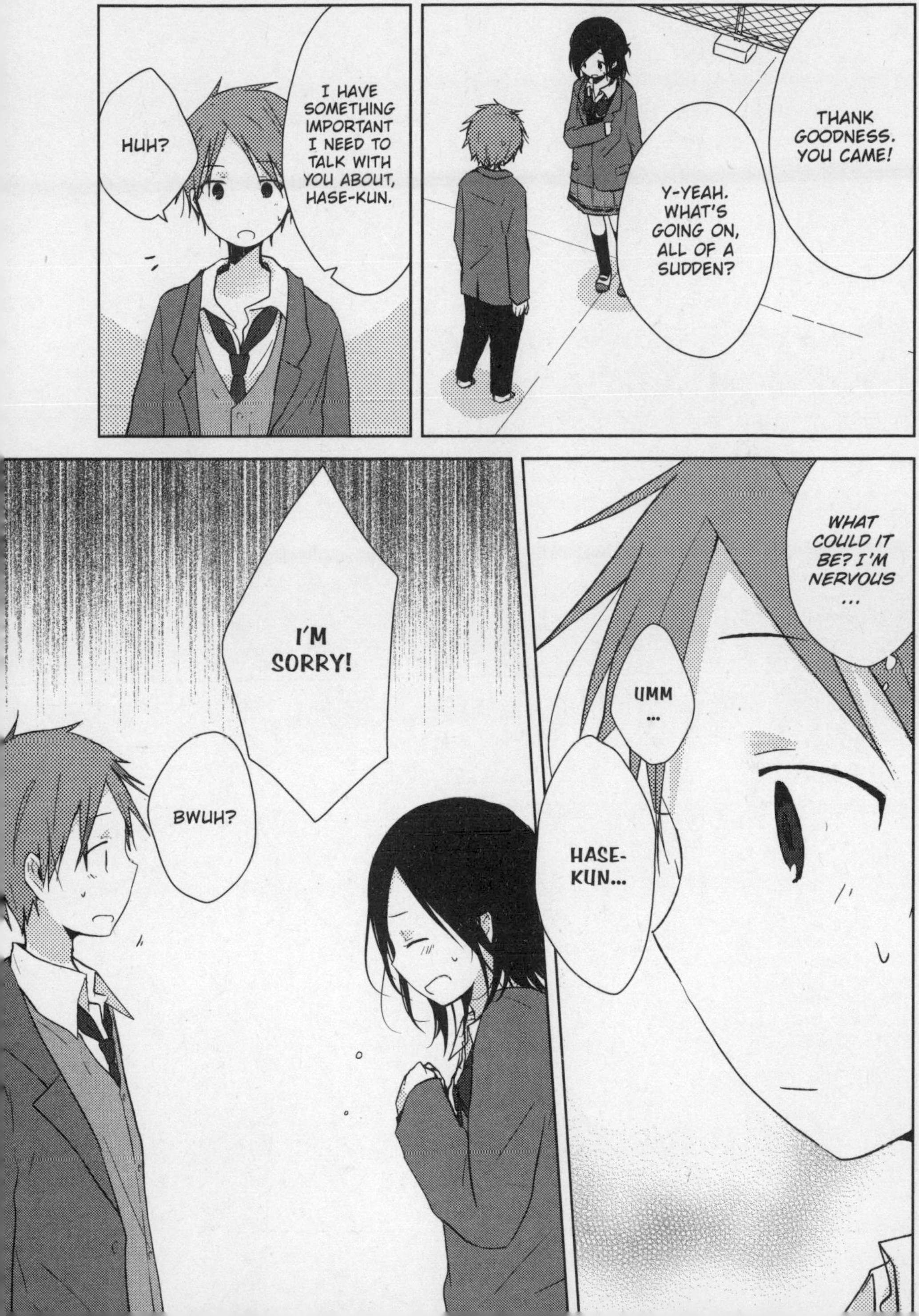
THANK GOODNESS. YOU CAME!
Y-YEAH. WHAT'S GOING ON, ALL OF A SUDDEN?
I HAVE SOMETHING IMPORTANT I NEED TO TALK WITH YOU ABOUT, HASE-KUN.
HUH?
WHAT COULD IT BE? I'M NERVOUS...
UMM...
HASE-KUN...
I'M SORRY!
BWUH?

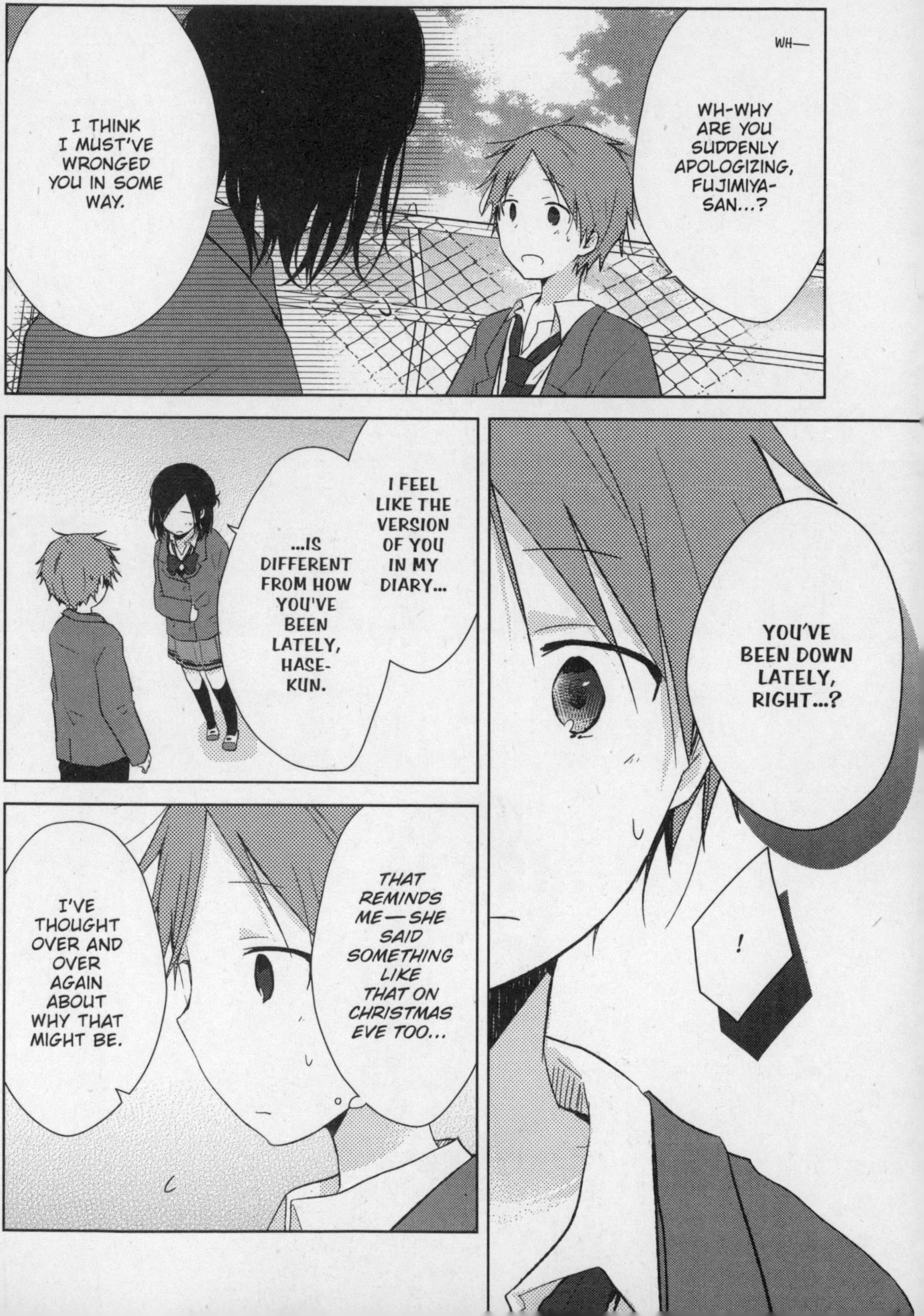
WH—
WH-WHY ARE YOU SUDDENLY APOLOGIZING, FUJIMIYA-SAN...?
I THINK I MUST'VE WRONGED YOU IN SOME WAY.
YOU'VE BEEN DOWN LATELY, RIGHT...?
!
I FEEL LIKE THE VERSION OF YOU IN MY DIARY...
...IS DIFFERENT FROM HOW YOU'VE BEEN LATELY, HASE-KUN.
THAT REMINDS ME—SHE SAID SOMETHING LIKE THAT ON CHRISTMAS EVE TOO...
I'VE THOUGHT OVER AND OVER AGAIN ABOUT WHY THAT MIGHT BE.

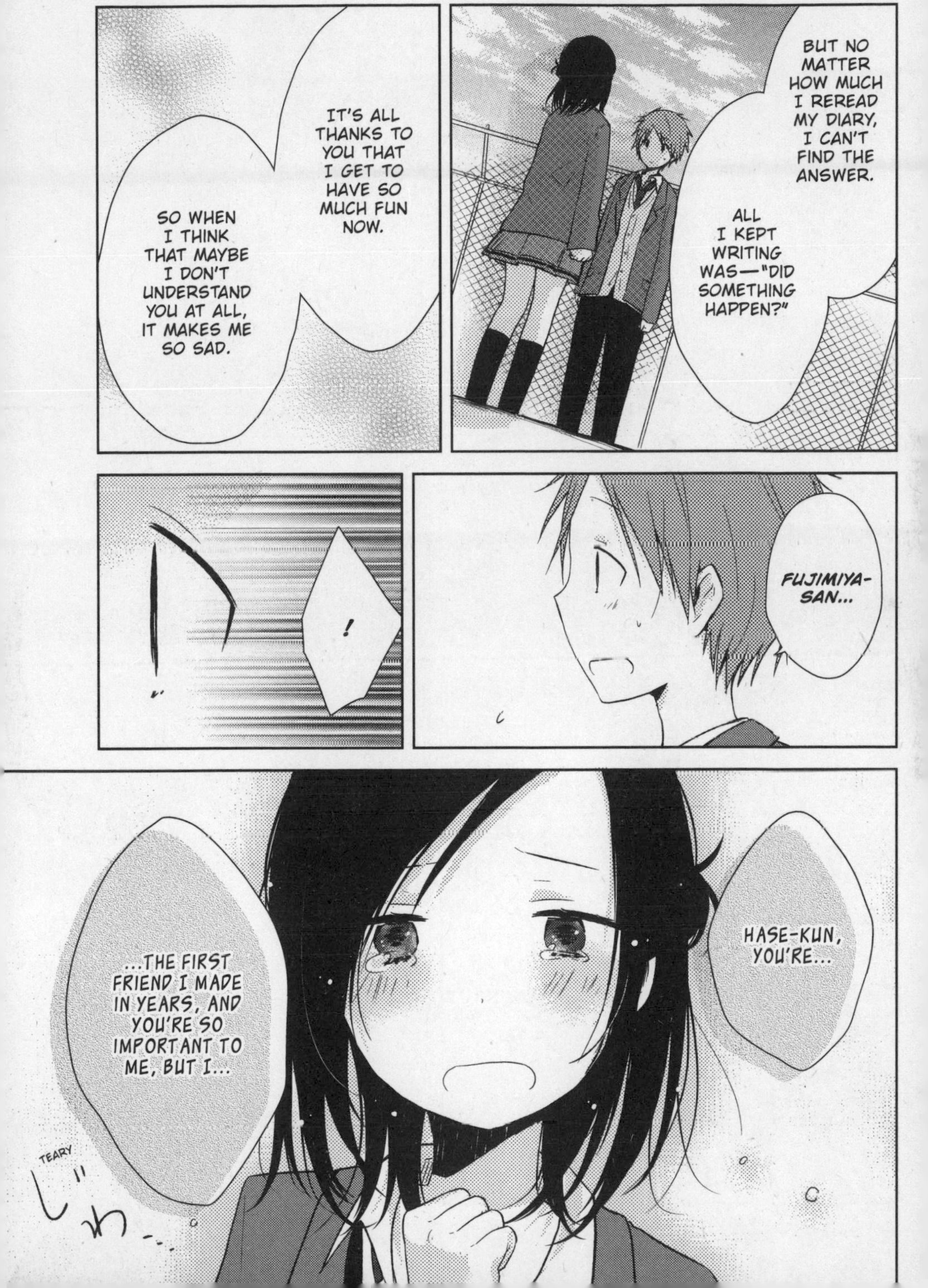
BUT NO MATTER HOW MUCH I REREAD MY DIARY, I CAN'T FIND THE ANSWER.
ALL I KEPT WRITING WAS—"DID SOMETHING HAPPEN?"
IT'S ALL THANKS TO YOU THAT I GET TO HAVE SO MUCH FUN NOW.
SO WHEN I THINK THAT MAYBE I DON'T UNDERSTAND YOU AT ALL, IT MAKES ME SO SAD.
FUJIMIYA-SAN...
!
HASE-KUN, YOU'RE...
...THE FIRST FRIEND I MADE IN YEARS, AND YOU'RE SO IMPORTANT TO ME, BUT I...
TEARY

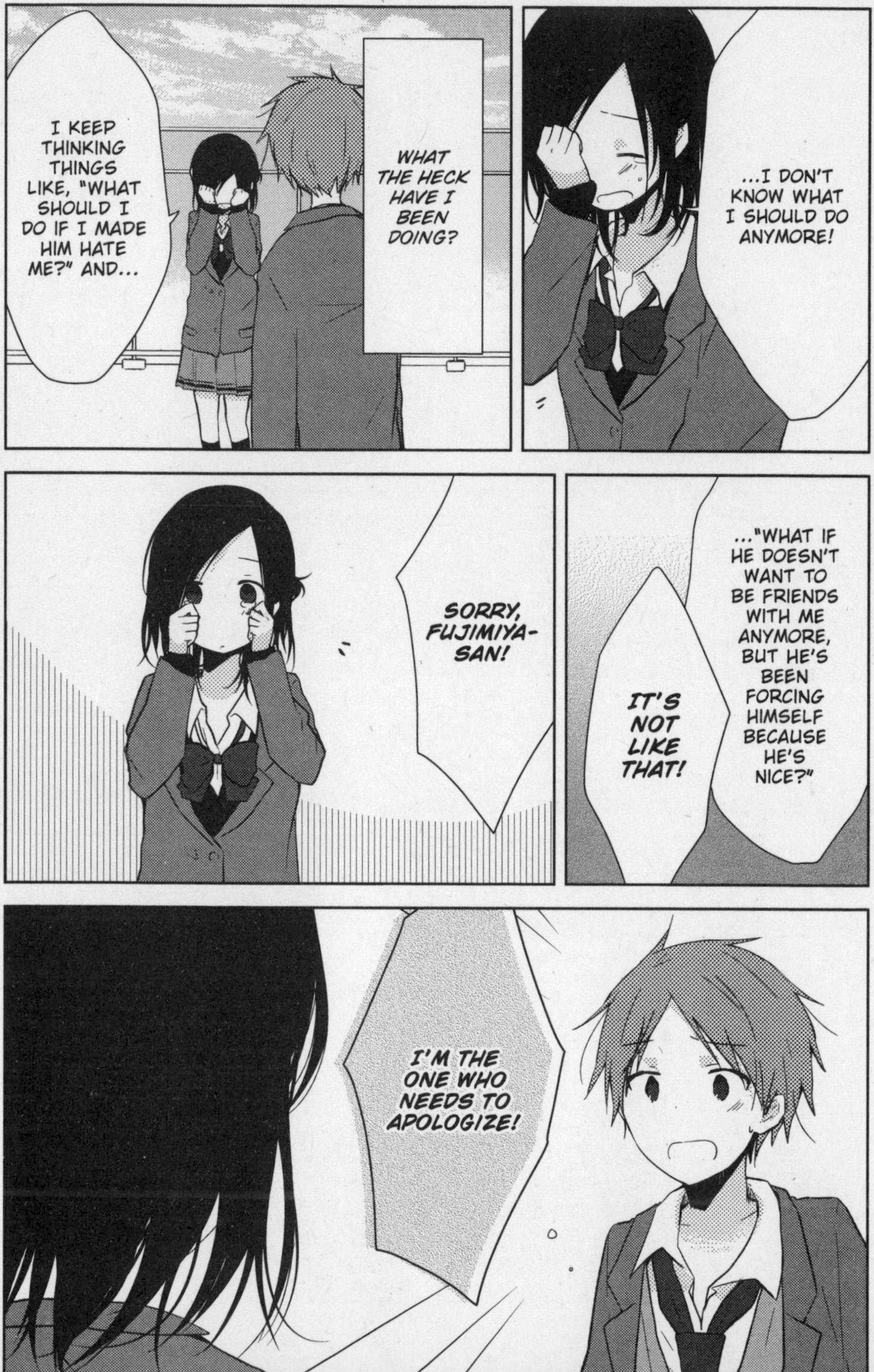
...I DON'T KNOW WHAT I SHOULD DO ANYMORE!
WHAT THE HECK HAVE I BEEN DOING?
I KEEP THINKING THINGS LIKE, "WHAT SHOULD I DO IF I MADE HIM HATE ME?" AND...
..."WHAT IF HE DOESN'T WANT TO BE FRIENDS WITH ME ANYMORE, BUT HE'S BEEN FORCING HIMSELF BECAUSE HE'S NICE?"
IT'S NOT LIKE THAT!
SORRY, FUJIMIYA-SAN!
I'M THE ONE WHO NEEDS TO APOLOGIZE!

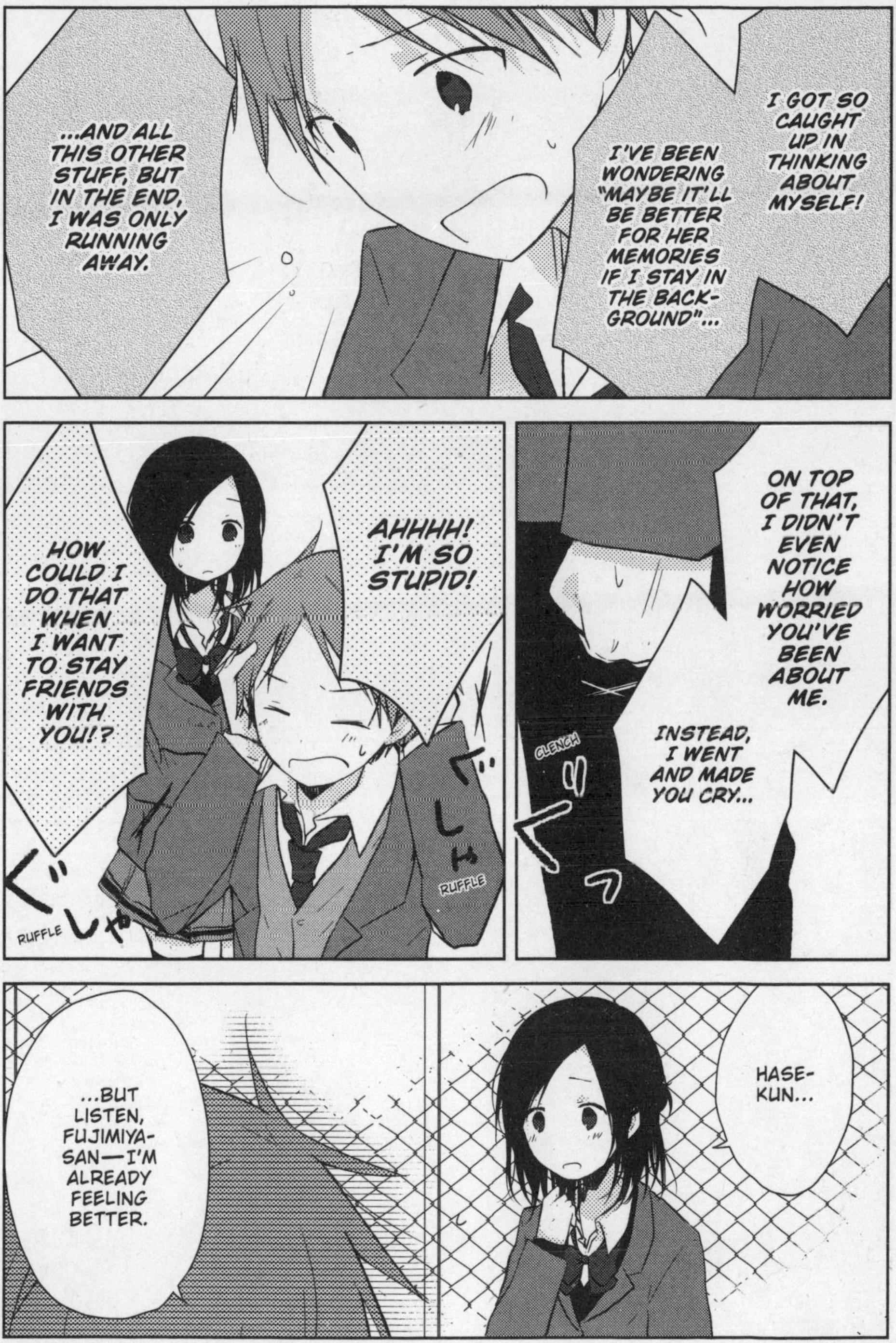
I GOT SO CAUGHT UP IN THINKING ABOUT MYSELF!
I'VE BEEN WONDERING "MAYBE IT'LL BE BETTER FOR HER MEMORIES IF I STAY IN THE BACK-GROUND"...
...AND ALL THIS OTHER STUFF, BUT IN THE END, I WAS ONLY RUNNING AWAY.
ON TOP OF THAT, I DIDN'T EVEN NOTICE HOW WORRIED YOU'VE BEEN ABOUT ME.
INSTEAD, I WENT AND MADE YOU CRY...
CLENCH
AHHHH! I'M SO STUPID!
HOW COULD I DO THAT WHEN I WANT TO STAY FRIENDS WITH YOU!?
RUFFLE
RUFFLE
HASE-KUN...
...BUT LISTEN, FUJIMIYA-SAN—I'M ALREADY FEELING BETTER.

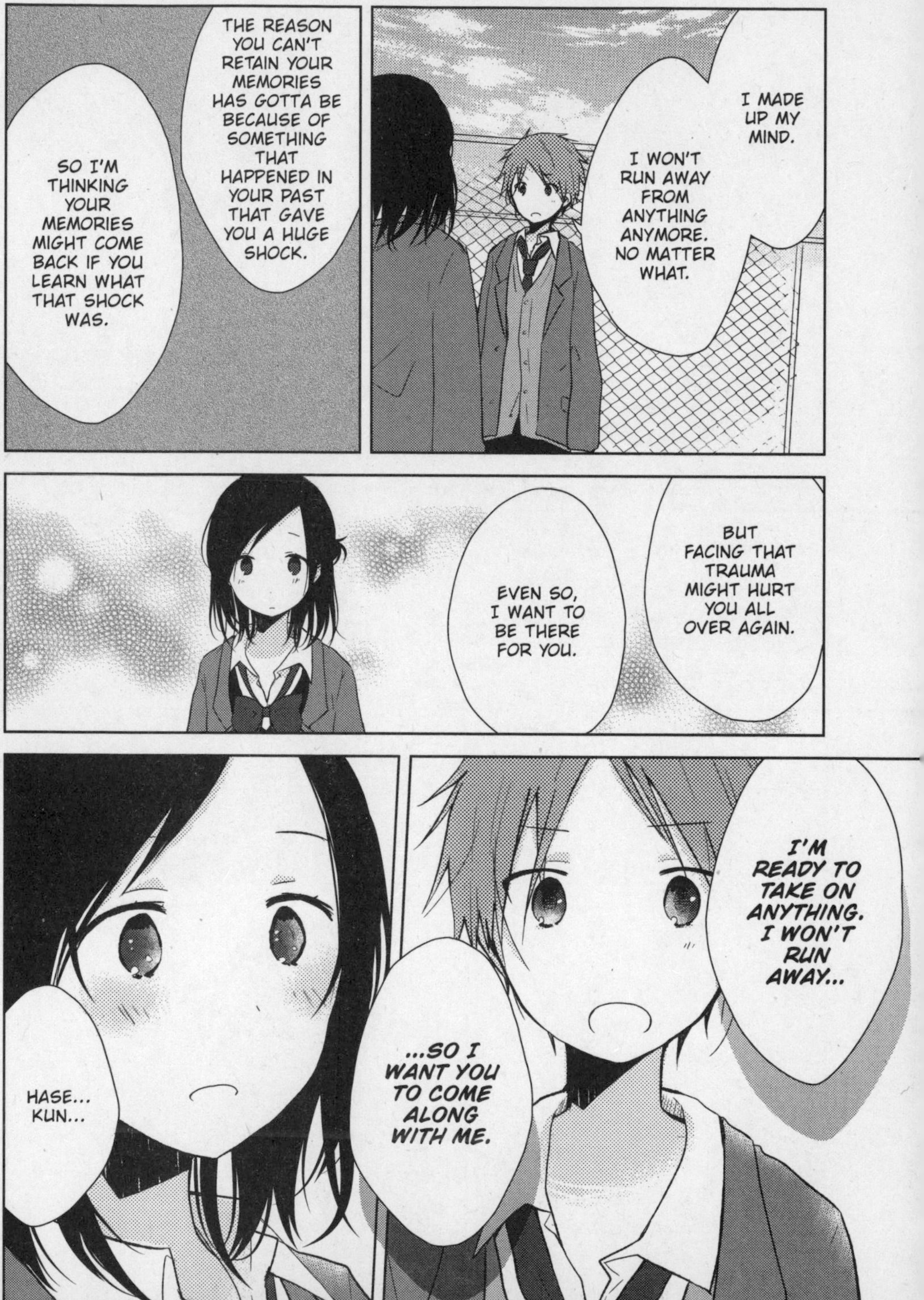
I MADE UP MY MIND. I WON'T RUN AWAY FROM ANYTHING ANYMORE. NO MATTER WHAT.
THE REASON YOU CAN'T RETAIN YOUR MEMORIES HAS GOTTA BE BECAUSE OF SOMETHING THAT HAPPENED IN YOUR PAST THAT GAVE YOU A HUGE SHOCK.
SO I'M THINKING YOUR MEMORIES MIGHT COME BACK IF YOU LEARN WHAT THAT SHOCK WAS.
BUT FACING THAT TRAUMA MIGHT HURT YOU ALL OVER AGAIN.
EVEN SO, I WANT TO BE THERE FOR YOU.
I'M READY TO TAKE ON ANYTHING. I WON'T RUN AWAY...
...SO I WANT YOU TO COME ALONG WITH ME.
HASE... KUN...

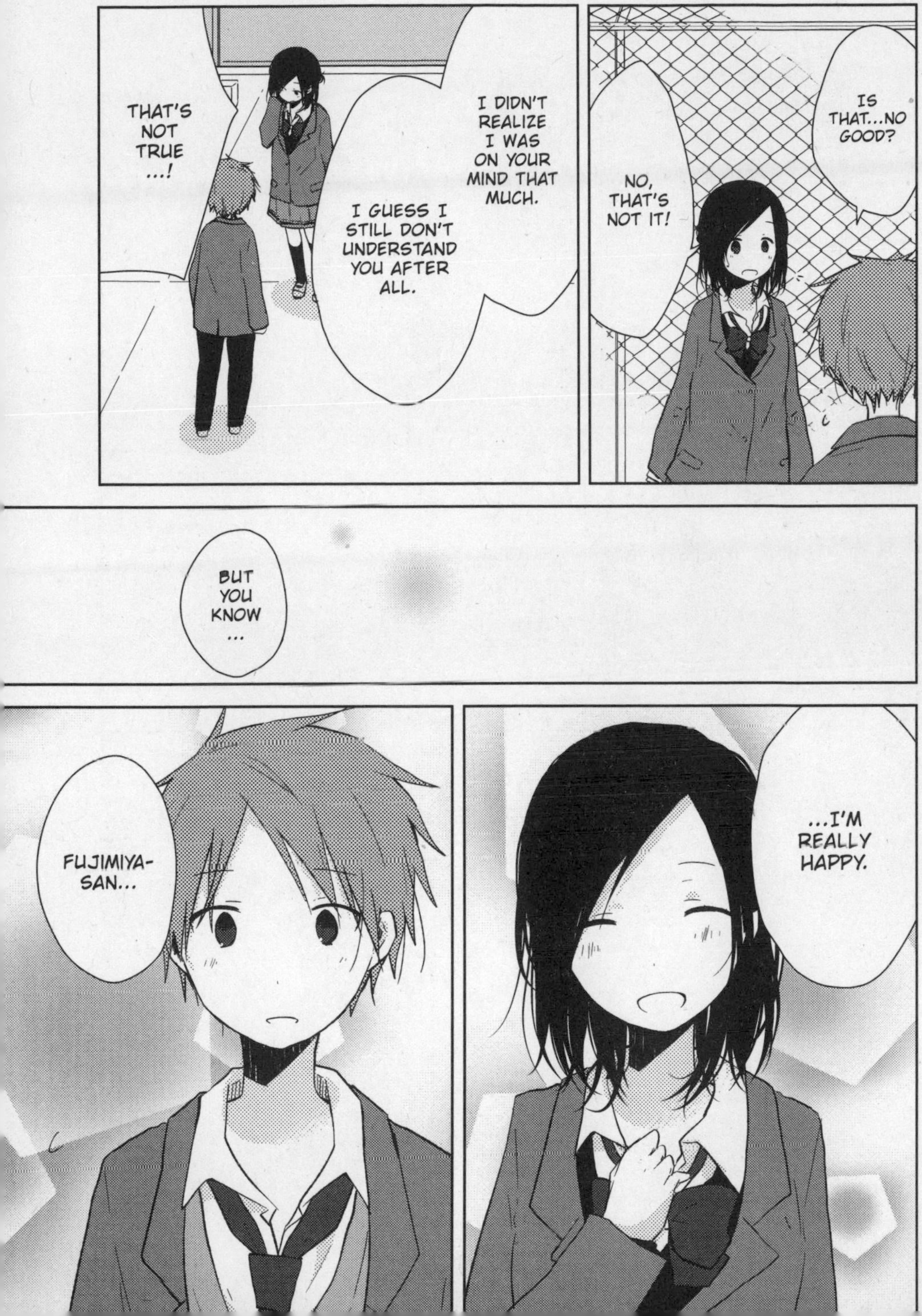
IS THAT...NO GOOD?
NO, THAT'S NOT IT!
I DIDN'T REALIZE I WAS ON YOUR MIND THAT MUCH.
I GUESS I STILL DON'T UNDERSTAND YOU AFTER ALL.
THAT'S NOT TRUE ...!
BUT YOU KNOW ...
...I'M REALLY HAPPY.
FUJIMIYA-SAN...

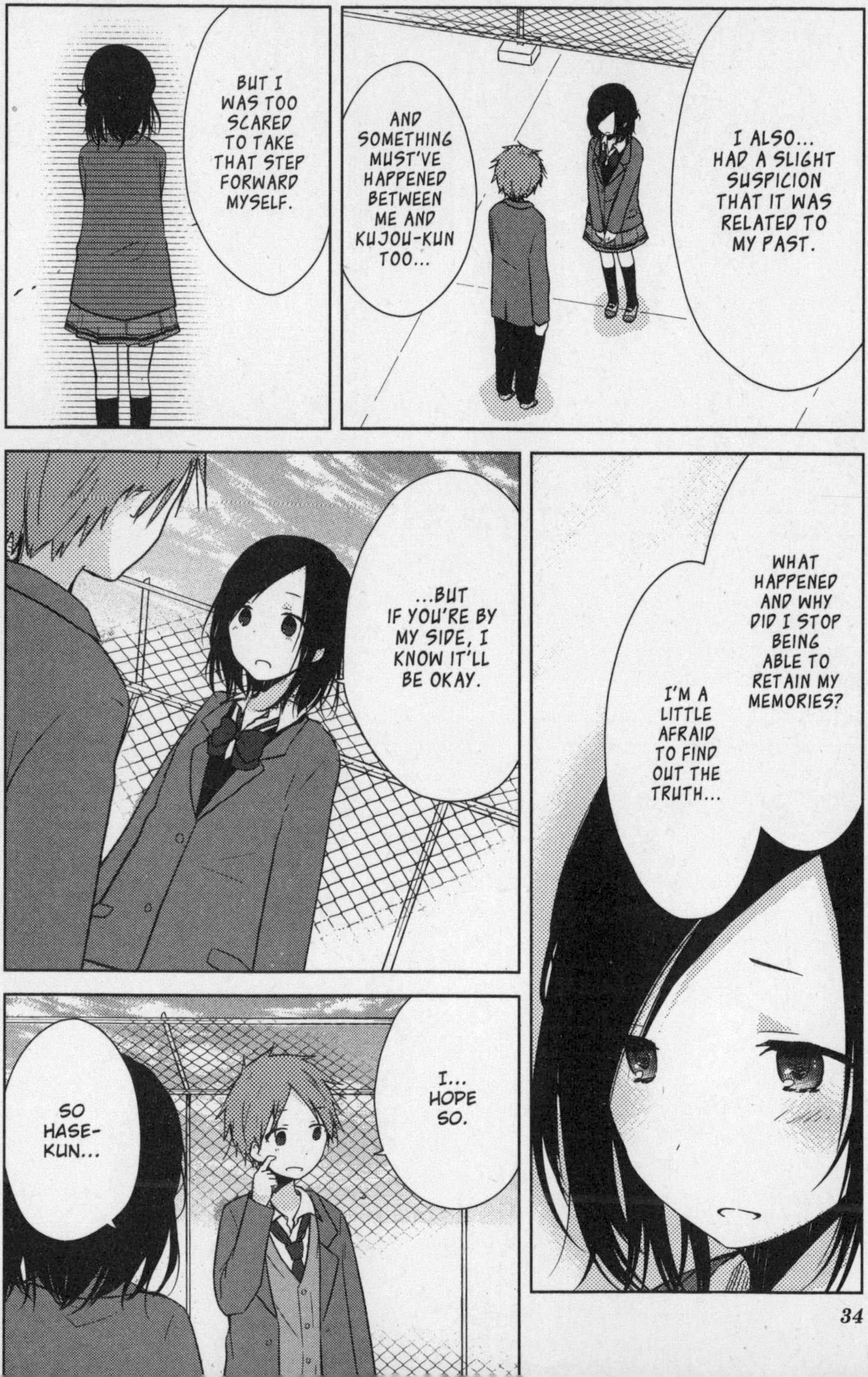
I ALSO... HAD A SLIGHT SUSPICION THAT IT WAS RELATED TO MY PAST.
AND SOMETHING MUST'VE HAPPENED BETWEEN ME AND KUJOU-KUN TOO...
BUT I WAS TOO SCARED TO TAKE THAT STEP FORWARD MYSELF.
WHAT HAPPENED AND WHY DID I STOP BEING ABLE TO RETAIN MY MEMORIES?
I'M A LITTLE AFRAID TO FIND OUT THE TRUTH...
...BUT IF YOU'RE BY MY SIDE, I KNOW IT'LL BE OKAY.
I... HOPE SO.
SO HASE-KUN...

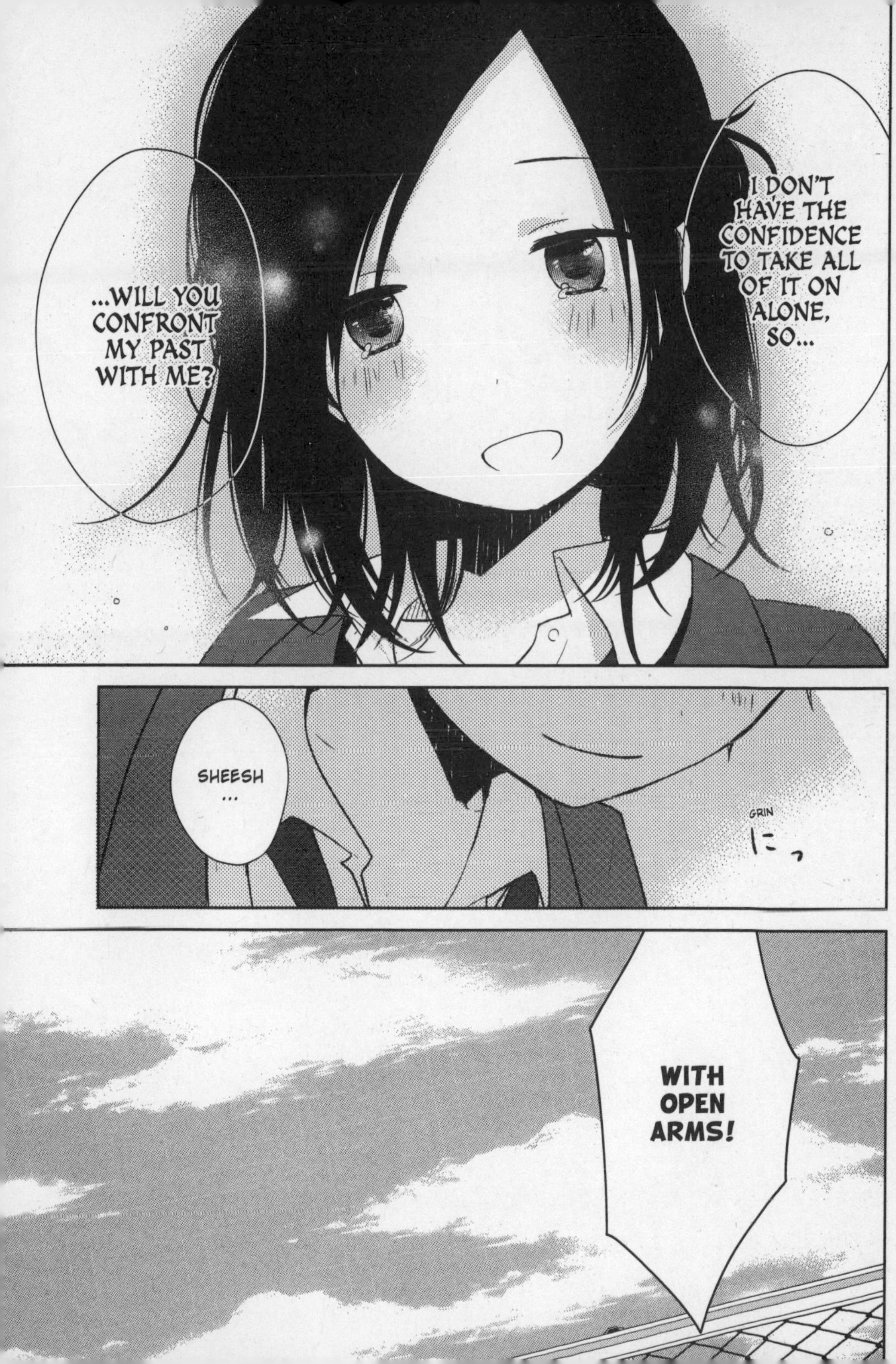
I DON'T HAVE THE CONFIDENCE TO TAKE ALL OF IT ON ALONE, SO...
...WILL YOU CONFRONT MY PAST WITH ME?
SHEESH ...
GRIN
にっ
WITH OPEN ARMS!

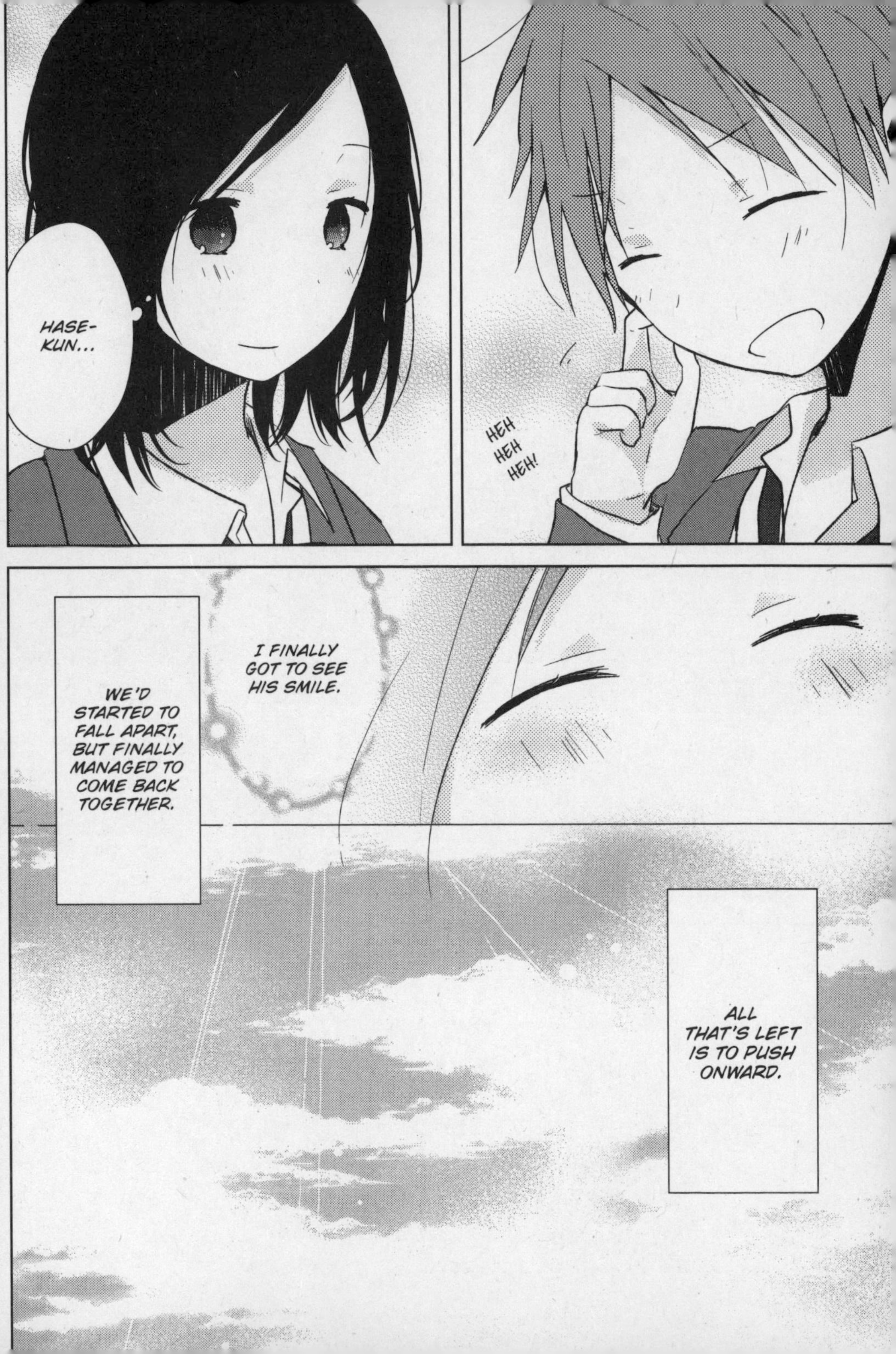
HEH HEH HEH!
HASE-KUN...
I FINALLY GOT TO SEE HIS SMILE.
WE'D STARTED TO FALL APART, BUT FINALLY MANAGED TO COME BACK TOGETHER.
ALL THAT'S LEFT IS TO PUSH ONWARD.

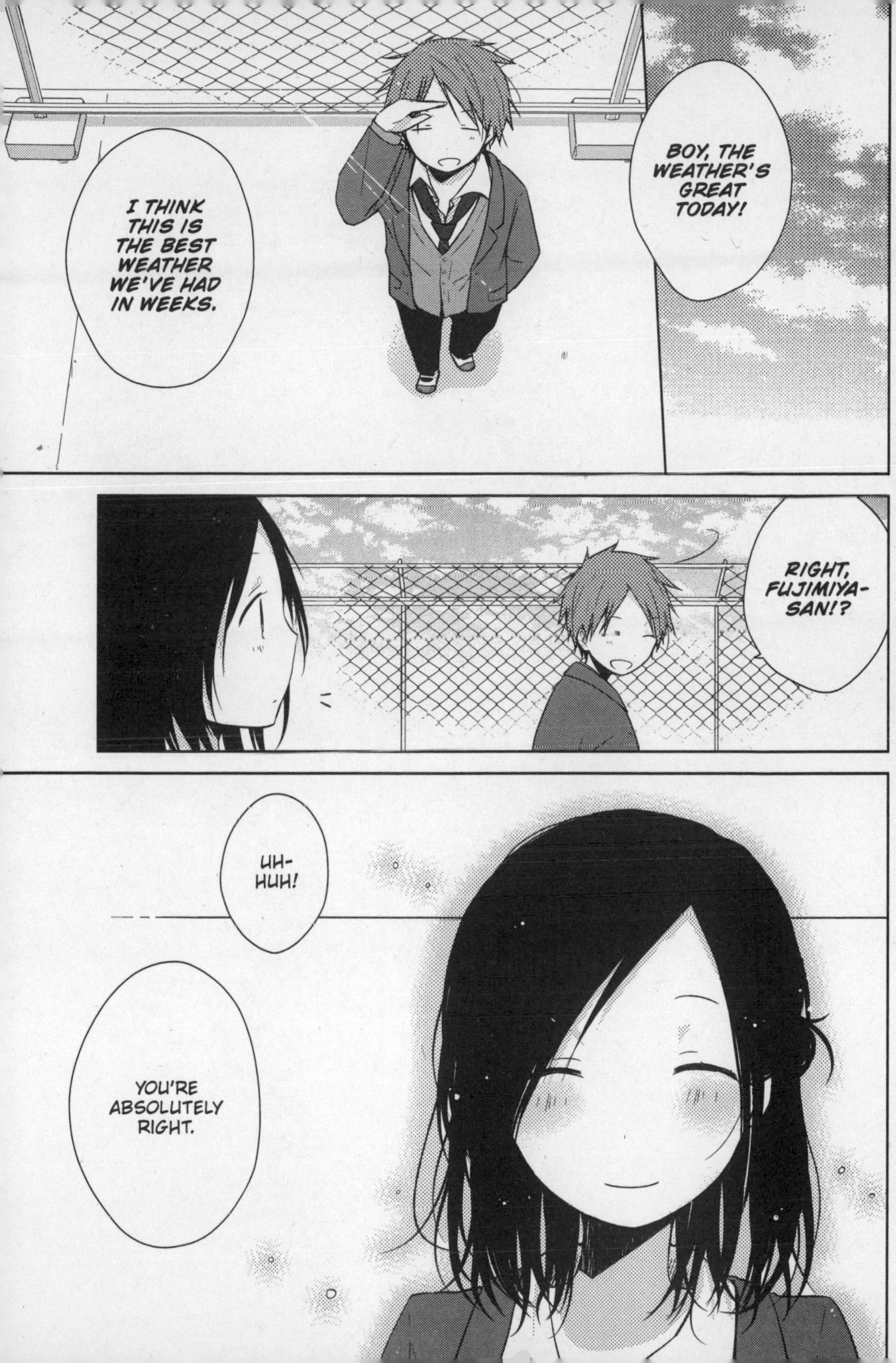
BOY, THE WEATHER'S GREAT TODAY!
I THINK THIS IS THE BEST WEATHER WE'VE HAD IN WEEKS.
RIGHT, FUJIMIYA-SAN!?
UH-HUH!
YOU'RE ABSOLUTELY RIGHT.

CHAPTER 34
SURPRISINGLY OKAY

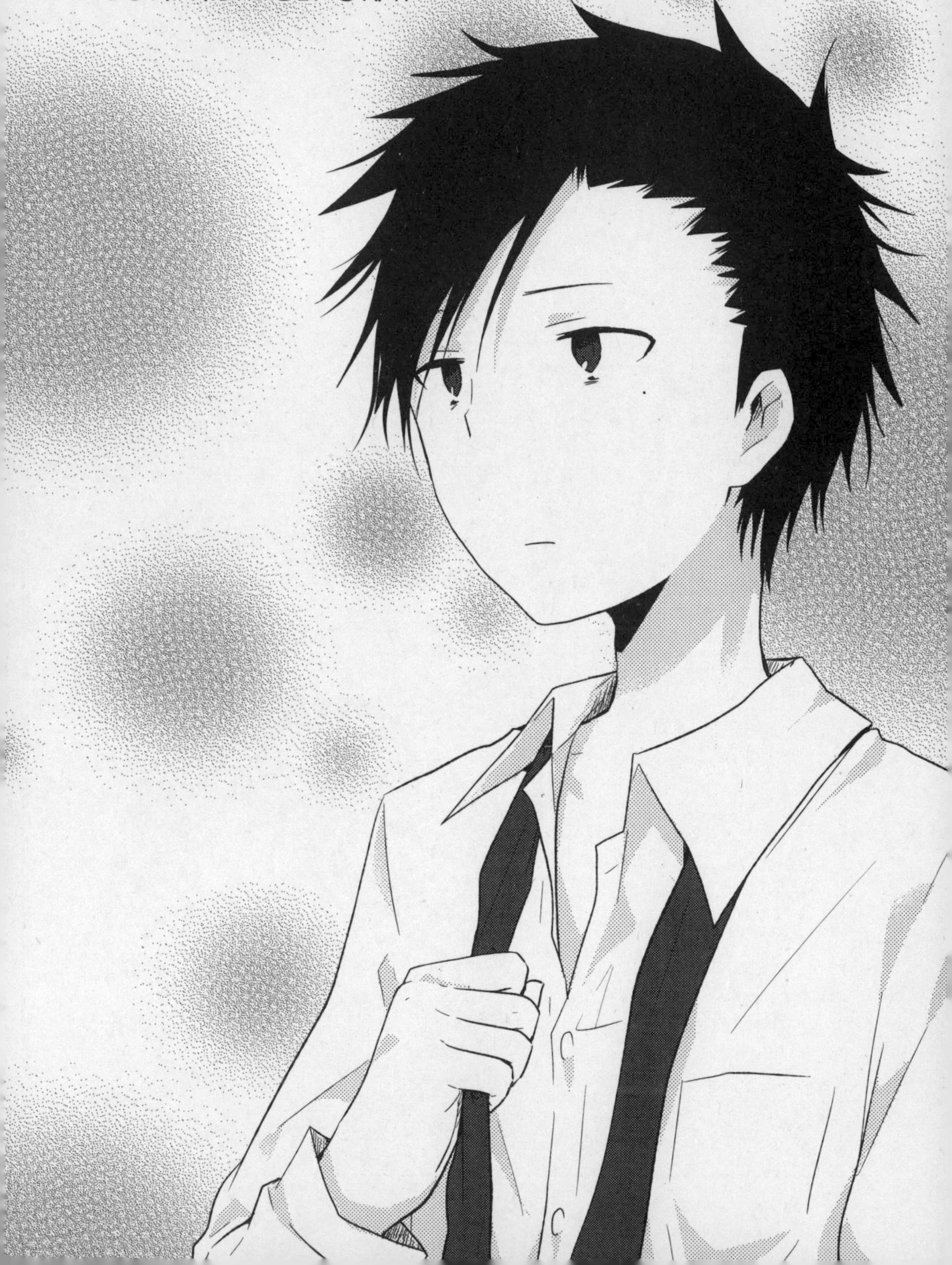

LUCKY

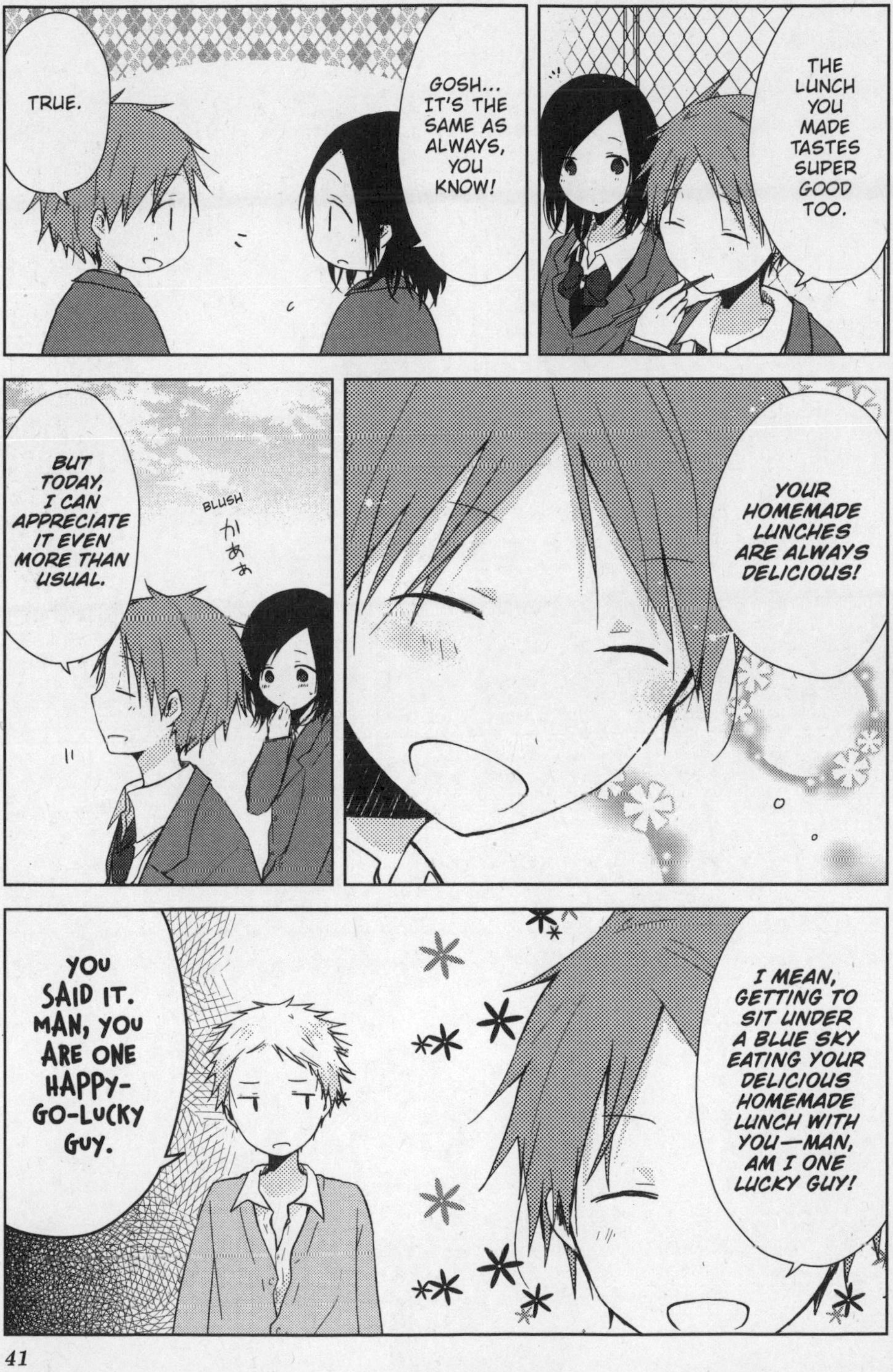
THE LUNCH YOU MADE TASTES SUPER GOOD TOO.
GOSH... IT'S THE SAME AS ALWAYS, YOU KNOW!
TRUE.
YOUR HOMEMADE LUNCHES ARE ALWAYS DELICIOUS!
BUT TODAY, I CAN APPRECIATE IT EVEN MORE THAN USUAL.
BLUSH
かああ
I MEAN, GETTING TO SIT UNDER A BLUE SKY EATING YOUR DELICIOUS HOMEMADE LUNCH WITH YOU—MAN, AM I ONE LUCKY GUY!
YOU SAID IT. MAN, YOU ARE ONE HAPPY-GO-LUCKY GUY.

RETURN OF THIS OLD VIBE

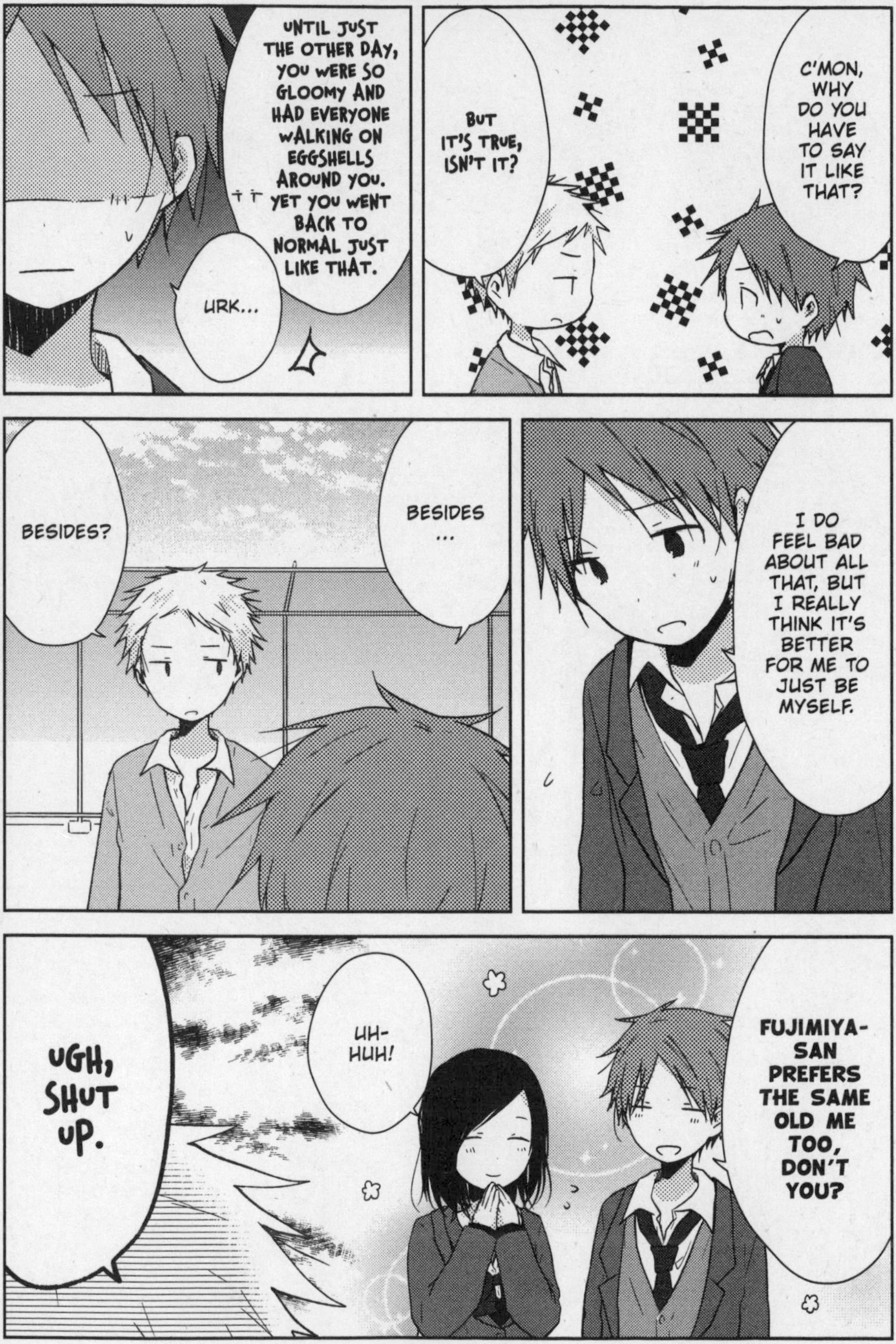
C'MON, WHY DO YOU HAVE TO SAY IT LIKE THAT?
BUT IT'S TRUE, ISN'T IT?
UNTIL JUST THE OTHER DAY, YOU WERE SO GLOOMY AND HAD EVERYONE WALKING ON EGGSHELLS AROUND YOU. YET YOU WENT BACK TO NORMAL JUST LIKE THAT.
URK...
I DO FEEL BAD ABOUT ALL THAT, BUT I REALLY THINK IT'S BETTER FOR ME TO JUST BE MYSELF.
BESIDES...
BESIDES?
FUJIMIYA-SAN PREFERS THE SAME OLD ME TOO, DON'T YOU?
UH-HUH!
UGH, SHUT UP.

NOSTALGIC

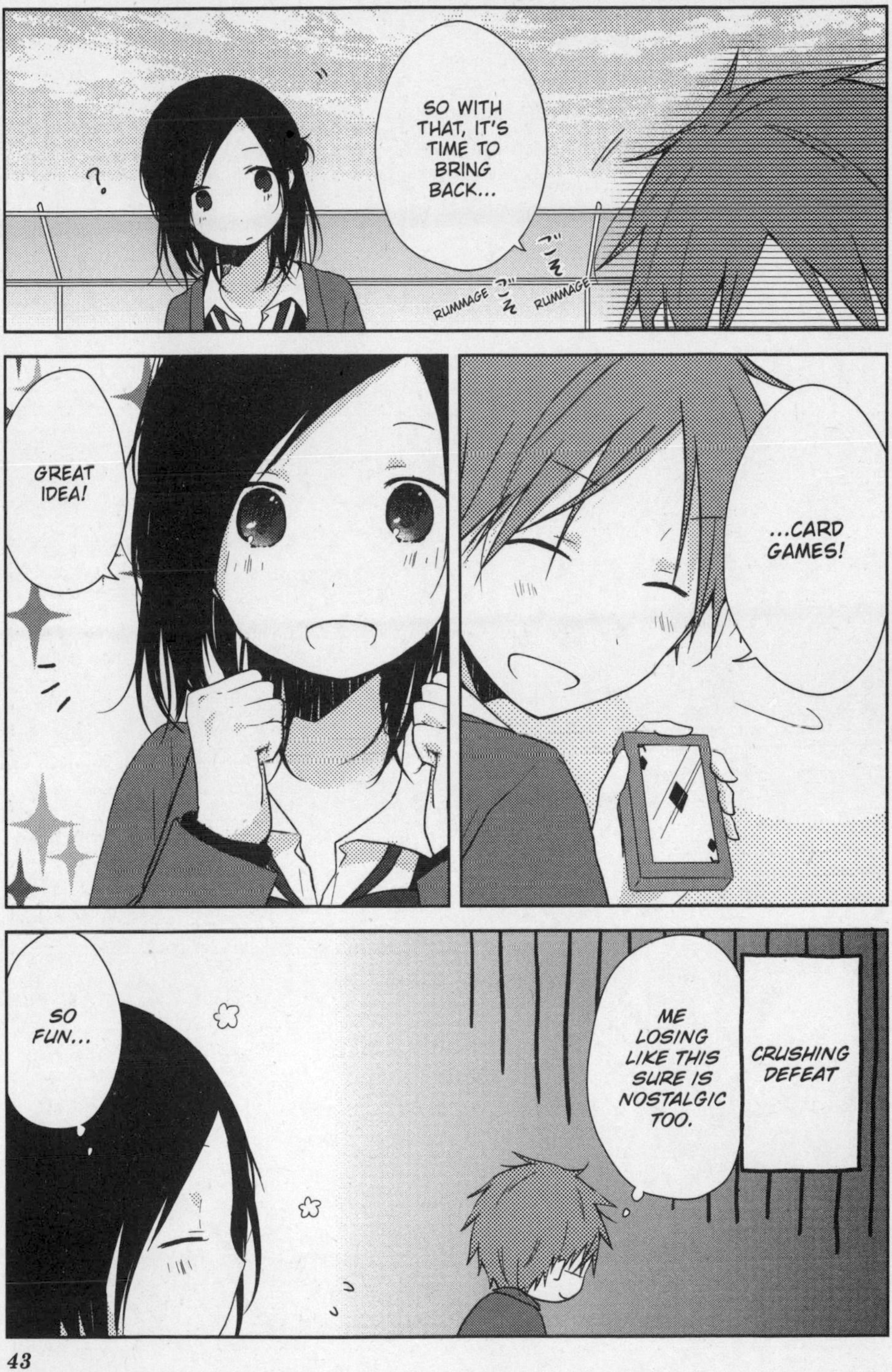
SO WITH THAT, IT'S TIME TO BRING BACK...
?
RUMMAGE RUMMAGE
...CARD GAMES!
GREAT IDEA!
CRUSHING DEFEAT
ME LOSING LIKE THIS SURE IS NOSTALGIC TOO.
SO FUN...

COURAGE

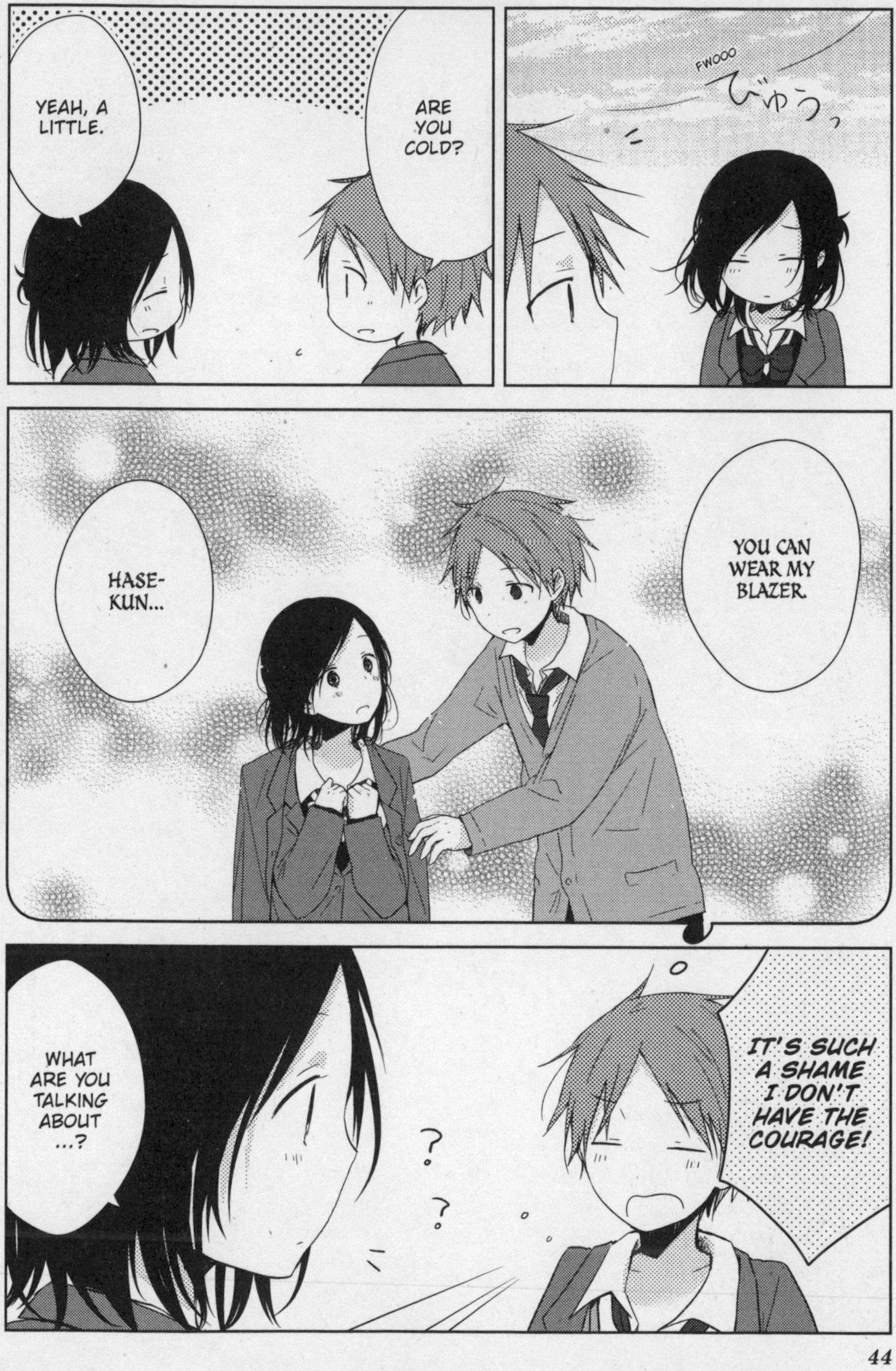

FWOOO
びゅうっ
ARE YOU COLD?
YEAH, A LITTLE.
YOU CAN WEAR MY BLAZER.
HASE-KUN...
IT'S SUCH A SHAME I DON'T HAVE THE COURAGE!
WHAT ARE YOU TALKING ABOUT ...?

LOOKING BACK

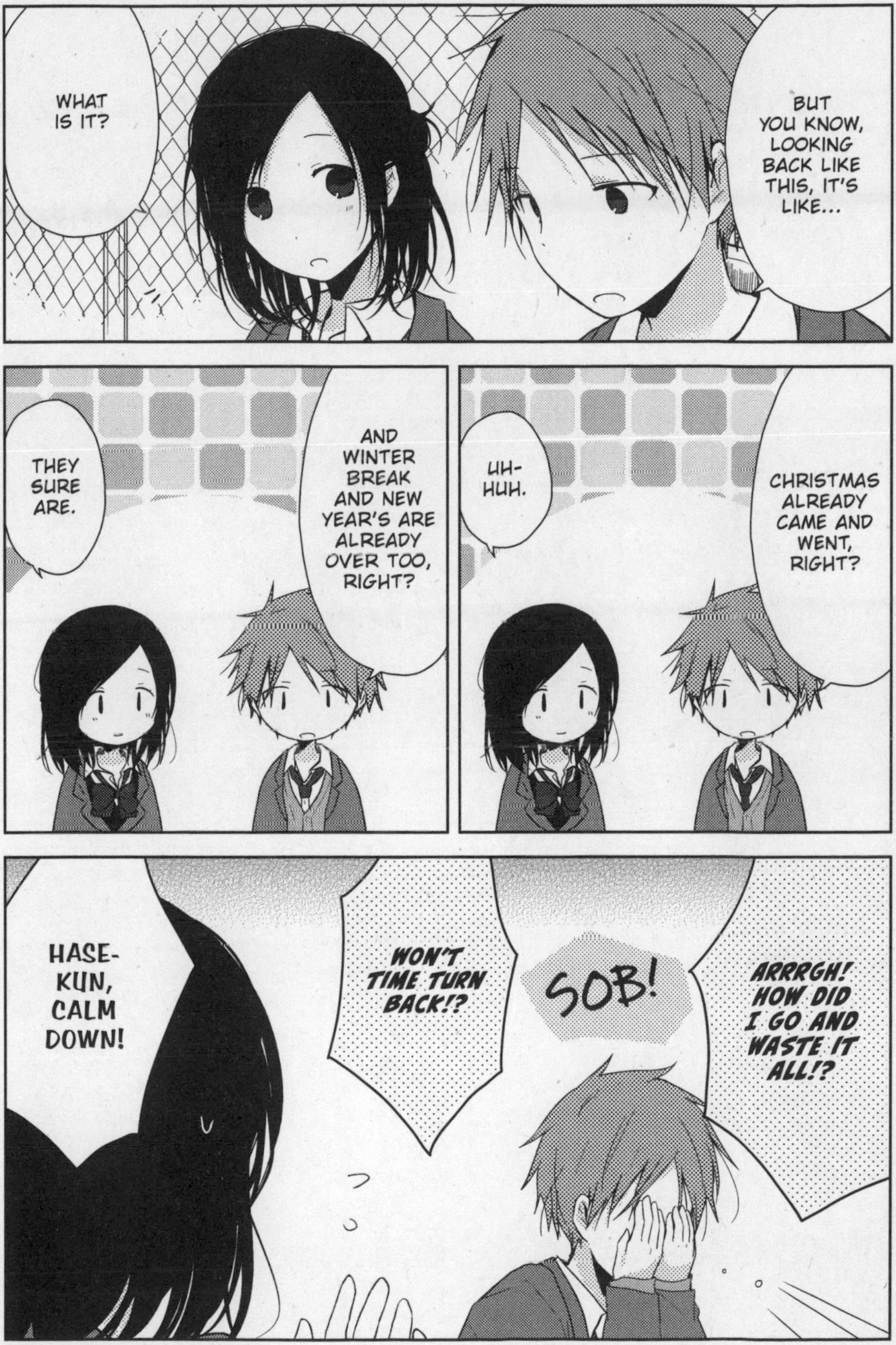

BUT YOU KNOW, LOOKING BACK LIKE THIS, IT'S LIKE...
WHAT IS IT?
CHRISTMAS ALREADY CAME AND WENT, RIGHT?
UH-HUH.
AND WINTER BREAK AND NEW YEAR'S ARE ALREADY OVER TOO, RIGHT?
THEY SURE ARE.
ARRRGH! HOW DID I GO AND WASTE IT ALL!?
SOB!
WON'T TIME TURN BACK!?
HASE-KUN, CALM DOWN!

A WAY TO CHEER UP

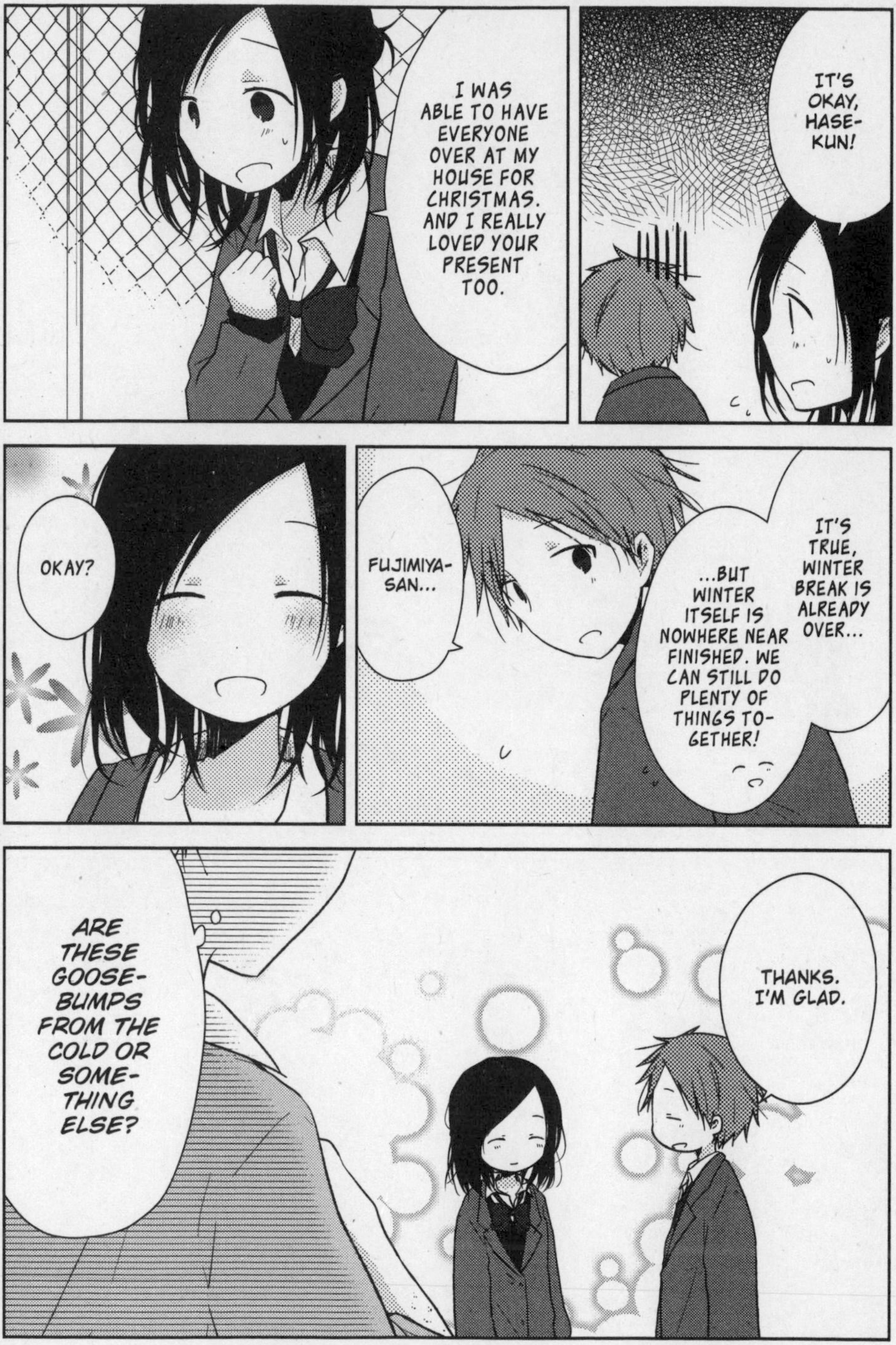
IT'S OKAY, HASE-KUN!
I WAS ABLE TO HAVE EVERYONE OVER AT MY HOUSE FOR CHRISTMAS. AND I REALLY LOVED YOUR PRESENT TOO.
IT'S TRUE, WINTER BREAK IS ALREADY OVER...
...BUT WINTER ITSELF IS NOWHERE NEAR FINISHED. WE CAN STILL DO PLENTY OF THINGS TO-GETHER!
FUJIMIYA-SAN...
OKAY?
THANKS. I'M GLAD.
ARE THESE GOOSE-BUMPS FROM THE COLD OR SOME-THING ELSE?

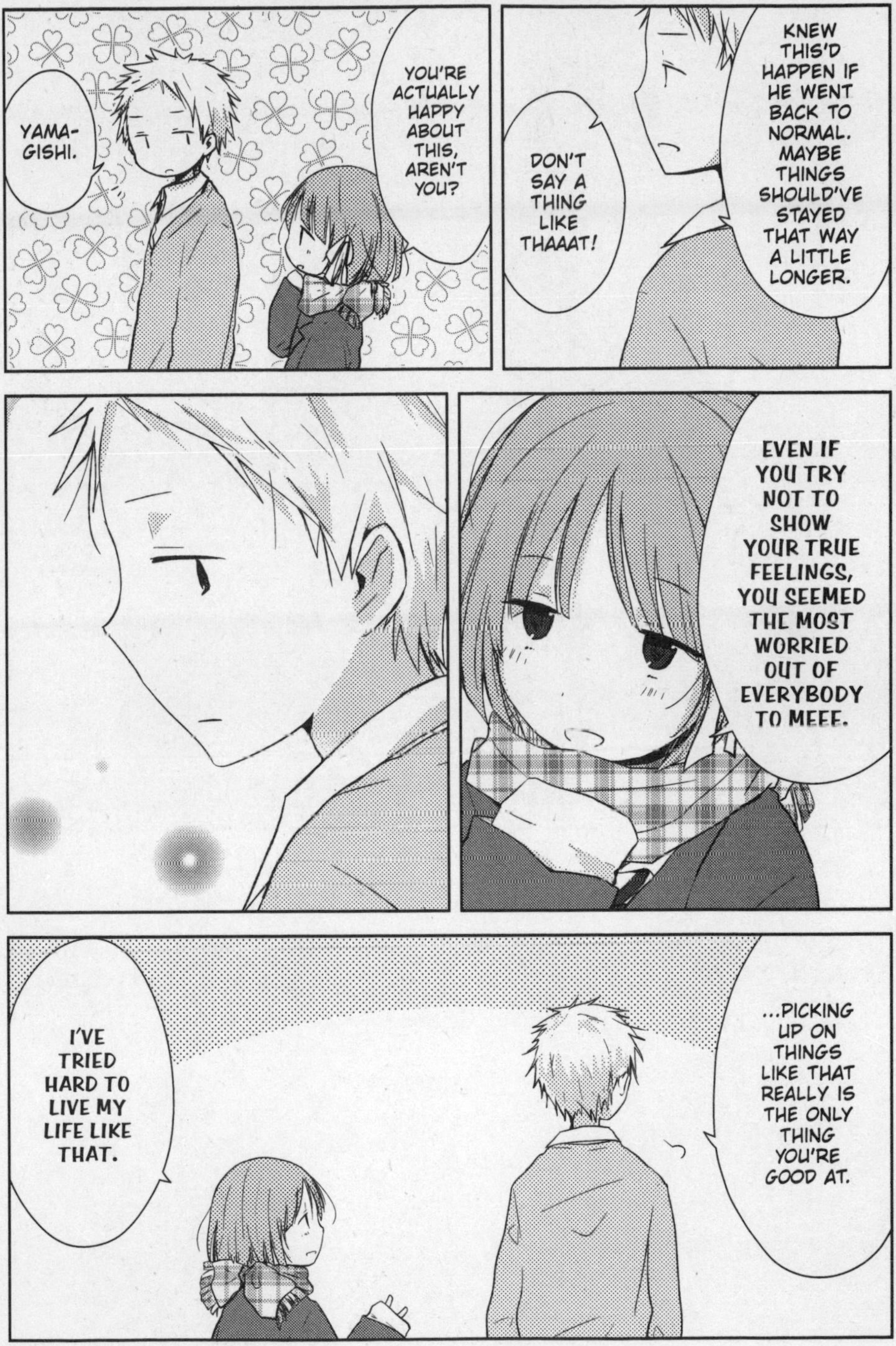
KNEW THIS'D HAPPEN IF HE WENT BACK TO NORMAL. MAYBE THINGS SHOULD'VE STAYED THAT WAY A LITTLE LONGER.
DON'T SAY A THING LIKE THAAAT!
YOU'RE ACTUALLY HAPPY ABOUT THIS, AREN'T YOU?
YAMA-GISHI.
EVEN IF YOU TRY NOT TO SHOW YOUR TRUE FEELINGS, YOU SEEMED THE MOST WORRIED OUT OF EVERYBODY TO MEEE.
...PICKING UP ON THINGS LIKE THAT REALLY IS THE ONLY THING YOU'RE GOOD AT.
I'VE TRIED HARD TO LIVE MY LIFE LIKE THAT.

THE GANG'S ALL HERE

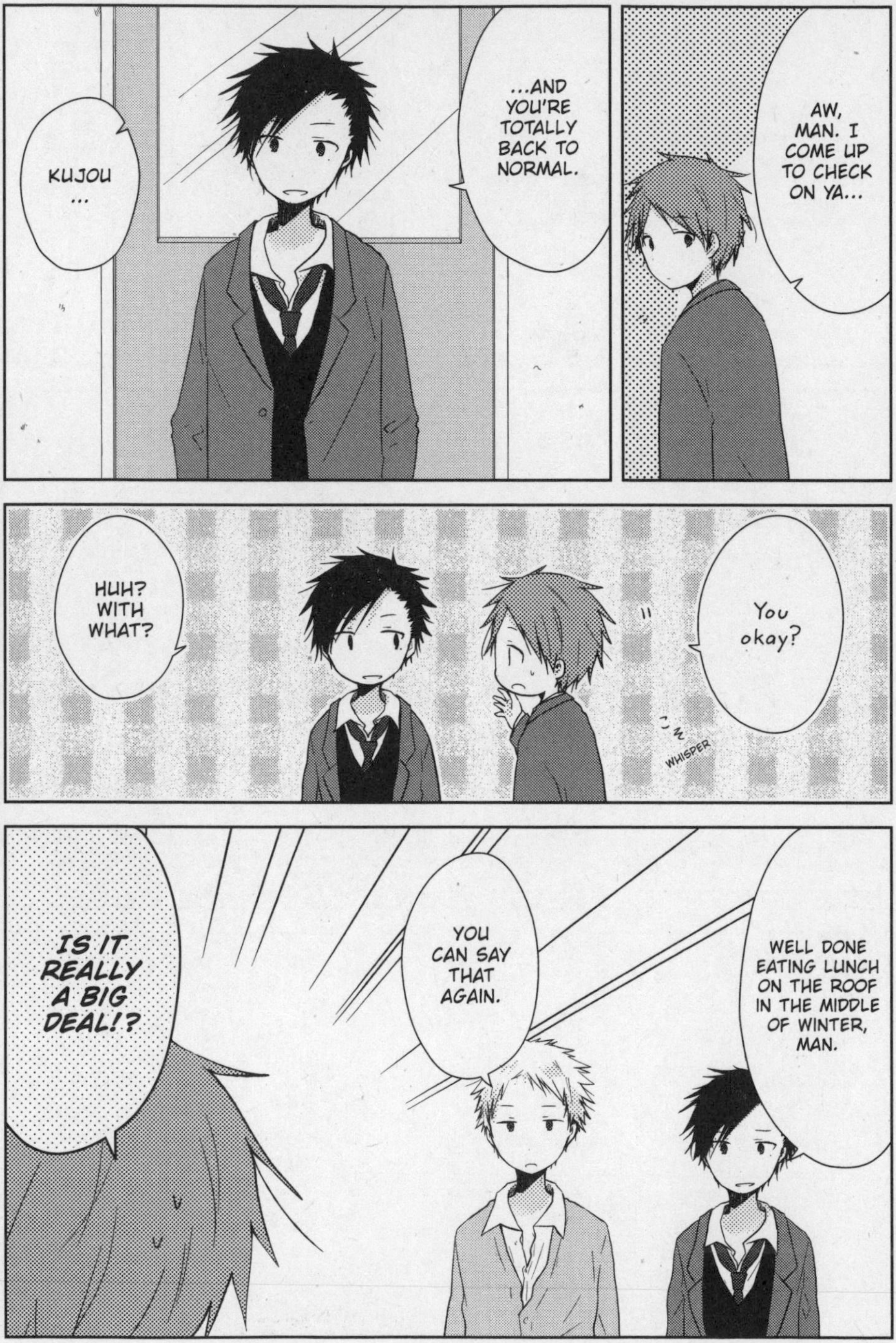
AW, MAN. I COME UP TO CHECK ON YA...
...AND YOU'RE TOTALLY BACK TO NORMAL.
KUJOU...
You okay?
WHISPER
HUH? WITH WHAT?
WELL DONE EATING LUNCH ON THE ROOF IN THE MIDDLE OF WINTER, MAN.
YOU CAN SAY THAT AGAIN.
IS IT REALLY A BIG DEAL!?

ABOUT THE COLD

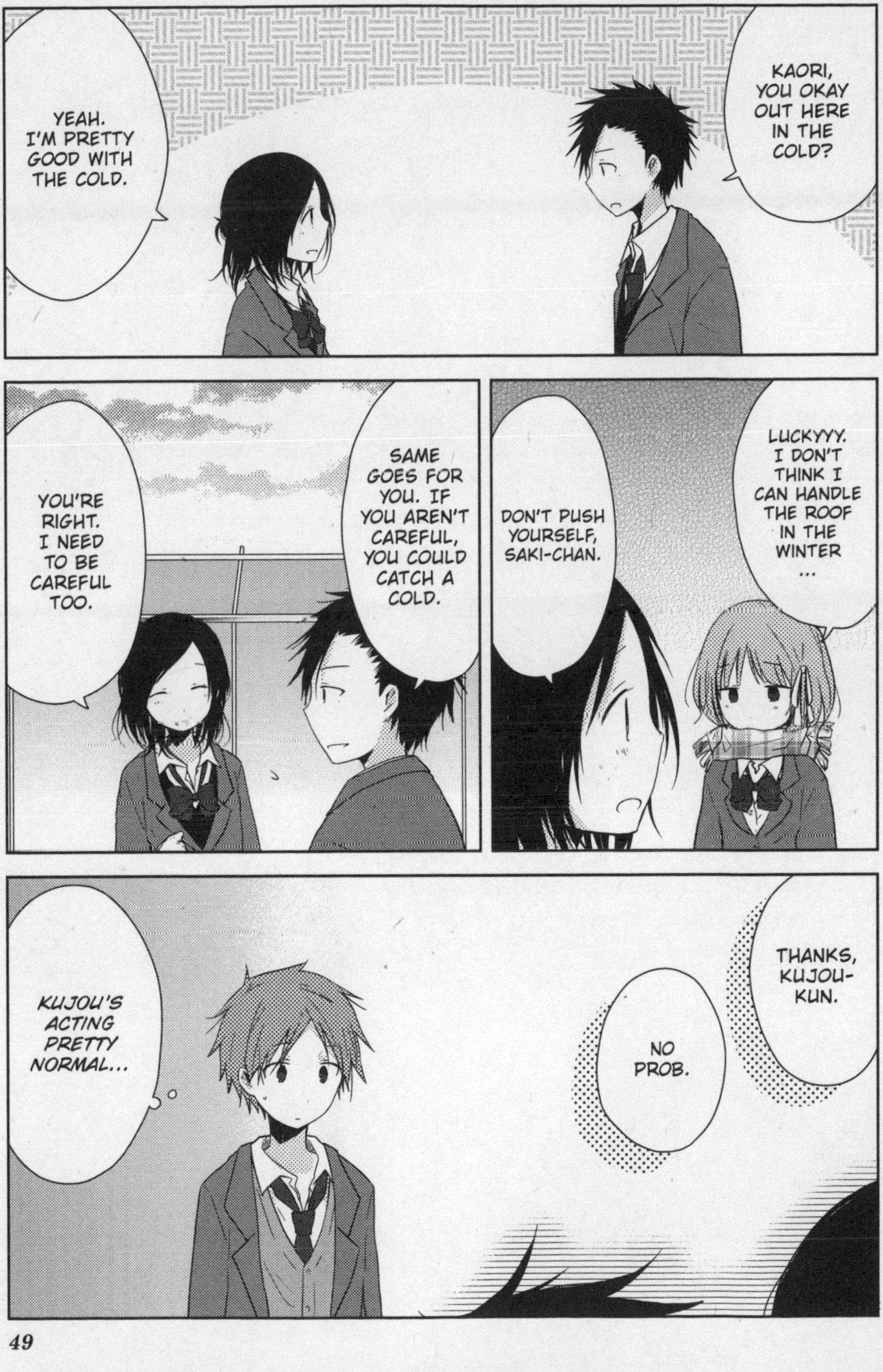
KAORI, YOU OKAY OUT HERE IN THE COLD?
YEAH. I'M PRETTY GOOD WITH THE COLD.
LUCKYYY. I DON'T THINK I CAN HANDLE THE ROOF IN THE WINTER ...
DON'T PUSH YOURSELF, SAKI-CHAN.
SAME GOES FOR YOU. IF YOU AREN'T CAREFUL, YOU COULD CATCH A COLD.
YOU'RE RIGHT. I NEED TO BE CAREFUL TOO.
THANKS, KUJOU-KUN.
NO PROB.
KUJOU'S ACTING PRETTY NORMAL...

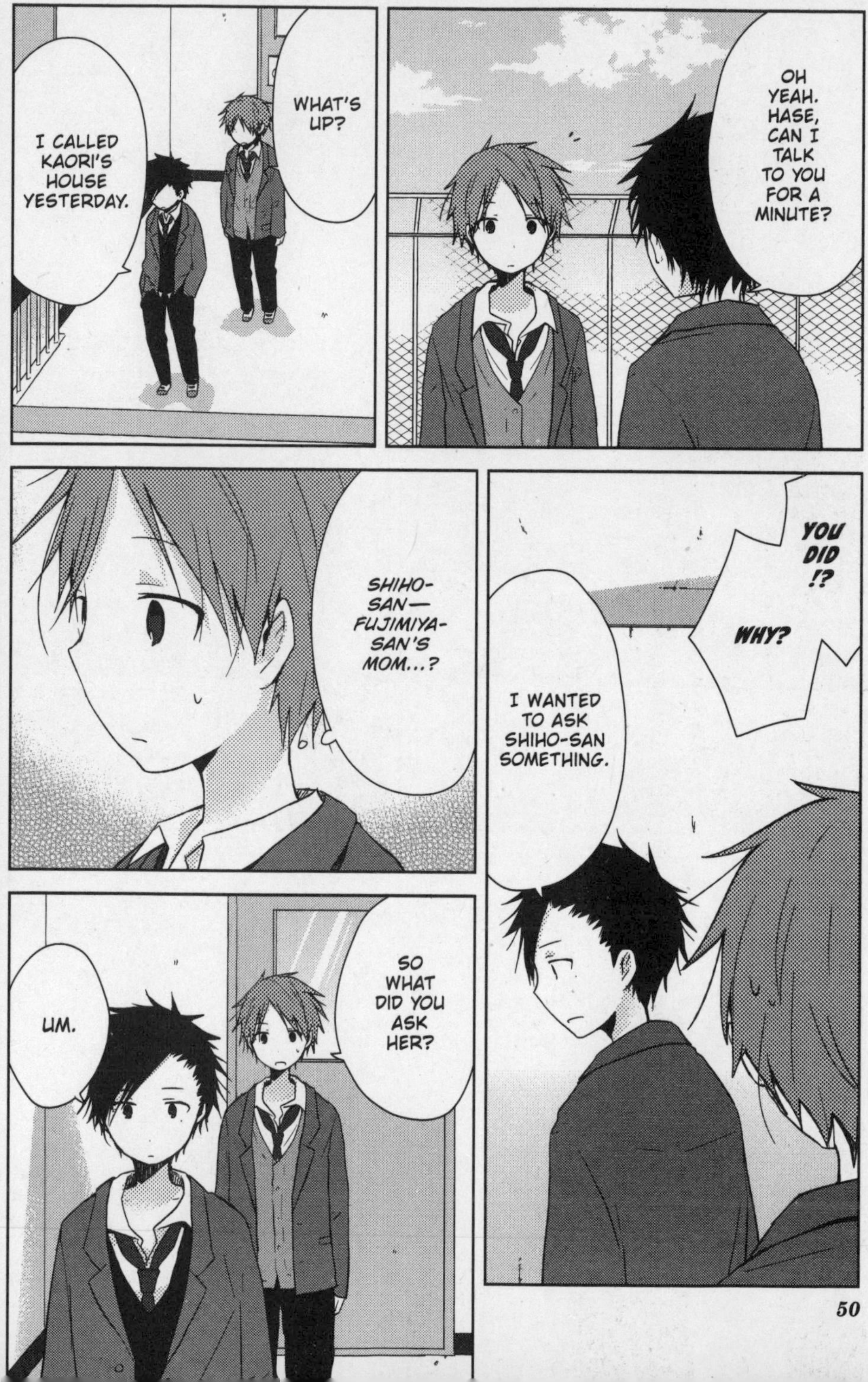
OH YEAH. HASE, CAN I TALK TO YOU FOR A MINUTE?
WHAT'S UP?
I CALLED KAORI'S HOUSE YESTERDAY.
YOU DID!?
WHY?
I WANTED TO ASK SHIHO-SAN SOMETHING.
SHIHO-SAN—FUJIMIYA-SAN'S MOM...?
SO WHAT DID YOU ASK HER?
UM.

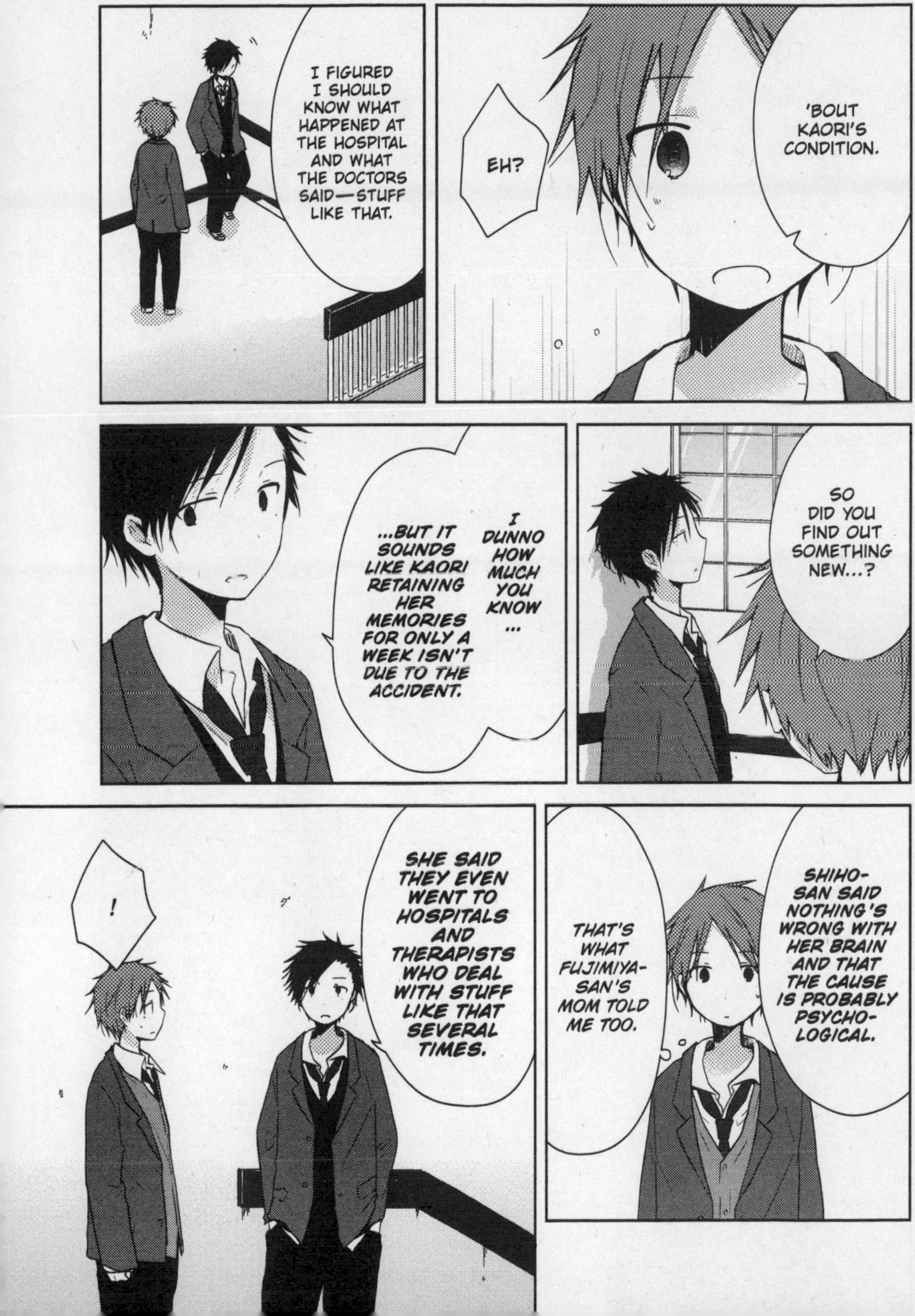
'BOUT KAORI'S CONDITION.
EH?
I FIGURED I SHOULD KNOW WHAT HAPPENED AT THE HOSPITAL AND WHAT THE DOCTORS SAID—STUFF LIKE THAT.
SO DID YOU FIND OUT SOMETHING NEW...?
I DUNNO HOW MUCH YOU KNOW...
...BUT IT SOUNDS LIKE KAORI RETAINING HER MEMORIES FOR ONLY A WEEK ISN'T DUE TO THE ACCIDENT.
SHIHO-SAN SAID NOTHING'S WRONG WITH HER BRAIN AND THAT THE CAUSE IS PROBABLY PSYCHOLOGICAL.
THAT'S WHAT FUJIMIYA-SAN'S MOM TOLD ME TOO.
SHE SAID THEY EVEN WENT TO HOSPITALS AND THERAPISTS WHO DEAL WITH STUFF LIKE THAT SEVERAL TIMES.
!

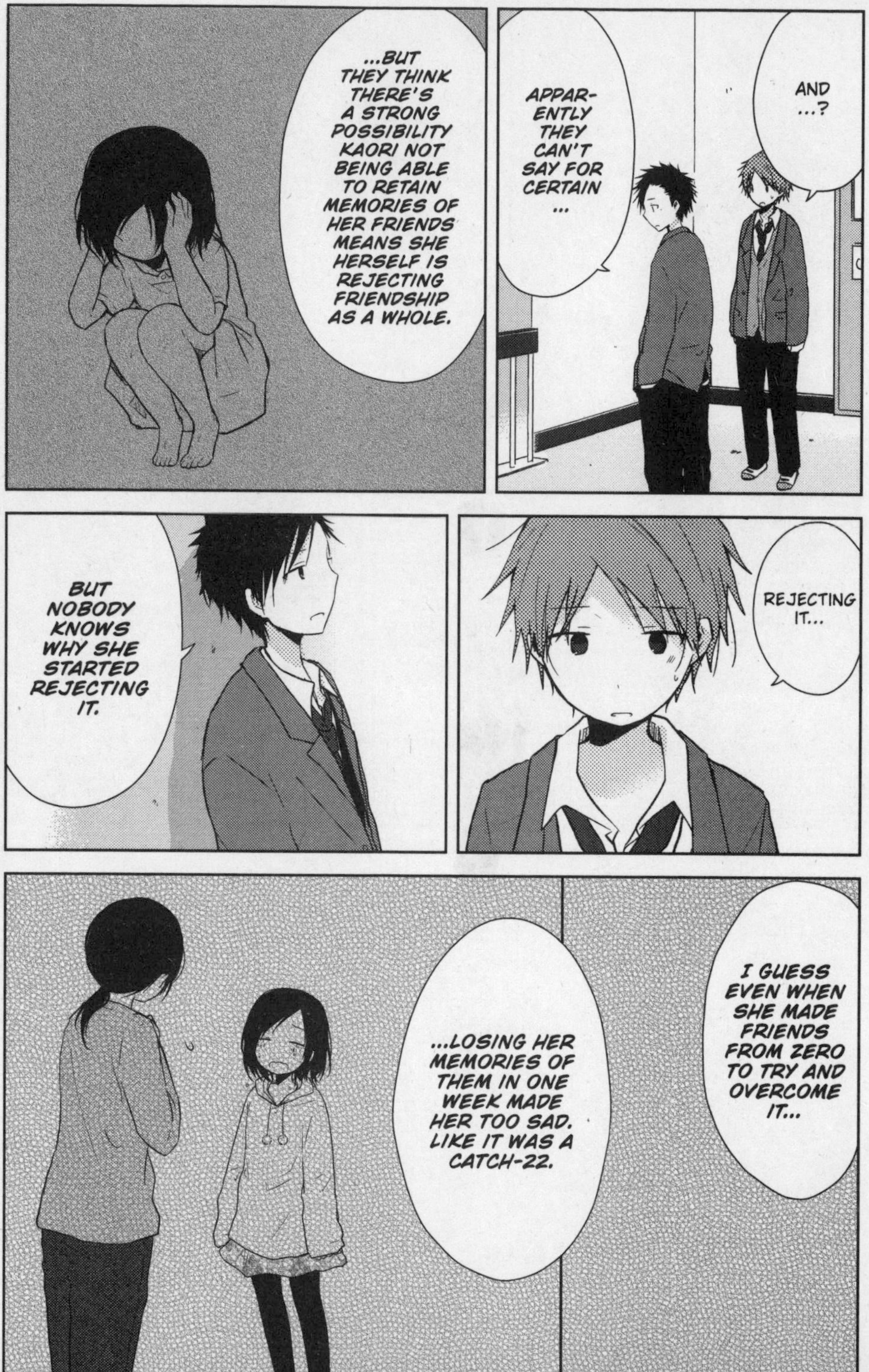
AND ...?
APPAR-ENTLY THEY CAN'T SAY FOR CERTAIN ...
...BUT THEY THINK THERE'S A STRONG POSSIBILITY KAORI NOT BEING ABLE TO RETAIN MEMORIES OF HER FRIENDS MEANS SHE HERSELF IS REJECTING FRIENDSHIP AS A WHOLE.
REJECTING IT...
BUT NOBODY KNOWS WHY SHE STARTED REJECTING IT.
I GUESS EVEN WHEN SHE MADE FRIENDS FROM ZERO TO TRY AND OVERCOME IT...
...LOSING HER MEMORIES OF THEM IN ONE WEEK MADE HER TOO SAD. LIKE IT WAS A CATCH-22.

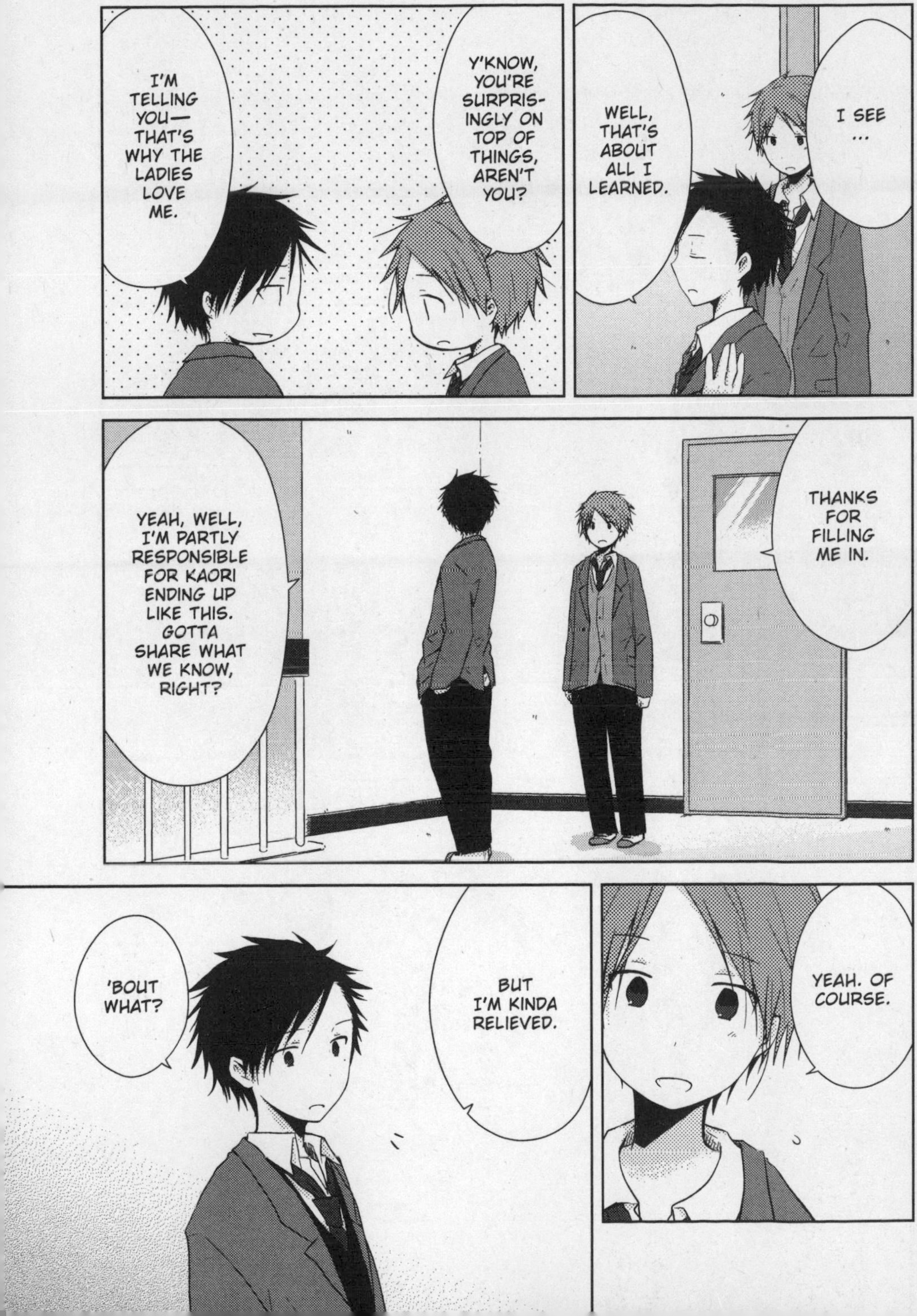
I SEE ...
WELL, THAT'S ABOUT ALL I LEARNED.
Y'KNOW, YOU'RE SURPRIS-INGLY ON TOP OF THINGS, AREN'T YOU?
I'M TELLING YOU—THAT'S WHY THE LADIES LOVE ME.
THANKS FOR FILLING ME IN.
YEAH, WELL, I'M PARTLY RESPONSIBLE FOR KAORI ENDING UP LIKE THIS. GOTTA SHARE WHAT WE KNOW, RIGHT?
YEAH. OF COURSE.
BUT I'M KINDA RELIEVED.
'BOUT WHAT?

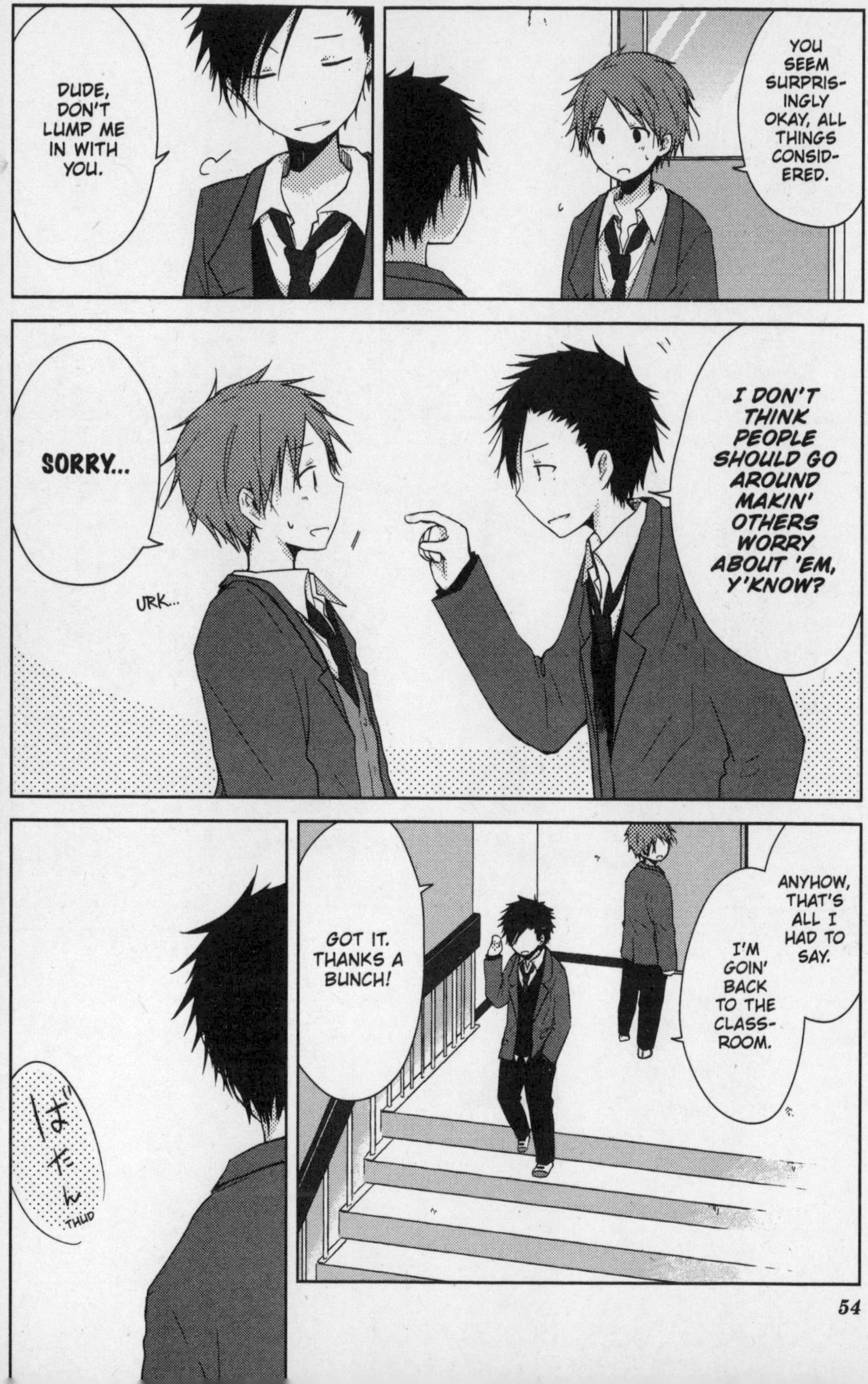
YOU SEEM SURPRISINGLY OKAY, ALL THINGS CONSIDERED.
DUDE, DON'T LUMP ME IN WITH YOU.
I DON'T THINK PEOPLE SHOULD GO AROUND MAKIN' OTHERS WORRY ABOUT 'EM, Y'KNOW?
SORRY...
URK...
ANYHOW, THAT'S ALL I HAD TO SAY.
I'M GOIN' BACK TO THE CLASSROOM.
GOT IT. THANKS A BUNCH!
ばたん
THUD

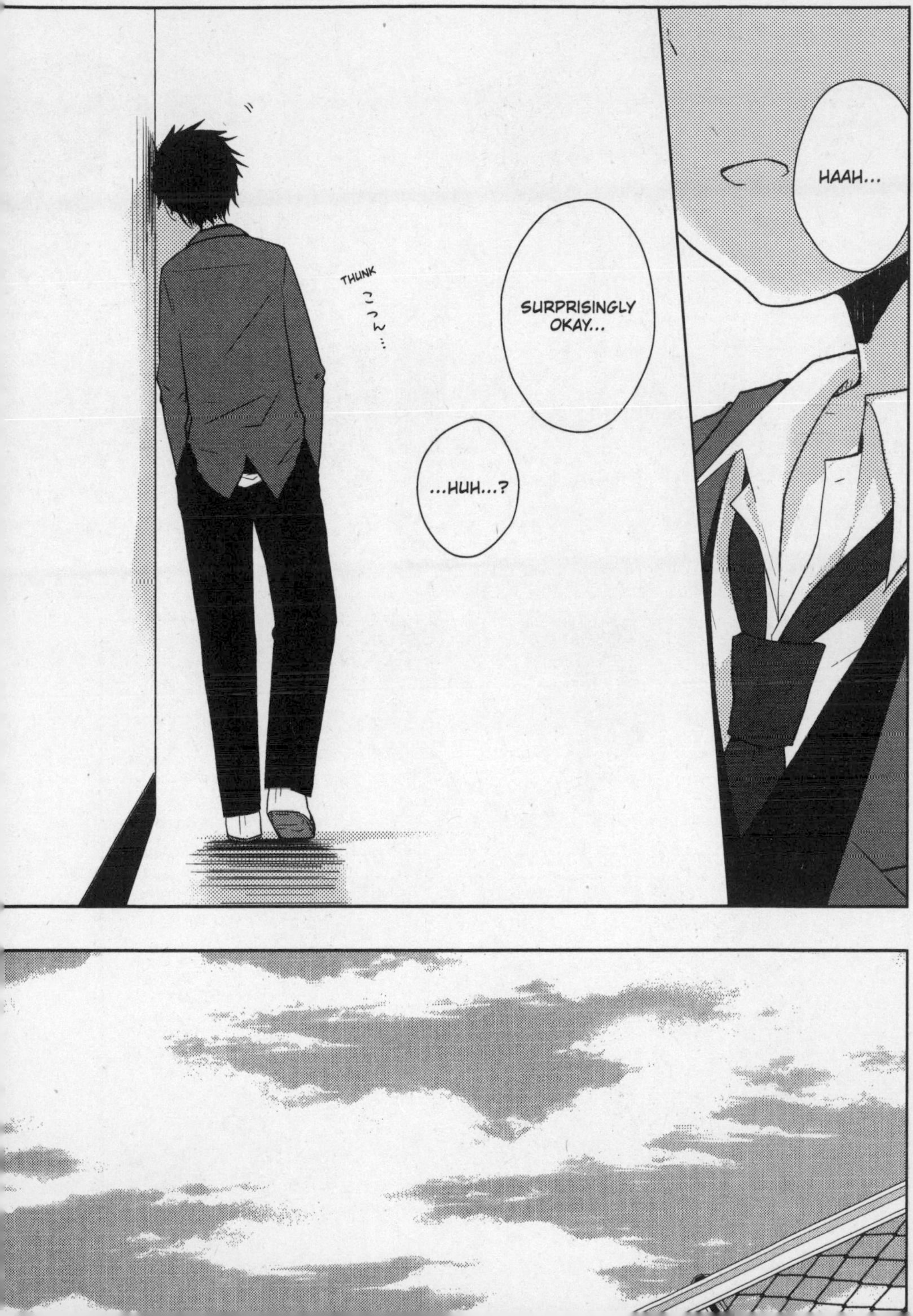
HAAH...
SURPRISINGLY OKAY...
...HUH...?
THUNK
こつん…

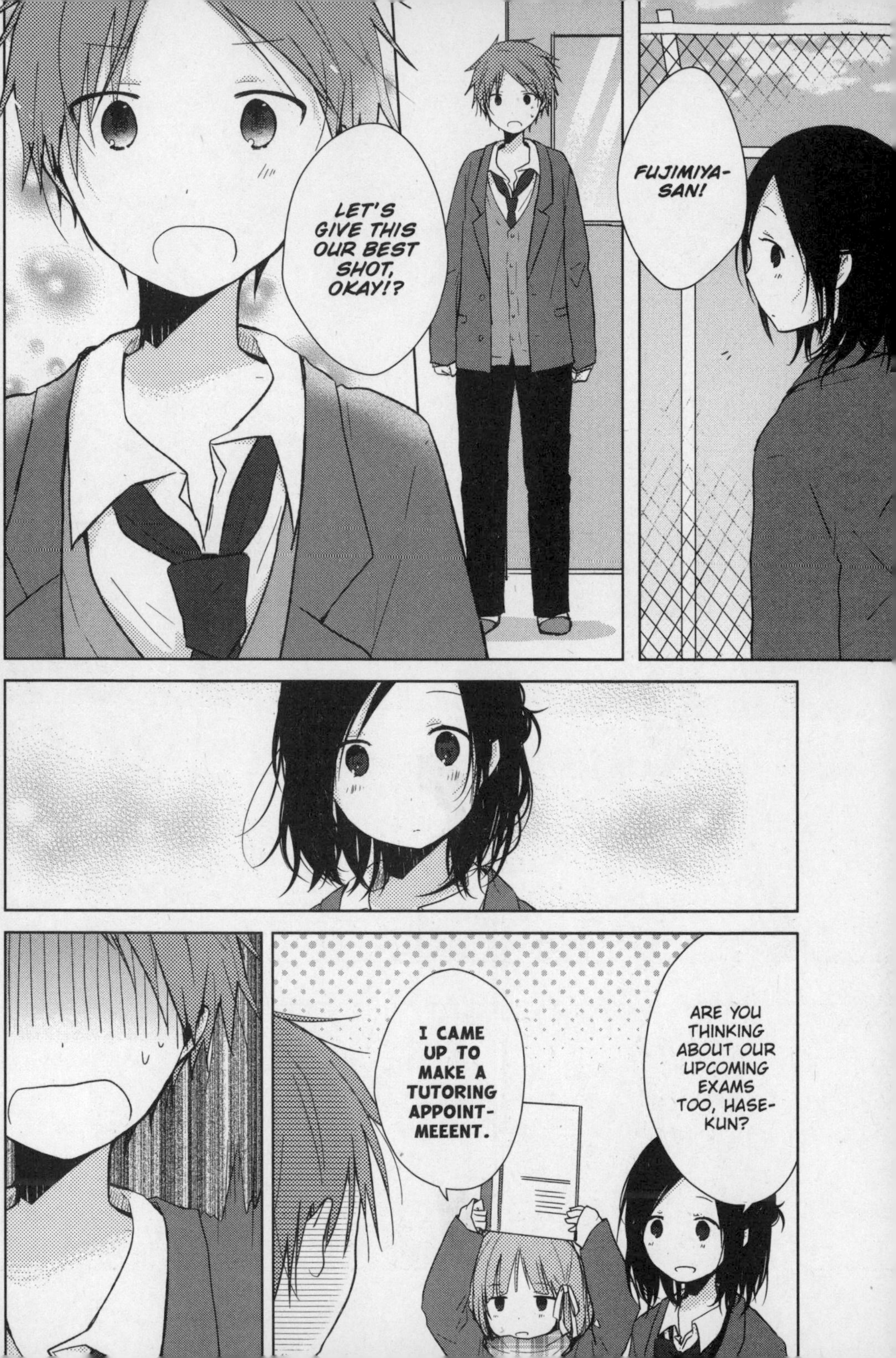
FUJIMIYA-SAN!
LET'S GIVE THIS OUR BEST SHOT, OKAY!?
ARE YOU THINKING ABOUT OUR UPCOMING EXAMS TOO, HASE-KUN?
I CAME UP TO MAKE A TUTORING APPOINT-MEEENT.

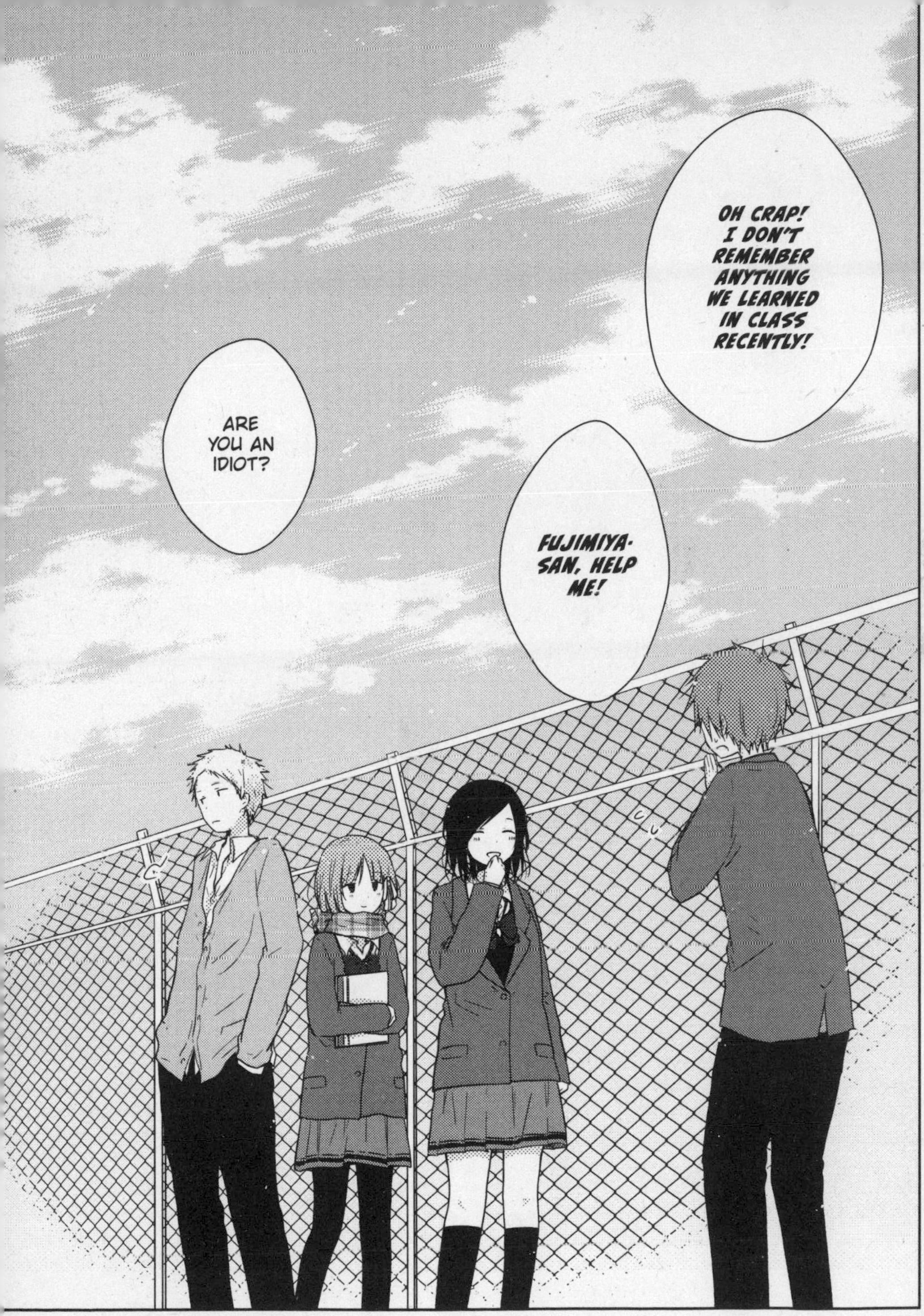

OH CRAP! I DON'T REMEMBER ANYTHING WE LEARNED IN CLASS RECENTLY!
FUJIMIYA-SAN, HELP ME!
ARE YOU AN IDIOT?

COME AGAIN ...?

A TWENTY-EIGHT...?

NAME YUUKI HASE

28

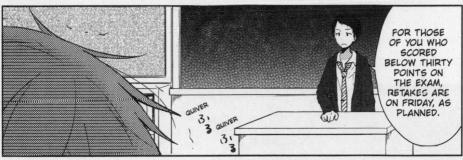

FOR THOSE OF YOU WHO SCORED BELOW THIRTY POINTS ON THE EXAM, RETAKES ARE ON FRIDAY, AS PLANNED.

QUIVER
い
り

QUIVER
い
り

WHYYY !?

HASE.

AREN'T YOU A REGULAR?

CHAPTER 35 COFFEE AND MILK

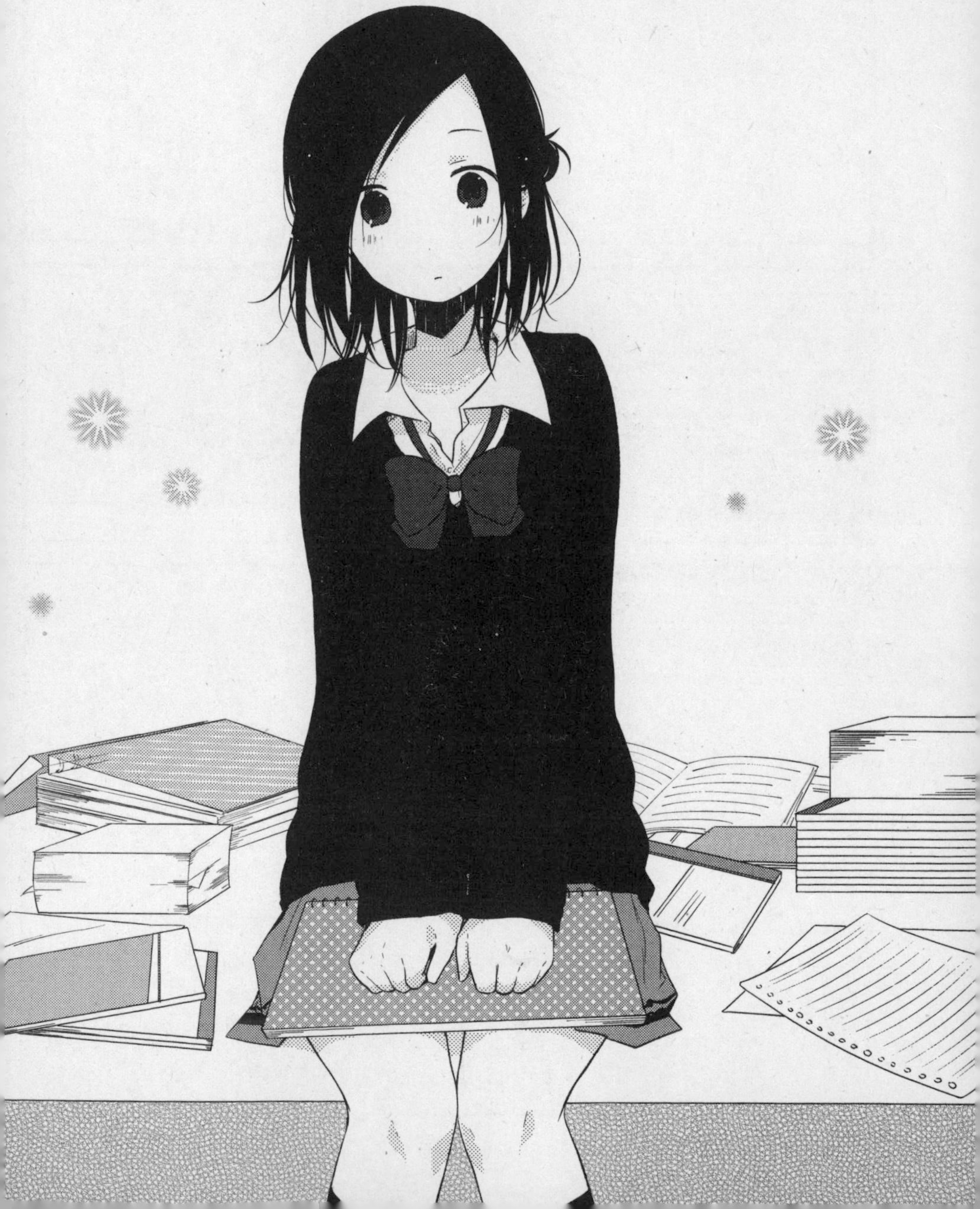

DOWN-TO-THE-WIRE BATTLE

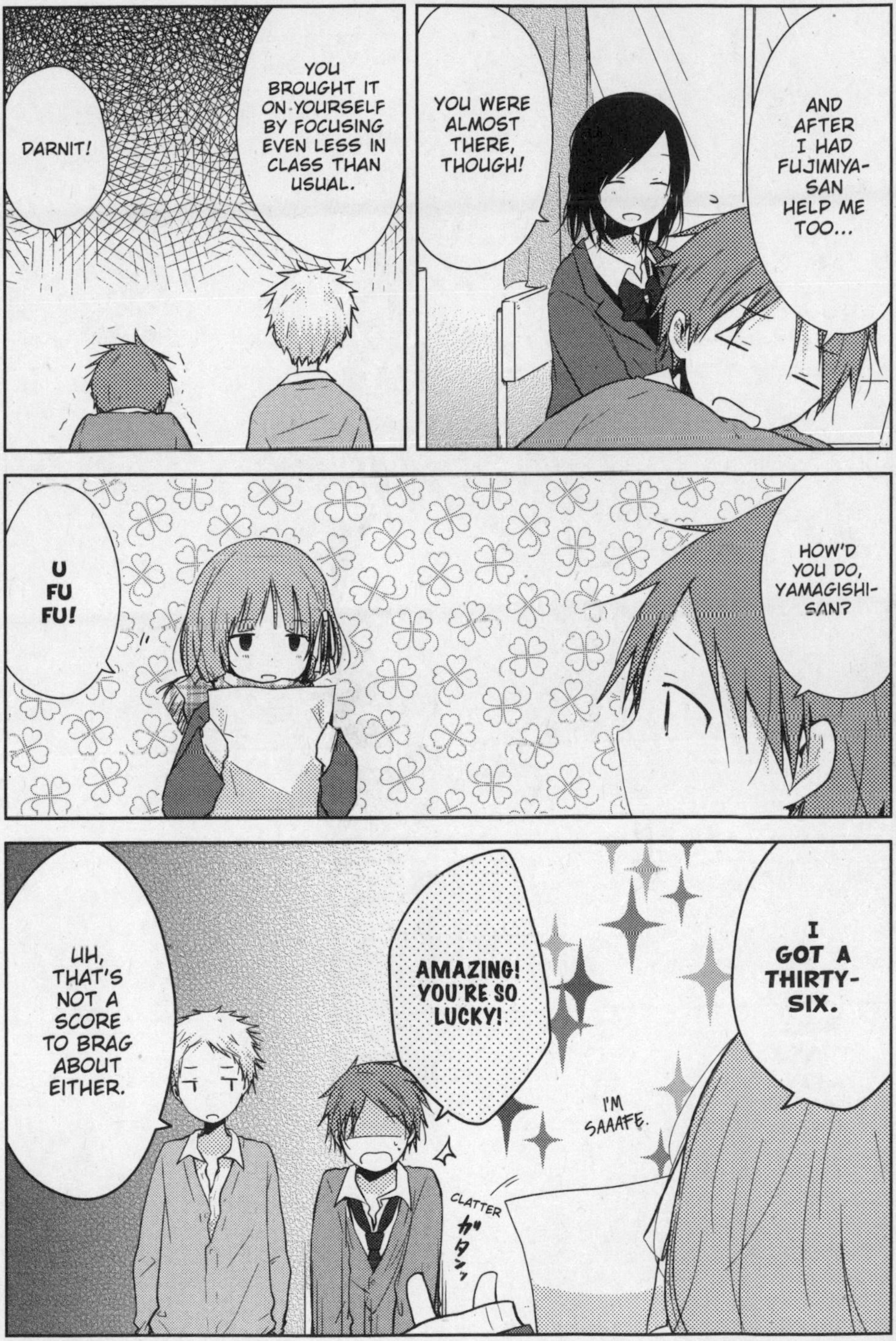

AND AFTER I HAD FUJIMIYA-SAN HELP ME TOO...
YOU WERE ALMOST THERE, THOUGH!
YOU BROUGHT IT ON YOURSELF BY FOCUSING EVEN LESS IN CLASS THAN USUAL.
DARNIT!
HOW'D YOU DO, YAMAGISHI-SAN?
U FU FU!
I GOT A THIRTY-SIX.
AMAZING! YOU'RE SO LUCKY!
I'M SAAAFE.
UH, THAT'S NOT A SCORE TO BRAG ABOUT EITHER.
CLATTER
ガタッ

EASILY MOTIVATED

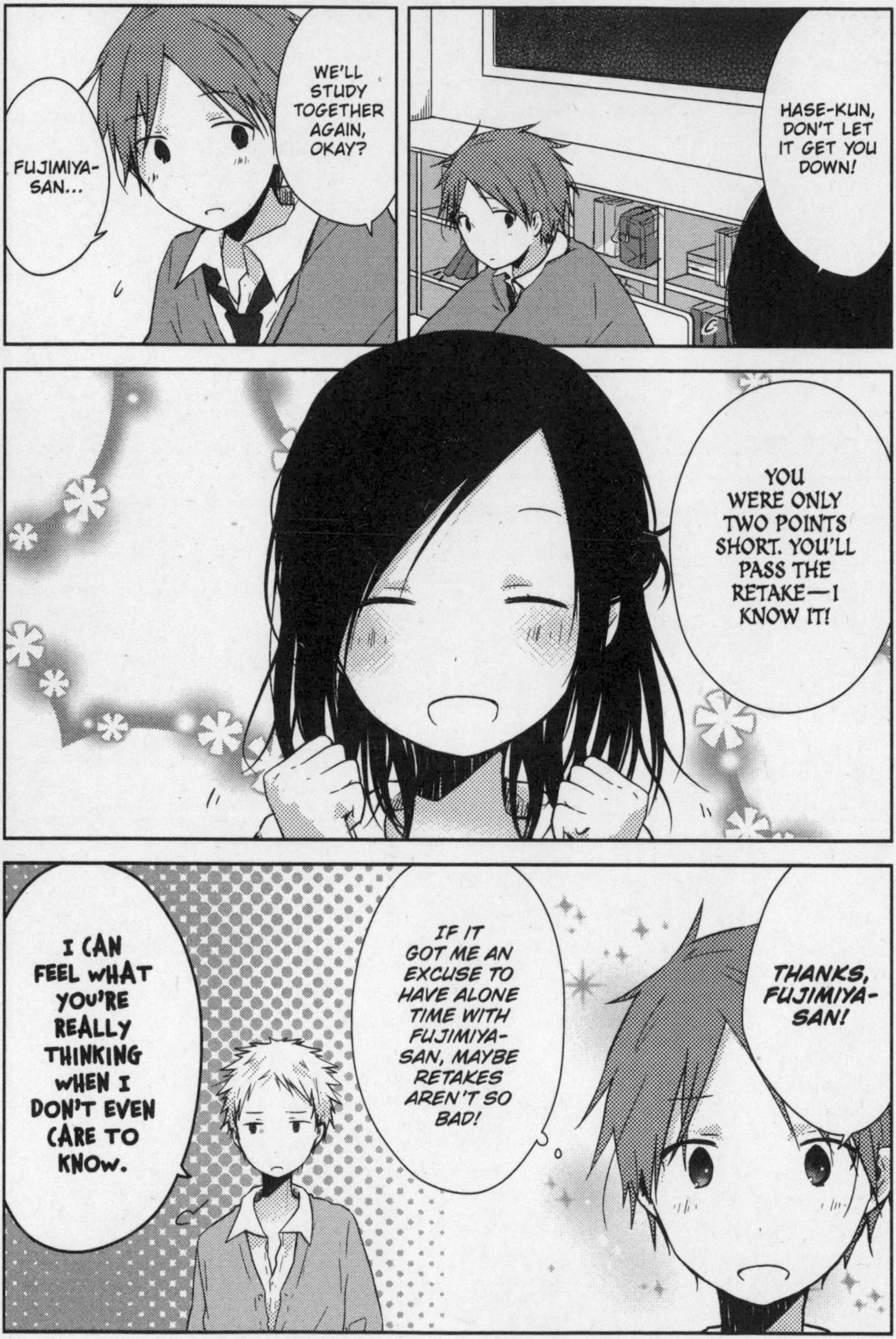
HASE-KUN, DON'T LET IT GET YOU DOWN!
WE'LL STUDY TOGETHER AGAIN, OKAY?
FUJIMIYA-SAN...
YOU WERE ONLY TWO POINTS SHORT. YOU'LL PASS THE RETAKE—I KNOW IT!
THANKS, FUJIMIYA-SAN!
IF IT GOT ME AN EXCUSE TO HAVE ALONE TIME WITH FUJIMIYA-SAN, MAYBE RETAKES AREN'T SO BAD!
I CAN FEEL WHAT YOU'RE REALLY THINKING WHEN I DON'T EVEN CARE TO KNOW.

HANG IN THERE, HASE-KUN

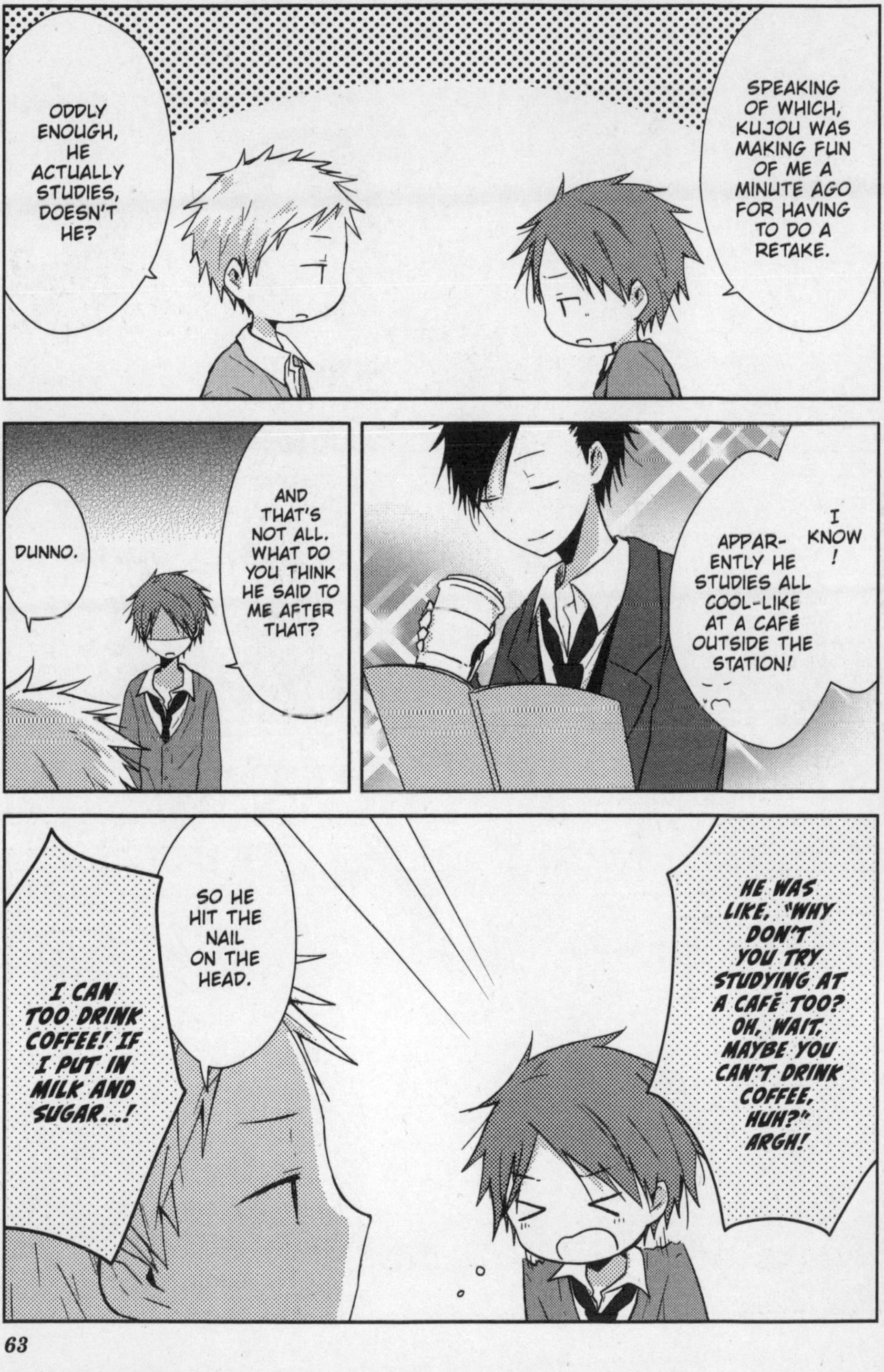

SPEAKING OF WHICH, KUJOU WAS MAKING FUN OF ME A MINUTE AGO FOR HAVING TO DO A RETAKE.
ODDLY ENOUGH, HE ACTUALLY STUDIES, DOESN'T HE?
I KNOW!
APPAR-ENTLY HE STUDIES ALL COOL-LIKE AT A CAFÉ OUTSIDE THE STATION!
AND THAT'S NOT ALL. WHAT DO YOU THINK HE SAID TO ME AFTER THAT?
DUNNO.
HE WAS LIKE, "WHY DON'T YOU TRY STUDYING AT A CAFÉ TOO? OH, WAIT, MAYBE YOU CAN'T DRINK COFFEE, HUH?" ARGH!
SO HE HIT THE NAIL ON THE HEAD.
I CAN TOO DRINK COFFEE! IF I PUT IN MILK AND SUGAR...!

BIG PANIC

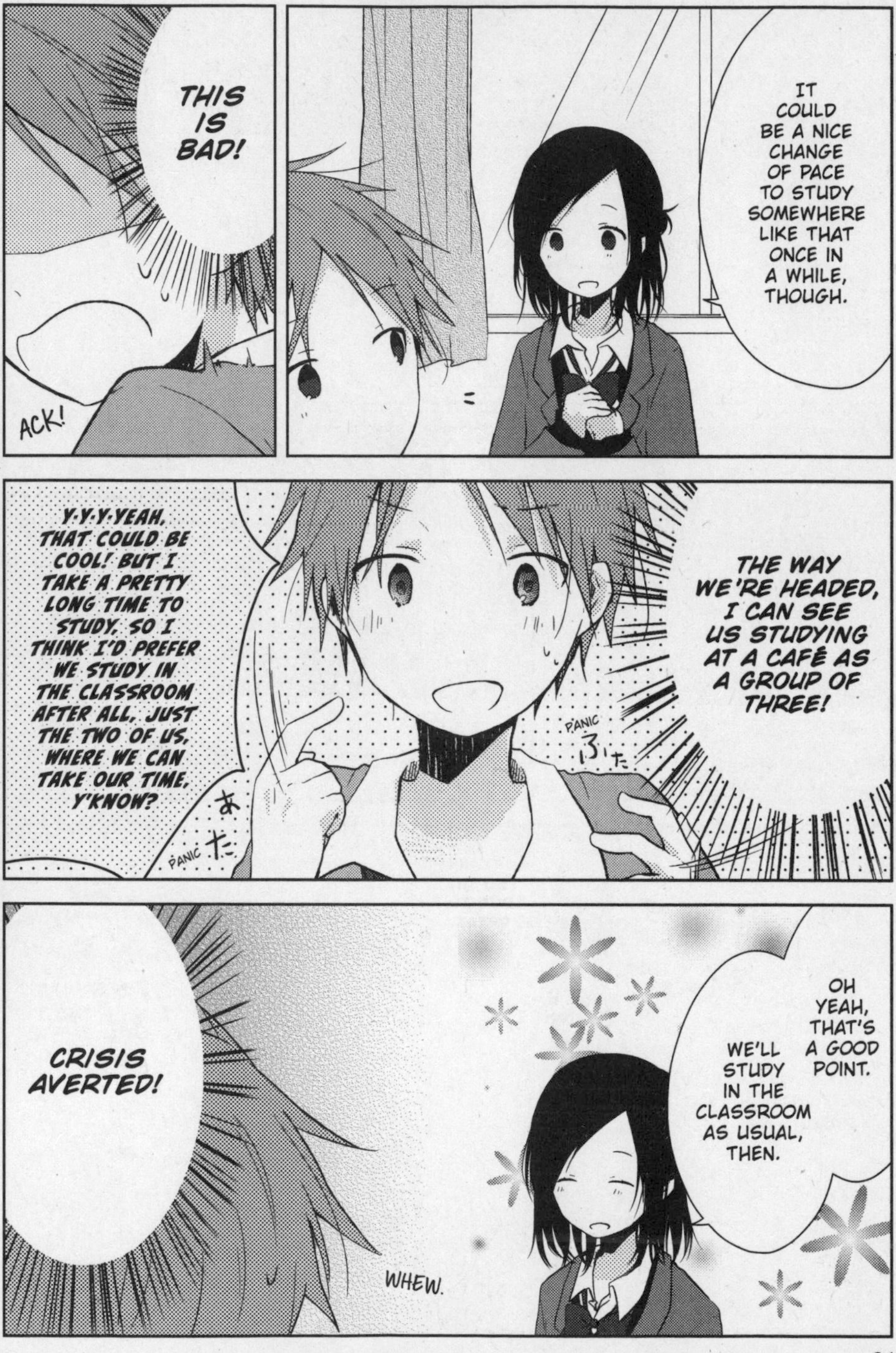

IT COULD BE A NICE CHANGE OF PACE TO STUDY SOMEWHERE LIKE THAT ONCE IN A WHILE, THOUGH.
THIS IS BAD!
ACK!
THE WAY WE'RE HEADED, I CAN SEE US STUDYING AT A CAFÉ AS A GROUP OF THREE!
Y-Y-Y-YEAH, THAT COULD BE COOL! BUT I TAKE A PRETTY LONG TIME TO STUDY, SO I THINK I'D PREFER WE STUDY IN THE CLASSROOM AFTER ALL, JUST THE TWO OF US, WHERE WE CAN TAKE OUR TIME, Y'KNOW?
PANIC ふた
PANIC あた
OH YEAH, THAT'S A GOOD POINT.
WE'LL STUDY IN THE CLASSROOM AS USUAL, THEN.
CRISIS AVERTED!
WHEW.

TODAY'S PLANS

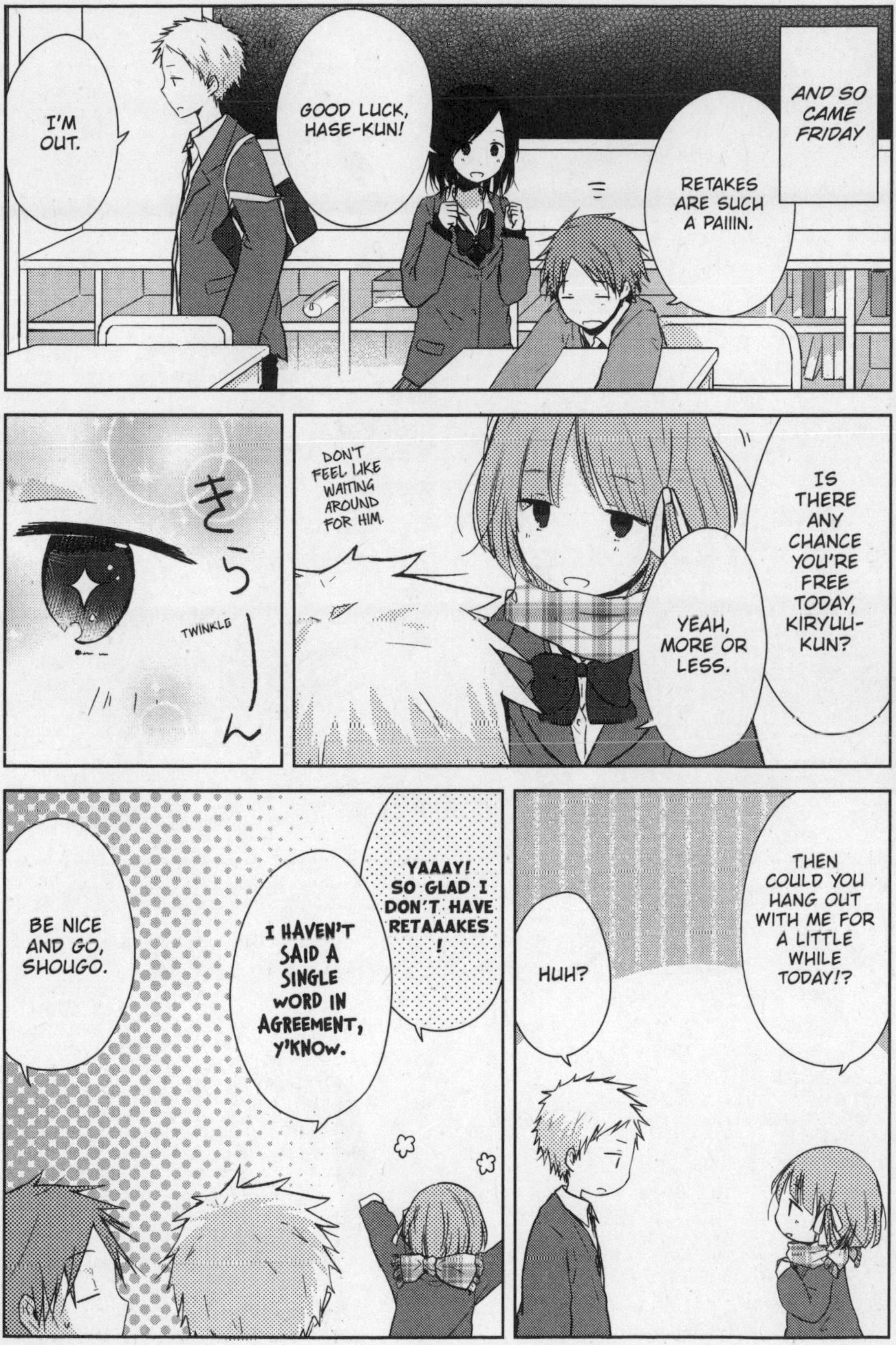
AND SO CAME FRIDAY
RETAKES ARE SUCH A PAIIIN.
GOOD LUCK, HASE-KUN!
I'M OUT.
IS THERE ANY CHANCE YOU'RE FREE TODAY, KIRYUU-KUN?
YEAH, MORE OR LESS.
DON'T FEEL LIKE WAITING AROUND FOR HIM.
きらーん
TWINKLE
THEN COULD YOU HANG OUT WITH ME FOR A LITTLE WHILE TODAY!?
HUH?
YAAAY! SO GLAD I DON'T HAVE RETAAAKES!
I HAVEN'T SAID A SINGLE WORD IN AGREEMENT, Y'KNOW.
BE NICE AND GO, SHOUGO.

CAN'T HOLD IT IN

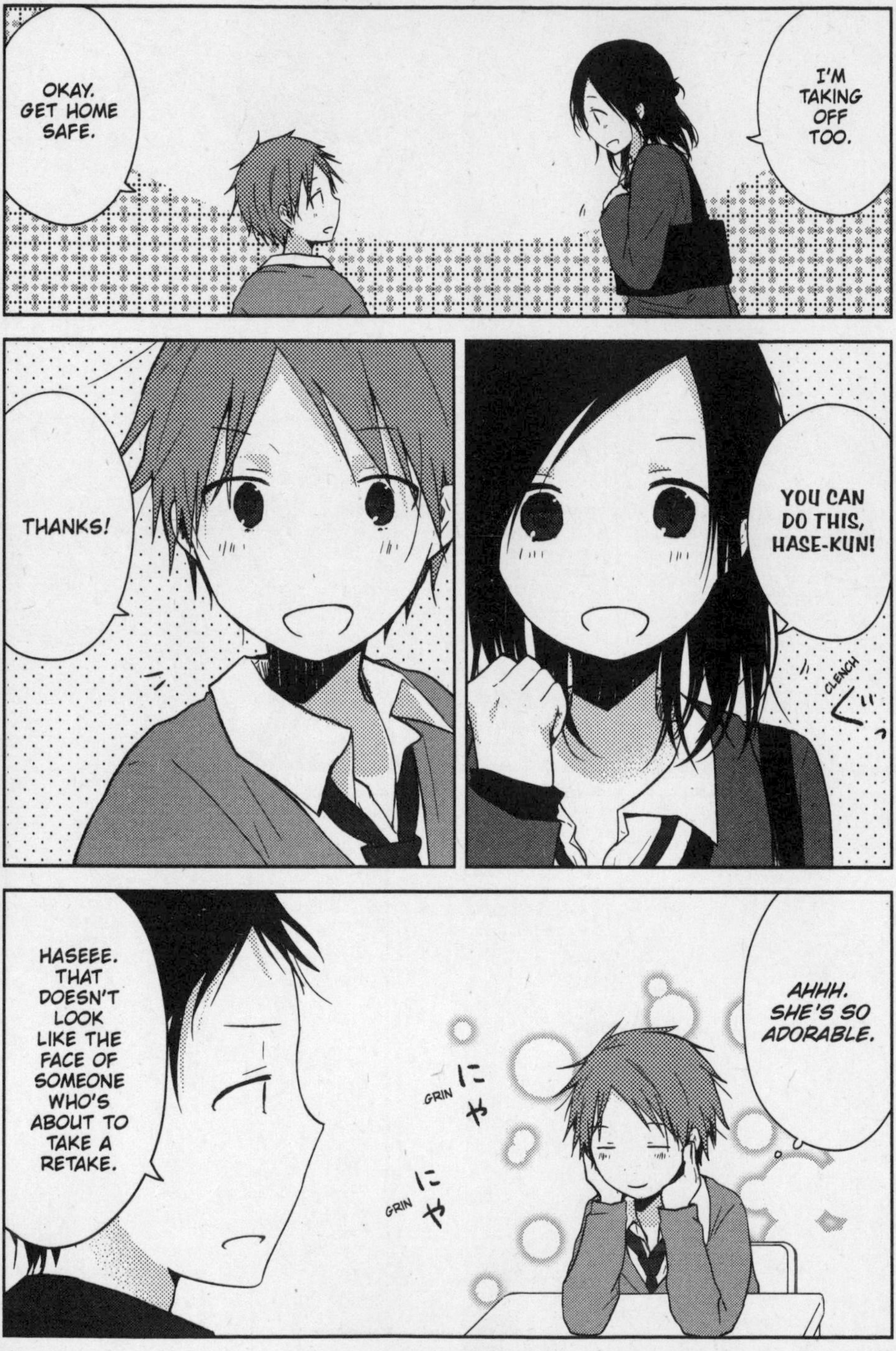

I'M TAKING OFF TOO.
OKAY. GET HOME SAFE.
YOU CAN DO THIS, HASE-KUN!
CLENCH
THANKS!
AHHH. SHE'S SO ADORABLE.
GRIN
GRIN
HASEEE. THAT DOESN'T LOOK LIKE THE FACE OF SOMEONE WHO'S ABOUT TO TAKE A RETAKE.

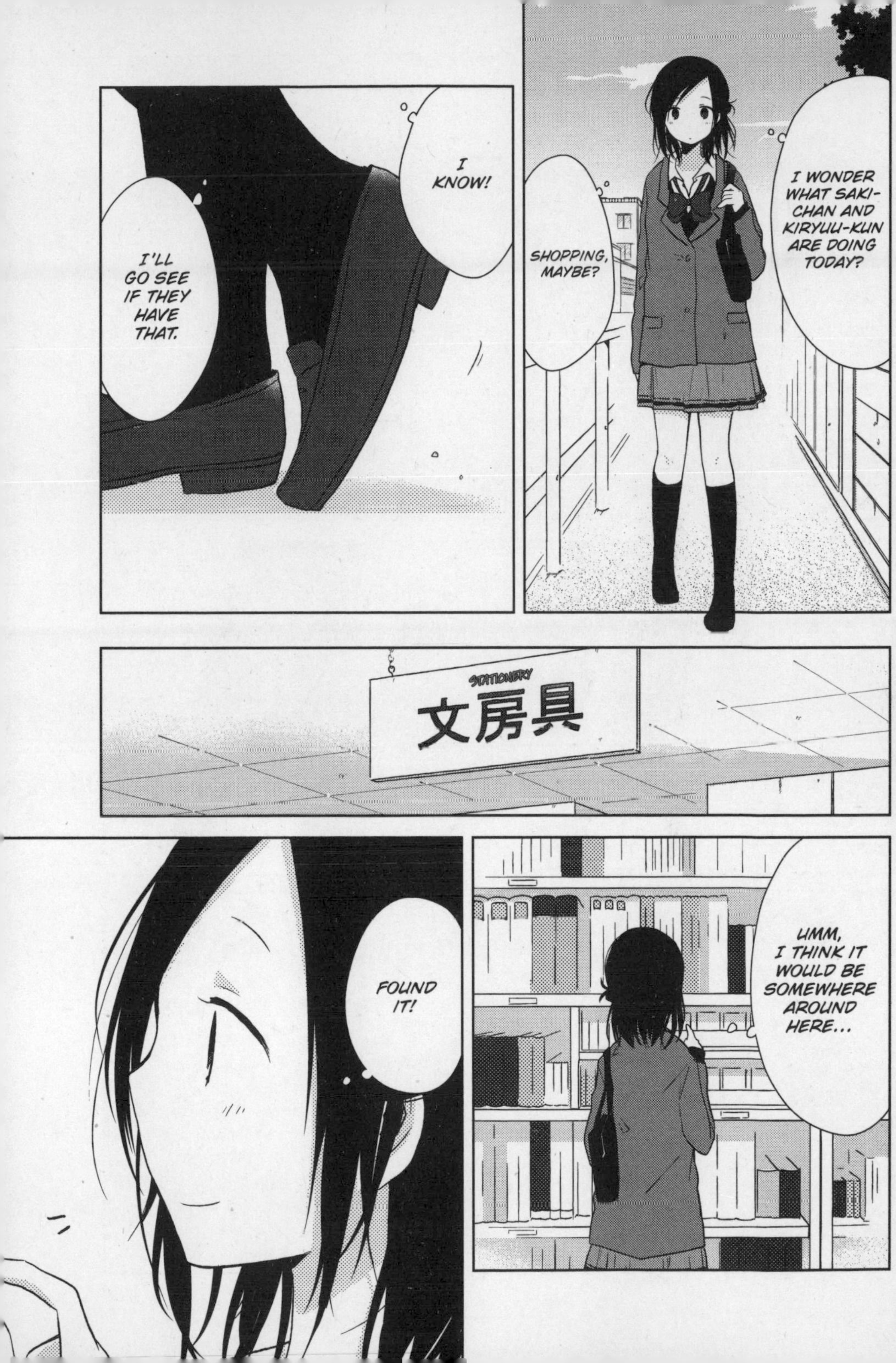
I WONDER WHAT SAKI-CHAN AND KIRYUU-KUN ARE DOING TODAY?
SHOPPING, MAYBE?
I KNOW!
I'LL GO SEE IF THEY HAVE THAT.
STATIONERY
文房具
UMM, I THINK IT WOULD BE SOMEWHERE AROUND HERE...
FOUND IT!

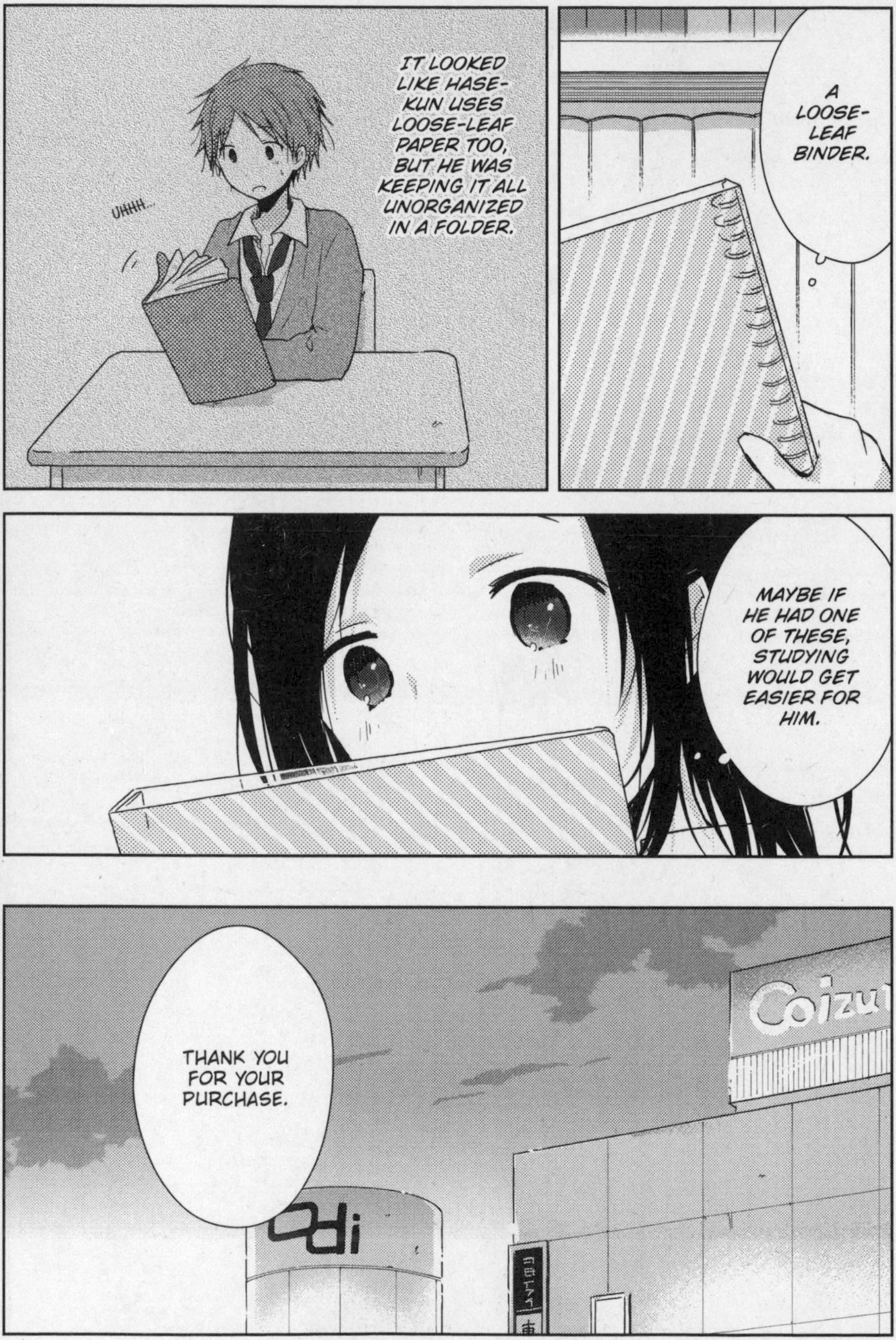
A LOOSE-LEAF BINDER.
IT LOOKED LIKE HASE-KUN USES LOOSE-LEAF PAPER TOO, BUT HE WAS KEEPING IT ALL UNORGANIZED IN A FOLDER.
UHHH...
MAYBE IF HE HAD ONE OF THESE, STUDYING WOULD GET EASIER FOR HIM.
THANK YOU FOR YOUR PURCHASE.

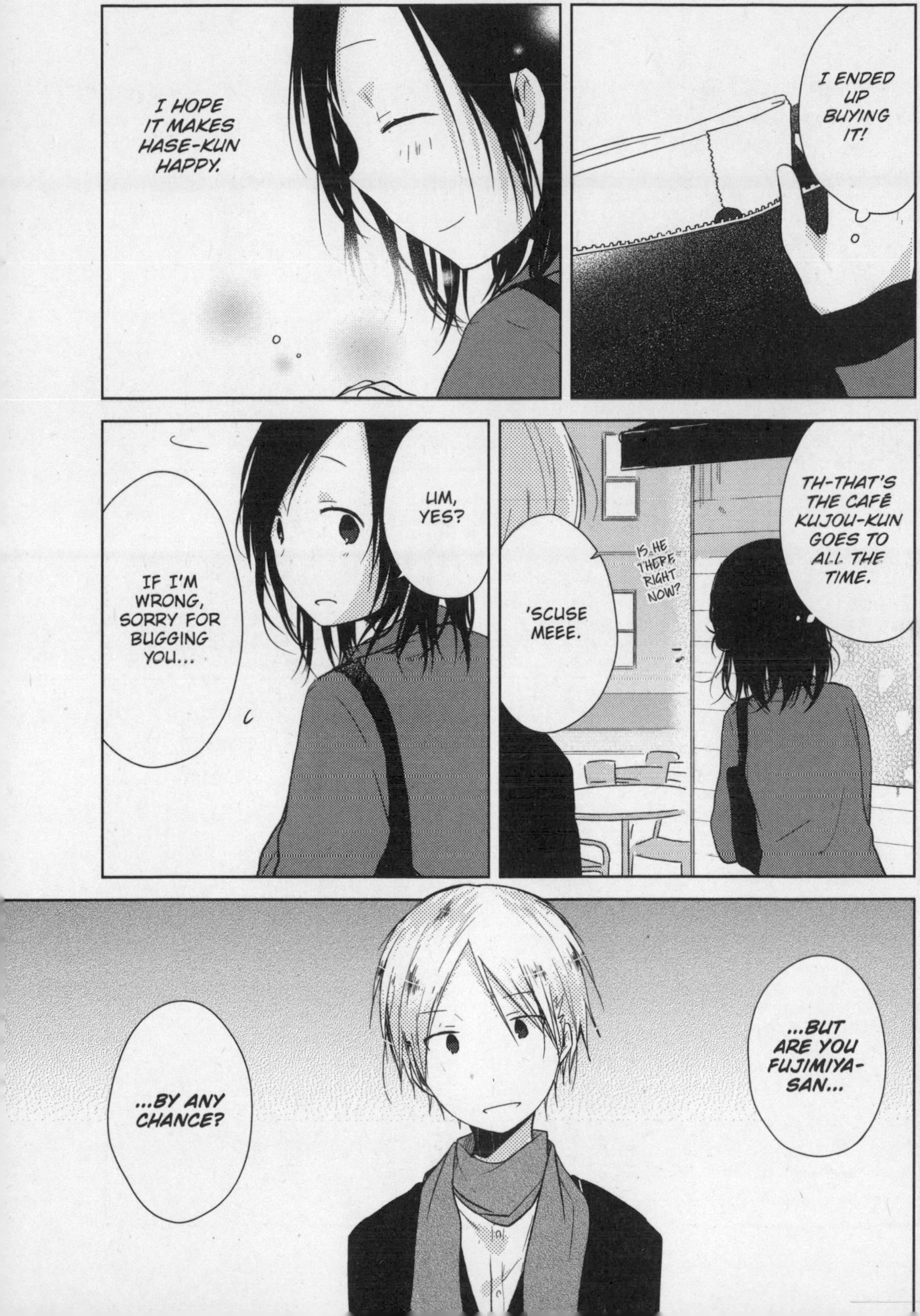
I ENDED UP BUYING IT!
I HOPE IT MAKES HASE-KUN HAPPY.
TH-THAT'S THE CAFÉ KUJOU-KUN GOES TO ALL THE TIME.
IS HE THERE RIGHT NOW?
'SCUSE MEEE.
UM, YES?
IF I'M WRONG, SORRY FOR BUGGING YOU...
...BUT ARE YOU FUJIMIYA-SAN...
...BY ANY CHANCE?

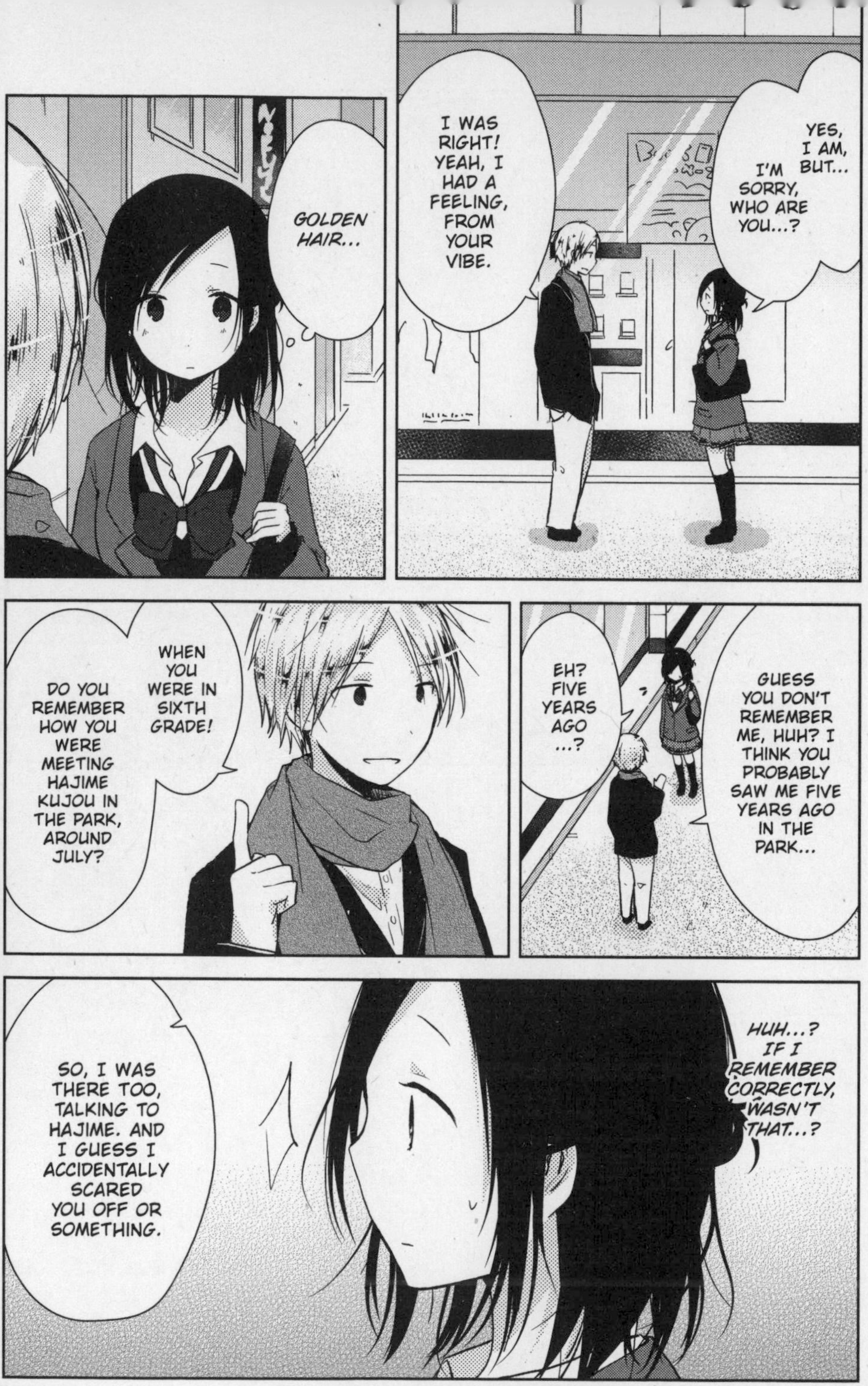
YES, I AM, BUT... I'M SORRY, WHO ARE YOU...?
I WAS RIGHT! YEAH, I HAD A FEELING, FROM YOUR VIBE.
GOLDEN HAIR...
GUESS YOU DON'T REMEMBER ME, HUH? I THINK YOU PROBABLY SAW ME FIVE YEARS AGO IN THE PARK...
EH? FIVE YEARS AGO...?
WHEN YOU WERE IN SIXTH GRADE!
DO YOU REMEMBER HOW YOU WERE MEETING HAJIME KUJOU IN THE PARK, AROUND JULY?
HUH...? IF I REMEMBER CORRECTLY, WASN'T THAT...?
SO, I WAS THERE TOO, TALKING TO HAJIME. AND I GUESS I ACCIDENTALLY SCARED YOU OFF OR SOMETHING.

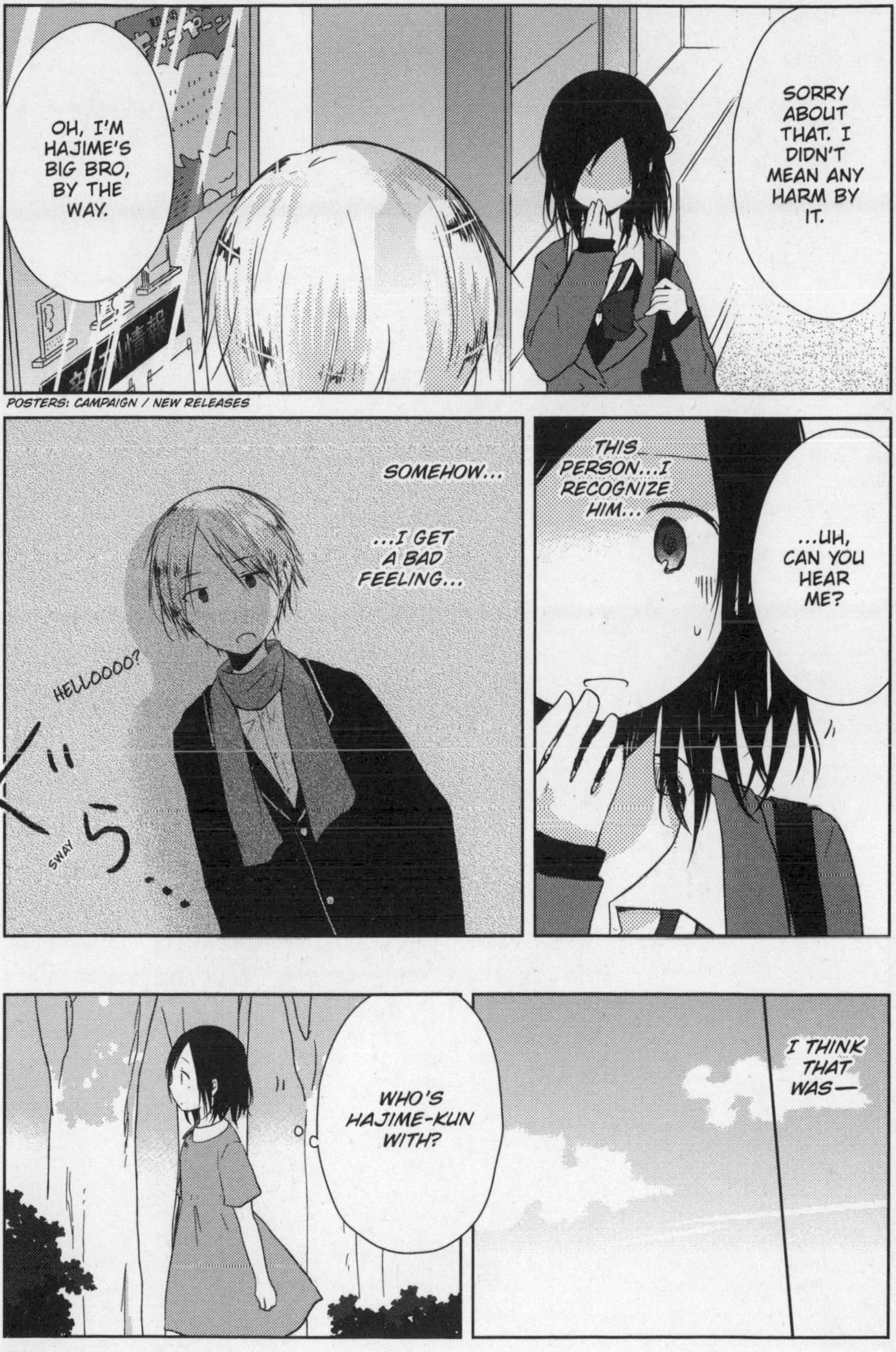
SORRY ABOUT THAT. I DIDN'T MEAN ANY HARM BY IT.
OH, I'M HAJIME'S BIG BRO, BY THE WAY.
POSTERS: CAMPAIGN / NEW RELEASES
THIS PERSON...I RECOGNIZE HIM...
...UH, CAN YOU HEAR ME?
SOMEHOW...
...I GET A BAD FEELING...
HELLOOOO?
SWAY
I THINK THAT WAS—
WHO'S HAJIME-KUN WITH?

AN OLDER BOY...
...WITH GOLDEN HAIR...
I CAN PLAY A LIIITTLE...
...TRICK ON HER FOR YA.
BADUM
—OW...
!
HUH? WHAT'S WRONG ALL OF A SUDDEN?
FUJIMIYA-SAN?

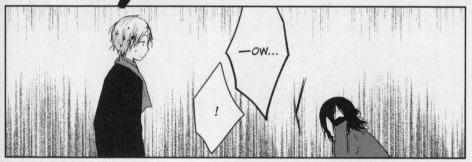

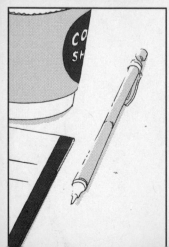

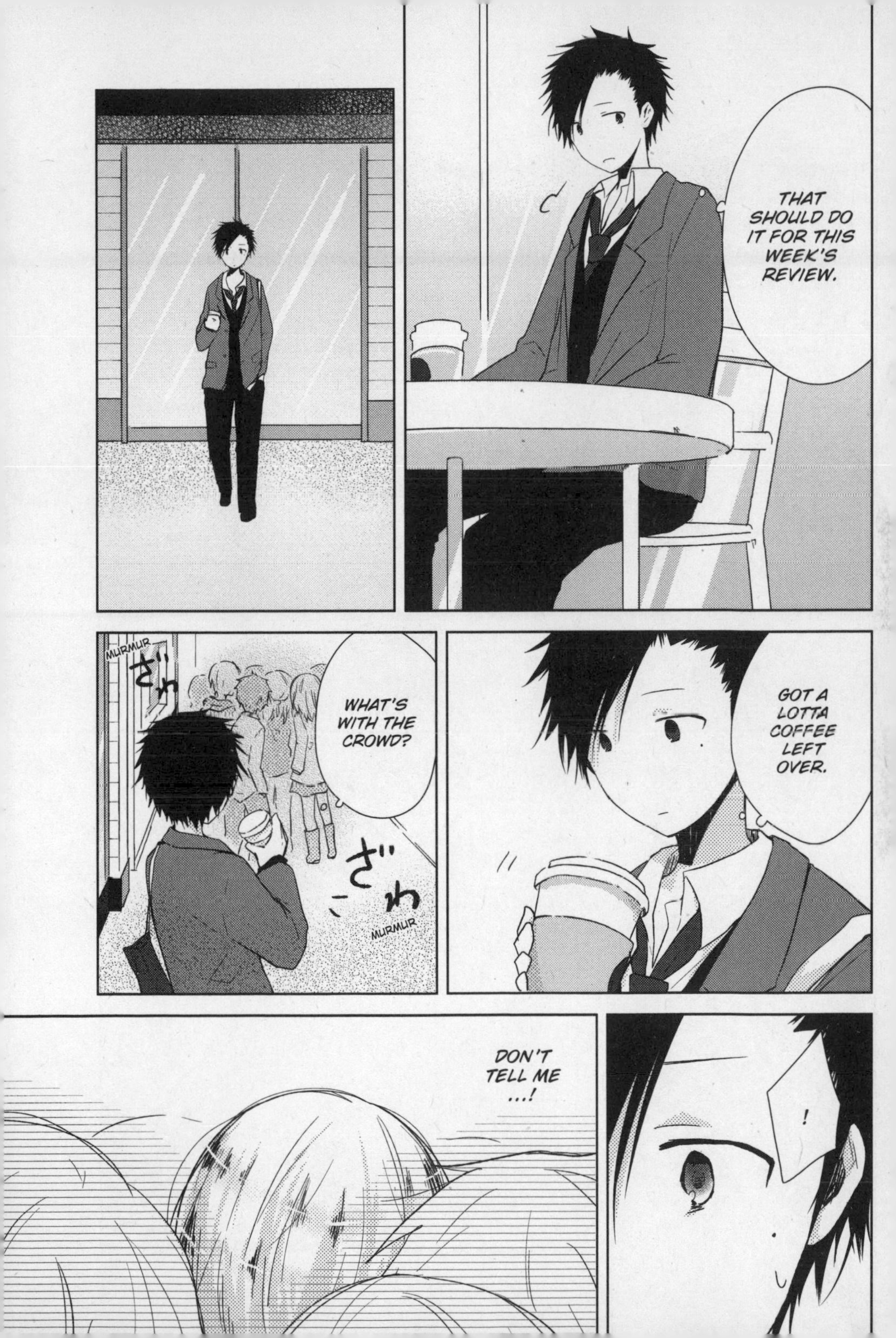
THAT SHOULD DO IT FOR THIS WEEK'S REVIEW.
GOT A LOTTA COFFEE LEFT OVER.
MURMUR
ざわ
WHAT'S WITH THE CROWD?
ざわ
MURMUR
!
DON'T TELL ME ...!

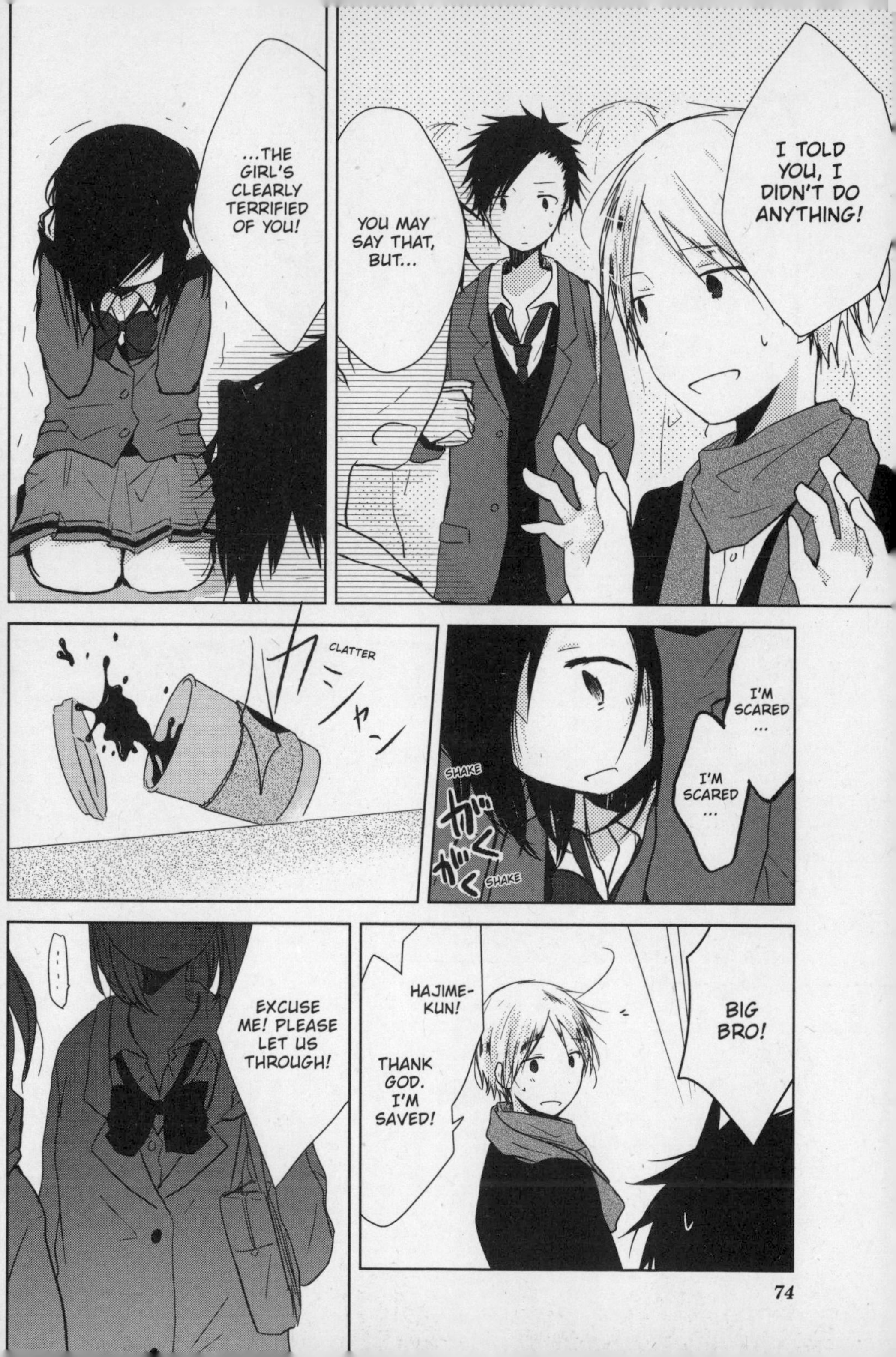
I TOLD YOU, I DIDN'T DO ANYTHING!
YOU MAY SAY THAT, BUT...
...THE GIRL'S CLEARLY TERRIFIED OF YOU!
I'M SCARED...
I'M SCARED...
SHAKE
SHAKE
CLATTER
BIG BRO!
HAJIME-KUN!
THANK GOD. I'M SAVED!
...
EXCUSE ME! PLEASE LET US THROUGH!

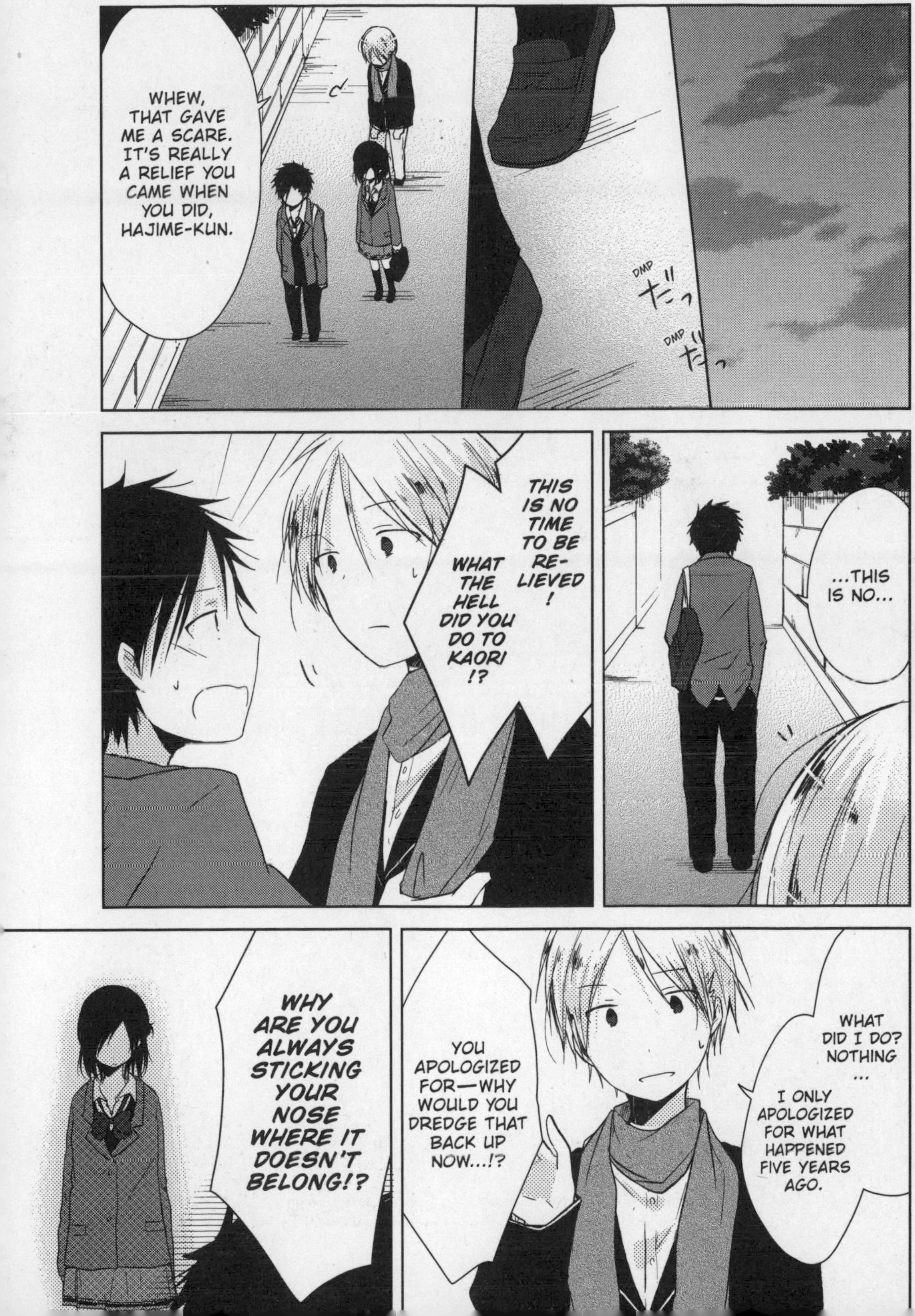
DMP だっ
DMP だっ
WHEW, THAT GAVE ME A SCARE. IT'S REALLY A RELIEF YOU CAME WHEN YOU DID, HAJIME-KUN.
...THIS IS NO...
THIS IS NO TIME TO BE RE-LIEVED!
WHAT THE HELL DID YOU DO TO KAORI!?
WHAT DID I DO? NOTHING...
I ONLY APOLOGIZED FOR WHAT HAPPENED FIVE YEARS AGO.
YOU APOLOGIZED FOR—WHY WOULD YOU DREDGE THAT BACK UP NOW...!?
WHY ARE YOU ALWAYS STICKING YOUR NOSE WHERE IT DOESN'T BELONG!?

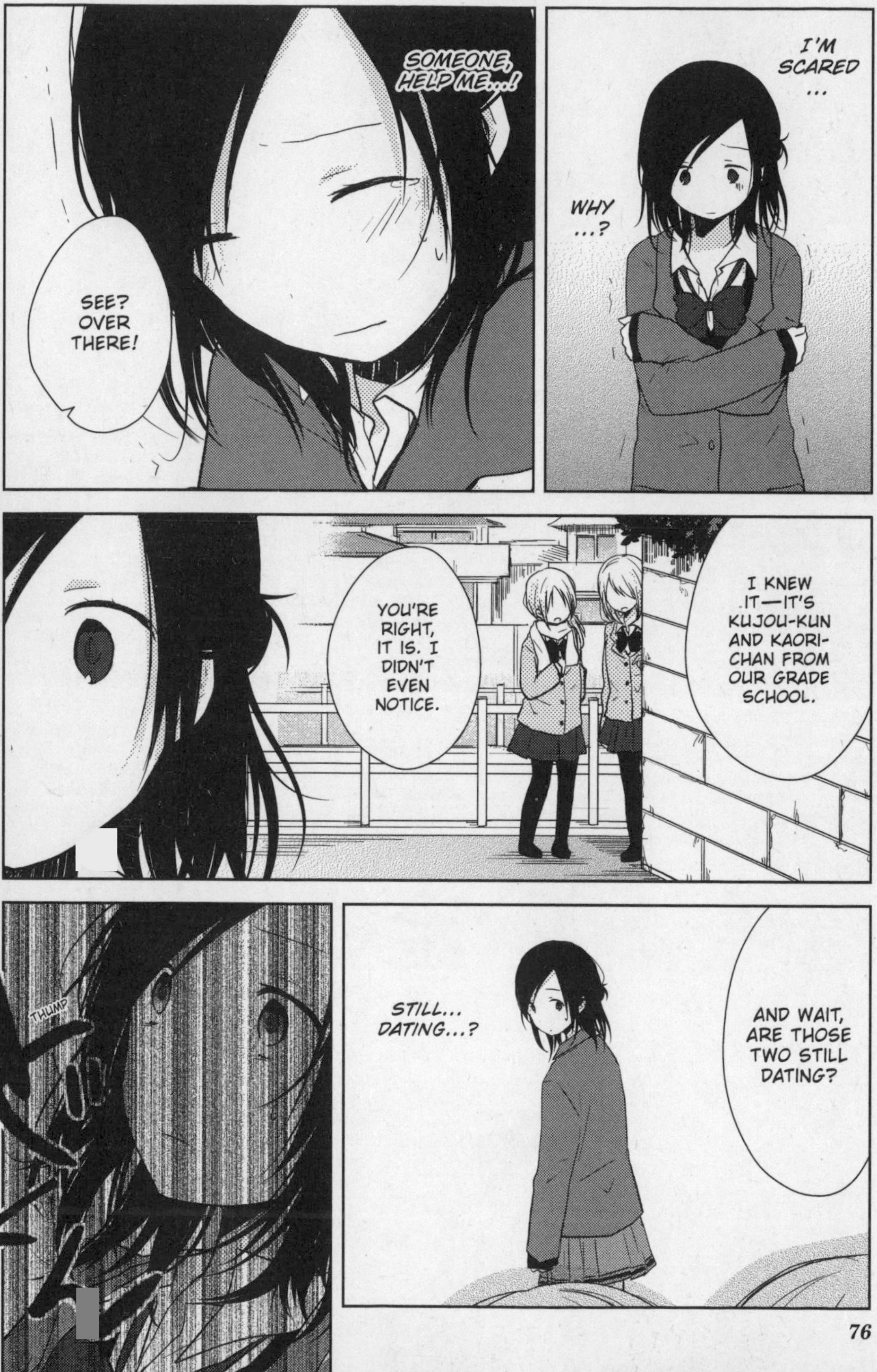
I'M SCARED ...
WHY ...?
SOMEONE, HELP ME...!
SEE? OVER THERE!
I KNEW IT—IT'S KUJOU-KUN AND KAORI-CHAN FROM OUR GRADE SCHOOL.
YOU'RE RIGHT, IT IS. I DIDN'T EVEN NOTICE.
AND WAIT, ARE THOSE TWO STILL DATING?
STILL... DATING...?
THUMP

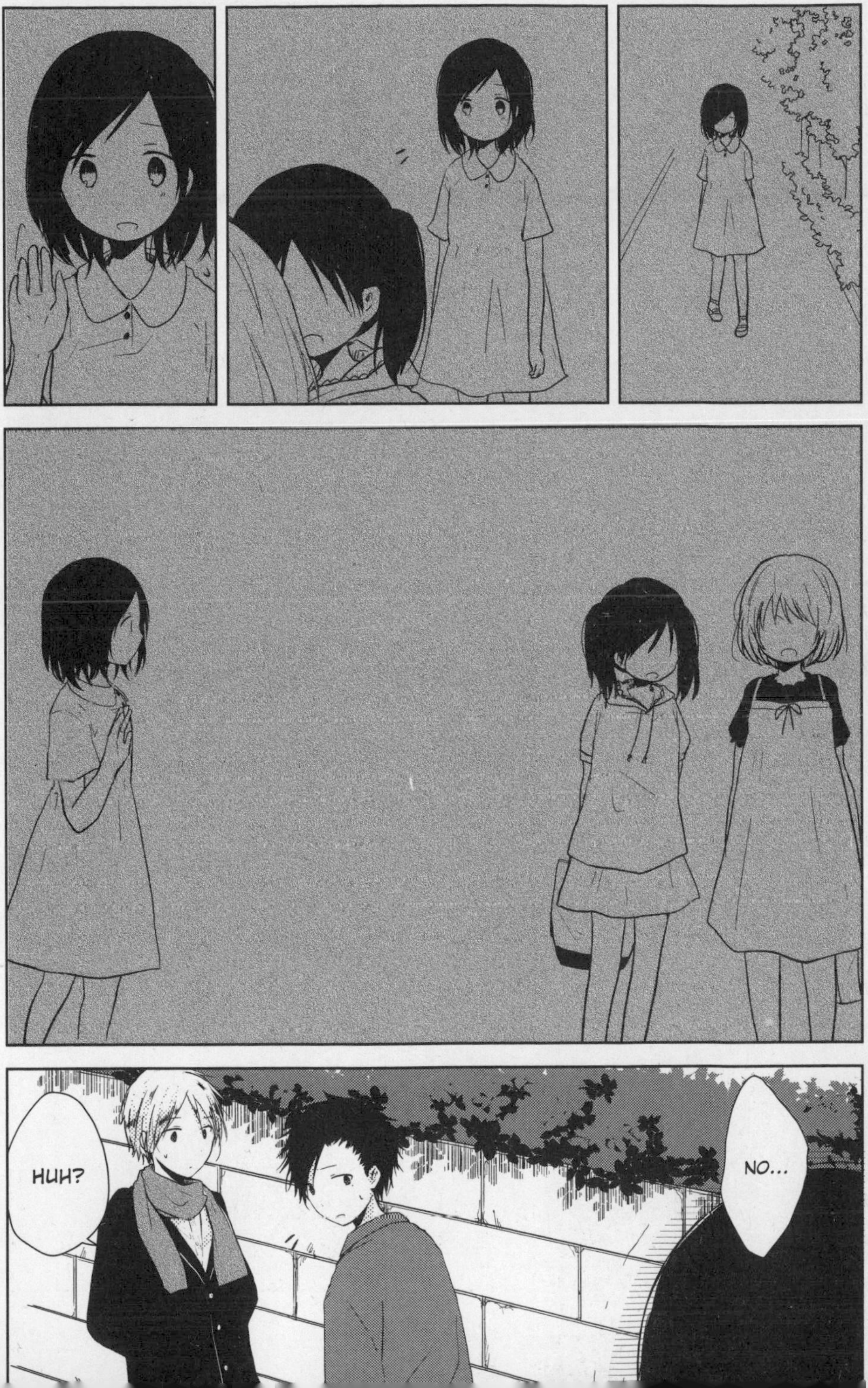
NO...
HUH?

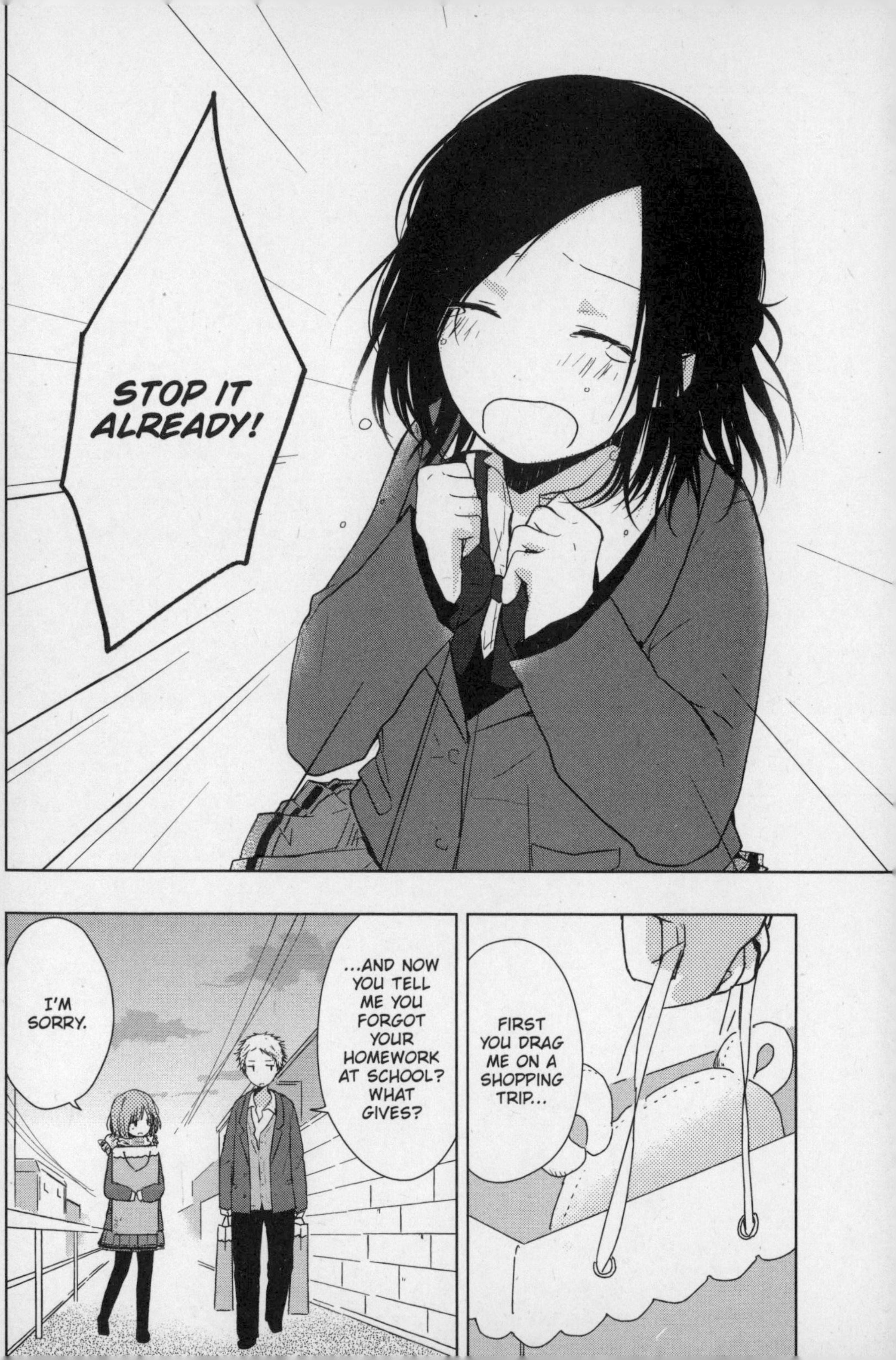
STOP IT ALREADY!
FIRST YOU DRAG ME ON A SHOPPING TRIP...
...AND NOW YOU TELL ME YOU FORGOT YOUR HOMEWORK AT SCHOOL? WHAT GIVES?
I'M SORRY.

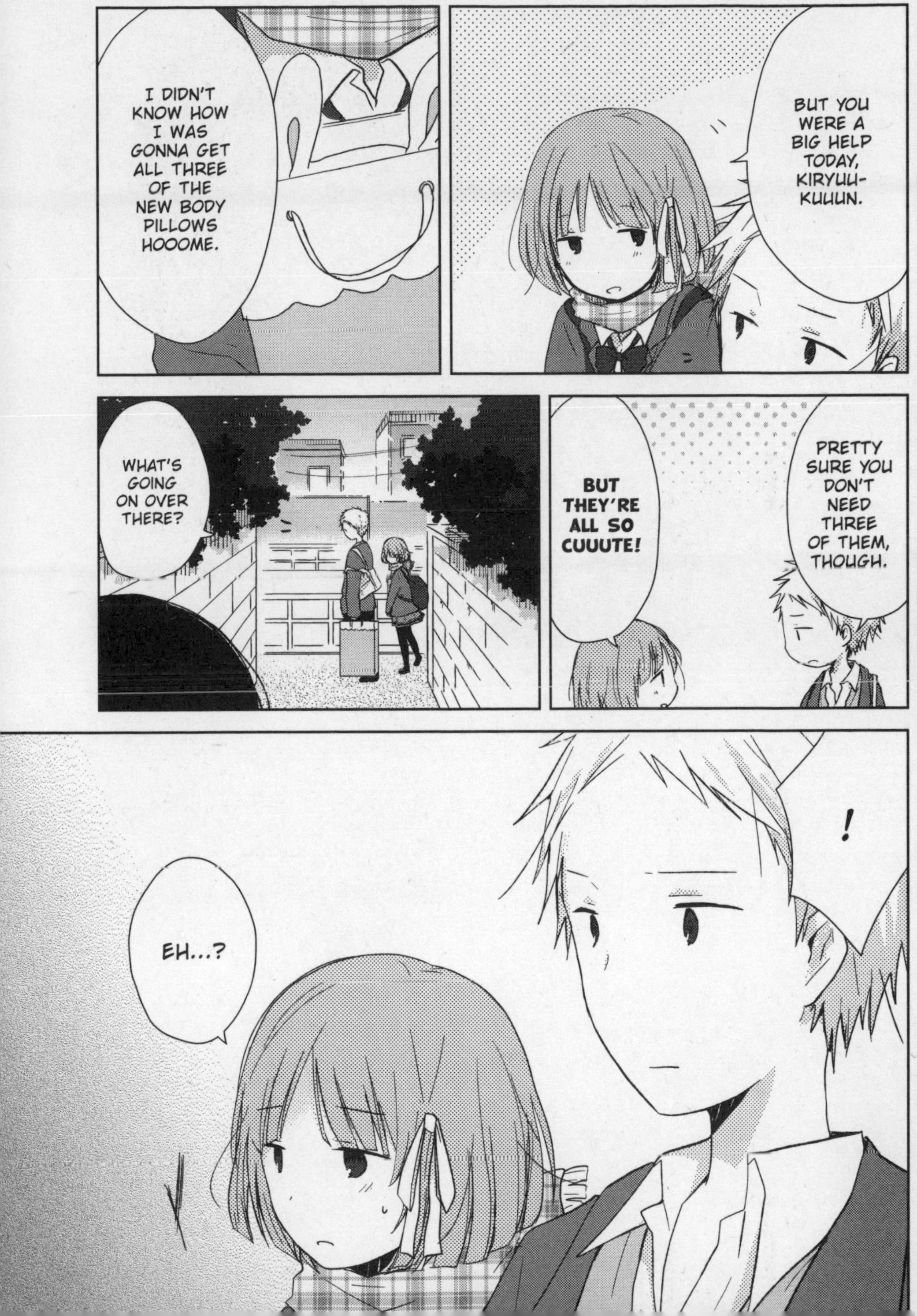
BUT YOU WERE A BIG HELP TODAY, KIRYUU-KUUUN.
I DIDN'T KNOW HOW I WAS GONNA GET ALL THREE OF THE NEW BODY PILLOWS HOOOME.
PRETTY SURE YOU DON'T NEED THREE OF THEM, THOUGH.
BUT THEY'RE ALL SO CUUUTE!
WHAT'S GOING ON OVER THERE?
!
EH...?

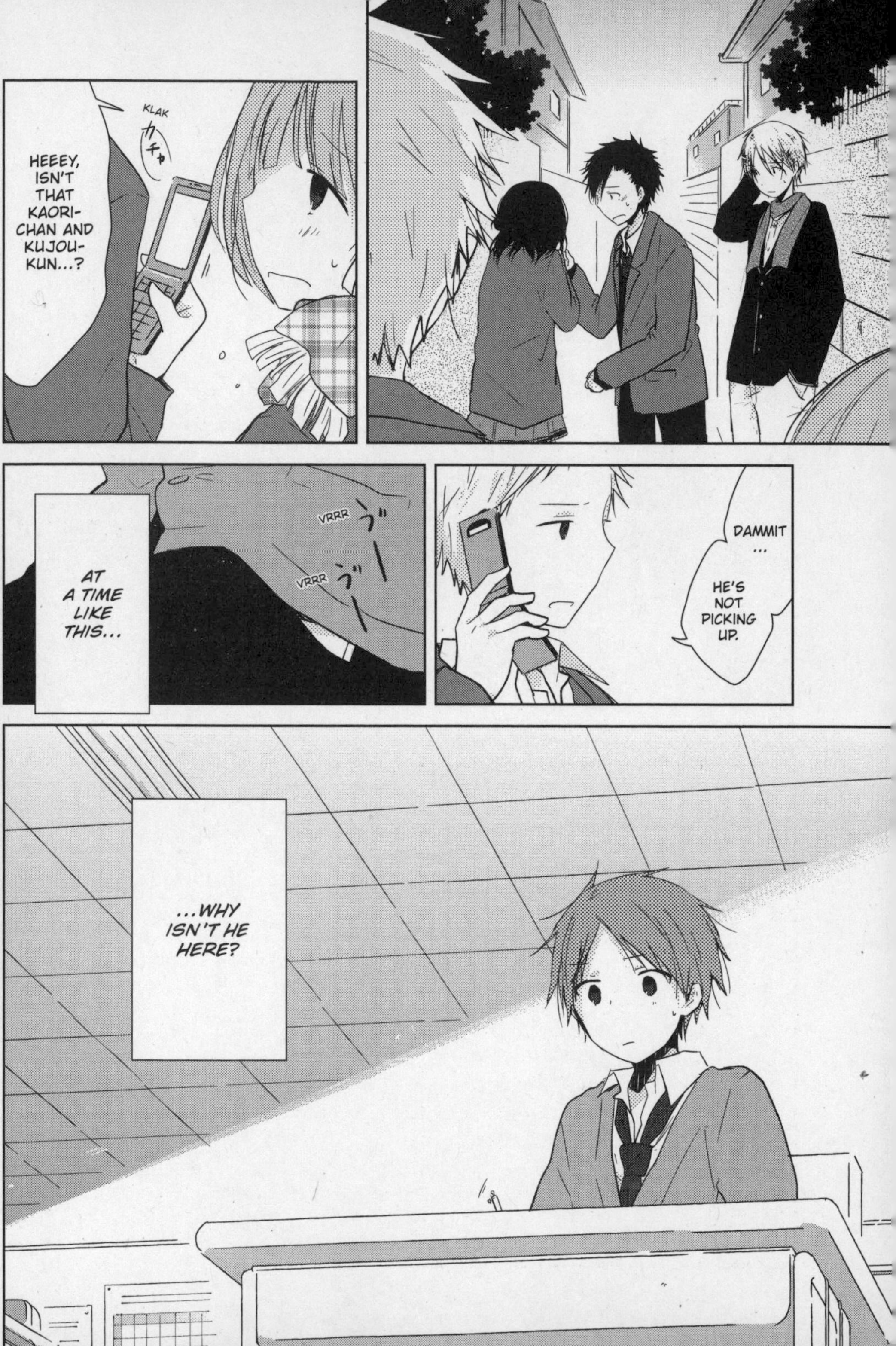
KLAK
カチャ
HEEEY, ISN'T THAT KAORI-CHAN AND KUJOU-KUN...?
DAMMIT ... HE'S NOT PICKING UP.
VRRR
ヴー
VRRR
ヴー
AT A TIME LIKE THIS...
...WHY ISN'T HE HERE?

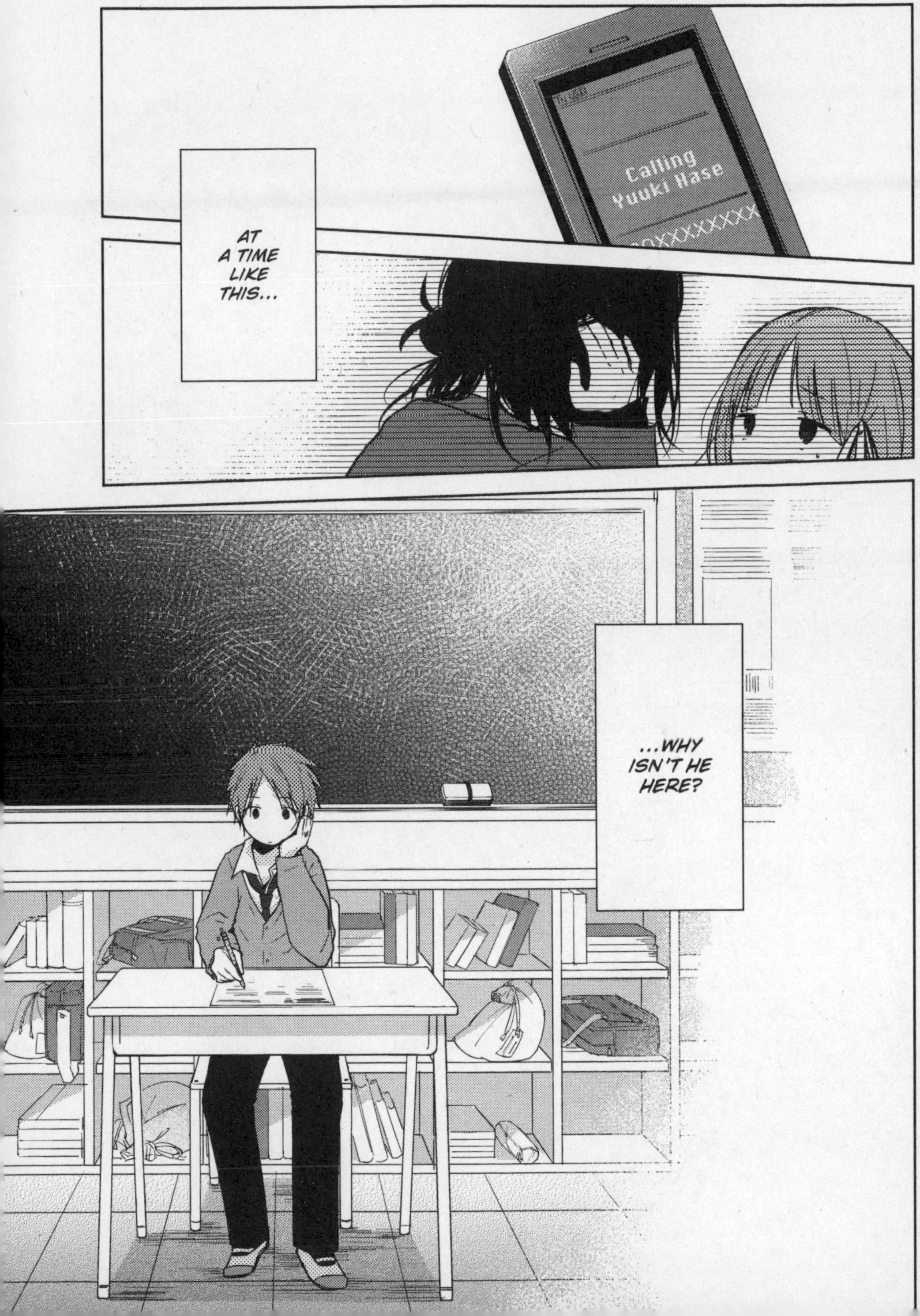
Calling
Yuuki Hase
AT A TIME LIKE THIS...
...WHY ISN'T HE HERE?

CHAPTER 36
I REMEMBER EVERYTHING

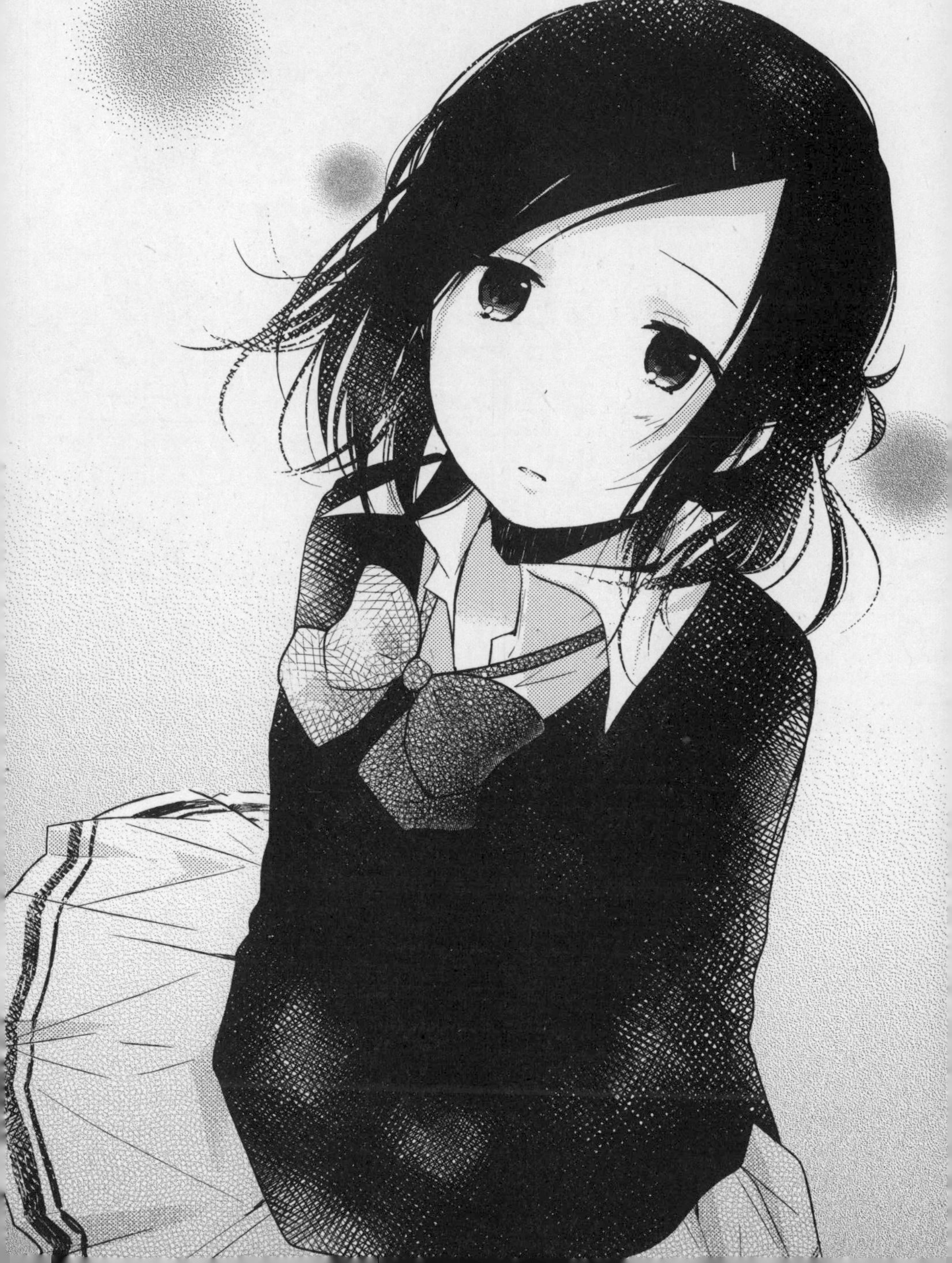

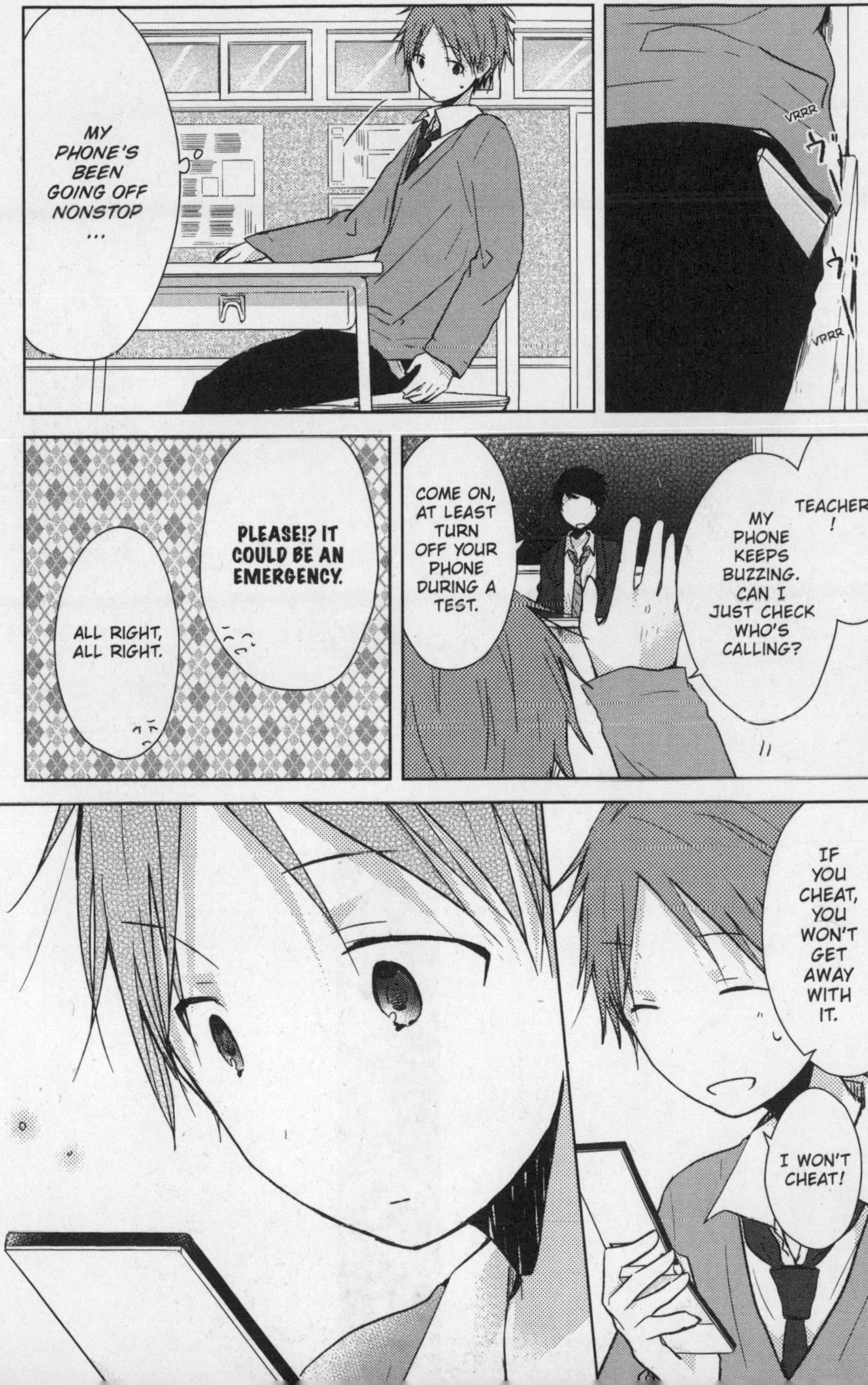
VRRR
VRRR
MY PHONE'S BEEN GOING OFF NONSTOP ...
TEACHER!
MY PHONE KEEPS BUZZING. CAN I JUST CHECK WHO'S CALLING?
COME ON, AT LEAST TURN OFF YOUR PHONE DURING A TEST.
PLEASE!? IT COULD BE AN EMERGENCY.
ALL RIGHT, ALL RIGHT.
IF YOU CHEAT, YOU WON'T GET AWAY WITH IT.
I WON'T CHEAT!

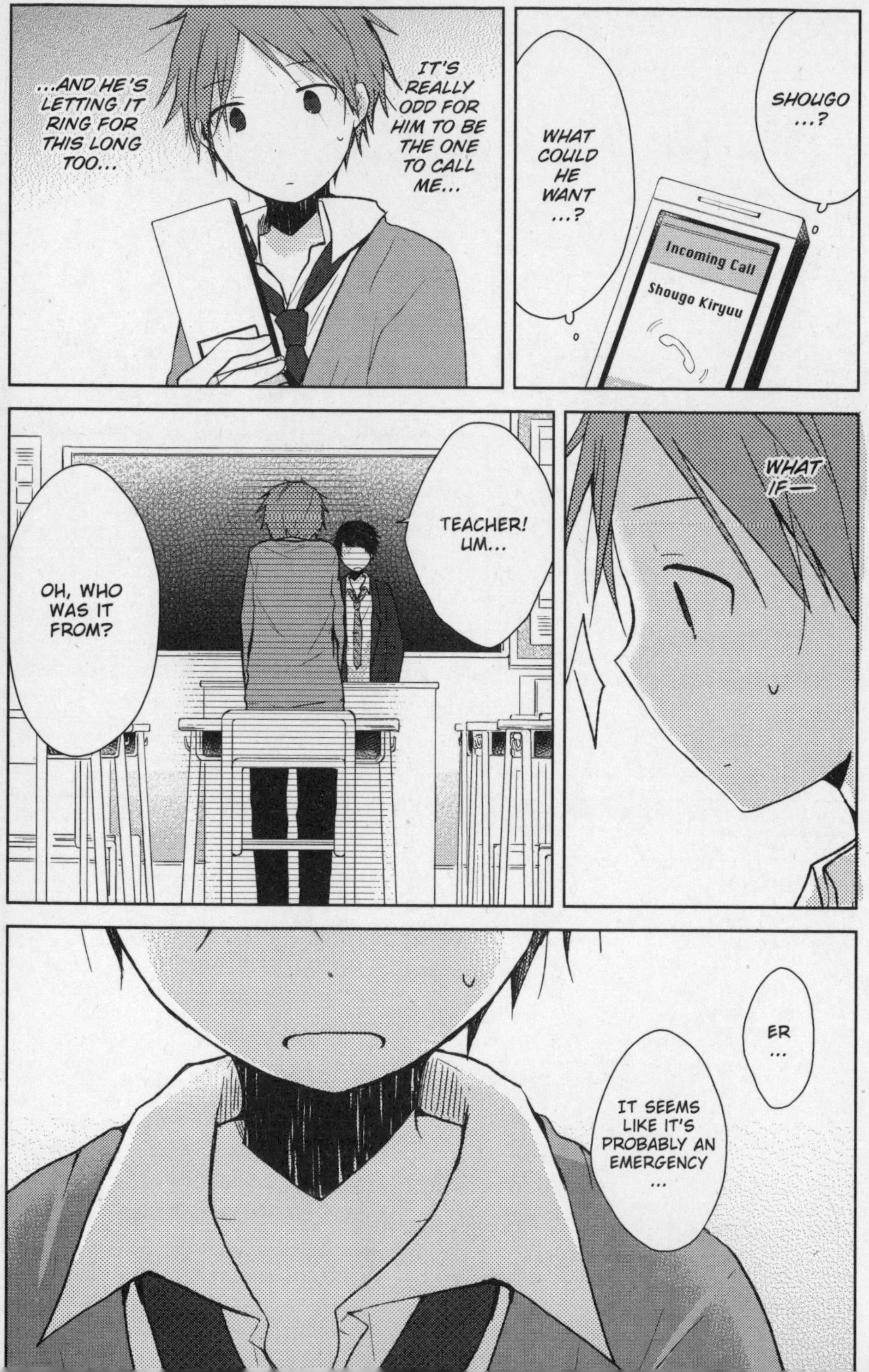
SHOUGO ...?
WHAT COULD HE WANT ...?
Incoming Call
Shougo Kiryuu
IT'S REALLY ODD FOR HIM TO BE THE ONE TO CALL ME...
...AND HE'S LETTING IT RING FOR THIS LONG TOO...
WHAT IF—
TEACHER! UM...
OH, WHO WAS IT FROM?
ER ...
IT SEEMS LIKE IT'S PROBABLY AN EMERGENCY ...

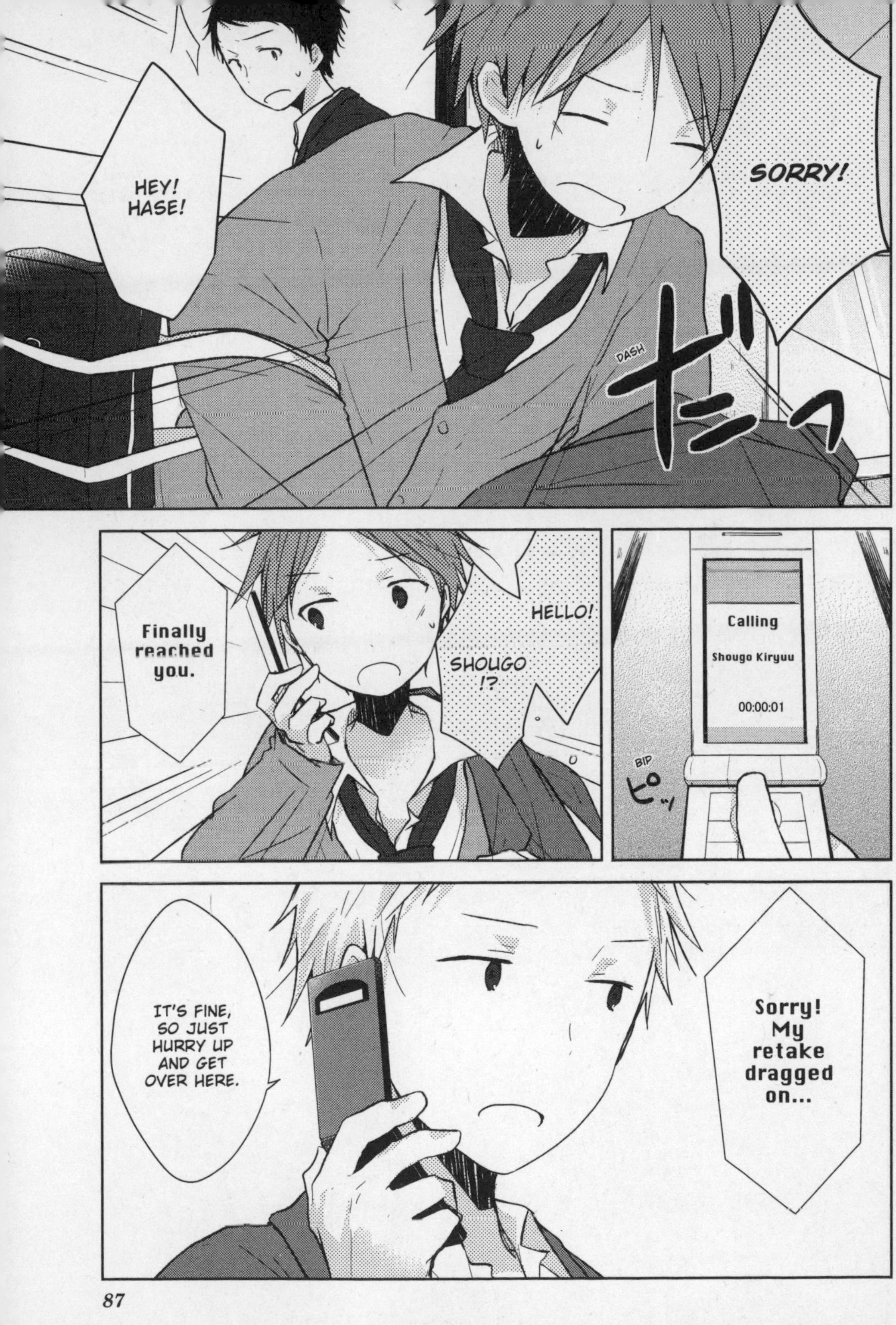
SORRY!
HEY! HASE!
DASH
ダッ
Calling
Shougo Kiryuu
00:00:01
BIP
ピッ
HELLO!
SHOUGO !?
Finally reached you.
Sorry! My retake dragged on...
IT'S FINE, SO JUST HURRY UP AND GET OVER HERE.

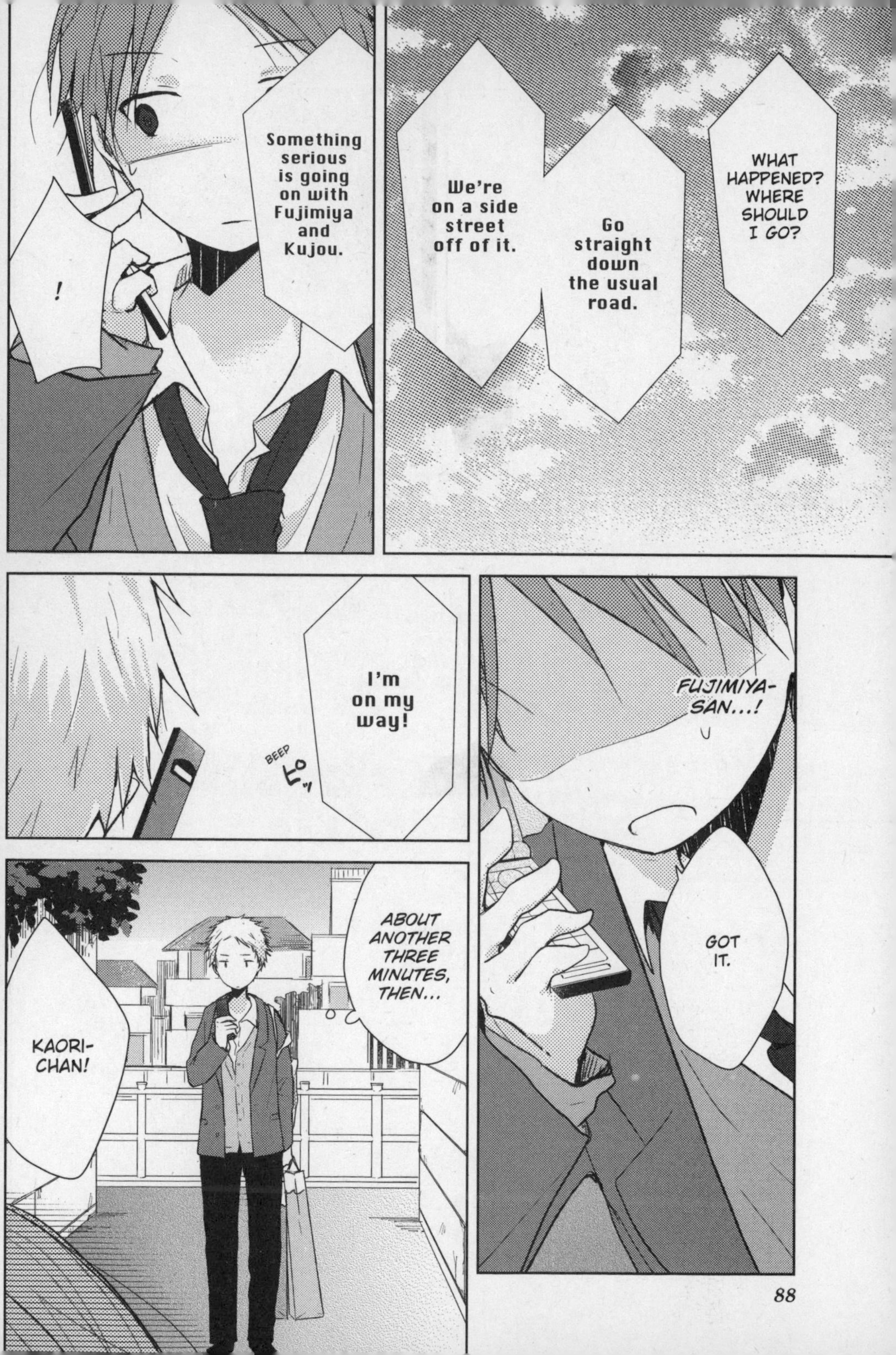
WHAT HAPPENED? WHERE SHOULD I GO?
Go straight down the usual road.
We're on a side street off of it.
Something serious is going on with Fujimiya and Kujou.
!
FUJIMIYA-SAN...!
GOT IT.
I'm on my way!
BEEP
ABOUT ANOTHER THREE MINUTES, THEN...
KAORI-CHAN!

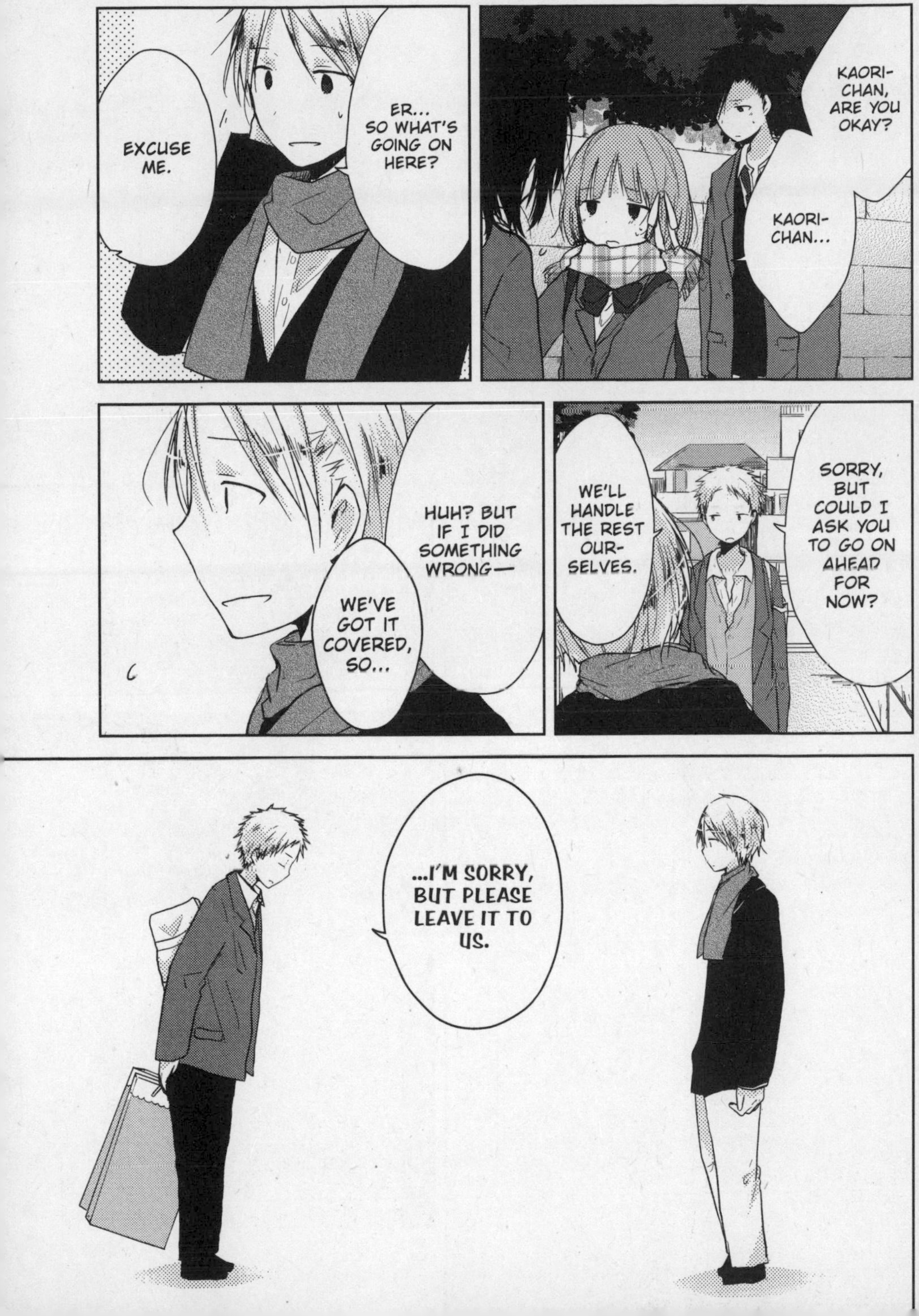
KAORI-CHAN, ARE YOU OKAY?
KAORI-CHAN...
ER... SO WHAT'S GOING ON HERE?
EXCUSE ME.
SORRY, BUT COULD I ASK YOU TO GO ON AHEAD FOR NOW?
WE'LL HANDLE THE REST OUR-SELVES.
HUH? BUT IF I DID SOMETHING WRONG—
WE'VE GOT IT COVERED, SO...
...I'M SORRY, BUT PLEASE LEAVE IT TO US.

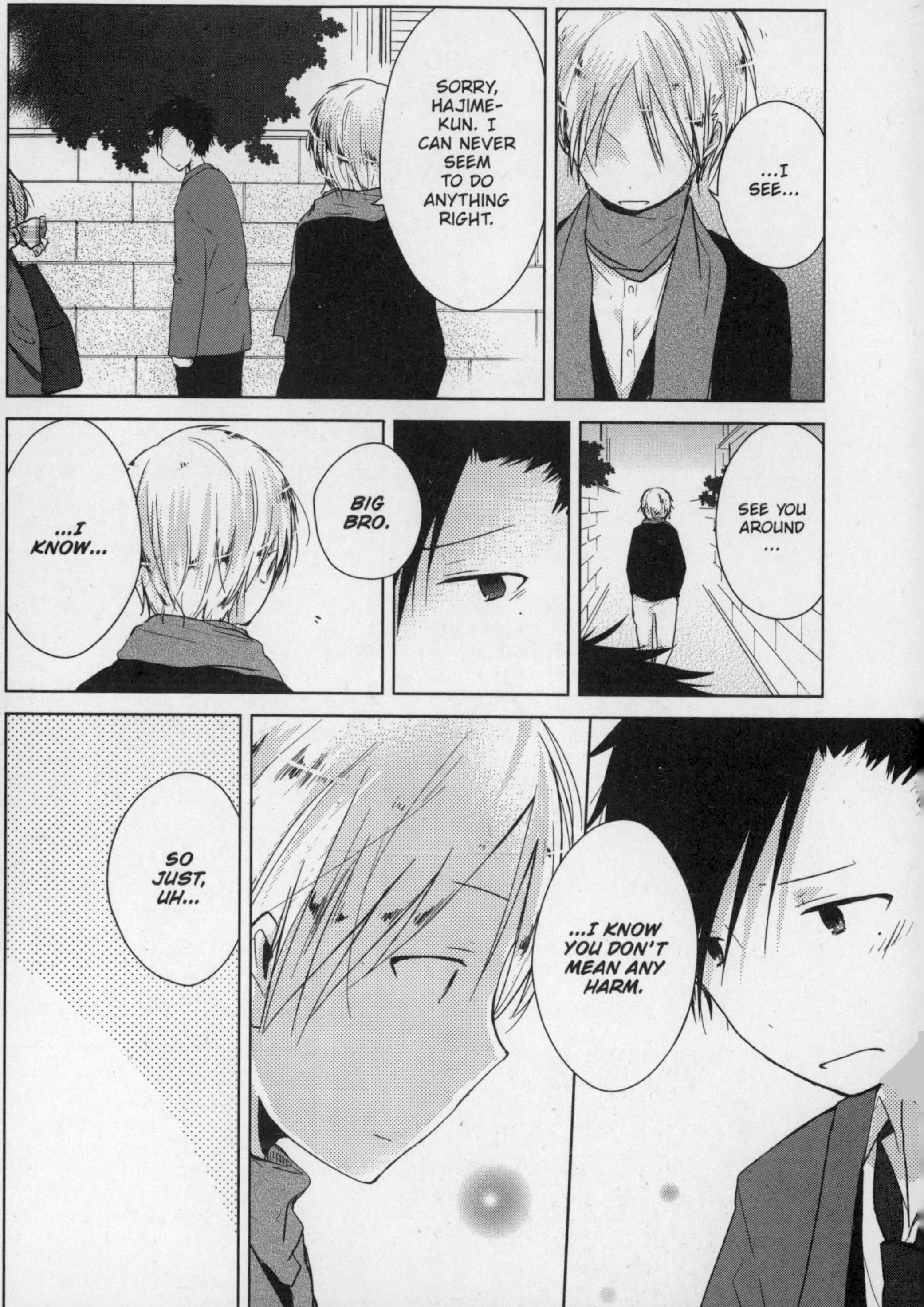
...I SEE...
SORRY, HAJIME-KUN. I CAN NEVER SEEM TO DO ANYTHING RIGHT.
SEE YOU AROUND ...
BIG BRO.
...I KNOW...
...I KNOW YOU DON'T MEAN ANY HARM.
SO JUST, UH...

...SHOW UP AT HOME EVERY ONCE IN A WHILE TOO.

...YEAH.

ALL RIGHT.

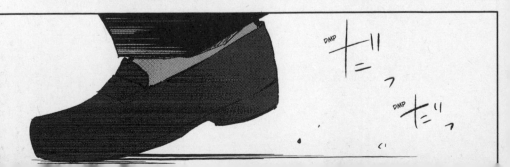

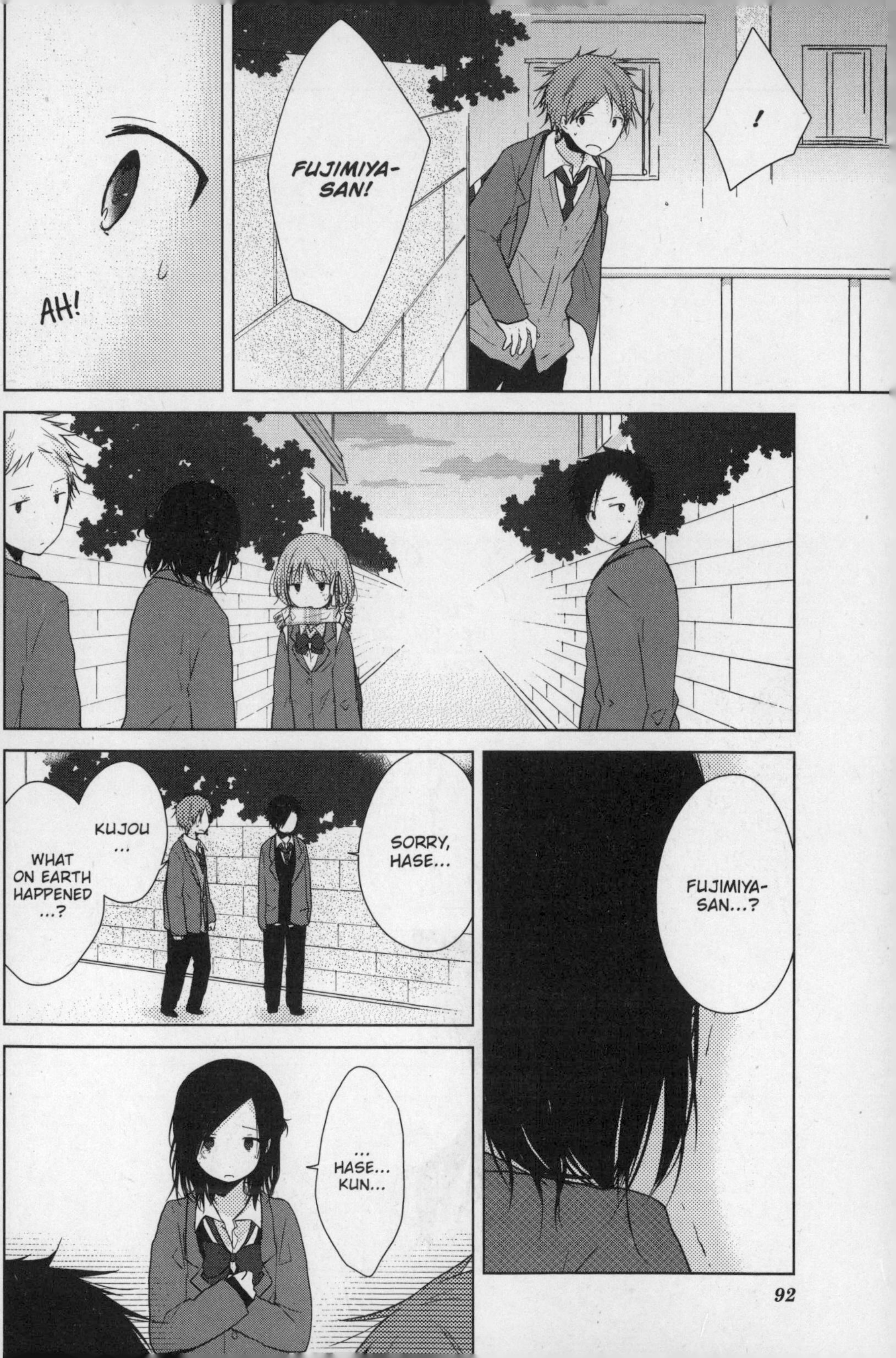
!
FUJIMIYA-SAN!
AH!
FUJIMIYA-SAN...?
SORRY, HASE...
KUJOU...
WHAT ON EARTH HAPPENED...?
... HASE... KUN...

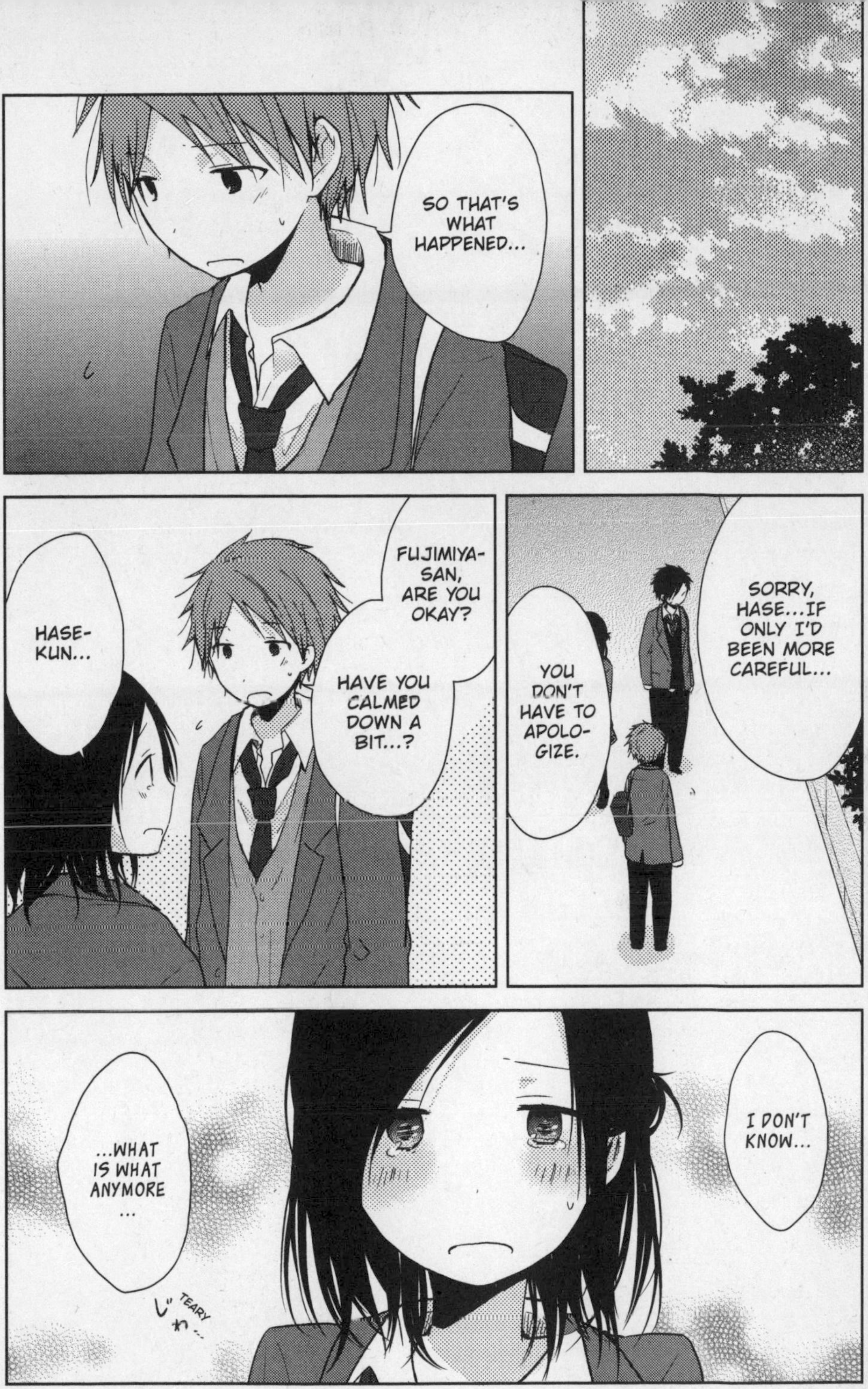

SO THAT'S WHAT HAPPENED...
SORRY, HASE...IF ONLY I'D BEEN MORE CAREFUL...
YOU DON'T HAVE TO APOLOGIZE.
FUJIMIYA-SAN, ARE YOU OKAY?
HAVE YOU CALMED DOWN A BIT...?
HASE-KUN...
I DON'T KNOW...
...WHAT IS WHAT ANYMORE ...
じわ...
TEARY

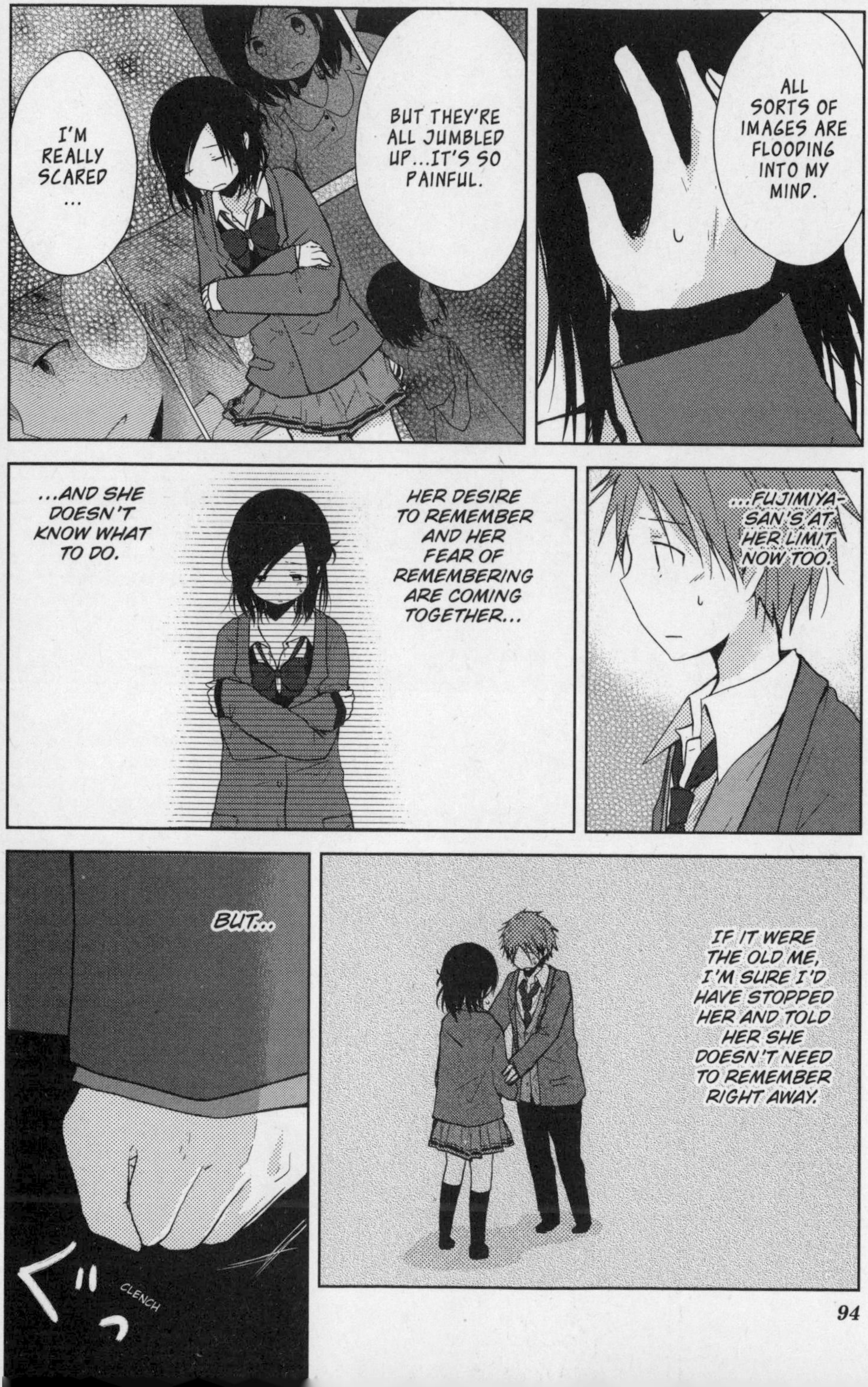
ALL SORTS OF IMAGES ARE FLOODING INTO MY MIND.
BUT THEY'RE ALL JUMBLED UP...IT'S SO PAINFUL.
I'M REALLY SCARED ...
...FUJIMIYA-SAN'S AT HER LIMIT NOW TOO.
HER DESIRE TO REMEMBER AND HER FEAR OF REMEMBERING ARE COMING TOGETHER...
...AND SHE DOESN'T KNOW WHAT TO DO.
IF IT WERE THE OLD ME, I'M SURE I'D HAVE STOPPED HER AND TOLD HER SHE DOESN'T NEED TO REMEMBER RIGHT AWAY.
BUT...
ぐっ
CLENCH

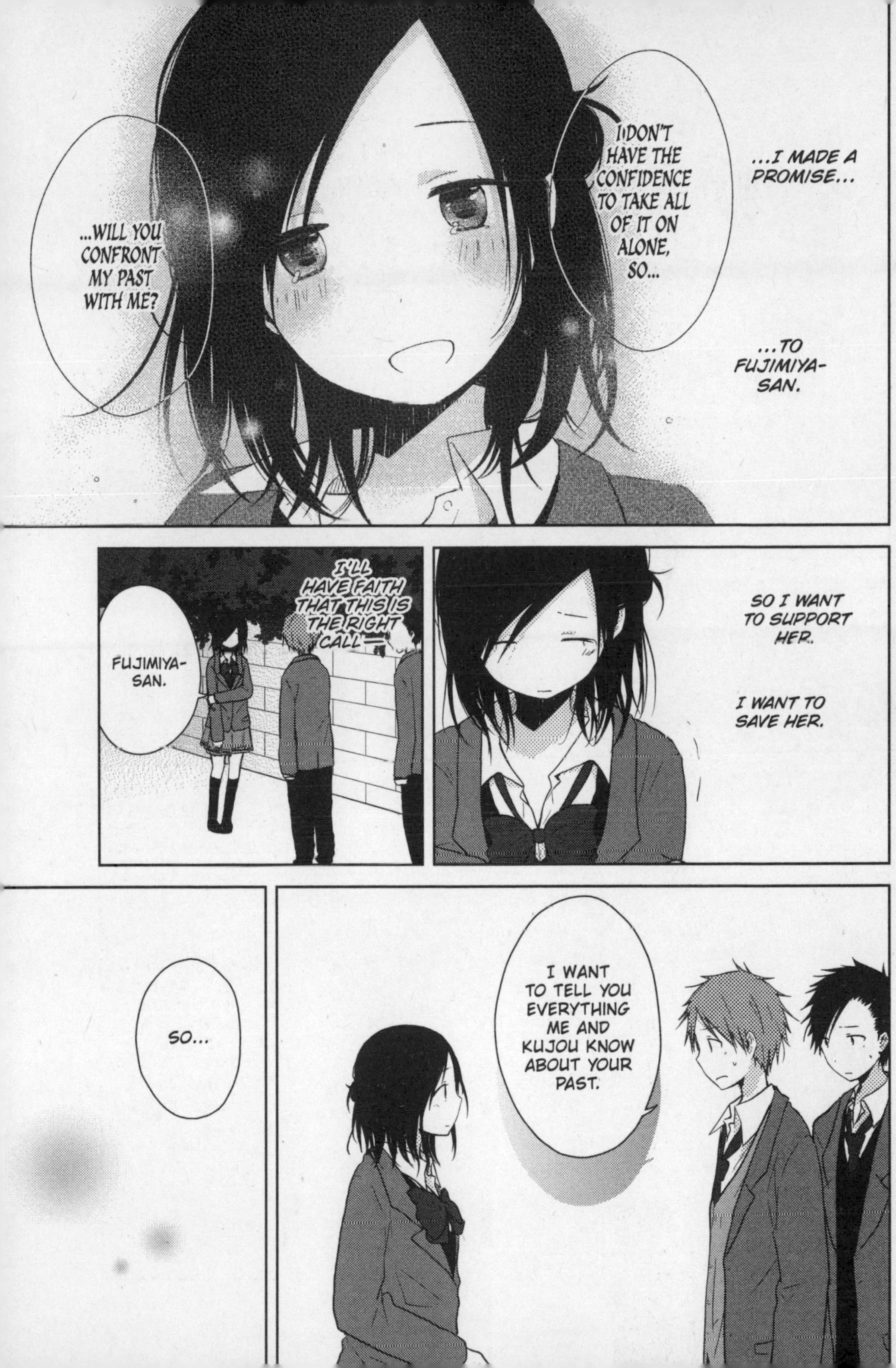
...I MADE A PROMISE...
...TO FUJIMIYA-SAN.
I DON'T HAVE THE CONFIDENCE TO TAKE ALL OF IT ON ALONE, SO...
...WILL YOU CONFRONT MY PAST WITH ME?
SO I WANT TO SUPPORT HER.
I WANT TO SAVE HER.
I'LL HAVE FAITH THAT THIS IS THE RIGHT CALL—
FUJIMIYA-SAN.
I WANT TO TELL YOU EVERYTHING ME AND KUJOU KNOW ABOUT YOUR PAST.
SO...

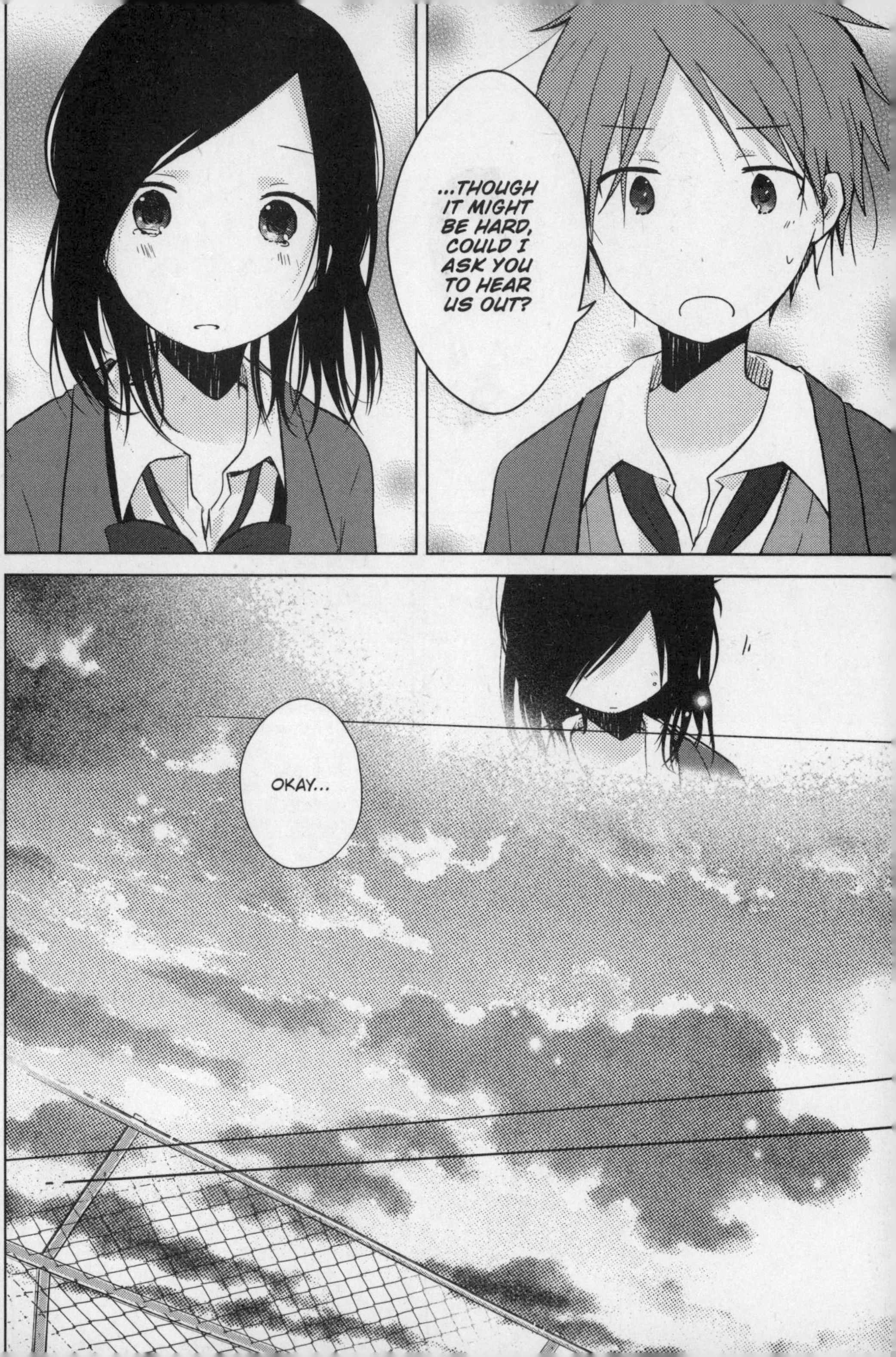
...THOUGH IT MIGHT BE HARD, COULD I ASK YOU TO HEAR US OUT?
OKAY...

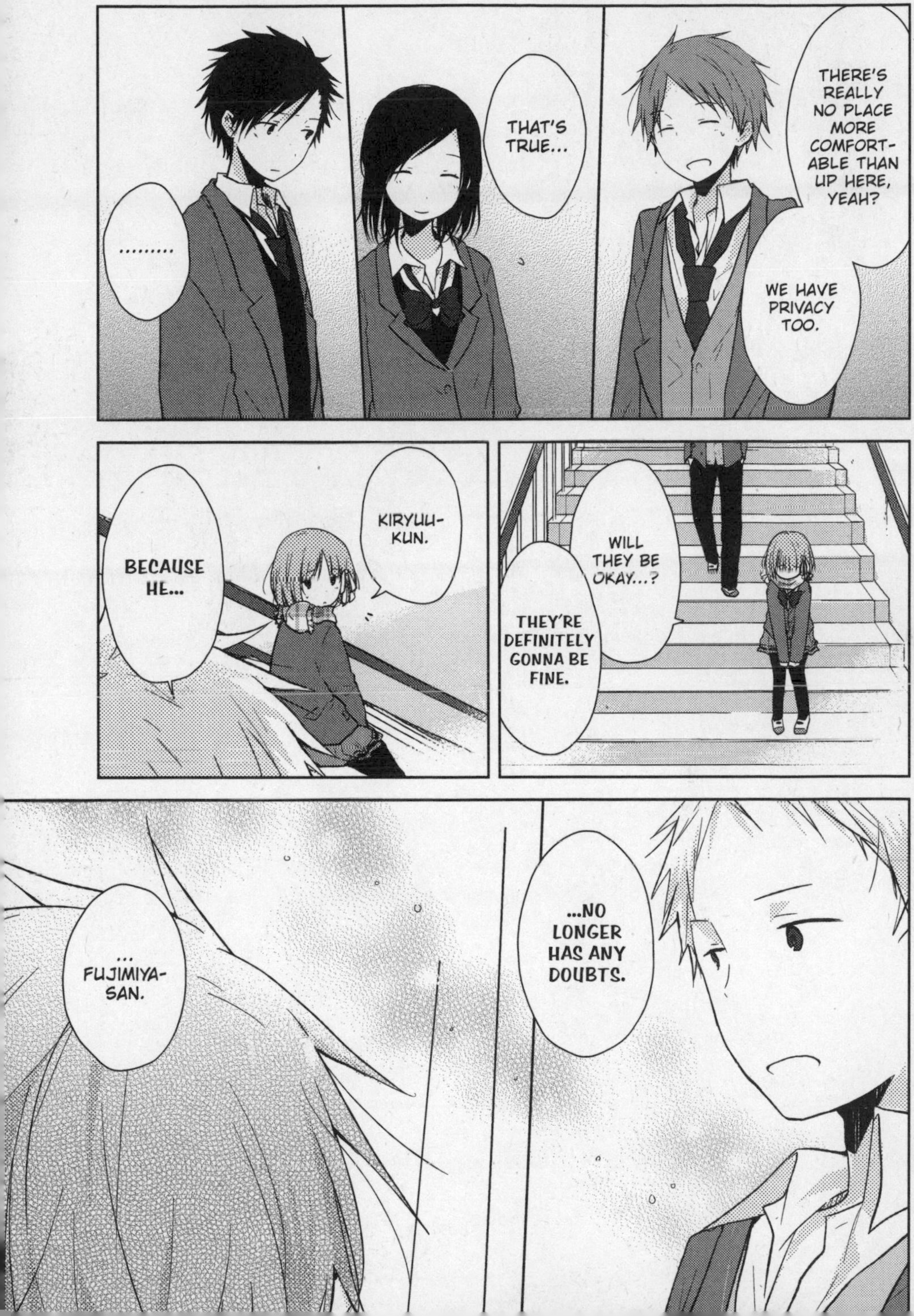
THERE'S REALLY NO PLACE MORE COMFORT-ABLE THAN UP HERE, YEAH?
WE HAVE PRIVACY TOO.
THAT'S TRUE...
....
WILL THEY BE OKAY...?
THEY'RE DEFINITELY GONNA BE FINE.
KIRYUU-KUN.
BECAUSE HE...
...NO LONGER HAS ANY DOUBTS.
... FUJIMIYA-SAN.

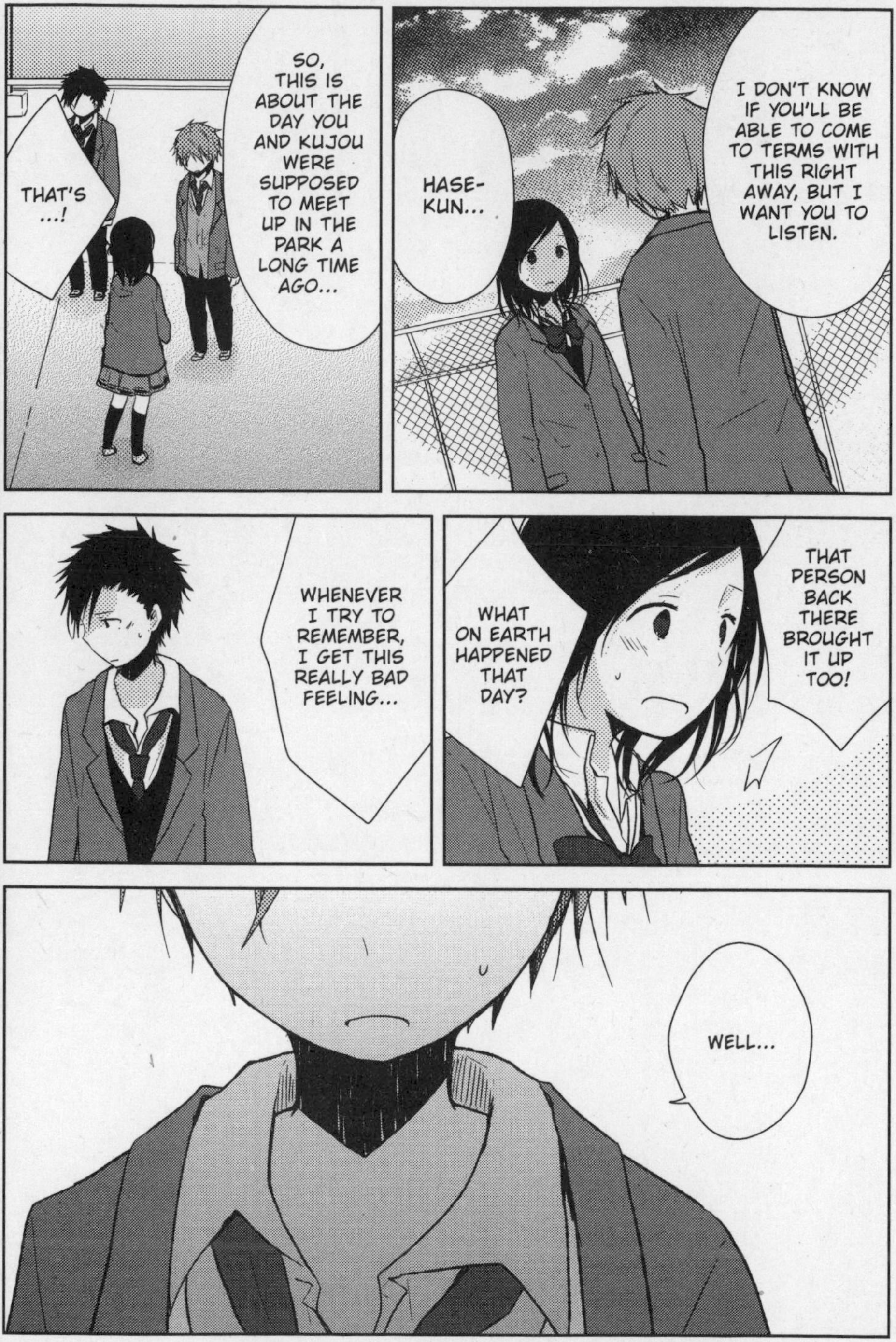
I DON'T KNOW IF YOU'LL BE ABLE TO COME TO TERMS WITH THIS RIGHT AWAY, BUT I WANT YOU TO LISTEN.
HASE-KUN...
SO, THIS IS ABOUT THE DAY YOU AND KUJOU WERE SUPPOSED TO MEET UP IN THE PARK A LONG TIME AGO...
THAT'S ...!
THAT PERSON BACK THERE BROUGHT IT UP TOO!
WHAT ON EARTH HAPPENED THAT DAY?
WHENEVER I TRY TO REMEMBER, I GET THIS REALLY BAD FEELING...
WELL...

HASE
...

!

KUJOU WILL TELL YOU ALL ABOUT IT.

... THANKS.

YOU'D HONESTLY RATHER BE THE ONE TO TELL HER, RIGHT, KUJOU?

WE'D PROMISED TO MEET IN THE PARK THAT DAY.

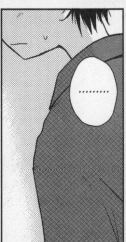
....

KAORI
...

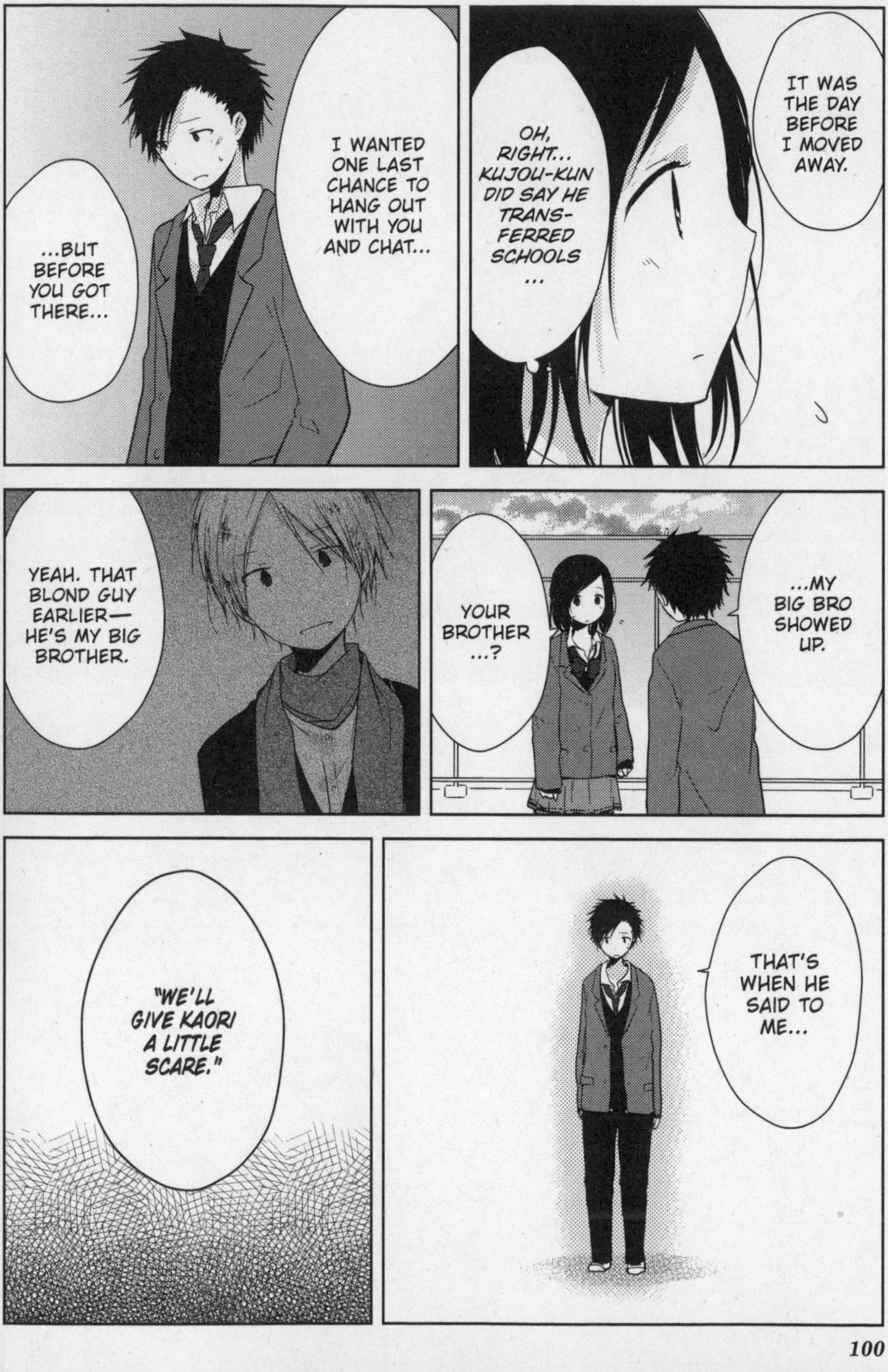
IT WAS THE DAY BEFORE I MOVED AWAY.
OH, RIGHT... KUJOU-KUN DID SAY HE TRANS-FERRED SCHOOLS...
I WANTED ONE LAST CHANCE TO HANG OUT WITH YOU AND CHAT...
...BUT BEFORE YOU GOT THERE...
...MY BIG BRO SHOWED UP.
YOUR BROTHER...?
YEAH. THAT BLOND GUY EARLIER—HE'S MY BIG BROTHER.
THAT'S WHEN HE SAID TO ME...
"WE'LL GIVE KAORI A LITTLE SCARE."

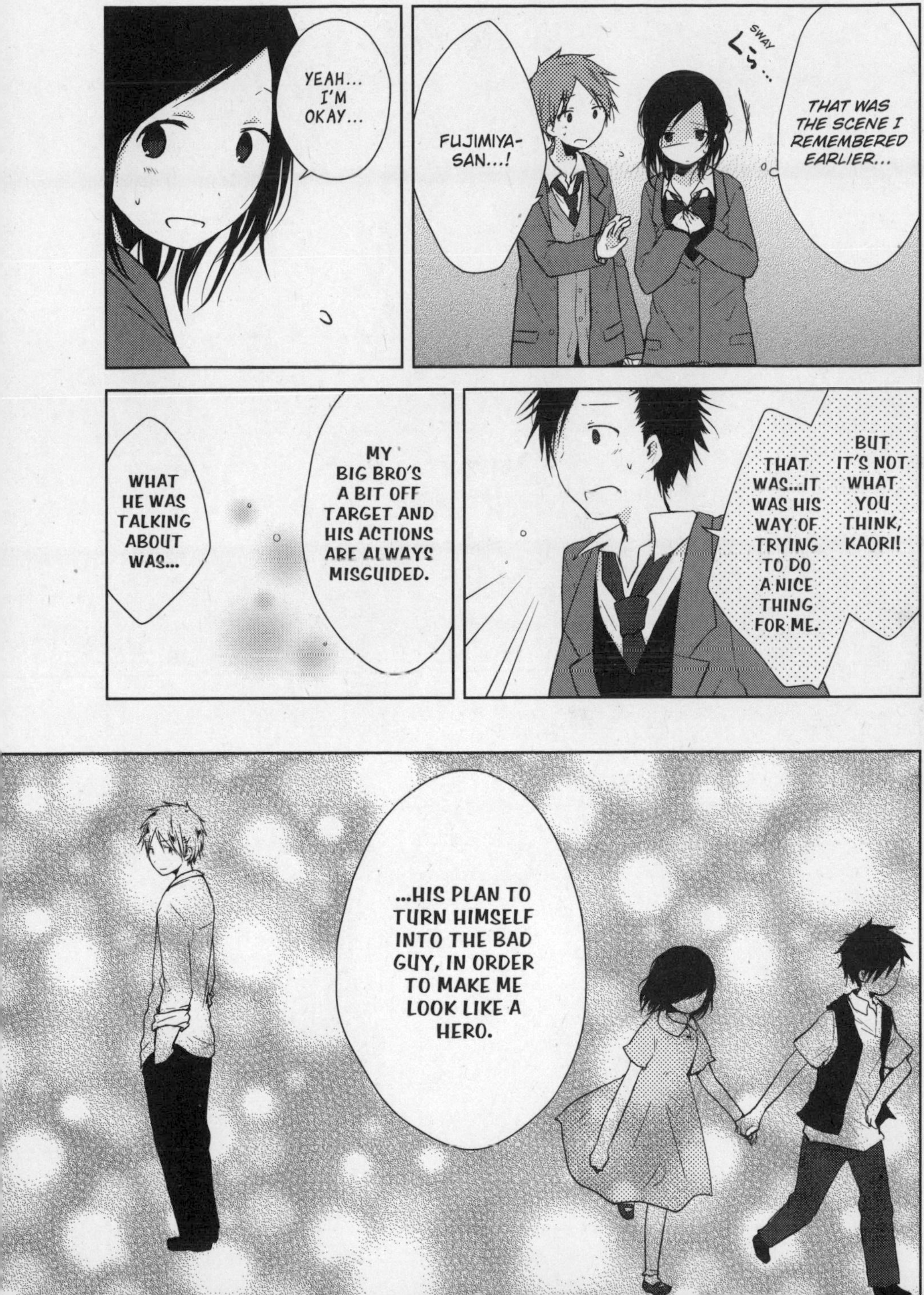
THAT WAS THE SCENE I REMEMBERED EARLIER...
SWAY
くら…
FUJIMIYA-SAN...!
YEAH... I'M OKAY...
BUT IT'S NOT WHAT YOU THINK, KAORI!
THAT WAS...IT WAS HIS WAY OF TRYING TO DO A NICE THING FOR ME.
MY BIG BRO'S A BIT OFF TARGET AND HIS ACTIONS ARE ALWAYS MISGUIDED.
WHAT HE WAS TALKING ABOUT WAS...
...HIS PLAN TO TURN HIMSELF INTO THE BAD GUY, IN ORDER TO MAKE ME LOOK LIKE A HERO.

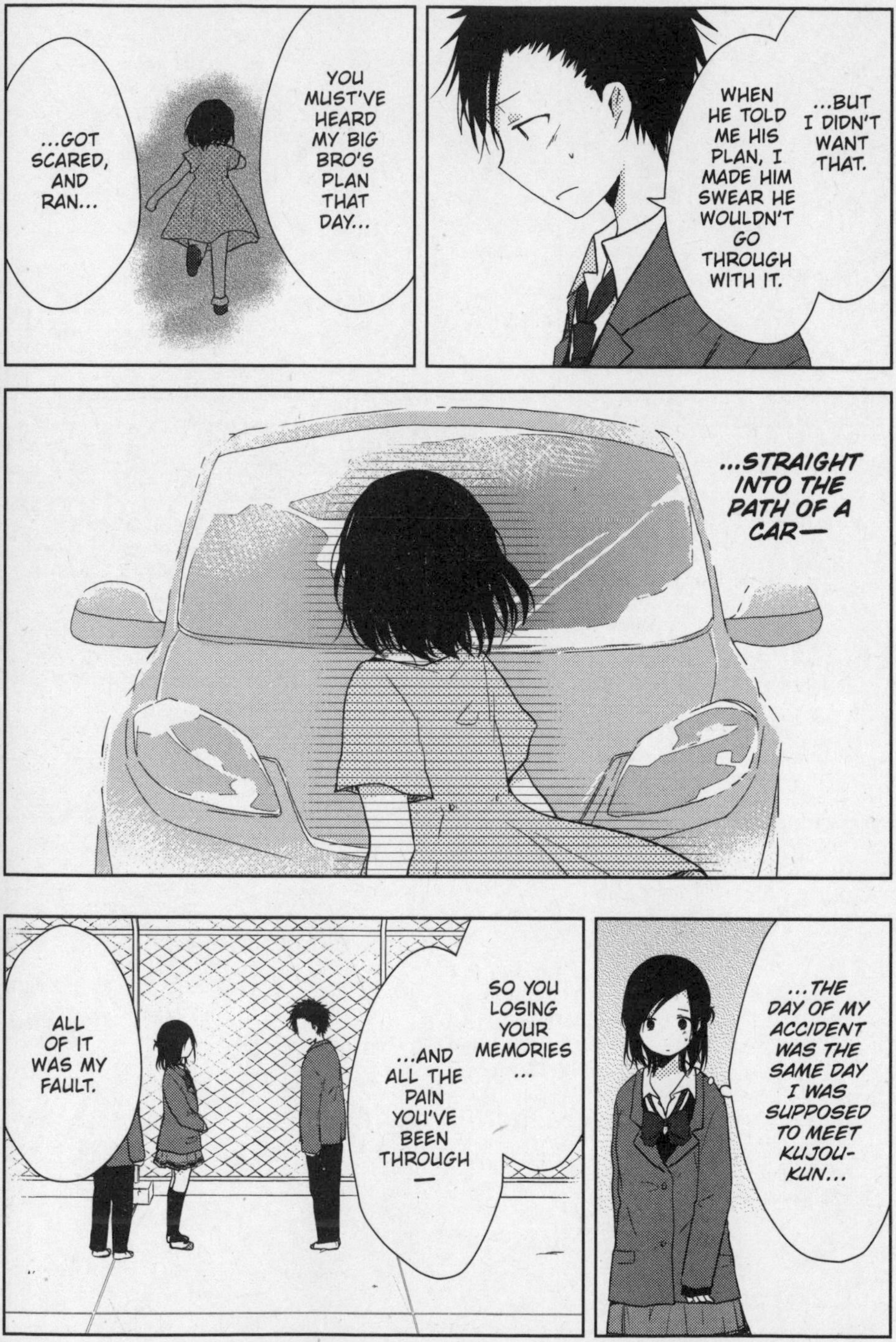
...BUT I DIDN'T WANT THAT.
WHEN HE TOLD ME HIS PLAN, I MADE HIM SWEAR HE WOULDN'T GO THROUGH WITH IT.
YOU MUST'VE HEARD MY BIG BRO'S PLAN THAT DAY...
...GOT SCARED, AND RAN...
...STRAIGHT INTO THE PATH OF A CAR—
...THE DAY OF MY ACCIDENT WAS THE SAME DAY I WAS SUPPOSED TO MEET KUJOU-KUN...
SO YOU LOSING YOUR MEMORIES...
...AND ALL THE PAIN YOU'VE BEEN THROUGH—
ALL OF IT WAS MY FAULT.

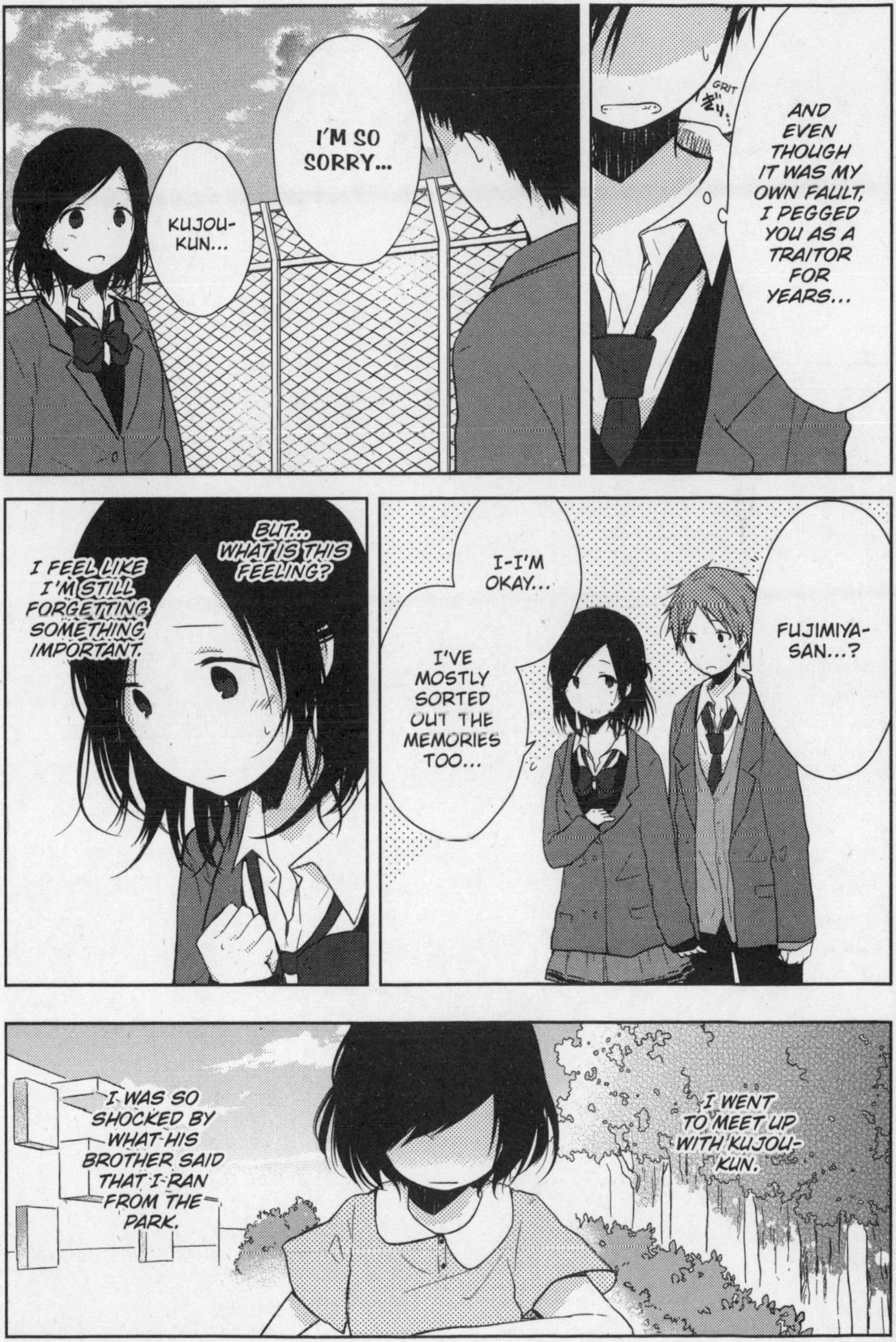
GRIT
AND EVEN THOUGH IT WAS MY OWN FAULT, I PEGGED YOU AS A TRAITOR FOR YEARS...
I'M SO SORRY...
KUJOU-KUN...
FUJIMIYA-SAN...?
I-I'M OKAY...
I'VE MOSTLY SORTED OUT THE MEMORIES TOO...
BUT... WHAT IS THIS FEELING?
I FEEL LIKE I'M STILL FORGETTING SOMETHING IMPORTANT.
I WENT TO MEET UP WITH KUJOU-KUN.
I WAS SO SHOCKED BY WHAT HIS BROTHER SAID THAT I RAN FROM THE PARK.

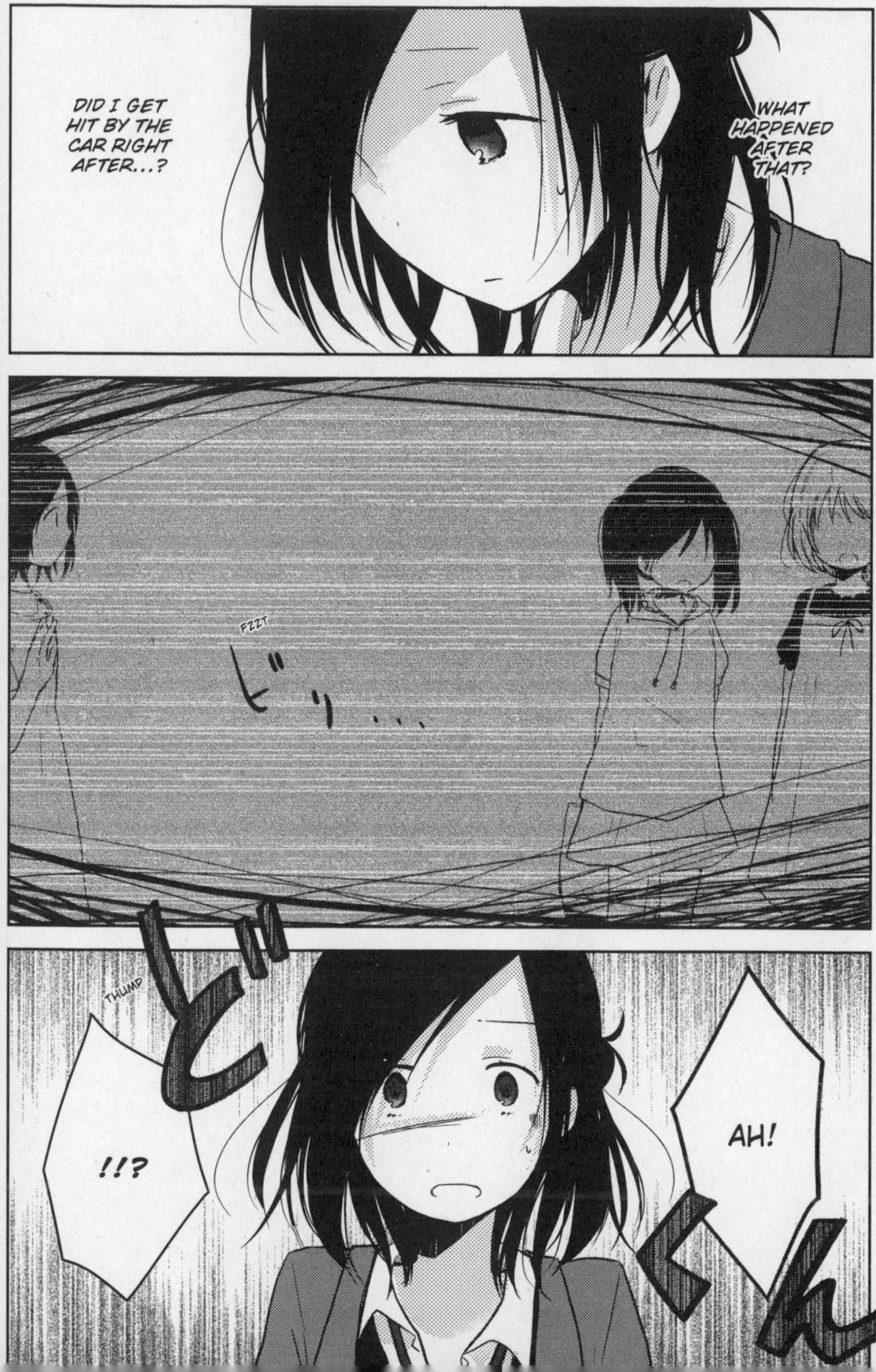
WHAT HAPPENED AFTER THAT?
DID I GET HIT BY THE CAR RIGHT AFTER...?
FZZT
THUMP
AH!
!!?

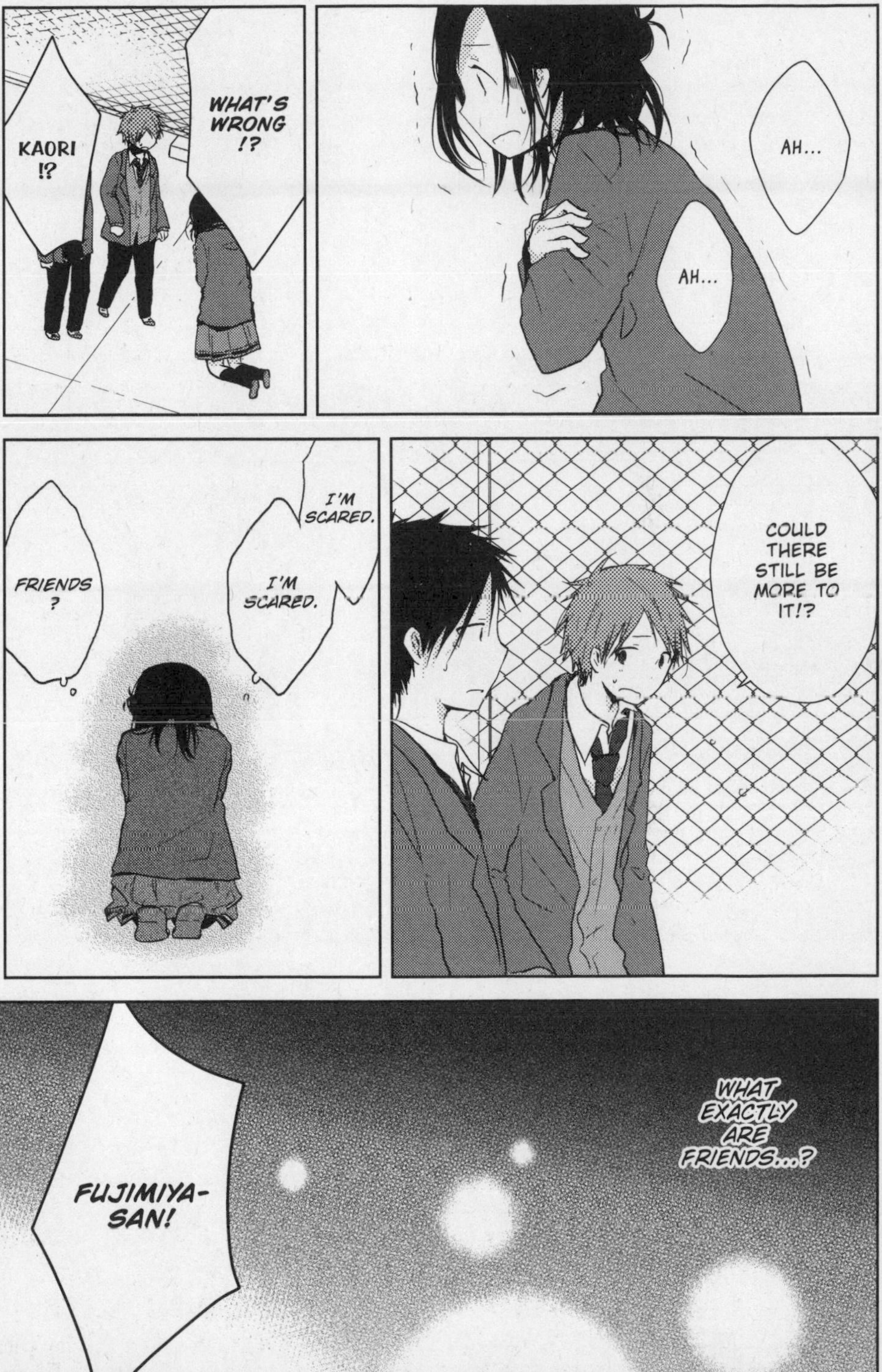
AH...
AH...
WHAT'S WRONG!?
KAORI!?
COULD THERE STILL BE MORE TO IT!?
I'M SCARED.
I'M SCARED.
FRIENDS?
WHAT EXACTLY ARE FRIENDS...?
FUJIMIYA-SAN!

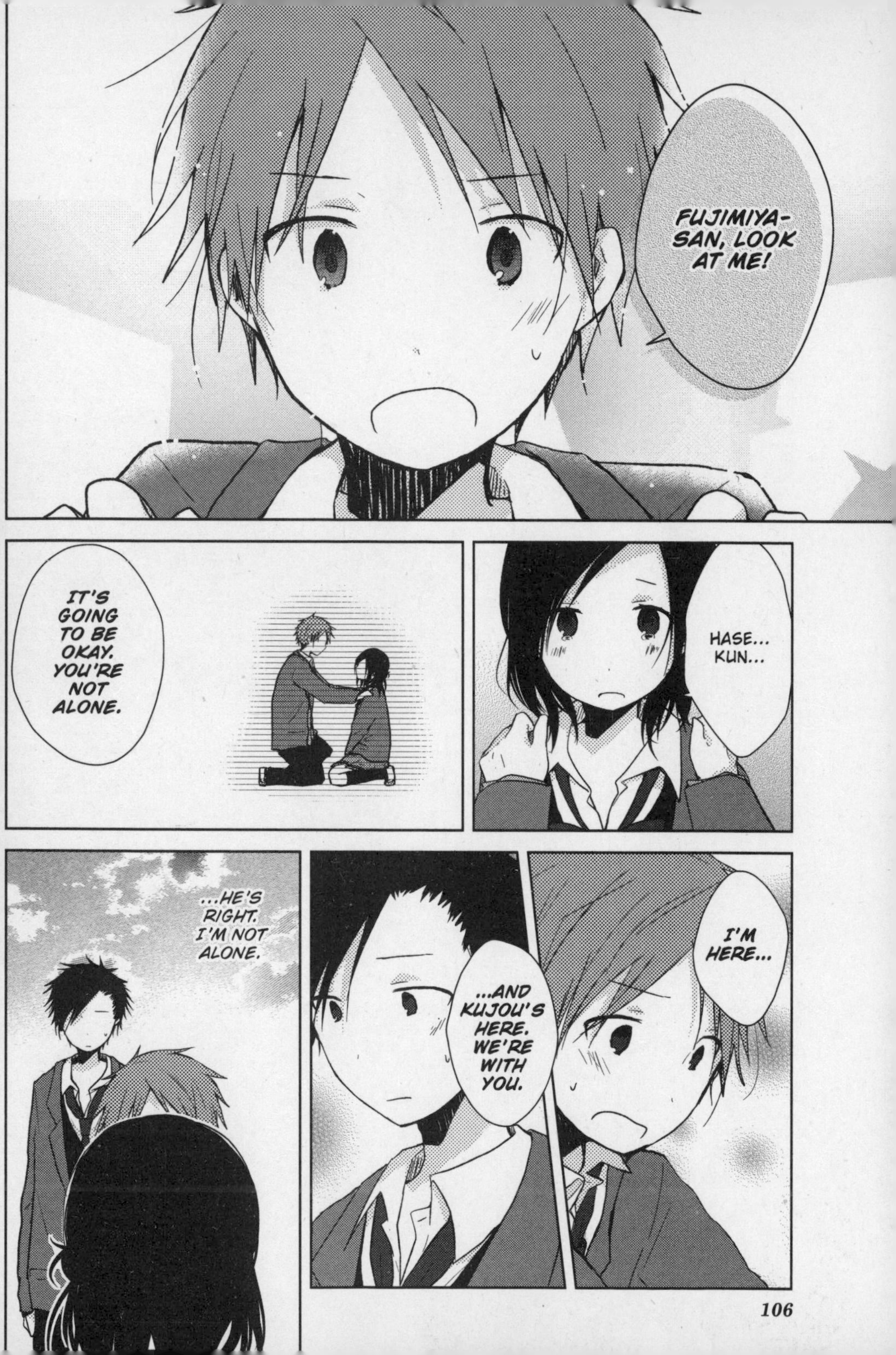
FUJIMIYA-SAN, LOOK AT ME!
HASE... KUN...
IT'S GOING TO BE OKAY. YOU'RE NOT ALONE.
I'M HERE...
...AND KUJOU'S HERE. WE'RE WITH YOU.
...HE'S RIGHT. I'M NOT ALONE.

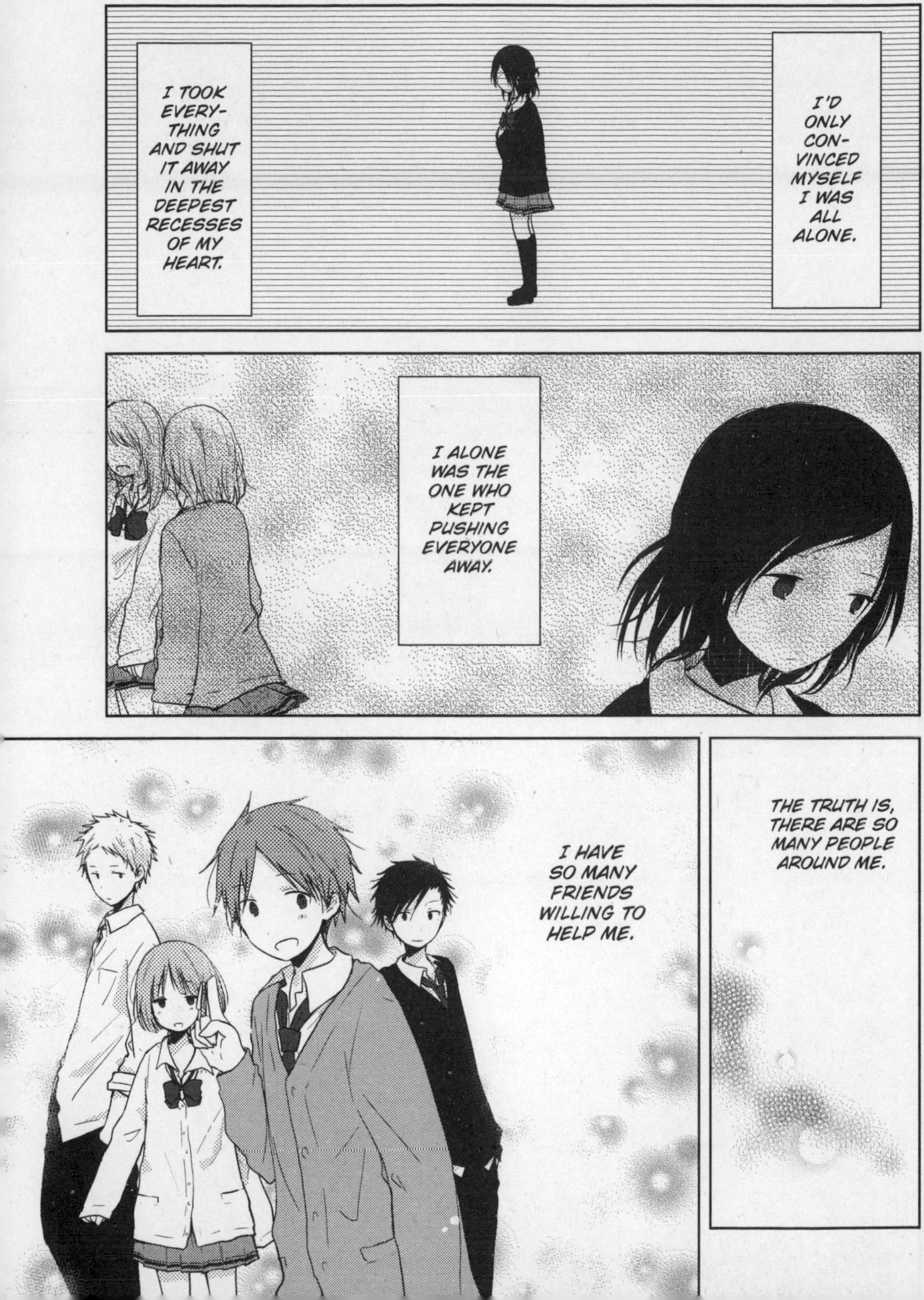

I'D ONLY CON-VINCED MYSELF I WAS ALL ALONE.
I TOOK EVERY-THING AND SHUT IT AWAY IN THE DEEPEST RECESSES OF MY HEART.
I ALONE WAS THE ONE WHO KEPT PUSHING EVERYONE AWAY.
THE TRUTH IS, THERE ARE SO MANY PEOPLE AROUND ME.
I HAVE SO MANY FRIENDS WILLING TO HELP ME.

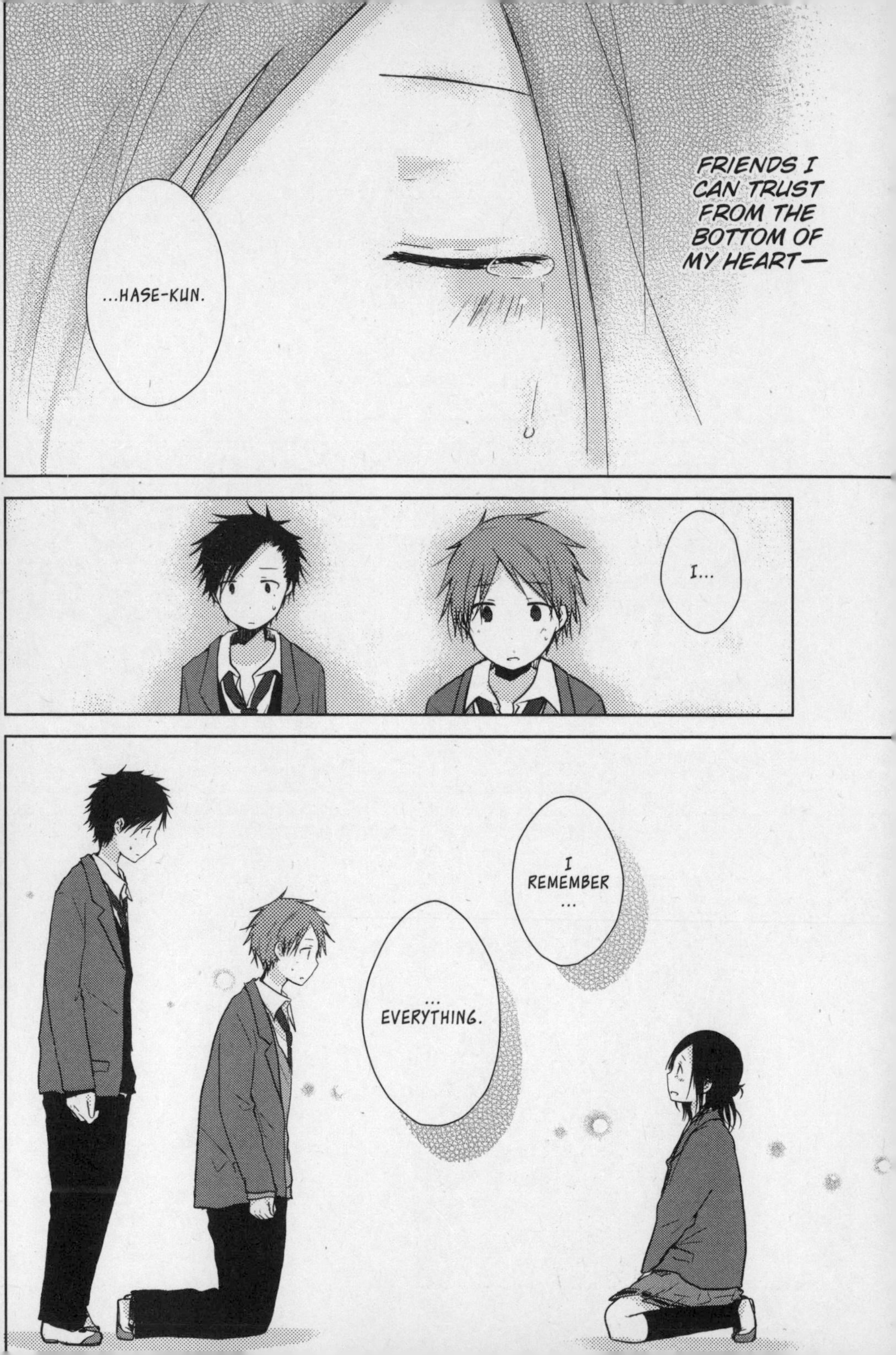
FRIENDS I CAN TRUST FROM THE BOTTOM OF MY HEART—
...HASE-KUN.
I...
I REMEMBER ...
... EVERYTHING.

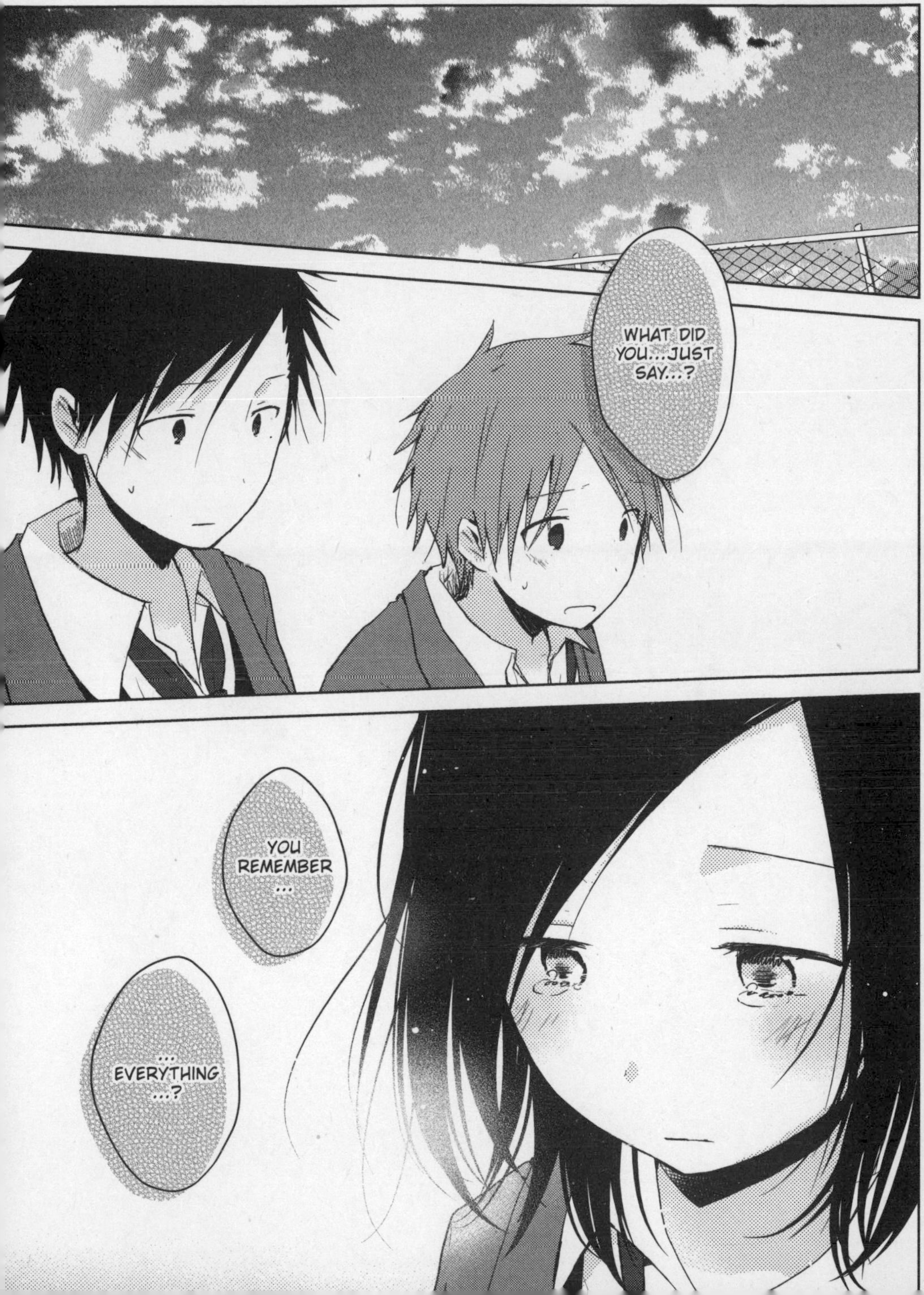
WHAT DID YOU...JUST SAY...?
YOU REMEMBER ...
... EVERYTHING ...?

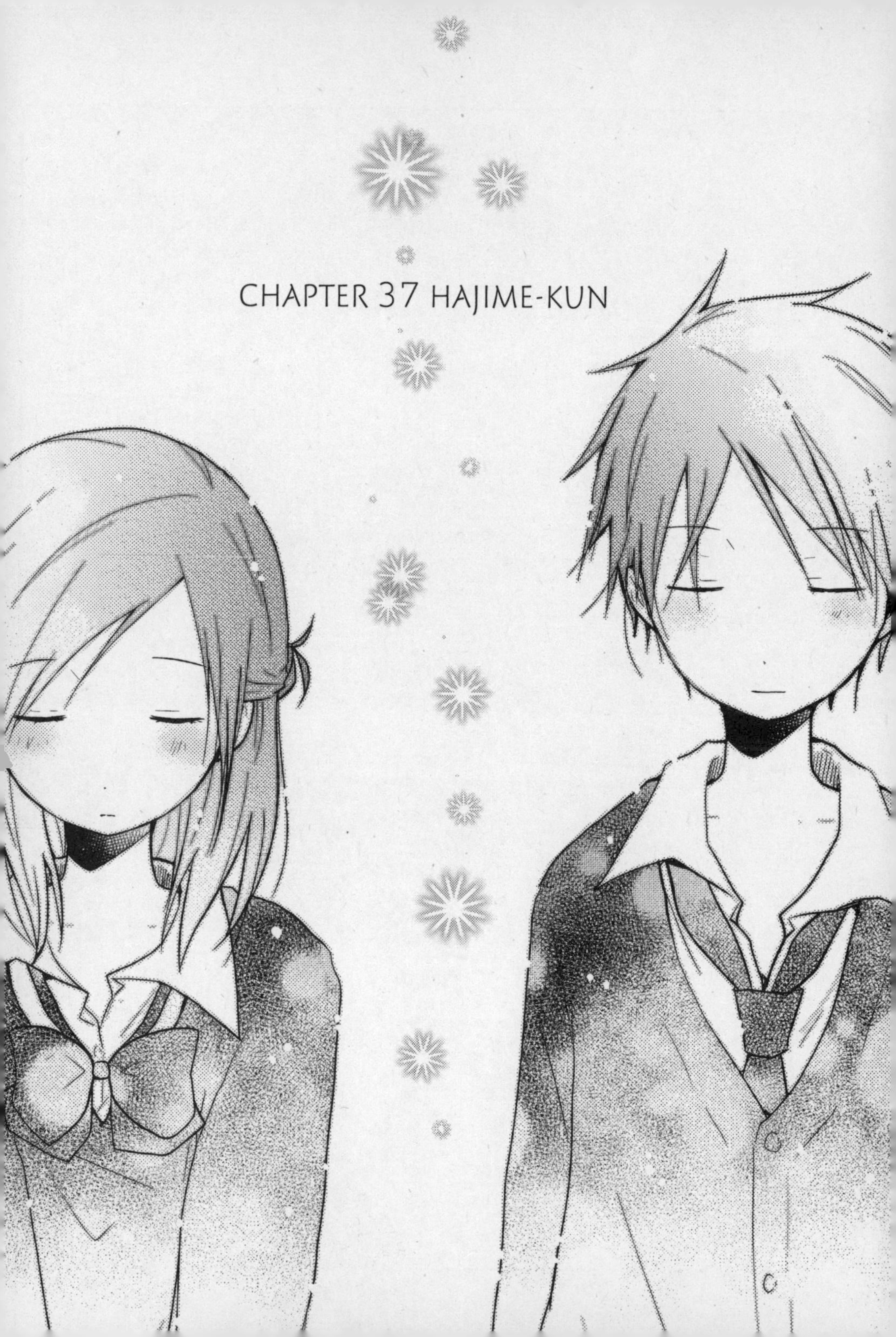
CHAPTER 37 HAJIME-KUN

WHEN YOU SAY YOU REMEMBER EVERYTHING, DOES THAT MEAN...

...YOU GOT YOUR MEMORIES BACK...?

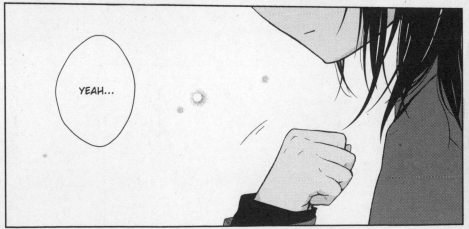

YEAH...

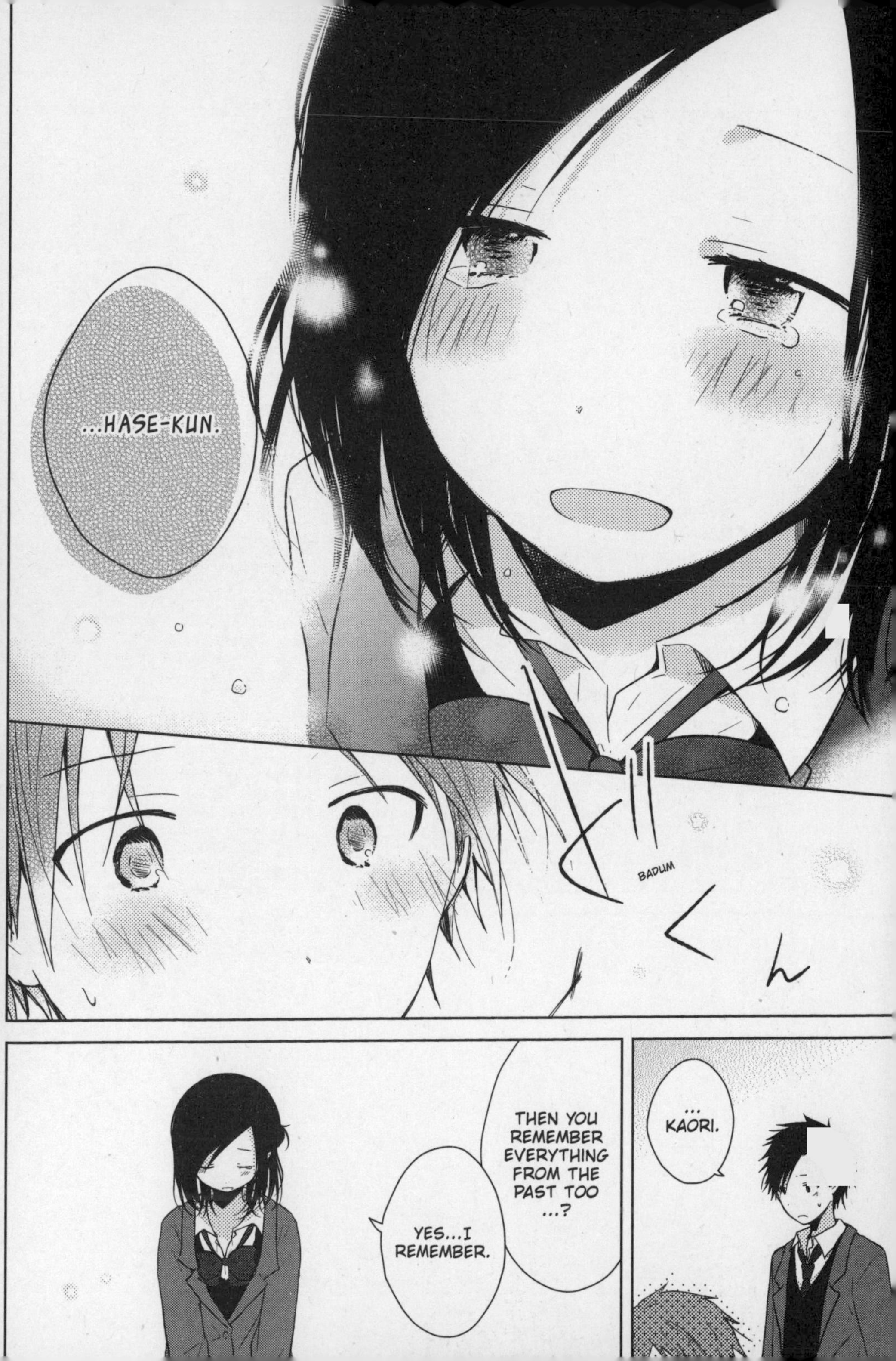
...HASE-KUN.
BADUM
...KAORI.
THEN YOU REMEMBER EVERYTHING FROM THE PAST TOO ...?
YES...I REMEMBER.

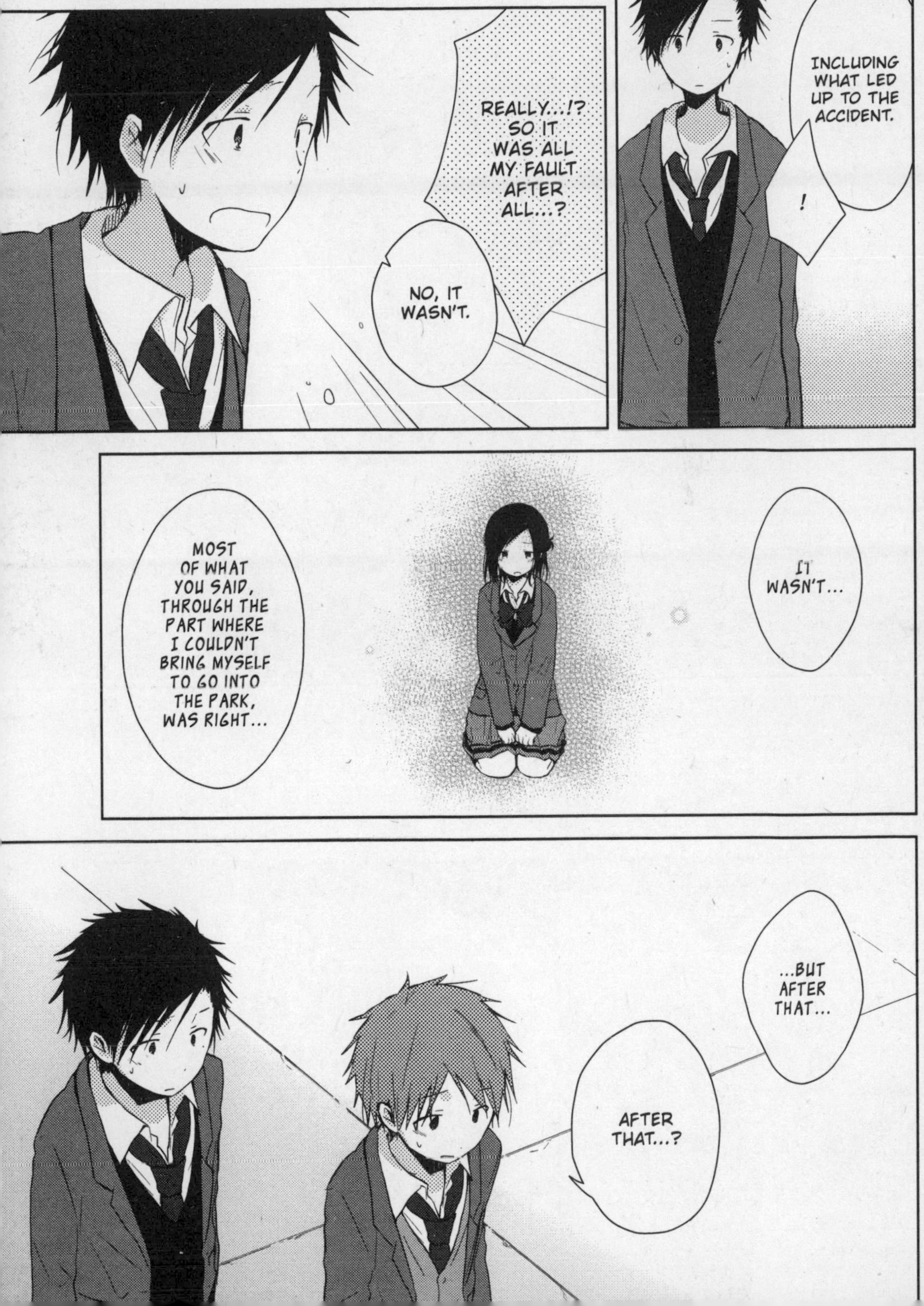
INCLUDING WHAT LED UP TO THE ACCIDENT.
!
REALLY...!? SO IT WAS ALL MY FAULT AFTER ALL...?
NO, IT WASN'T.
IT WASN'T...
MOST OF WHAT YOU SAID, THROUGH THE PART WHERE I COULDN'T BRING MYSELF TO GO INTO THE PARK, WAS RIGHT...
...BUT AFTER THAT...
AFTER THAT...?

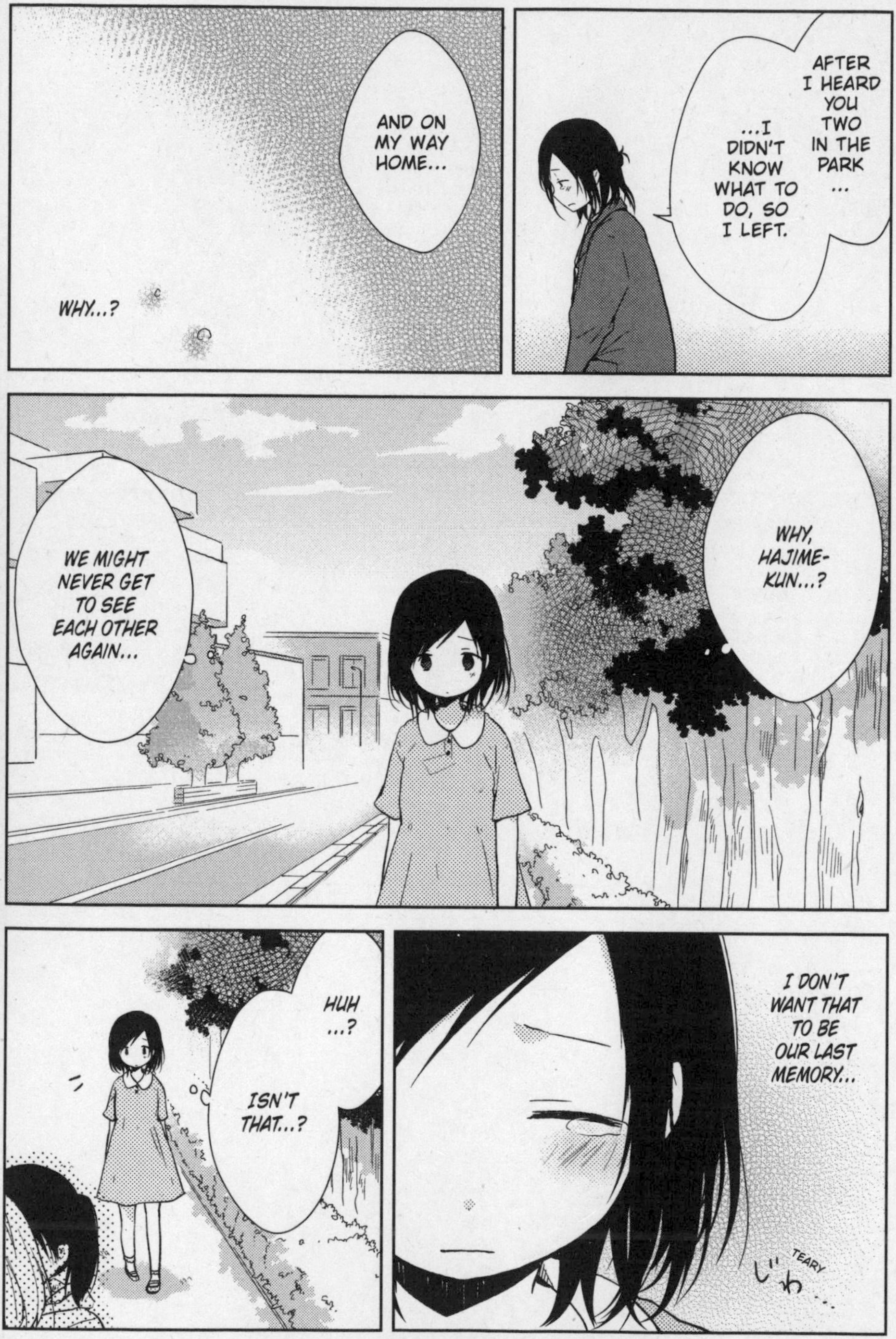
AFTER I HEARD YOU TWO IN THE PARK...
...I DIDN'T KNOW WHAT TO DO, SO I LEFT.
AND ON MY WAY HOME...
WHY...?
WHY, HAJIME-KUN...?
WE MIGHT NEVER GET TO SEE EACH OTHER AGAIN...
I DON'T WANT THAT TO BE OUR LAST MEMORY...
TEARY
じわ...
HUH...?
ISN'T THAT...?

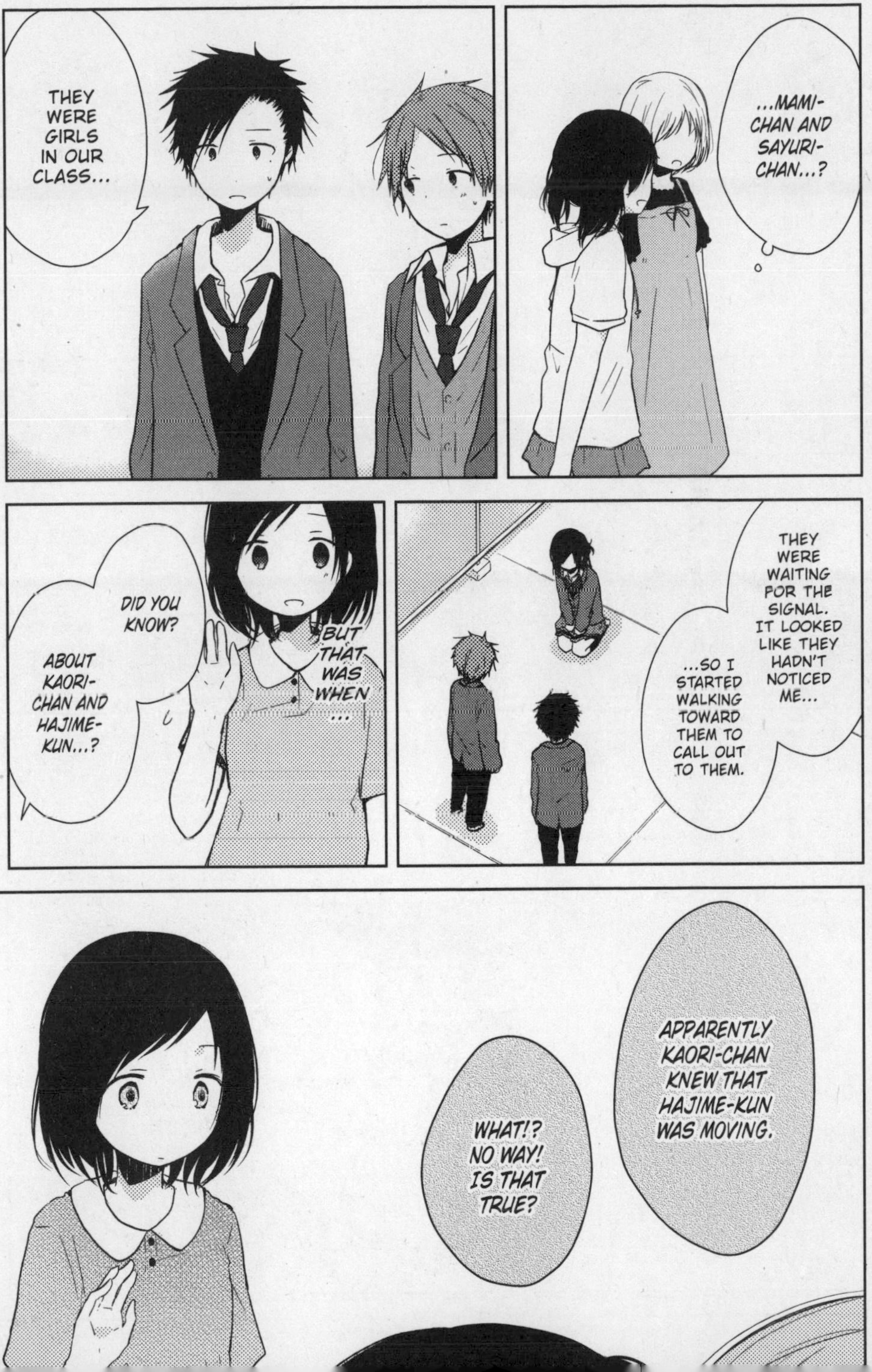
...MAMI-CHAN AND SAYURI-CHAN...?
THEY WERE GIRLS IN OUR CLASS...
THEY WERE WAITING FOR THE SIGNAL. IT LOOKED LIKE THEY HADN'T NOTICED ME...
...SO I STARTED WALKING TOWARD THEM TO CALL OUT TO THEM.
BUT THAT WAS WHEN...
DID YOU KNOW?
ABOUT KAORI-CHAN AND HAJIME-KUN...?
APPARENTLY KAORI-CHAN KNEW THAT HAJIME-KUN WAS MOVING.
WHAT!? NO WAY! IS THAT TRUE?

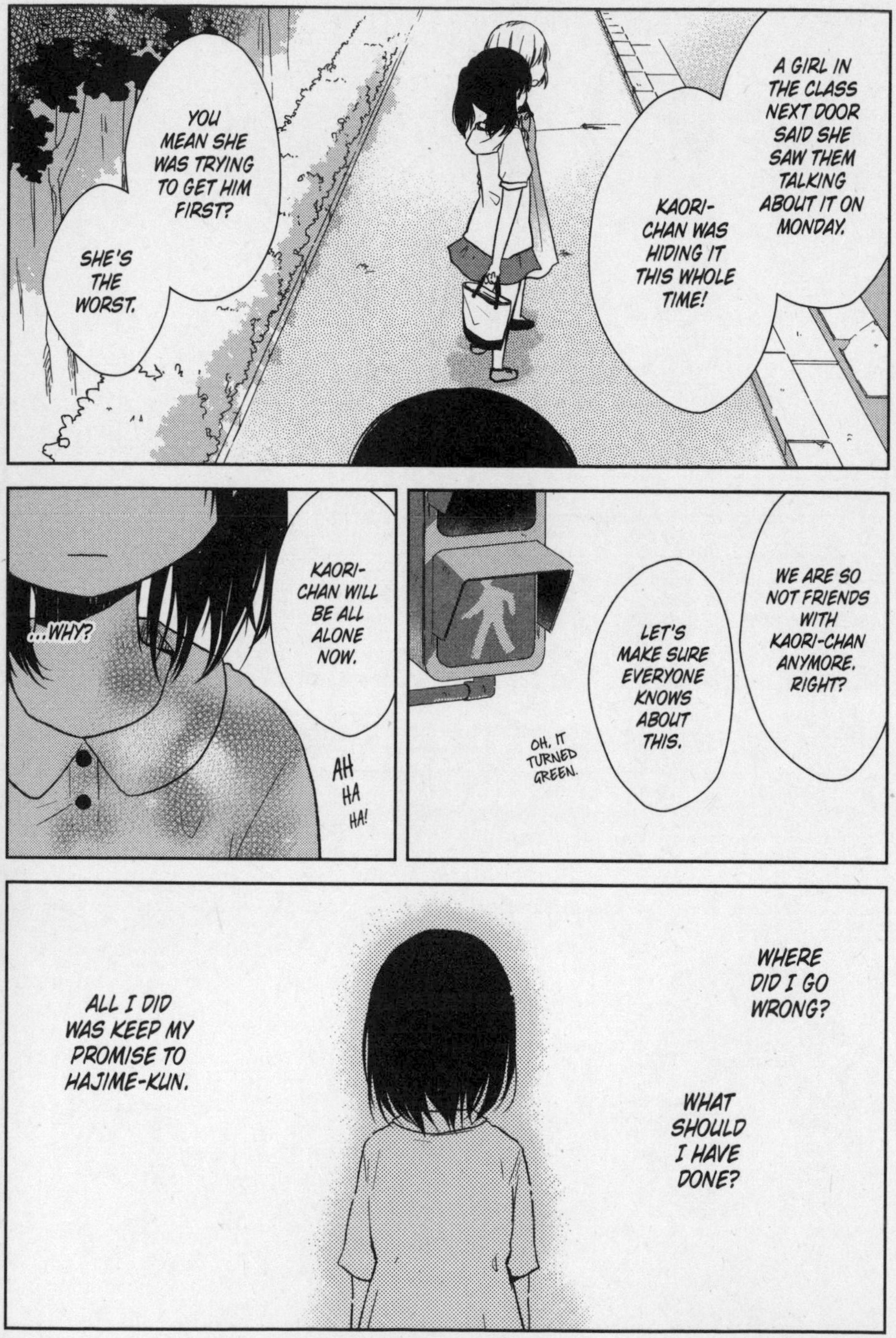
A GIRL IN THE CLASS NEXT DOOR SAID SHE SAW THEM TALKING ABOUT IT ON MONDAY.
KAORI-CHAN WAS HIDING IT THIS WHOLE TIME!
YOU MEAN SHE WAS TRYING TO GET HIM FIRST?
SHE'S THE WORST.
WE ARE SO NOT FRIENDS WITH KAORI-CHAN ANYMORE. RIGHT?
LET'S MAKE SURE EVERYONE KNOWS ABOUT THIS.
OH, IT TURNED GREEN.
KAORI-CHAN WILL BE ALL ALONE NOW.
AH HA HA!
...WHY?
WHERE DID I GO WRONG?
WHAT SHOULD I HAVE DONE?
ALL I DID WAS KEEP MY PROMISE TO HAJIME-KUN.

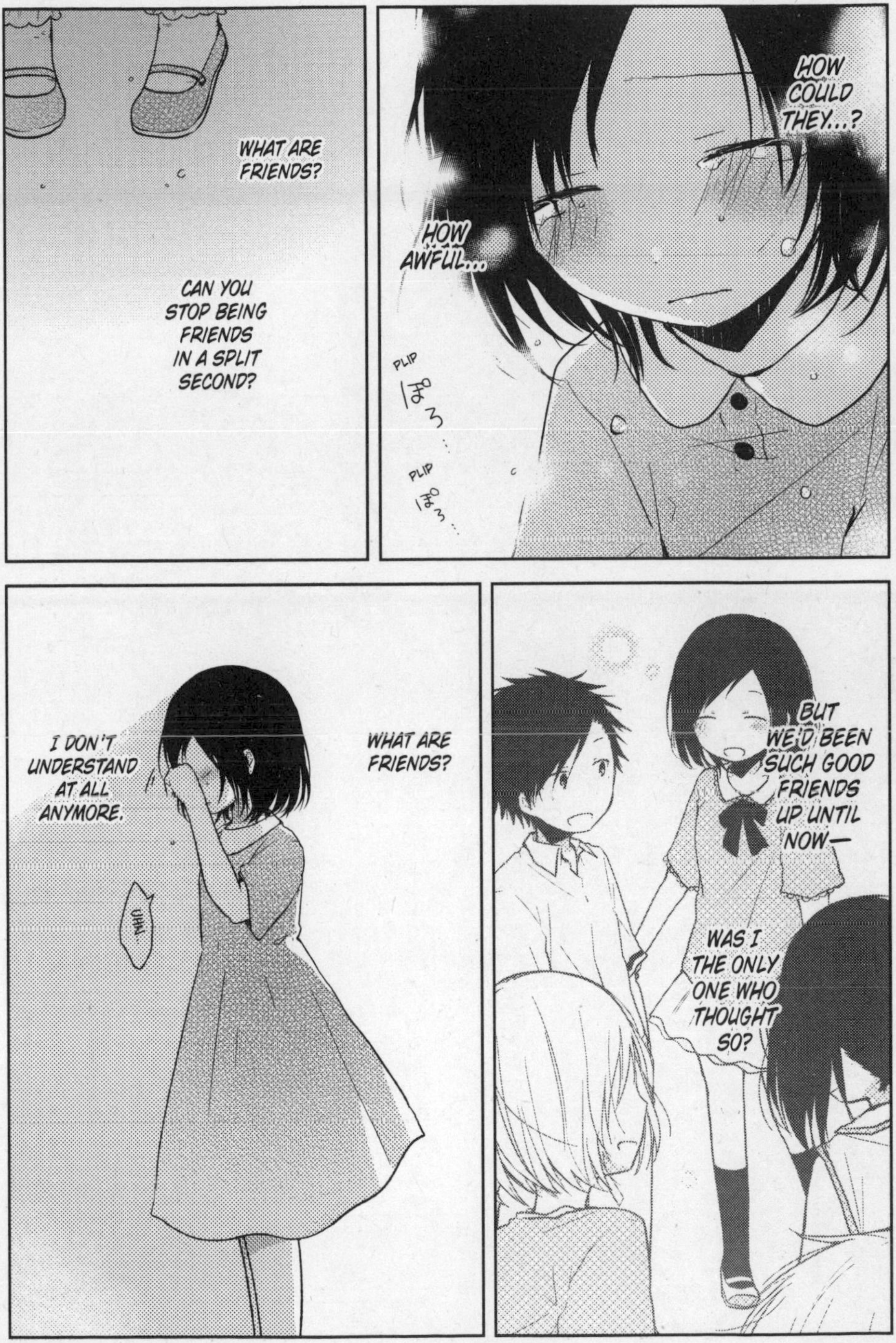
HOW COULD THEY...?
HOW AWFUL...
PLIP
ぽろ…
PLIP
ぽろ…
WHAT ARE FRIENDS?
CAN YOU STOP BEING FRIENDS IN A SPLIT SECOND?
BUT WE'D BEEN SUCH GOOD FRIENDS UP UNTIL NOW—
WAS I THE ONLY ONE WHO THOUGHT SO?
WHAT ARE FRIENDS?
I DON'T UNDERSTAND AT ALL ANYMORE.
UHH...

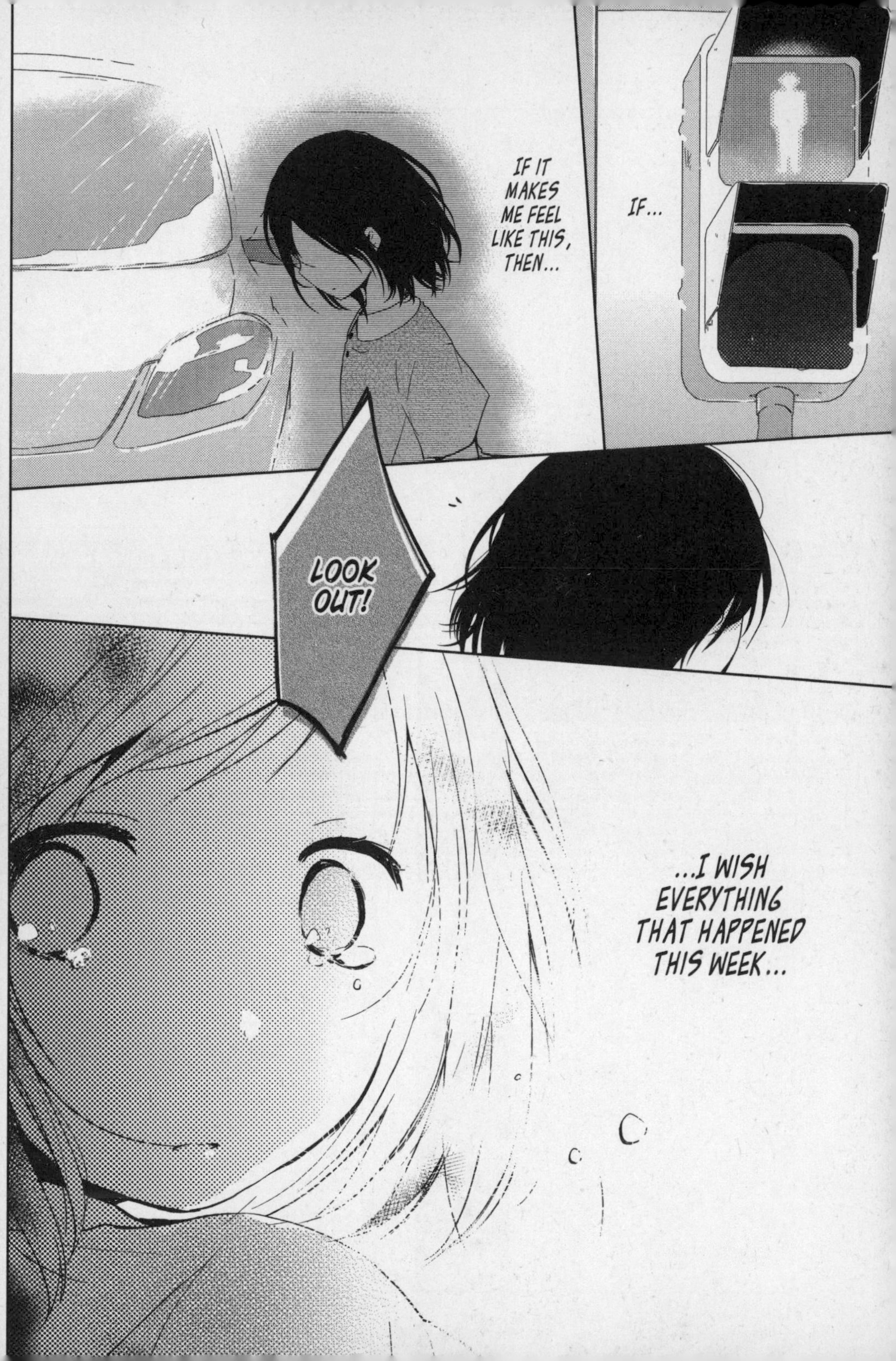
IF...
IF IT MAKES ME FEEL LIKE THIS, THEN...
LOOK OUT!
...I WISH EVERYTHING THAT HAPPENED THIS WEEK...

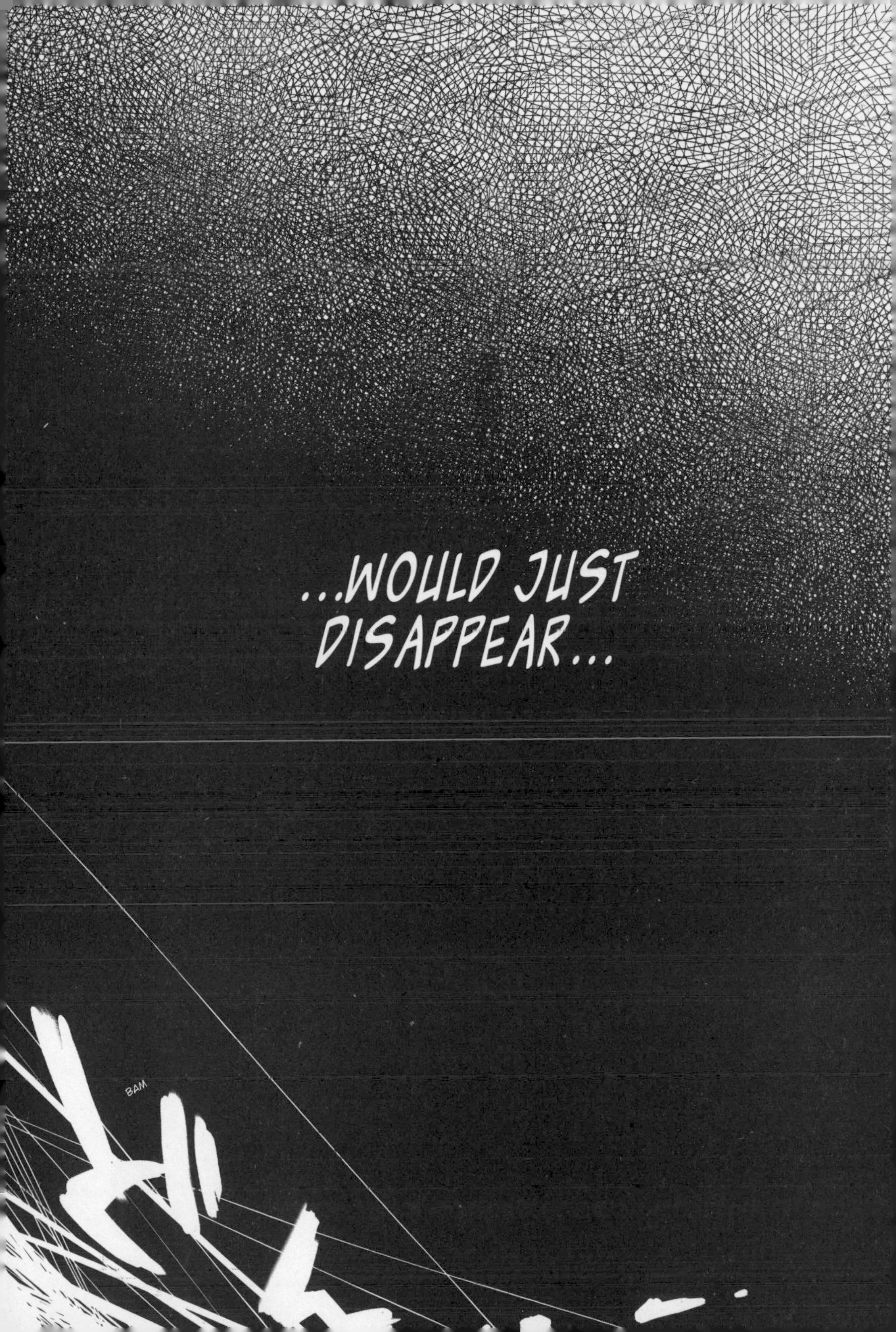
...WOULD JUST DISAPPEAR...
BAM

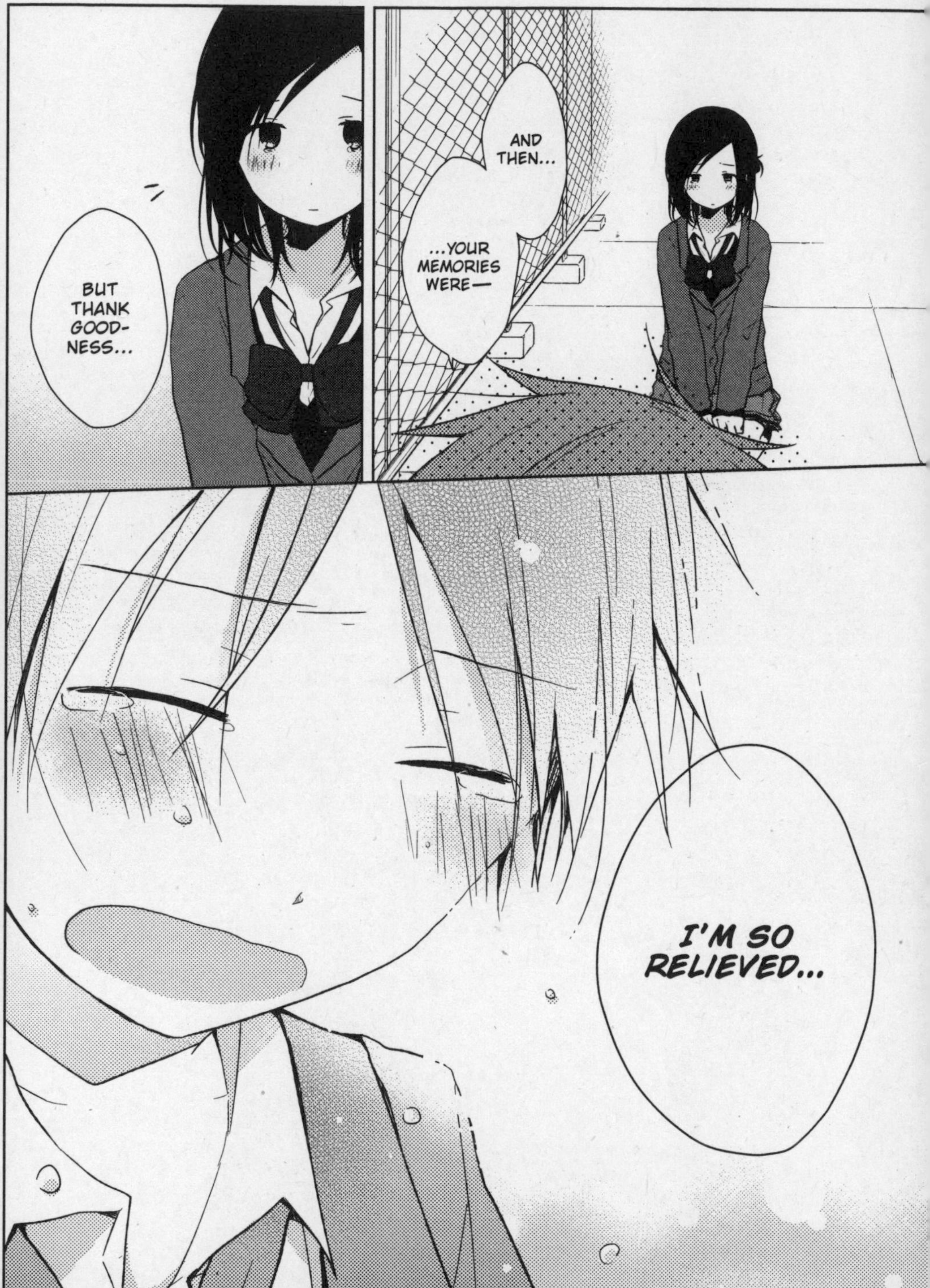
AND THEN...
...YOUR MEMORIES WERE—
BUT THANK GOOD-NESS...
I'M SO RELIEVED...

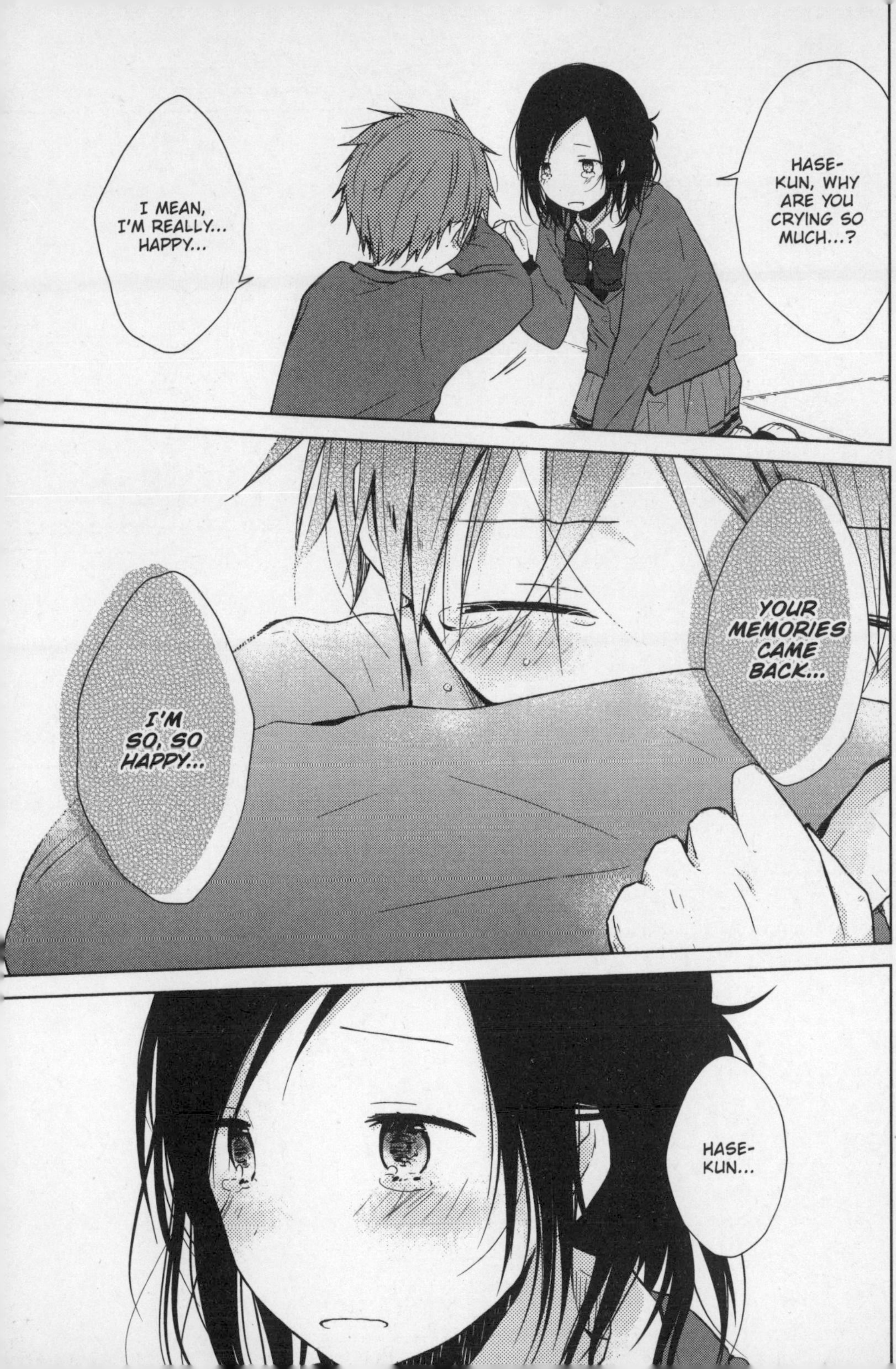
HASE-KUN, WHY ARE YOU CRYING SO MUCH...?
I MEAN, I'M REALLY... HAPPY...
YOUR MEMORIES CAME BACK...
I'M SO, SO HAPPY...
HASE-KUN...

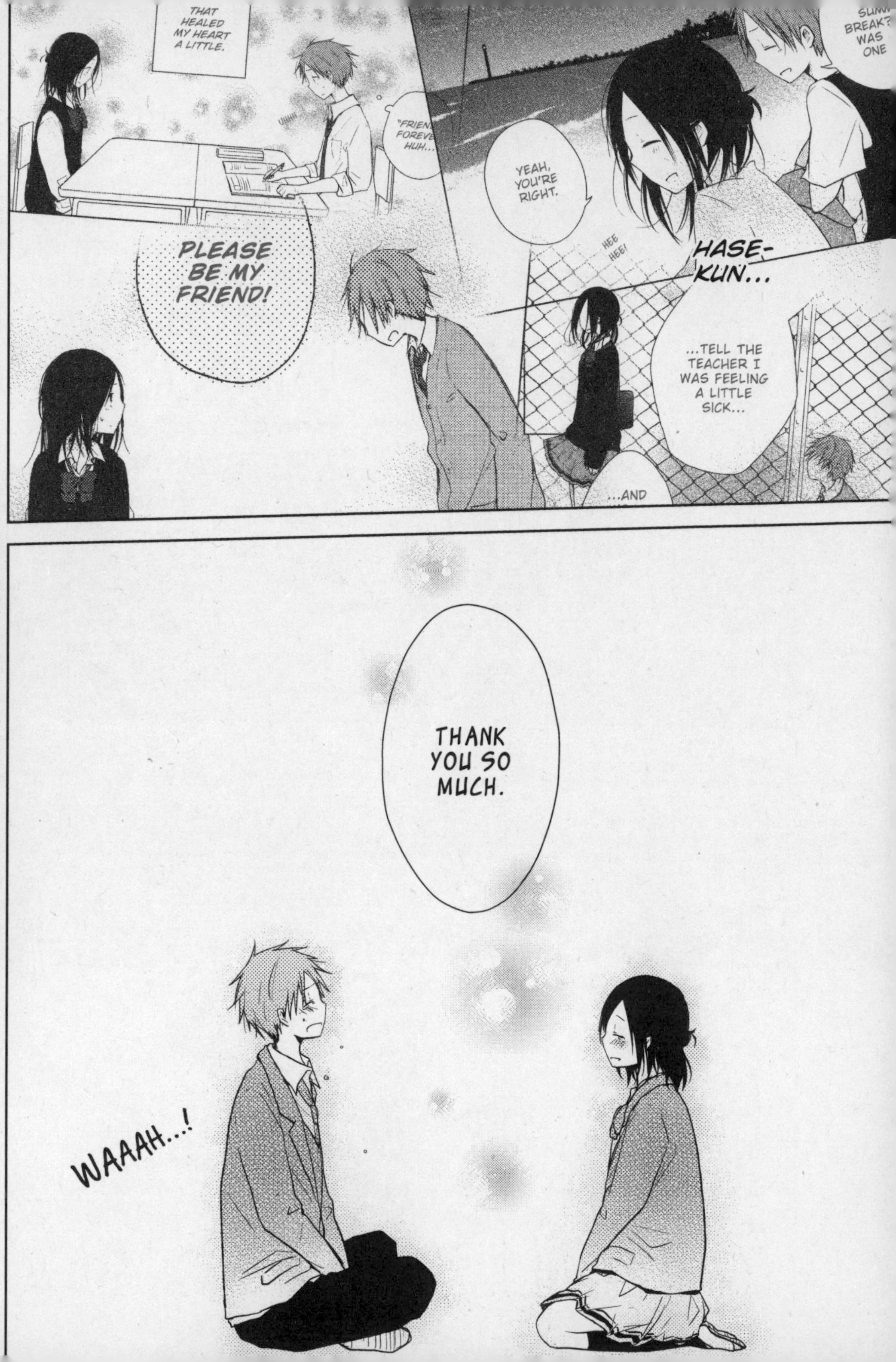
SUMM BREAK? WAS ONE
YEAH, YOU'RE RIGHT.
THAT HEALED MY HEART A LITTLE.
"FRIEN FOREVE HUH...
HASE-KUN...
...TELL THE TEACHER I WAS FEELING A LITTLE SICK...
...AND
HEE HEE!
PLEASE BE MY FRIEND!
THANK YOU SO MUCH.
WAAAH...!

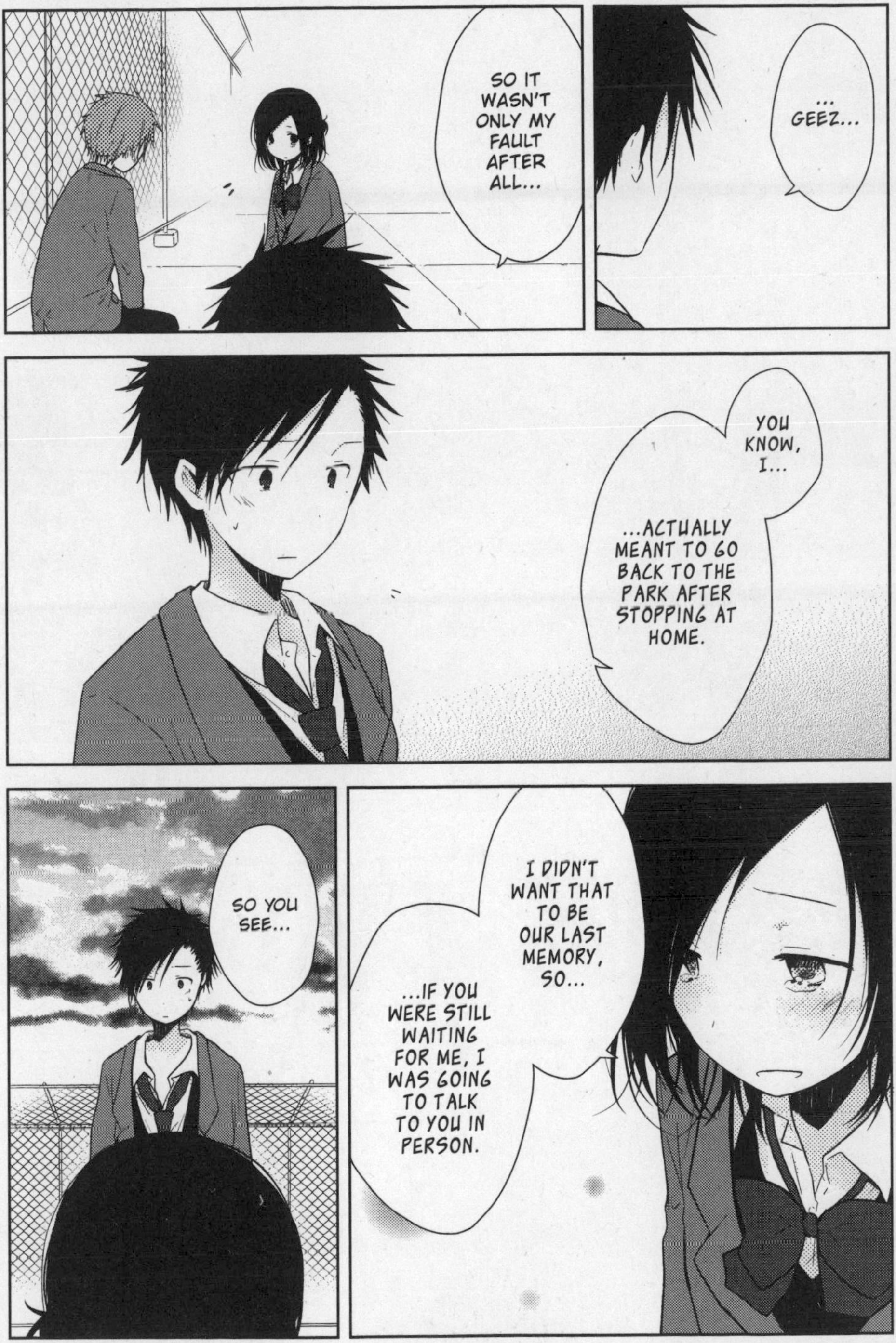
... GEEZ...
SO IT WASN'T ONLY MY FAULT AFTER ALL...
YOU KNOW, I...
...ACTUALLY MEANT TO GO BACK TO THE PARK AFTER STOPPING AT HOME.
I DIDN'T WANT THAT TO BE OUR LAST MEMORY, SO...
...IF YOU WERE STILL WAITING FOR ME, I WAS GOING TO TALK TO YOU IN PERSON.
SO YOU SEE...

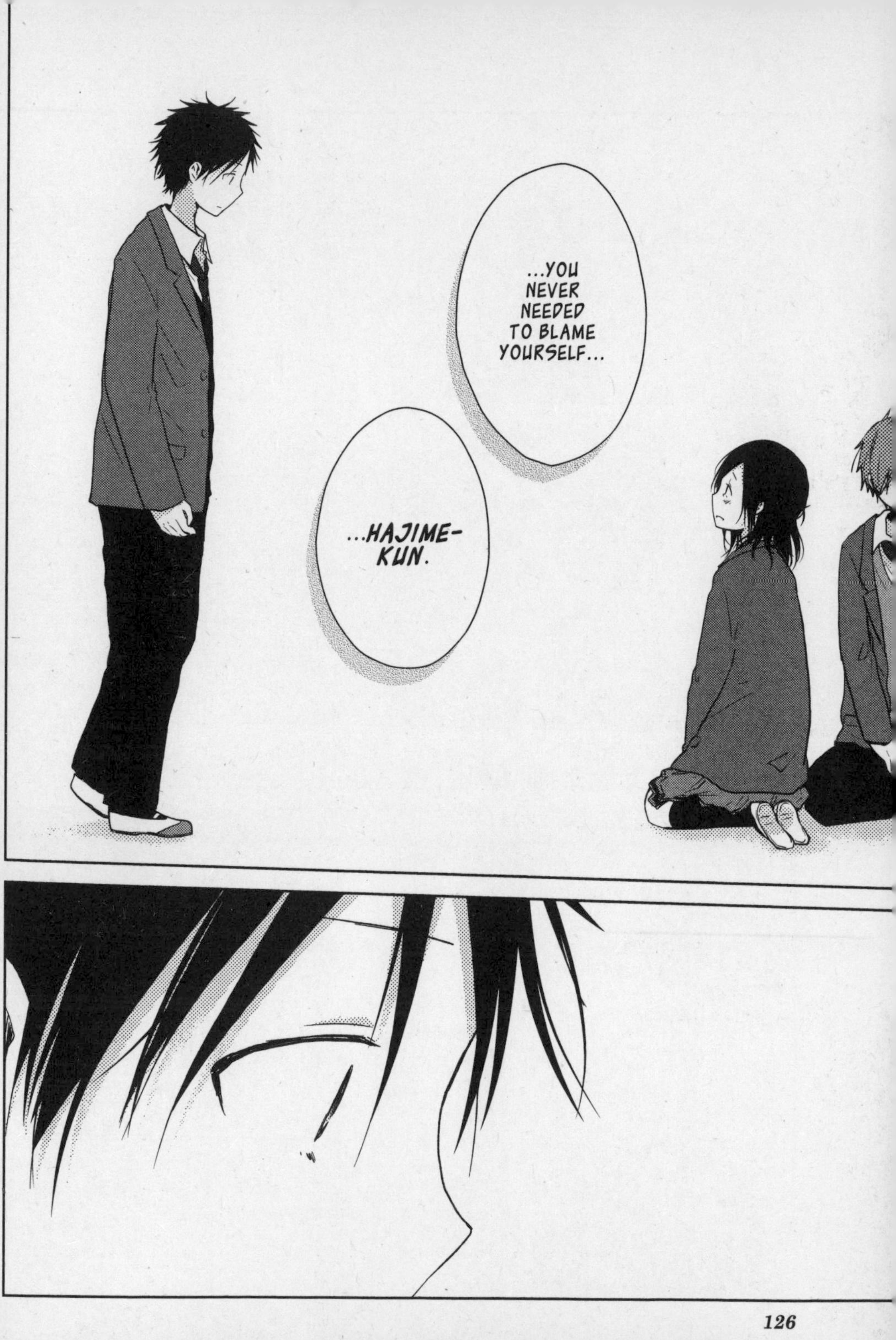
...YOU NEVER NEEDED TO BLAME YOURSELF...
...HAJIME-KUN.

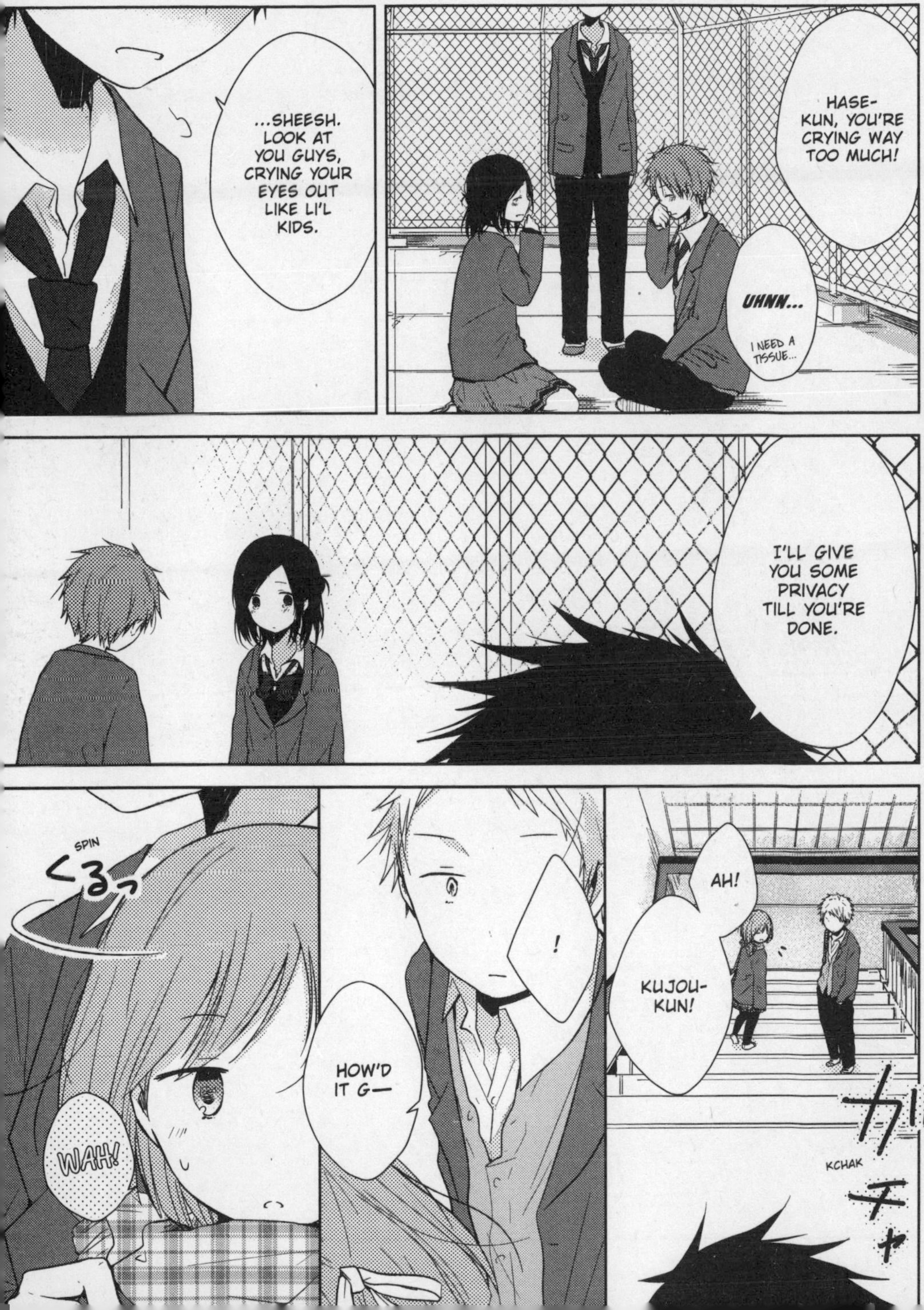
HASE-KUN, YOU'RE CRYING WAY TOO MUCH!
UHNN...
I NEED A TISSUE...
...SHEESH. LOOK AT YOU GUYS, CRYING YOUR EYES OUT LIKE LI'L KIDS.
I'LL GIVE YOU SOME PRIVACY TILL YOU'RE DONE.
カチャ
KCHAK
AH!
KUJOU-KUN!
!
HOW'D IT G—
くるっ
SPIN
WAH!

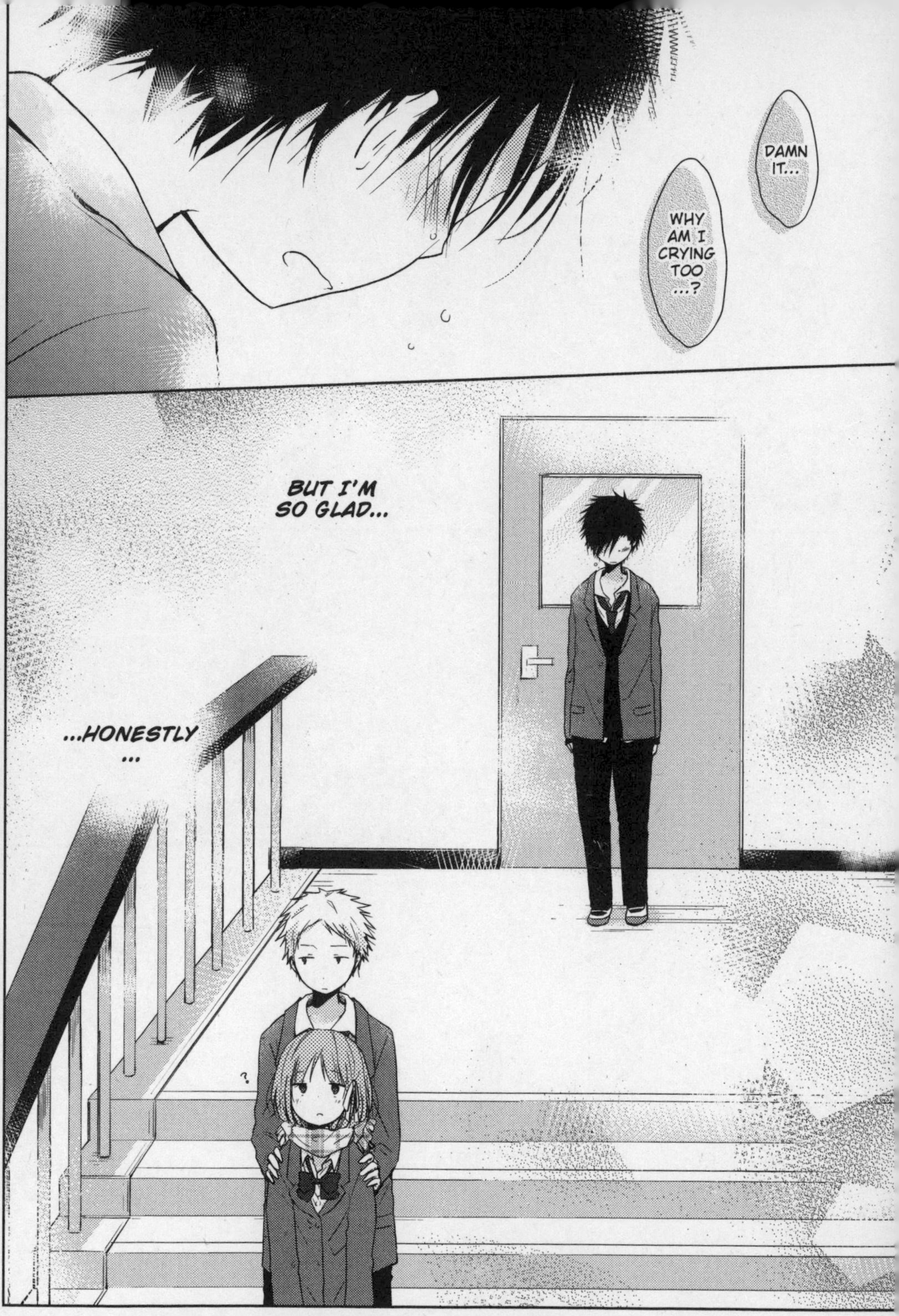

DAMN IT...
WHY AM I CRYING TOO ...?
BUT I'M SO GLAD...
...HONESTLY ...

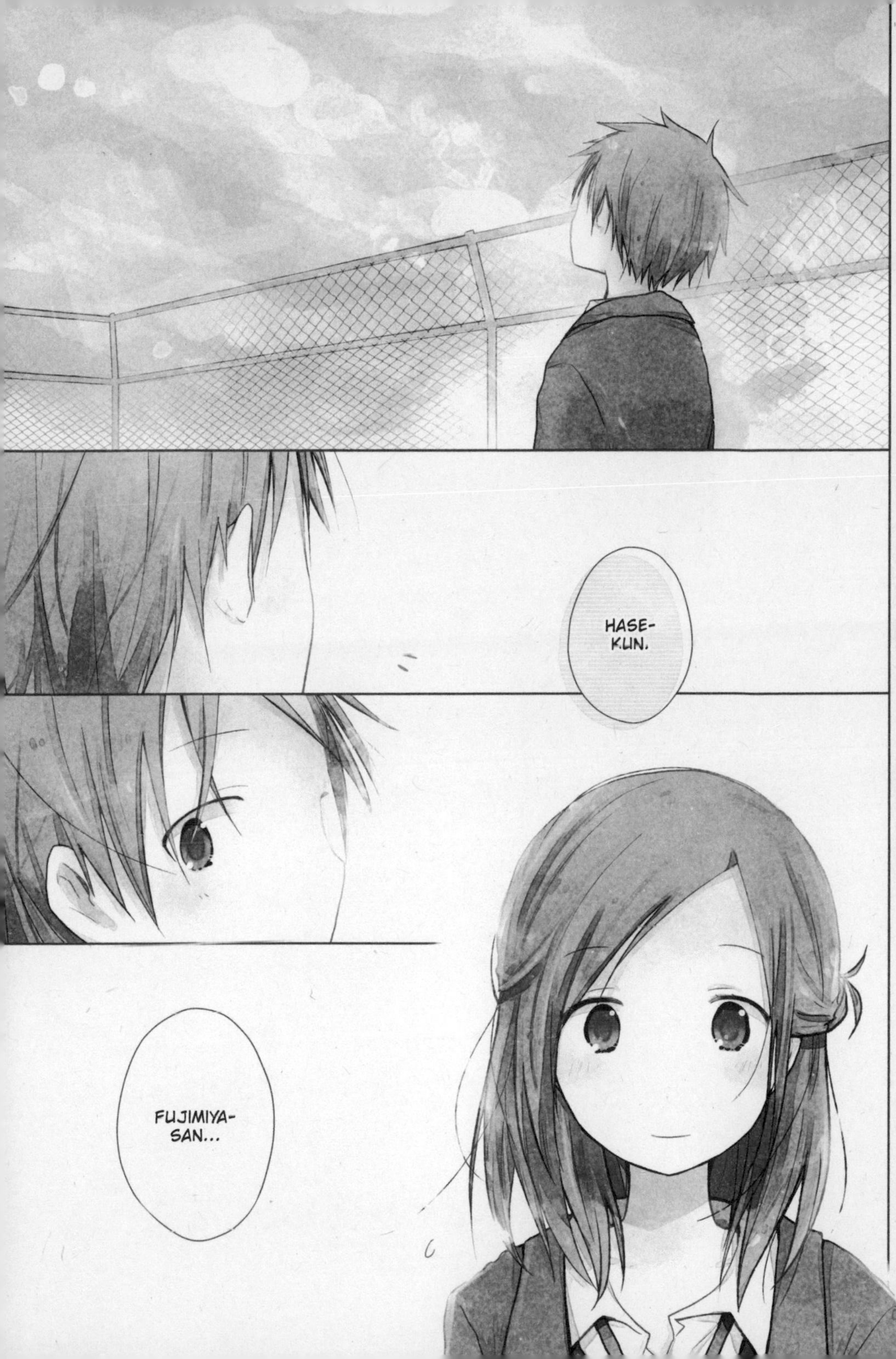
HASE-KUN.
FUJIMIYA-SAN...

FINAL CHAPTER PLEASE BE FRIENDS WITH ME AGAIN

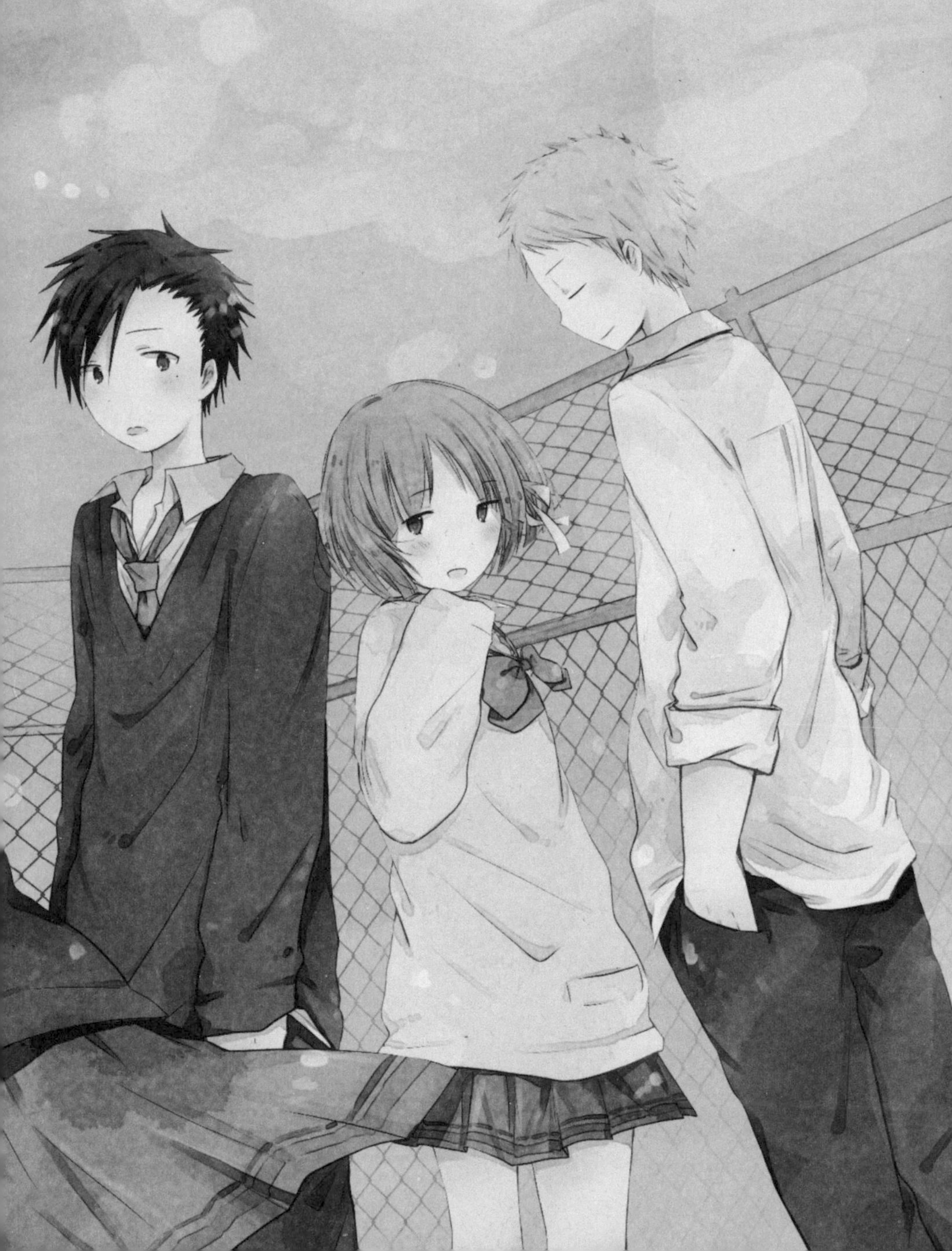

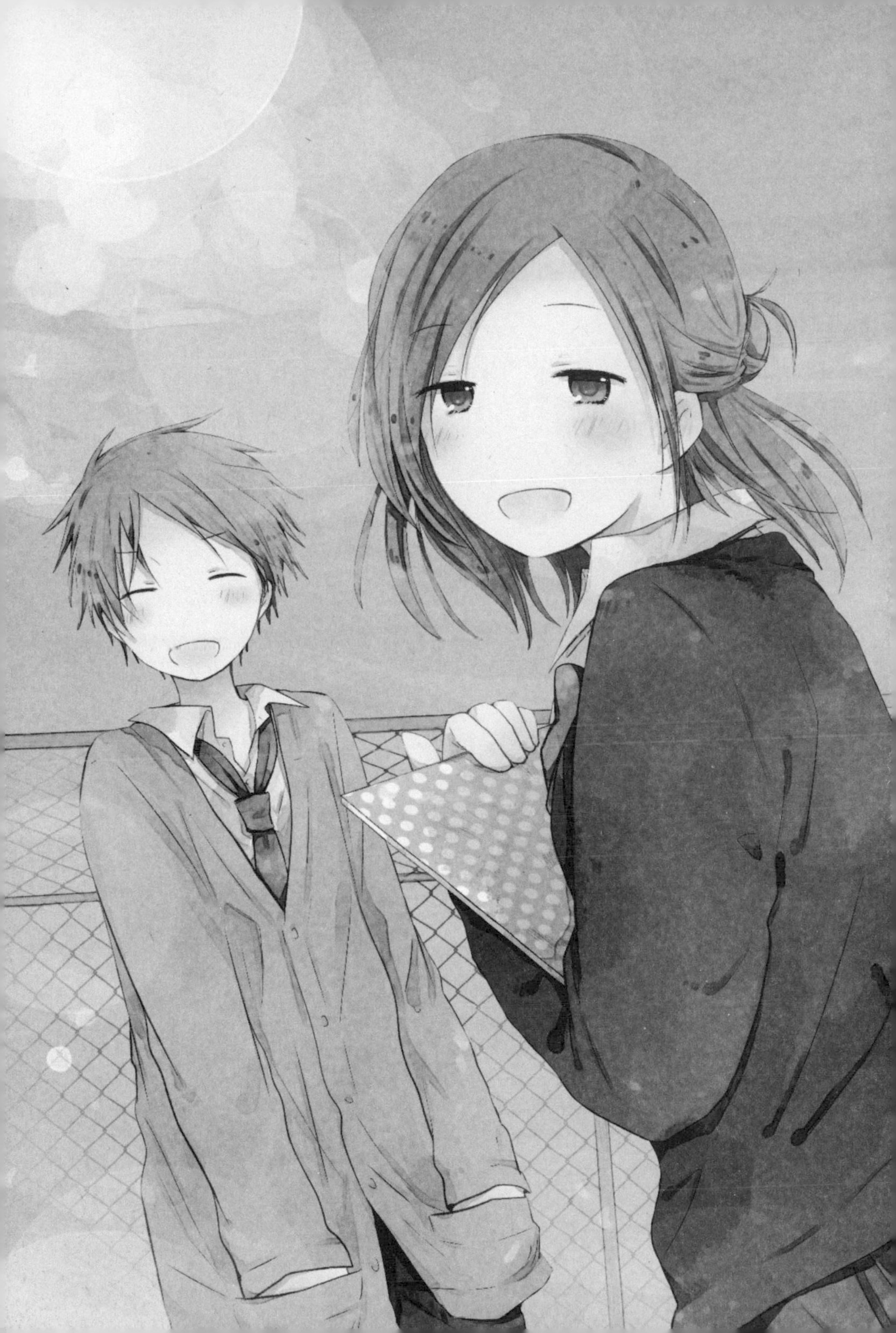

ONE
WEEK
FRIENDS

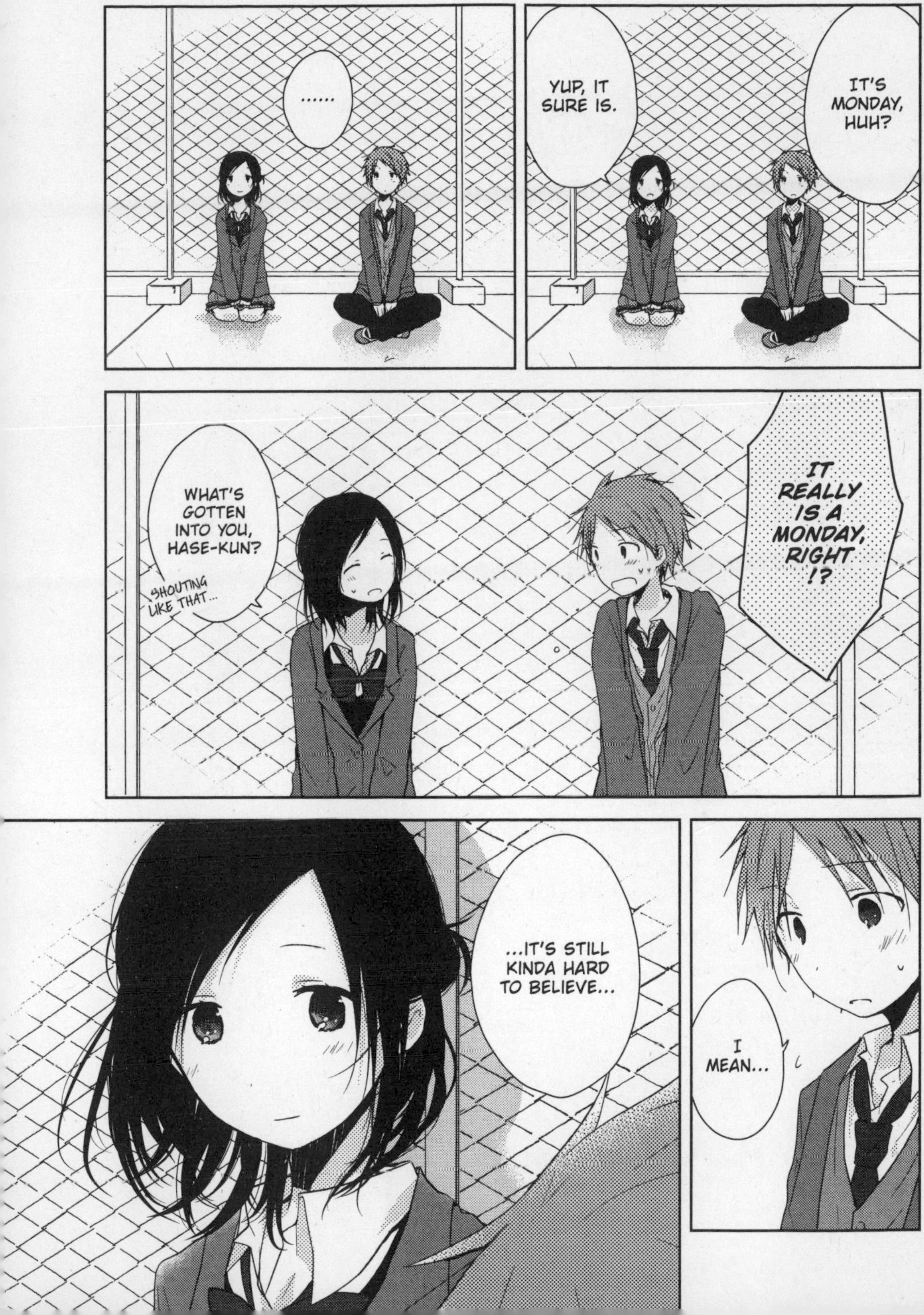
IT'S MONDAY, HUH?
YUP, IT SURE IS.
......
IT REALLY IS A MONDAY, RIGHT!?
WHAT'S GOTTEN INTO YOU, HASE-KUN?
SHOUTING LIKE THAT...
I MEAN...
...IT'S STILL KINDA HARD TO BELIEVE...

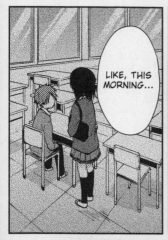

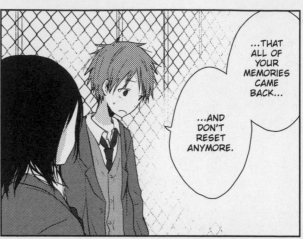

...THAT ALL OF YOUR MEMORIES CAME BACK...
...AND DON'T RESET ANYMORE.
LIKE, THIS MORNING...
HAVING YOU COME UP TO ME YOURSELF, FUJIMIYA-SAN—
I'M SO OVER THE MOON, I DON'T EVEN KNOW IF THIS IS A DREAM OR REALITY OR MAYBE EVEN A DELUSION...
AH HA HA!

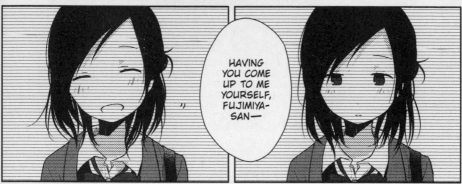

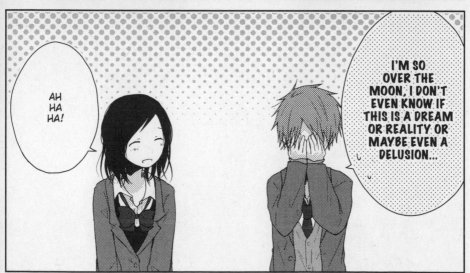

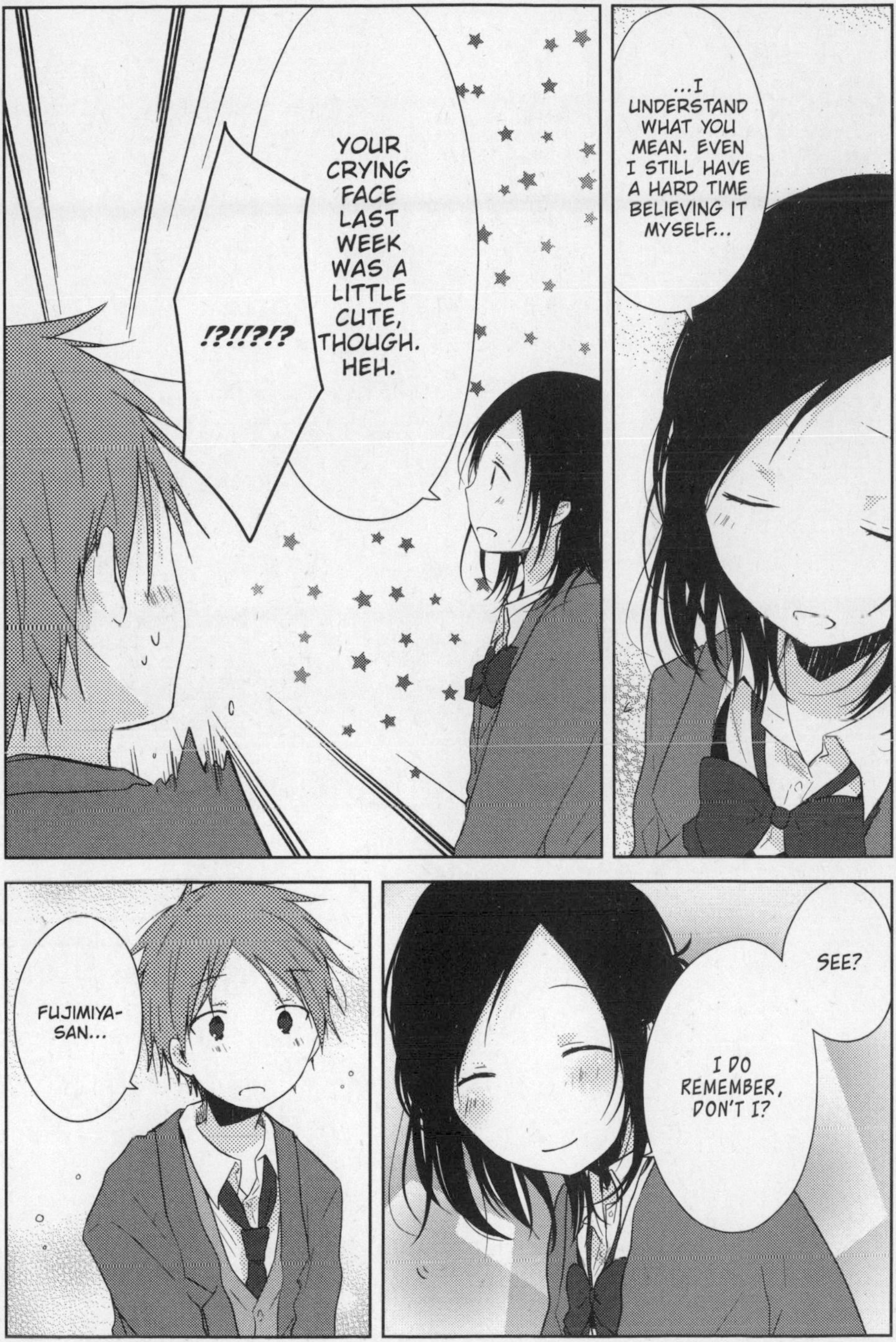
...I UNDERSTAND WHAT YOU MEAN. EVEN I STILL HAVE A HARD TIME BELIEVING IT MYSELF...
YOUR CRYING FACE LAST WEEK WAS A LITTLE CUTE, THOUGH. HEH.
!?!!?!?
SEE?
I DO REMEMBER, DON'T I?
FUJIMIYA-SAN...

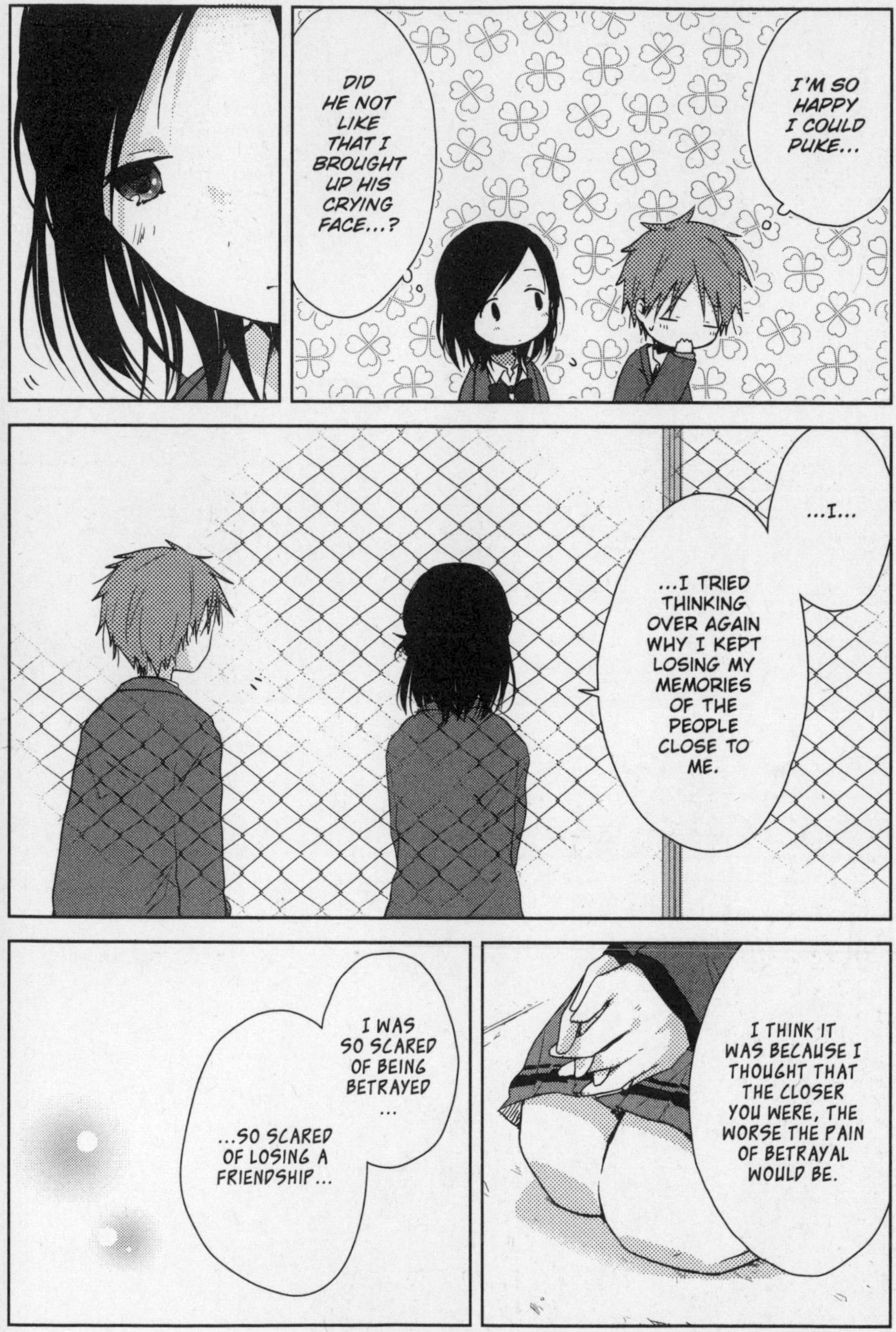
I'M SO HAPPY I COULD PUKE...
DID HE NOT LIKE THAT I BROUGHT UP HIS CRYING FACE...?
...I...
...I TRIED THINKING OVER AGAIN WHY I KEPT LOSING MY MEMORIES OF THE PEOPLE CLOSE TO ME.
I THINK IT WAS BECAUSE I THOUGHT THAT THE CLOSER YOU WERE, THE WORSE THE PAIN OF BETRAYAL WOULD BE.
I WAS SO SCARED OF BEING BETRAYED...
...SO SCARED OF LOSING A FRIENDSHIP...

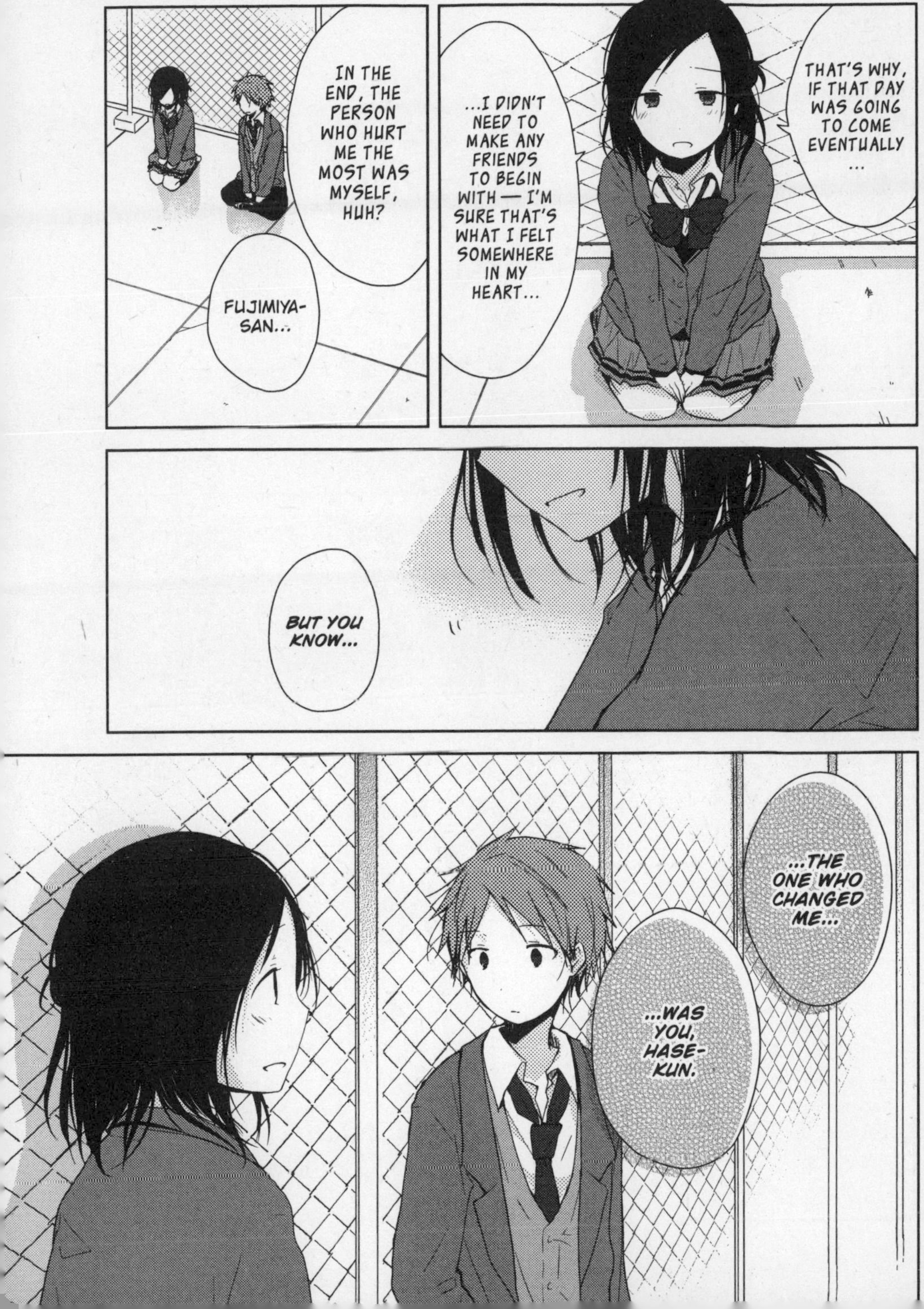
THAT'S WHY, IF THAT DAY WAS GOING TO COME EVENTUALLY ...
...I DIDN'T NEED TO MAKE ANY FRIENDS TO BEGIN WITH — I'M SURE THAT'S WHAT I FELT SOMEWHERE IN MY HEART...
IN THE END, THE PERSON WHO HURT ME THE MOST WAS MYSELF, HUH?
FUJIMIYA-SAN...
BUT YOU KNOW...
...THE ONE WHO CHANGED ME...
...WAS YOU, HASE-KUN.

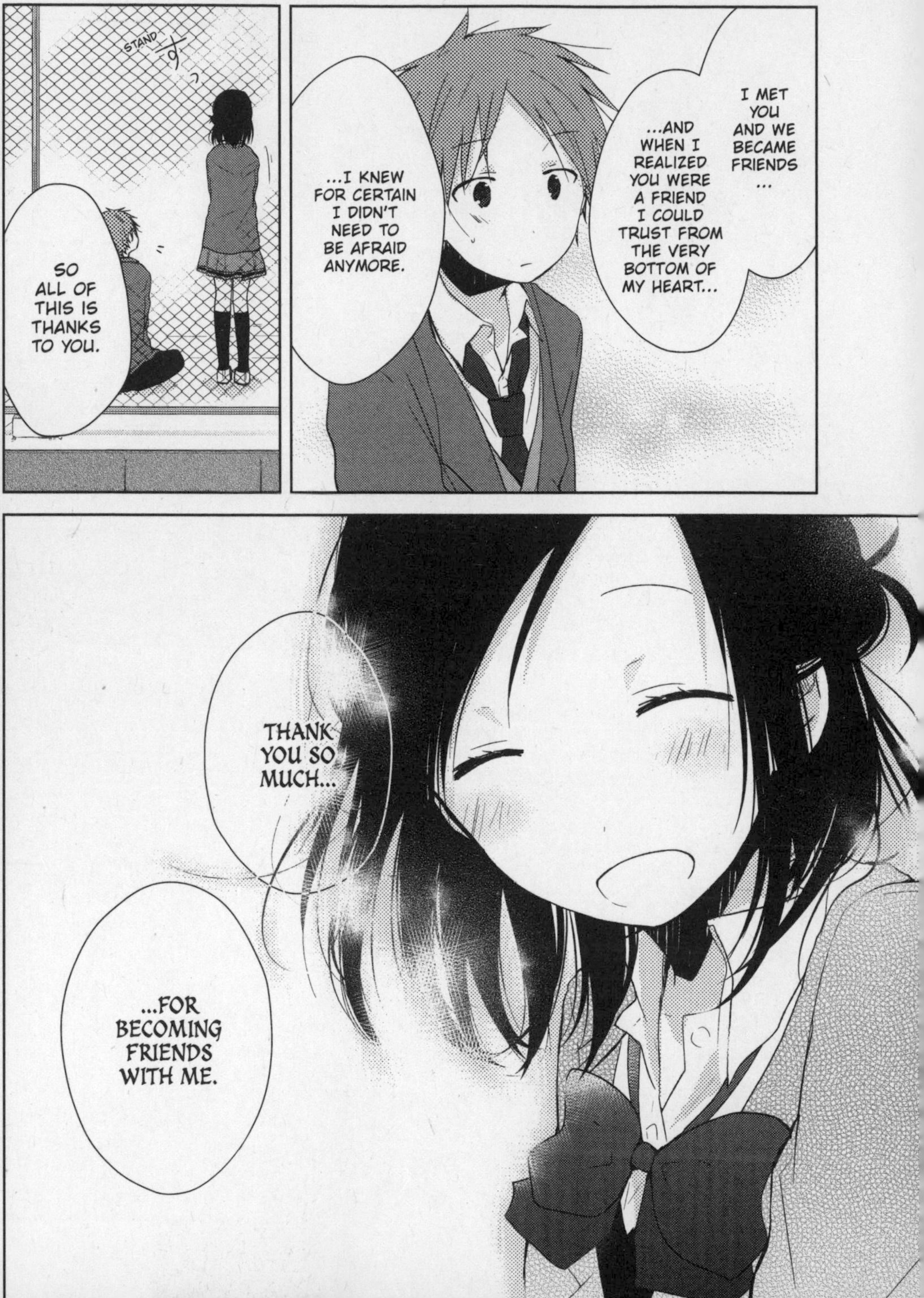
I MET YOU AND WE BECAME FRIENDS ...
...AND WHEN I REALIZED YOU WERE A FRIEND I COULD TRUST FROM THE VERY BOTTOM OF MY HEART...
...I KNEW FOR CERTAIN I DIDN'T NEED TO BE AFRAID ANYMORE.
STAND
SO ALL OF THIS IS THANKS TO YOU.
THANK YOU SO MUCH...
...FOR BECOMING FRIENDS WITH ME.

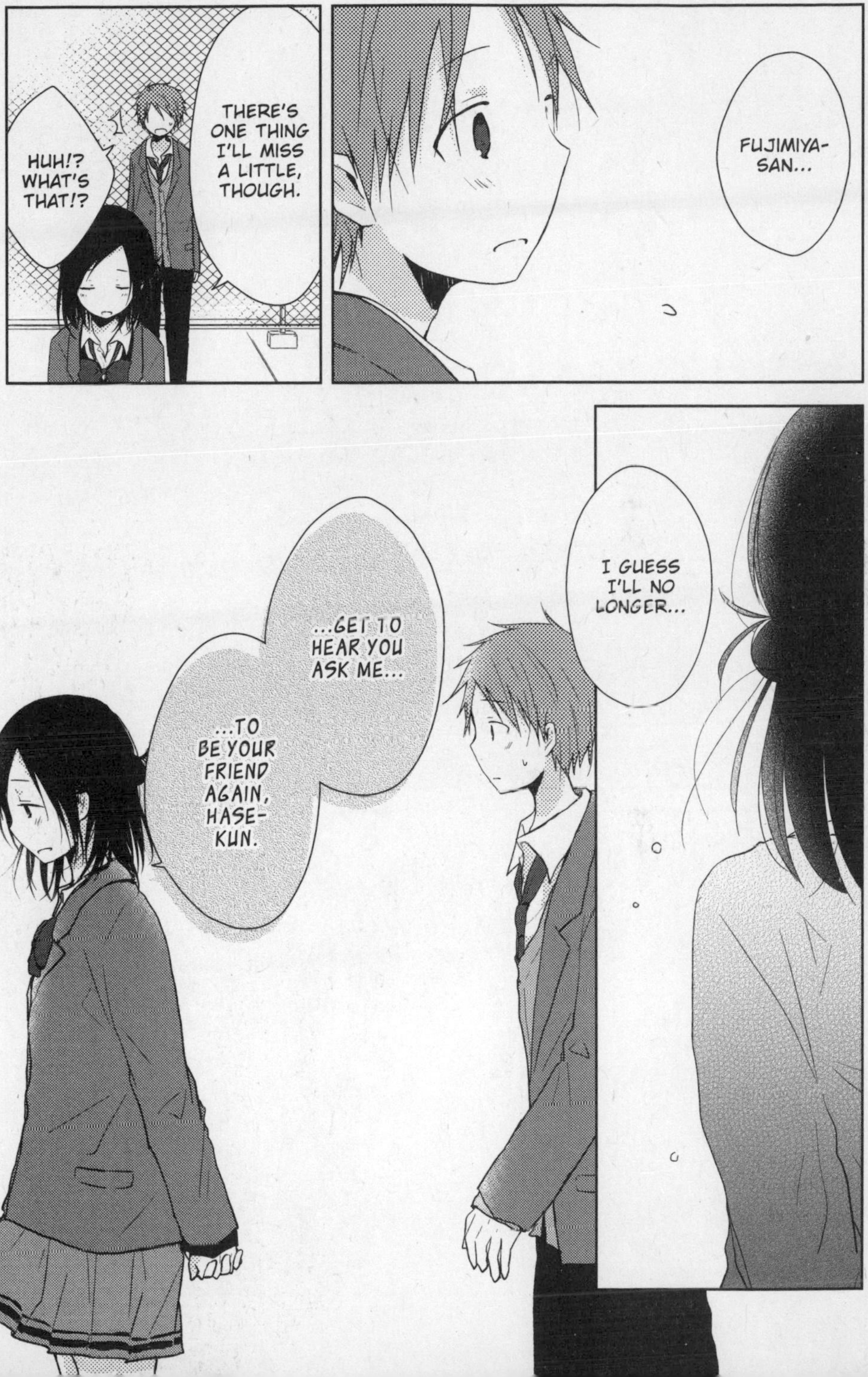
FUJIMIYA-SAN...
THERE'S ONE THING I'LL MISS A LITTLE, THOUGH.
HUH!? WHAT'S THAT!?
I GUESS I'LL NO LONGER...
...GET TO HEAR YOU ASK ME...
...TO BE YOUR FRIEND AGAIN, HASE-KUN.

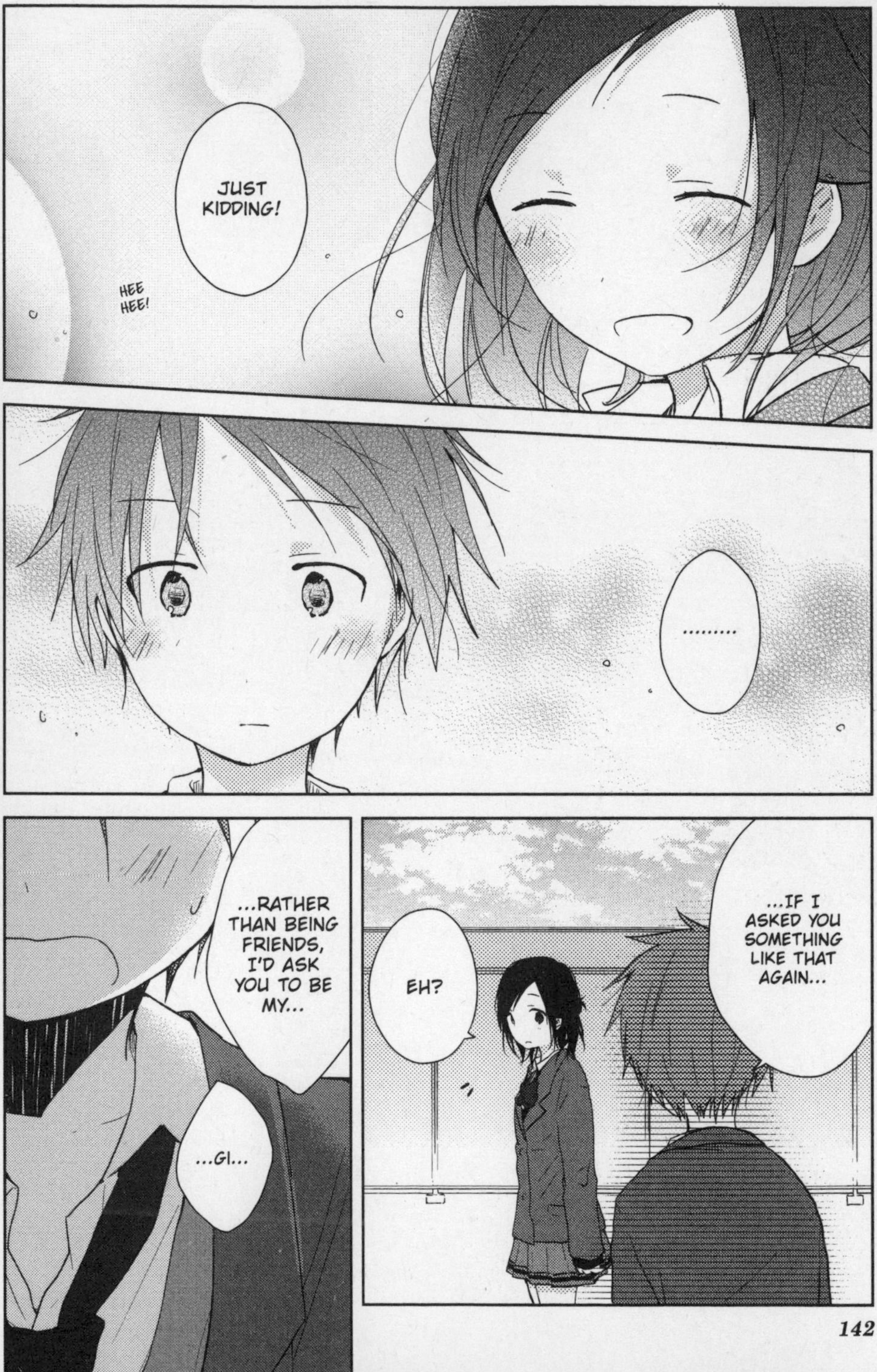
JUST KIDDING!
HEE HEE!
....
...IF I ASKED YOU SOMETHING LIKE THAT AGAIN...
EH?
...RATHER THAN BEING FRIENDS, I'D ASK YOU TO BE MY...
...GI...

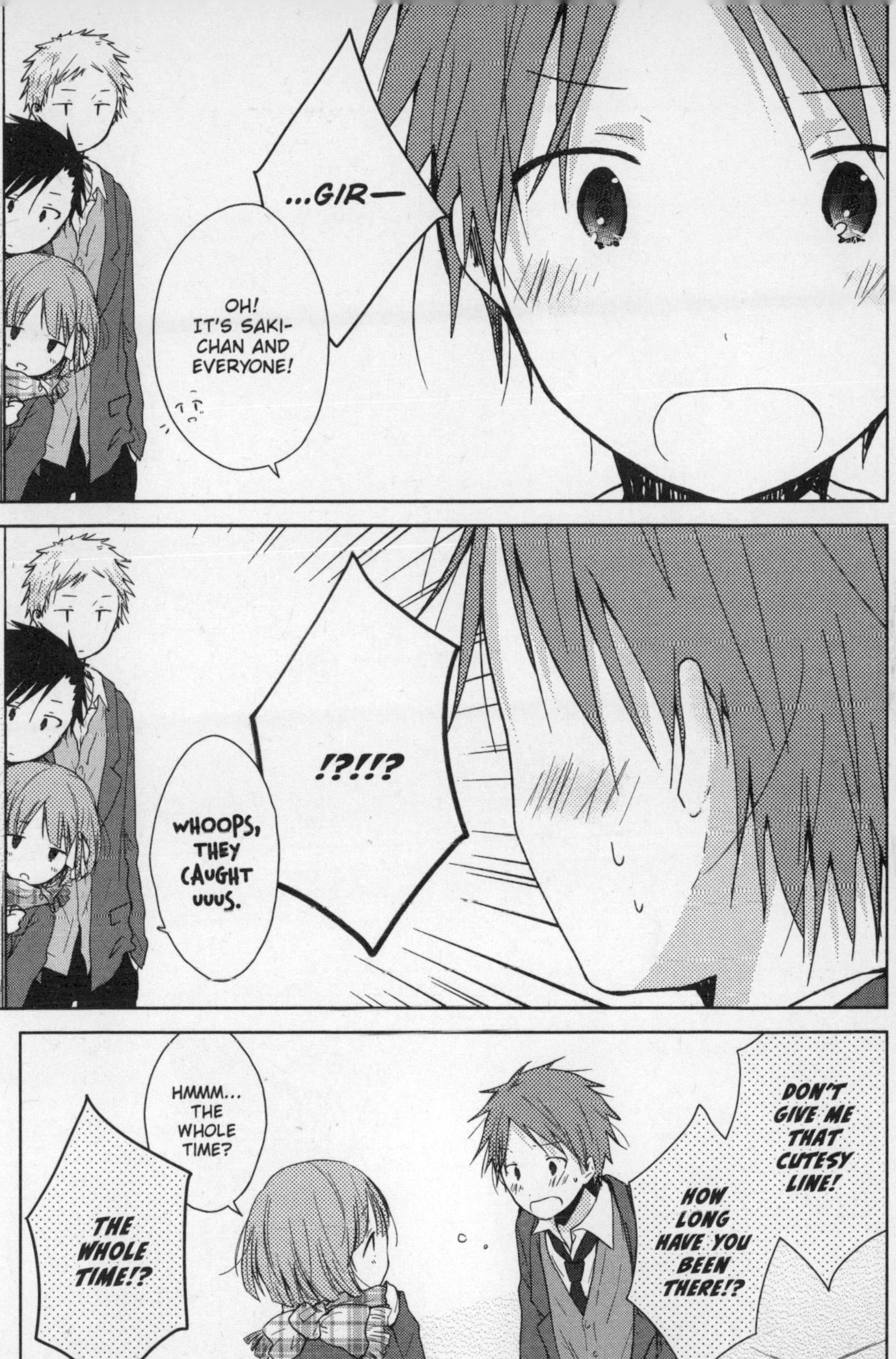
...GIR—
OH! IT'S SAKI-CHAN AND EVERYONE!
!?!!?
WHOOPS, THEY CAUGHT UUUS.
DON'T GIVE ME THAT CUTESY LINE!
HOW LONG HAVE YOU BEEN THERE!?
HMMM... THE WHOLE TIME?
THE WHOLE TIME!?

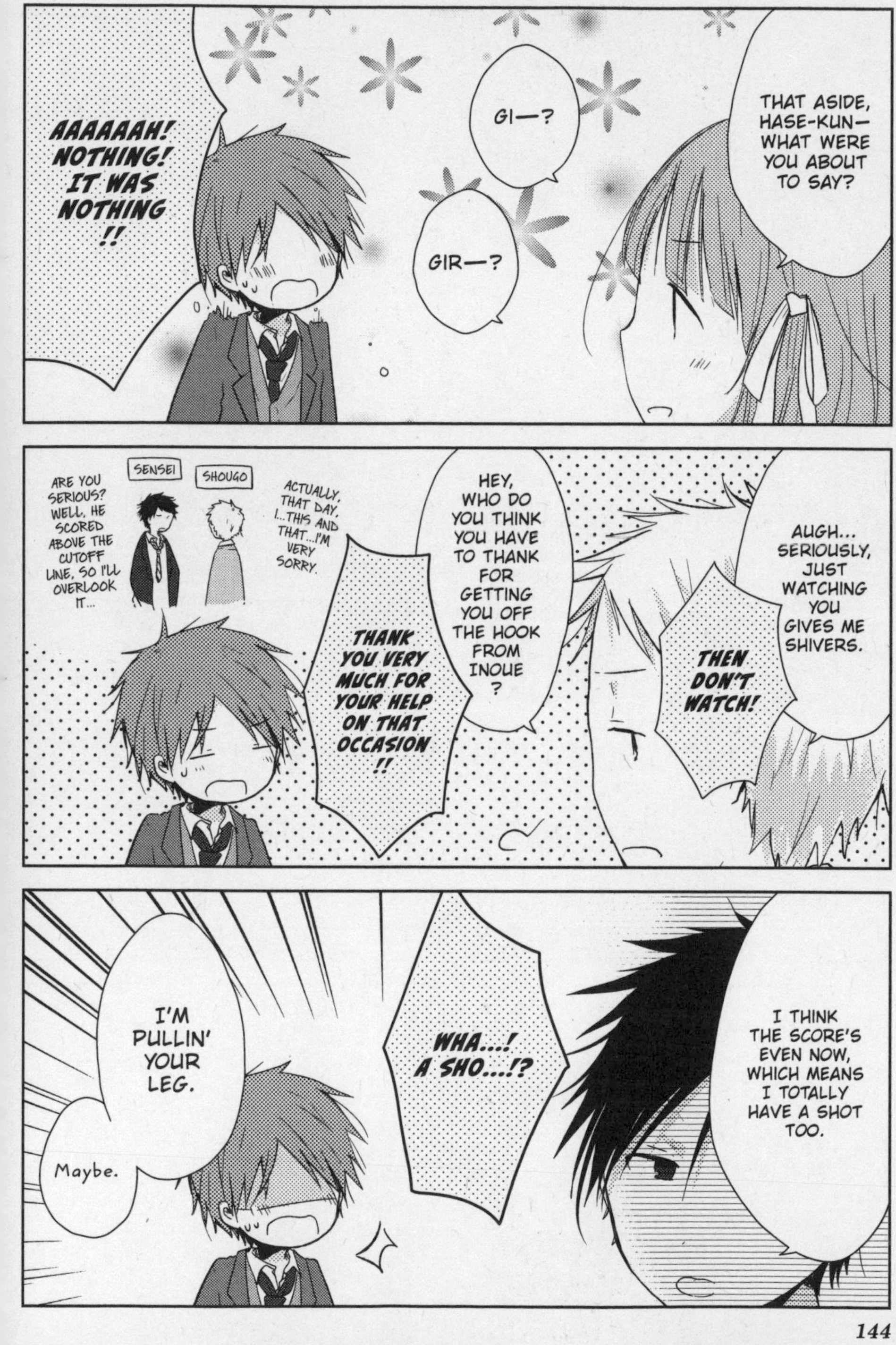
THAT ASIDE, HASE-KUN—WHAT WERE YOU ABOUT TO SAY?
GI—?
GIR—?
AAAAAAH! NOTHING! IT WAS NOTHING!!
AUGH... SERIOUSLY, JUST WATCHING YOU GIVES ME SHIVERS.
THEN DON'T WATCH!
HEY, WHO DO YOU THINK YOU HAVE TO THANK FOR GETTING YOU OFF THE HOOK FROM INOUE?
THANK YOU VERY MUCH FOR YOUR HELP ON THAT OCCASION!!
SHOUGO
ACTUALLY, THAT DAY, I...THIS AND THAT...I'M VERY SORRY.
SENSEI
ARE YOU SERIOUS? WELL, HE SCORED ABOVE THE CUTOFF LINE, SO I'LL OVERLOOK IT...
I THINK THE SCORE'S EVEN NOW, WHICH MEANS I TOTALLY HAVE A SHOT TOO.
WHA...! A SHO...!?
I'M PULLIN' YOUR LEG.
Maybe.

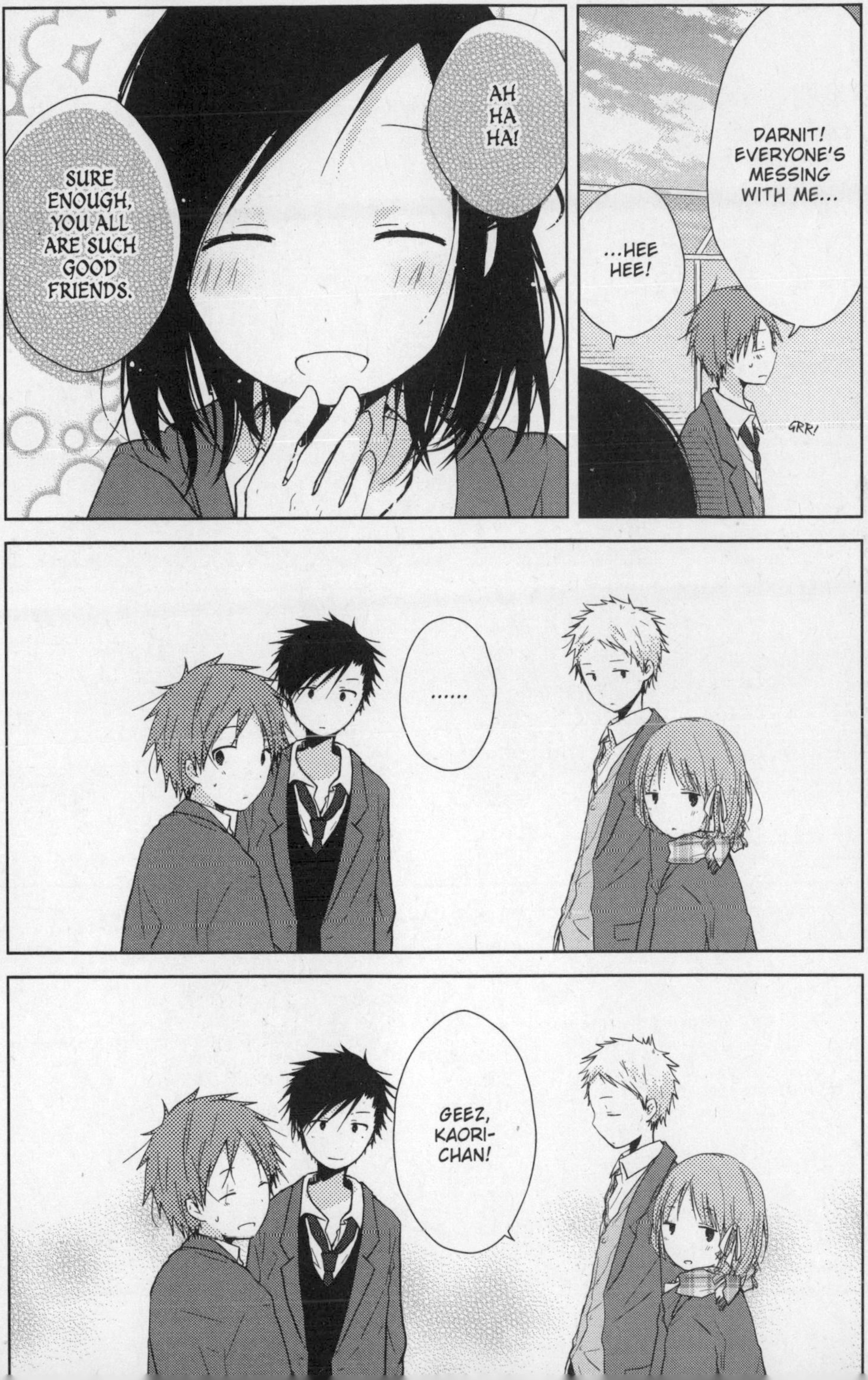
DARNIT! EVERYONE'S MESSING WITH ME...
...HEE HEE!
GRR!
AH HA HA!
SURE ENOUGH, YOU ALL ARE SUCH GOOD FRIENDS.
......
GEEZ, KAORI-CHAN!

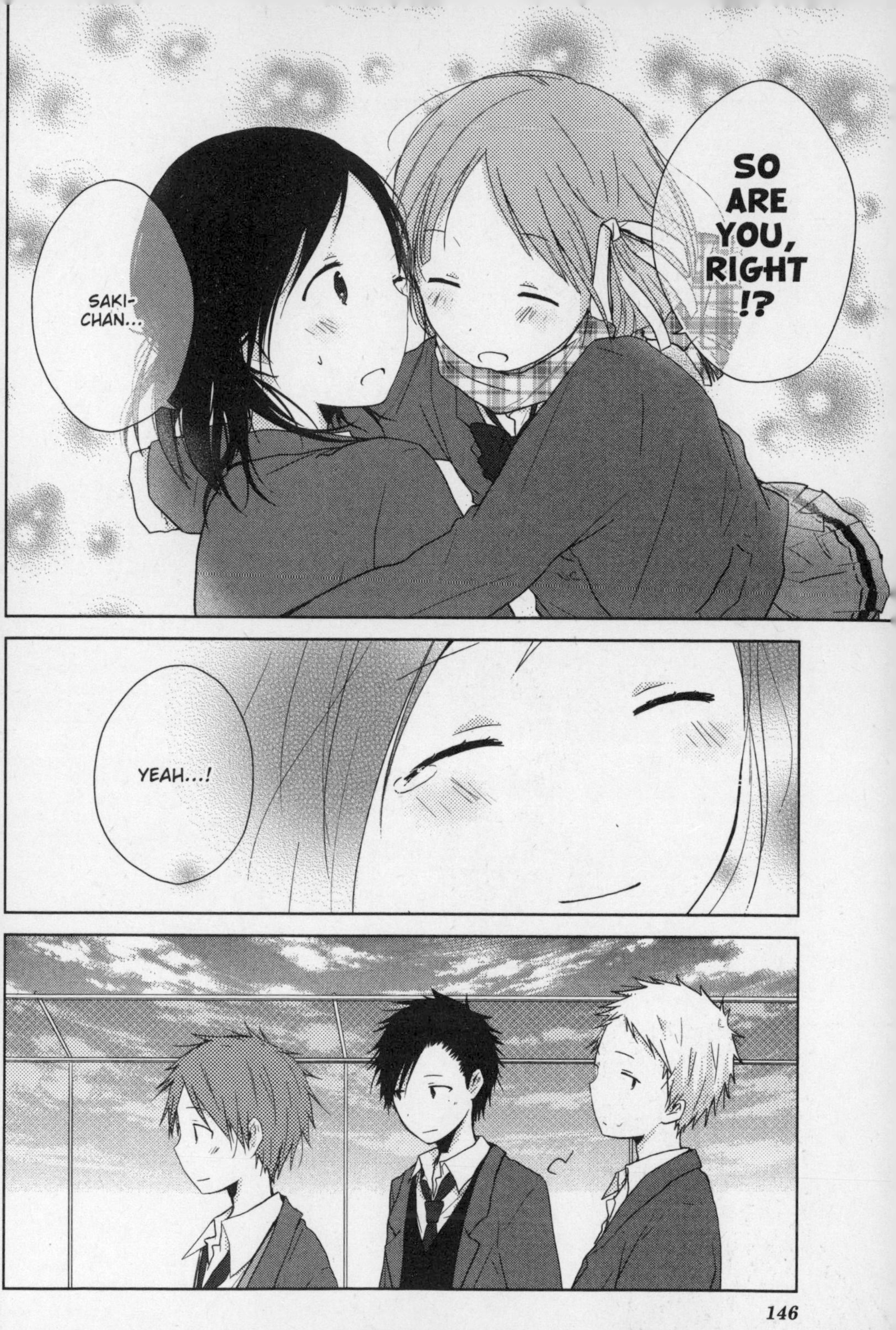
SO ARE YOU, RIGHT!?
SAKI-CHAN...
YEAH...!

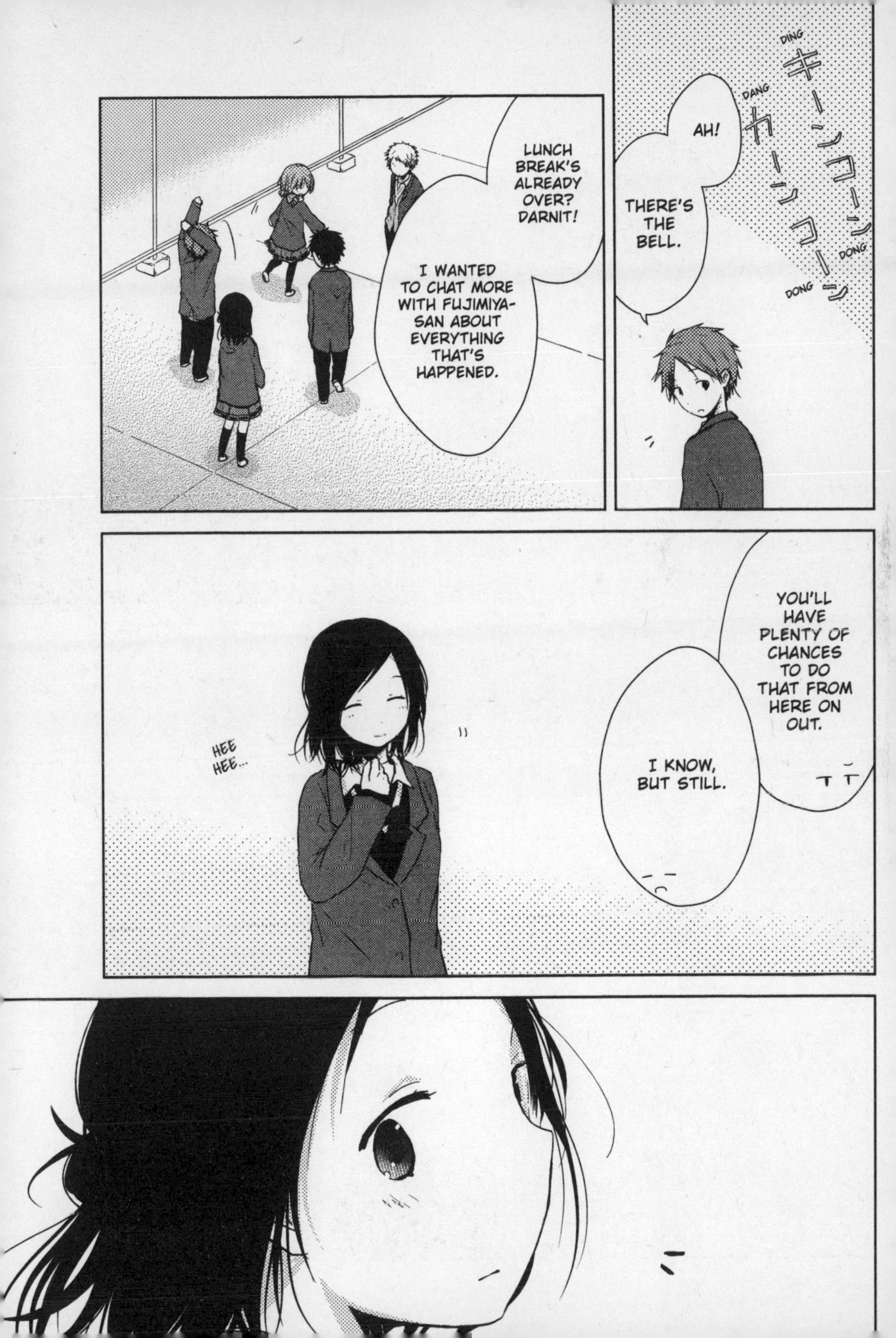
DING
DANG
DONG
DONG
AH!
THERE'S THE BELL.
LUNCH BREAK'S ALREADY OVER? DARNIT!
I WANTED TO CHAT MORE WITH FUJIMIYA-SAN ABOUT EVERYTHING THAT'S HAPPENED.
YOU'LL HAVE PLENTY OF CHANCES TO DO THAT FROM HERE ON OUT.
I KNOW, BUT STILL.
HEE HEE...

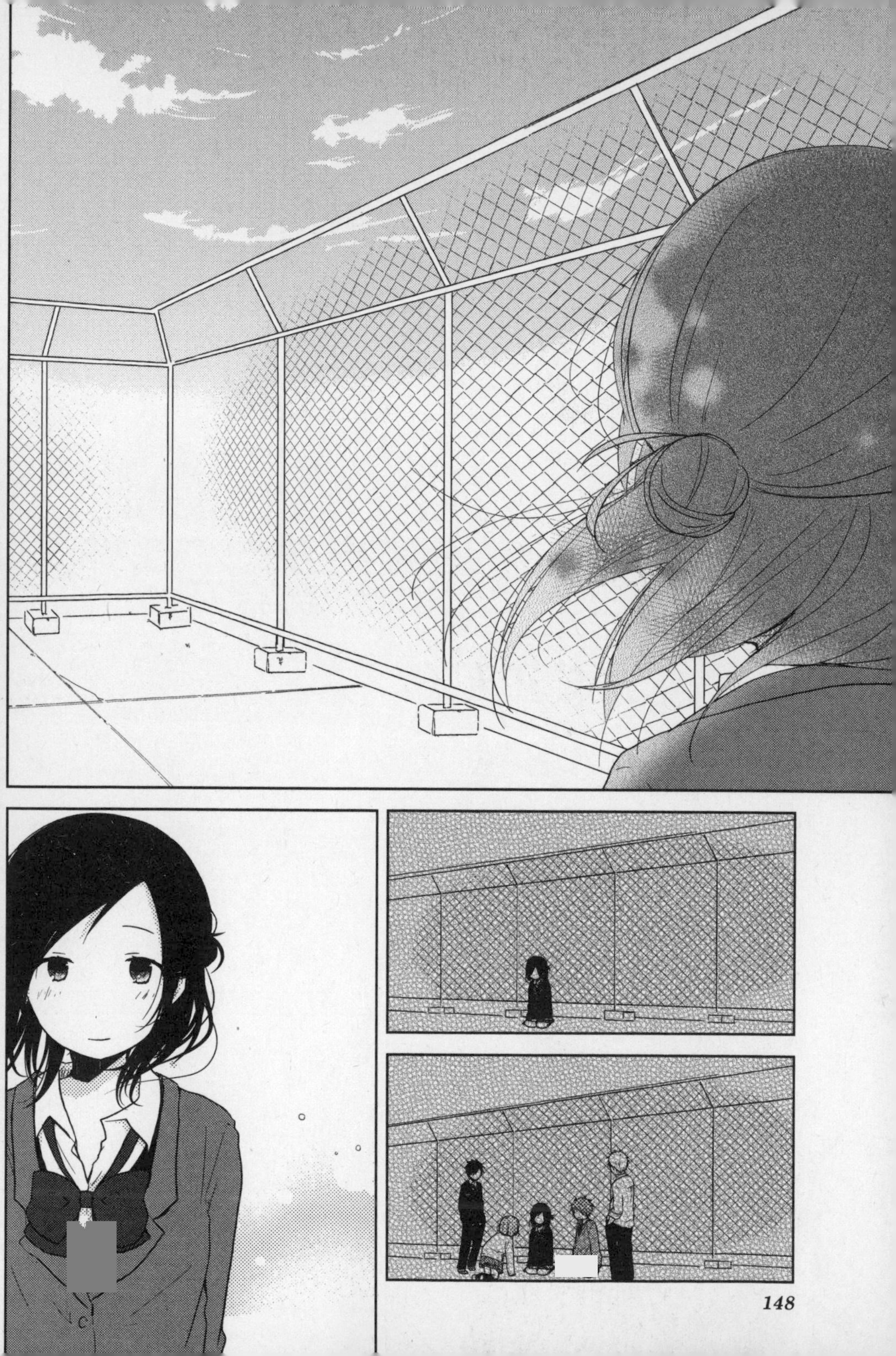

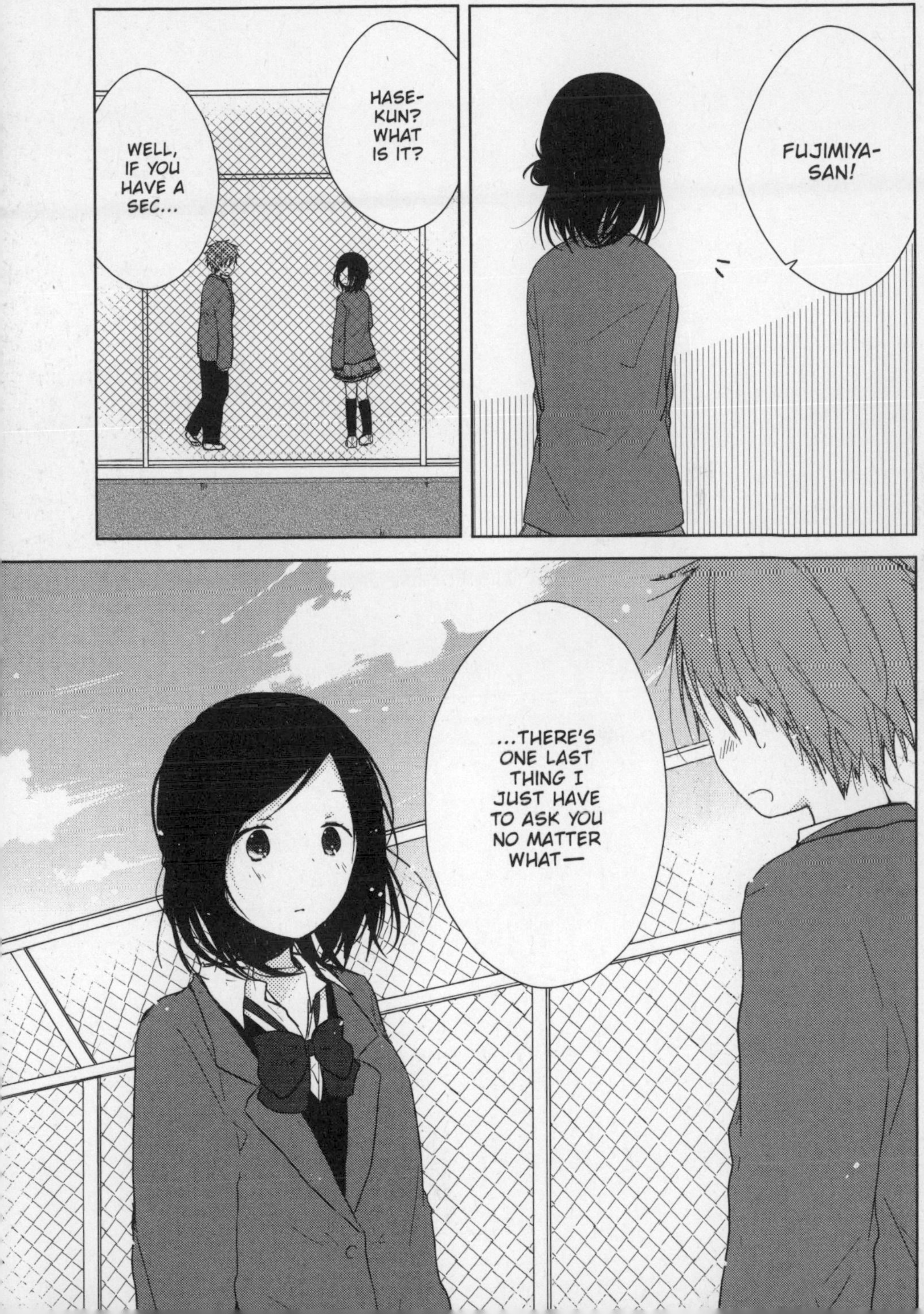
FUJIMIYA-SAN!
HASE-KUN? WHAT IS IT?
WELL, IF YOU HAVE A SEC...
...THERE'S ONE LAST THING I JUST HAVE TO ASK YOU NO MATTER WHAT—

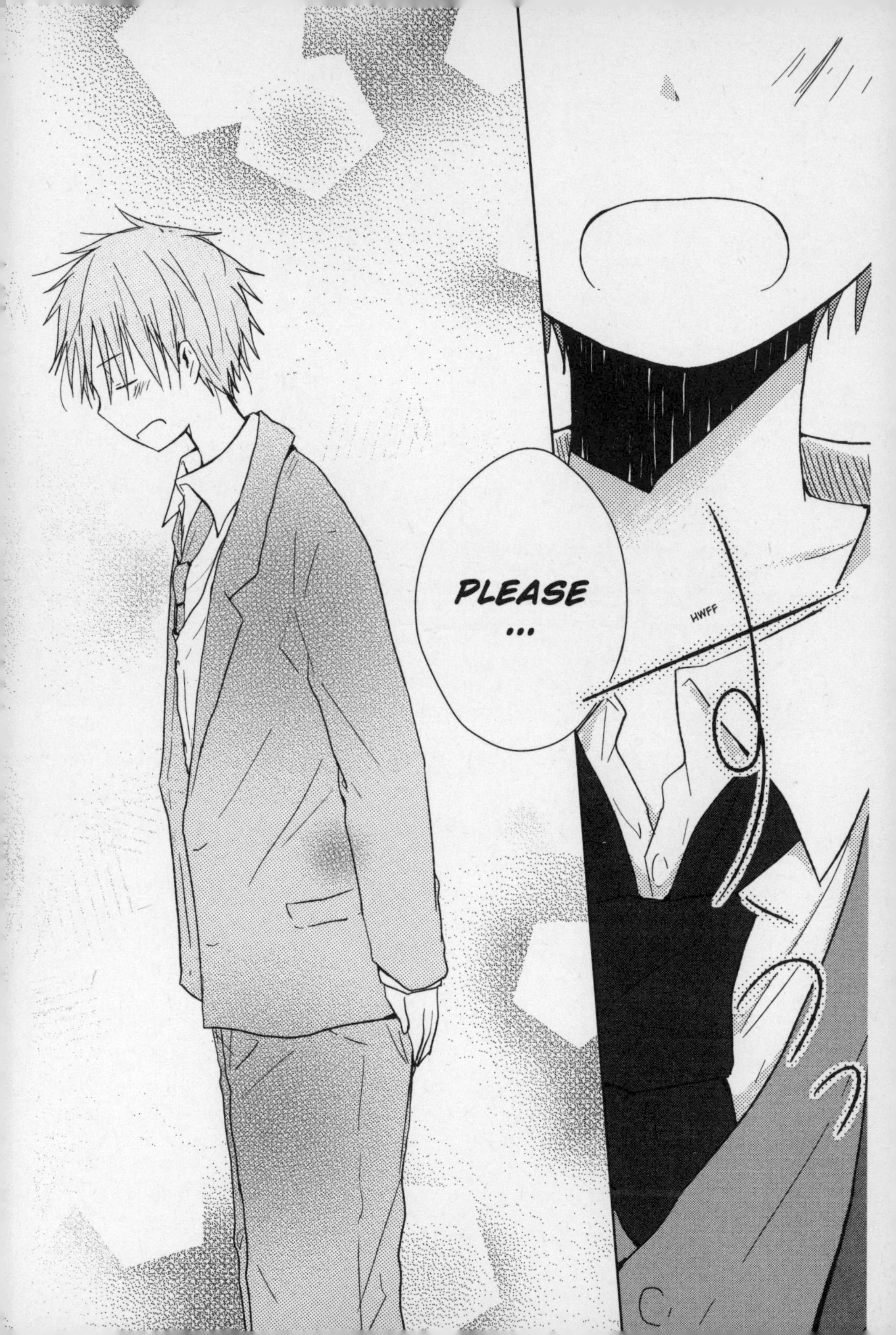
HWFF
PLEASE
...

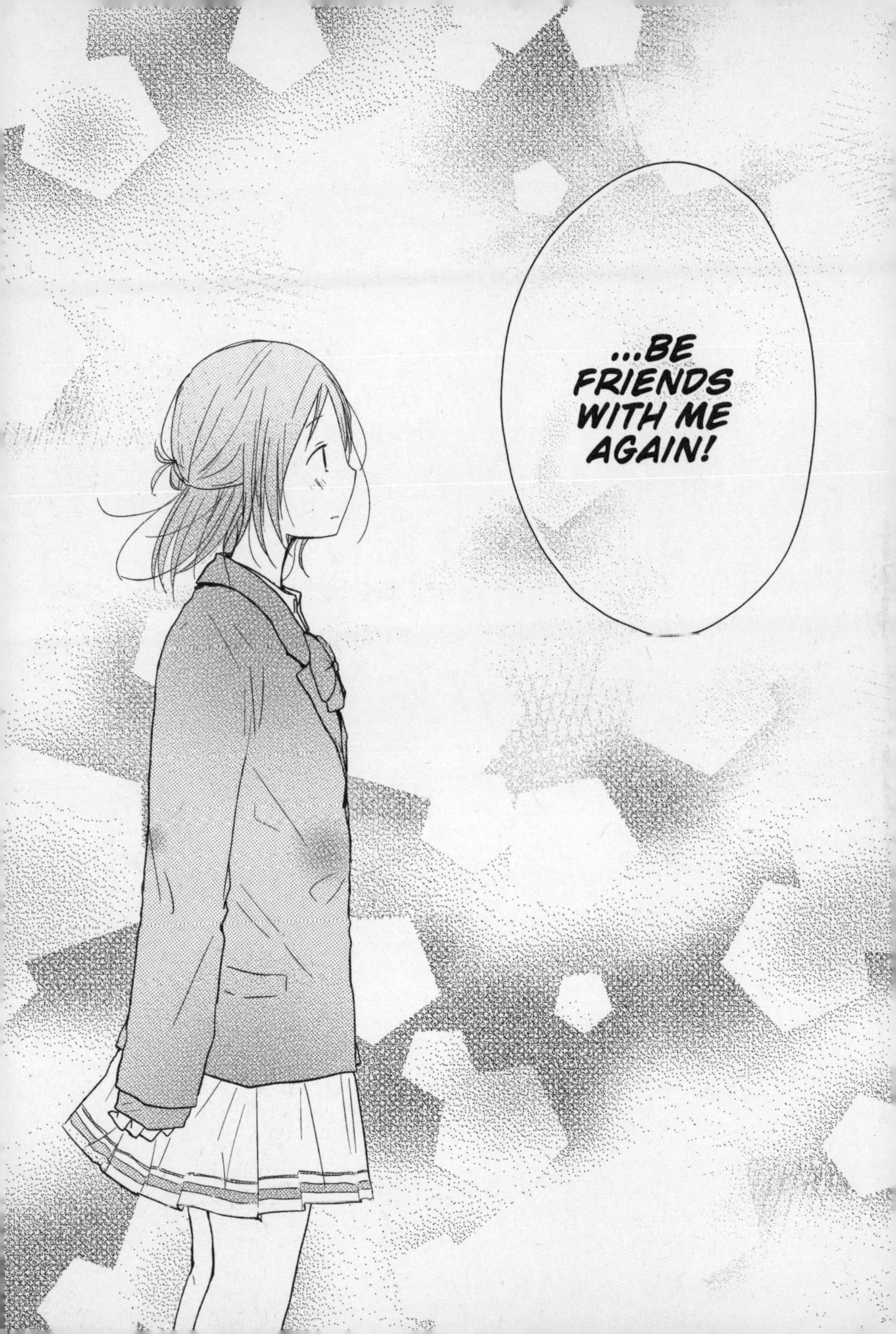
...BE FRIENDS WITH ME AGAIN!

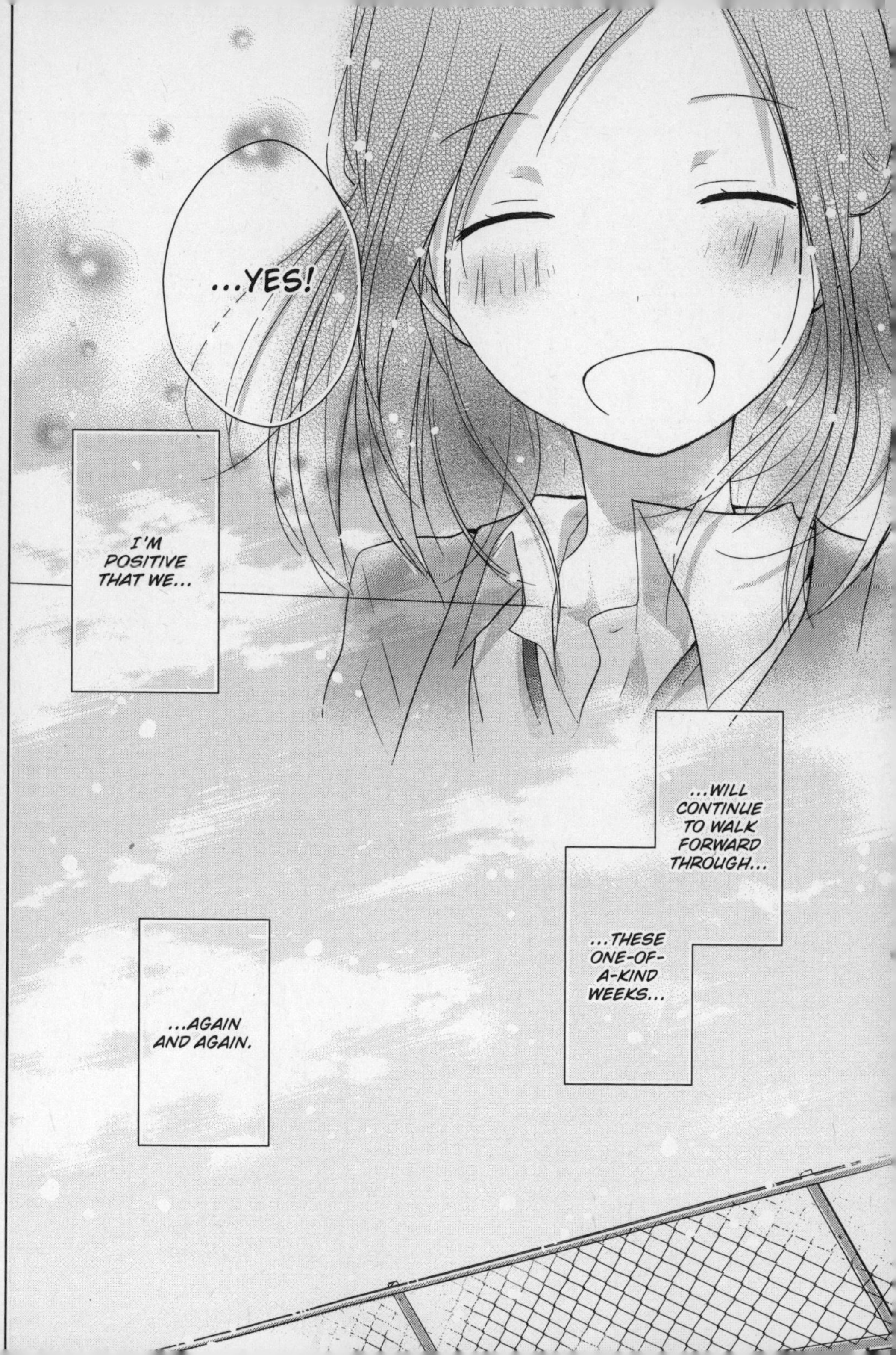
...YES!
I'M POSITIVE THAT WE...
...WILL CONTINUE TO WALK FORWARD THROUGH...
...THESE ONE-OF-A-KIND WEEKS...
...AGAIN AND AGAIN.

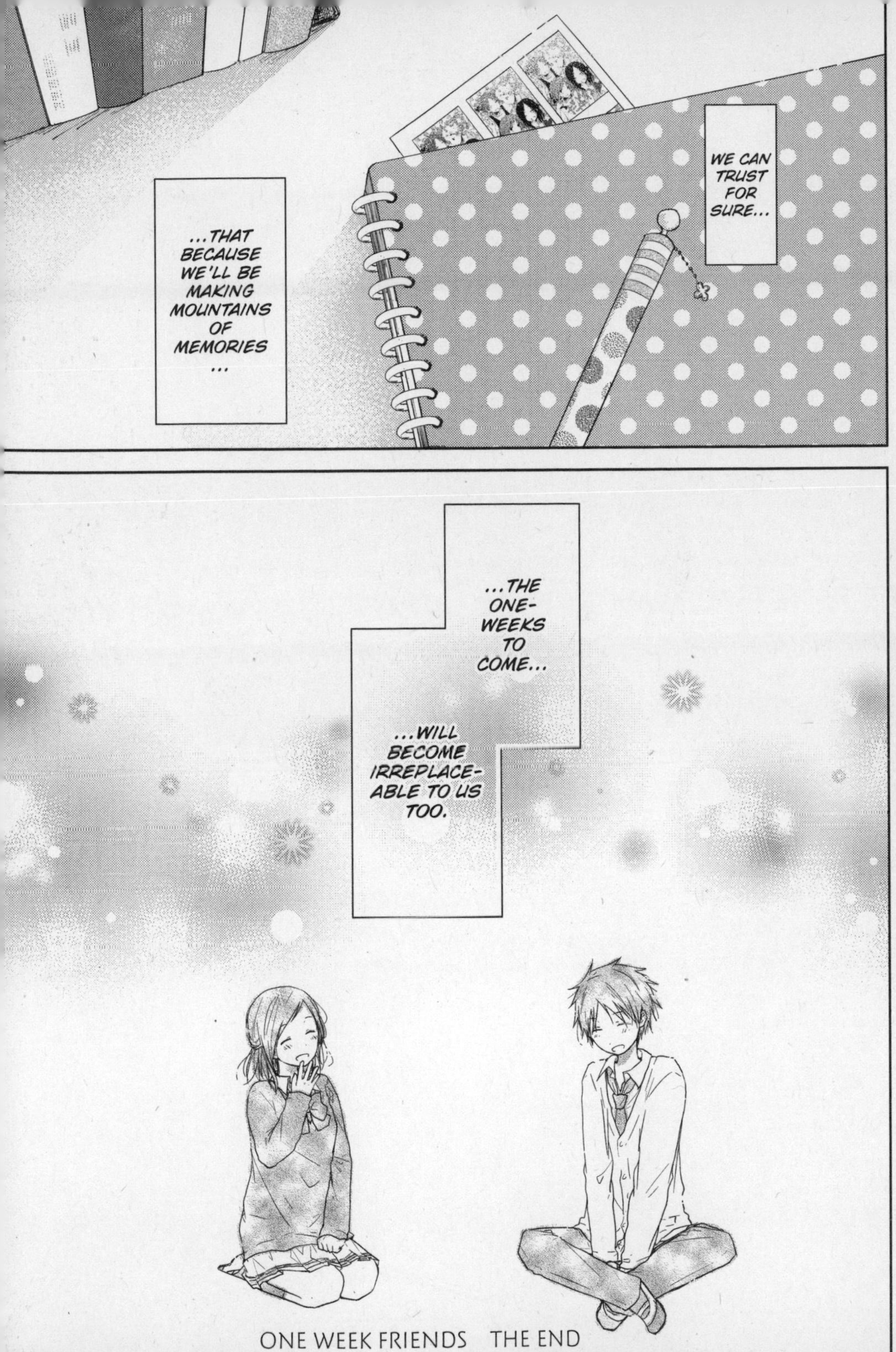
WE CAN TRUST FOR SURE...
...THAT BECAUSE WE'LL BE MAKING MOUNTAINS OF MEMORIES...
...THE ONE-WEEKS TO COME...
...WILL BECOME IRREPLACE-ABLE TO US TOO.

ONE WEEK FRIENDS THE END

ONE WEEK FRIENDS

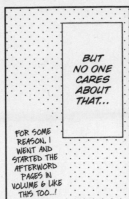

HELLO. IT'S ME, MATCHA HAZUKI, WHO FINALLY LEARNED HOW TO PUT IN CONTACTS RECENTLY.
ちゃき―――ん
TA-DAA
I STILL ONLY WEAR DISPOSABLE ONES ABOUT ONCE A MONTH, THOUGH.
BUT NO ONE CARES ABOUT THAT...
FOR SOME REASON, I WENT AND STARTED THE AFTERWORD PAGES IN VOLUME 6 LIKE THIS TOO...!
ONE WEEK FRIENDS IS OVER...!
POP
ぱ―ん
HOW WAS IT? REALLY, HOW WAS IT?
I STILL DON'T HAVE TIME TO GET SENTIMENTAL.
I'M SO NERVOUS ABOUT THE FACT THAT SO MANY PEOPLE WILL BE READING THE FINAL CHAPTER.
WHEEZE...
WHEEZE...
I MEAN, THE ENDING IS REALLY IMPORTANT, RIGHT?
IF YOU THOUGHT, "I'M GLAD I READ THIS TO THE END," FOR EVEN A SECOND, I WOULD BE TRULY HAPPY...

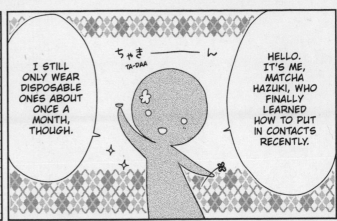

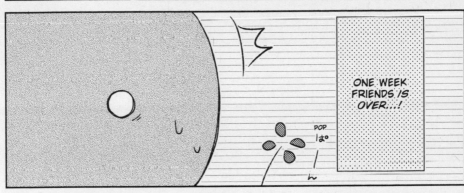

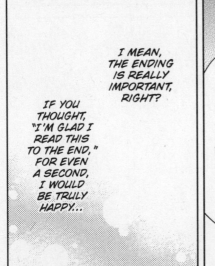

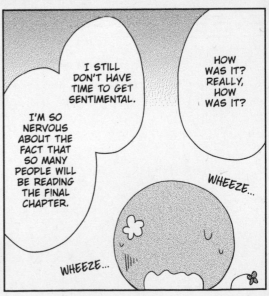

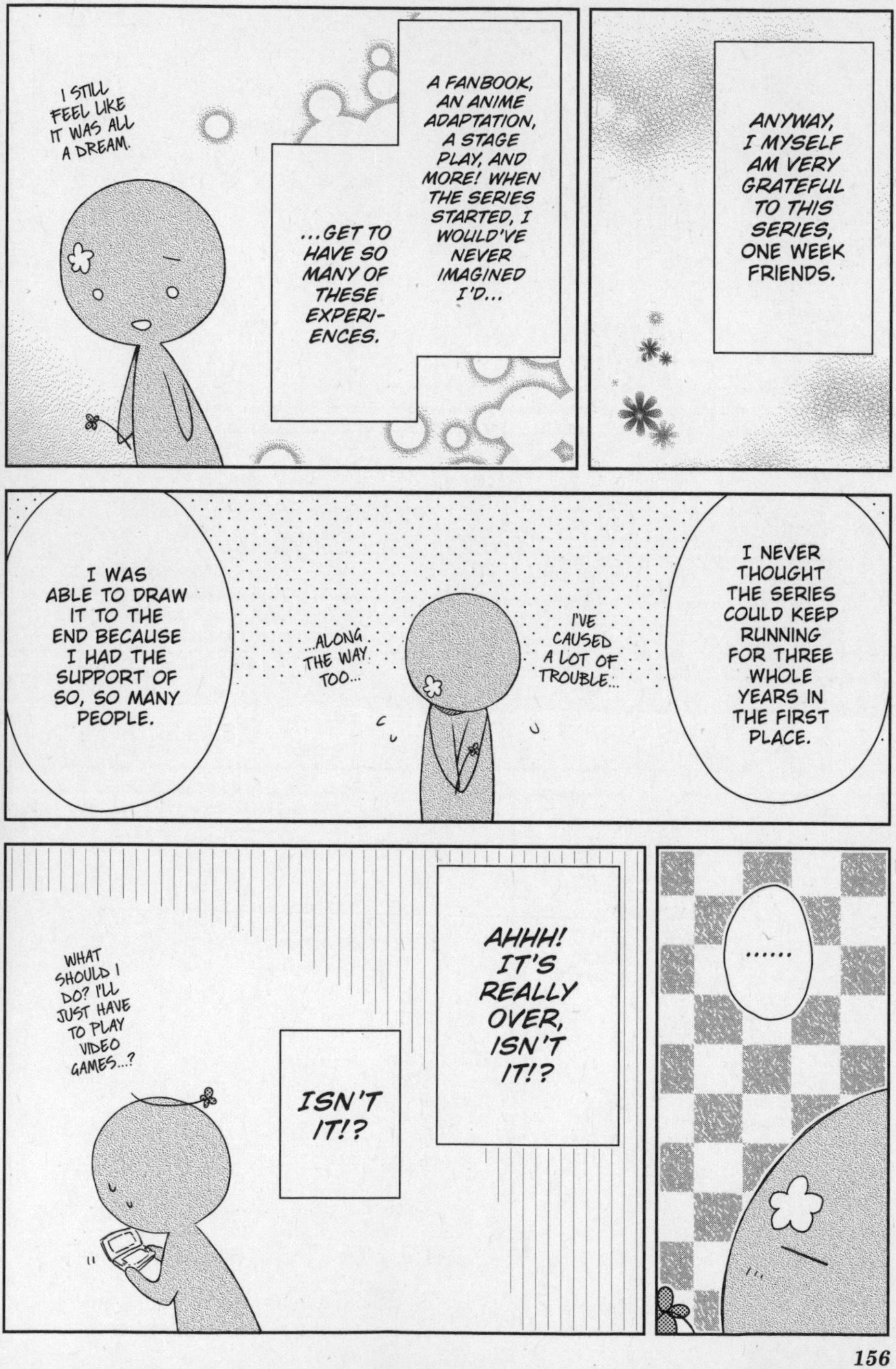
ANYWAY, I MYSELF AM VERY GRATEFUL TO THIS SERIES, ONE WEEK FRIENDS.
A FANBOOK, AN ANIME ADAPTATION, A STAGE PLAY, AND MORE! WHEN THE SERIES STARTED, I WOULD'VE NEVER IMAGINED I'D...
...GET TO HAVE SO MANY OF THESE EXPERIENCES.
I STILL FEEL LIKE IT WAS ALL A DREAM.
I NEVER THOUGHT THE SERIES COULD KEEP RUNNING FOR THREE WHOLE YEARS IN THE FIRST PLACE.
I'VE CAUSED A LOT OF TROUBLE...
...ALONG THE WAY TOO...
I WAS ABLE TO DRAW IT TO THE END BECAUSE I HAD THE SUPPORT OF SO, SO MANY PEOPLE.
......
AHHH! IT'S REALLY OVER, ISN'T IT!?
ISN'T IT!?
WHAT SHOULD I DO? I'LL JUST HAVE TO PLAY VIDEO GAMES...?

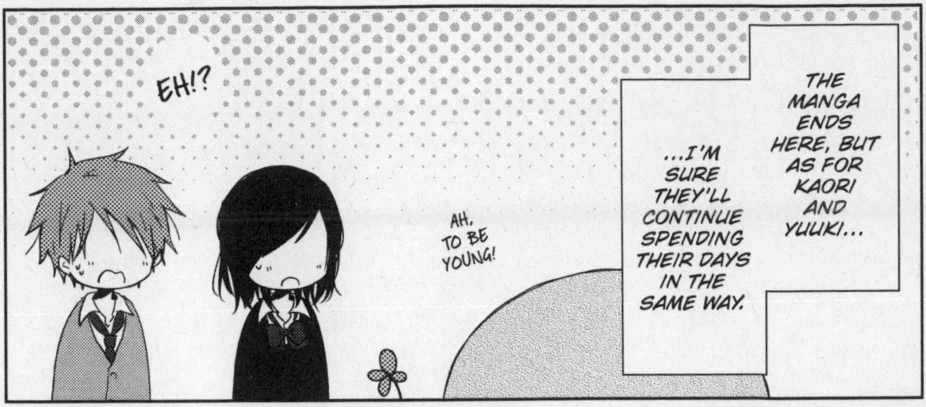
THE MANGA ENDS HERE, BUT AS FOR KAORI AND YUUKI...
...I'M SURE THEY'LL CONTINUE SPENDING THEIR DAYS IN THE SAME WAY.
AH, TO BE YOUNG!
EH!?

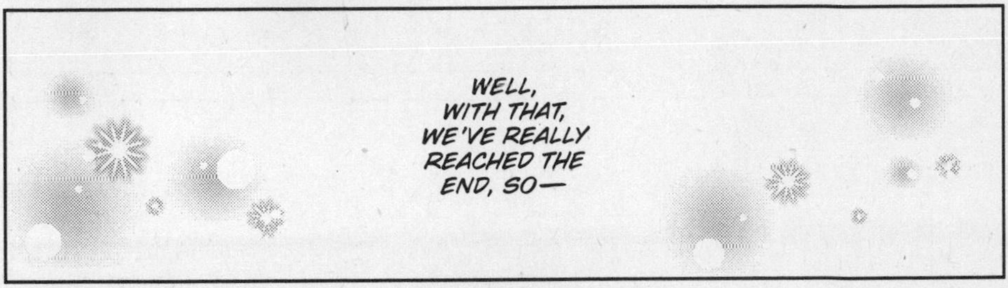
WELL, WITH THAT, WE'VE REALLY REACHED THE END, SO—

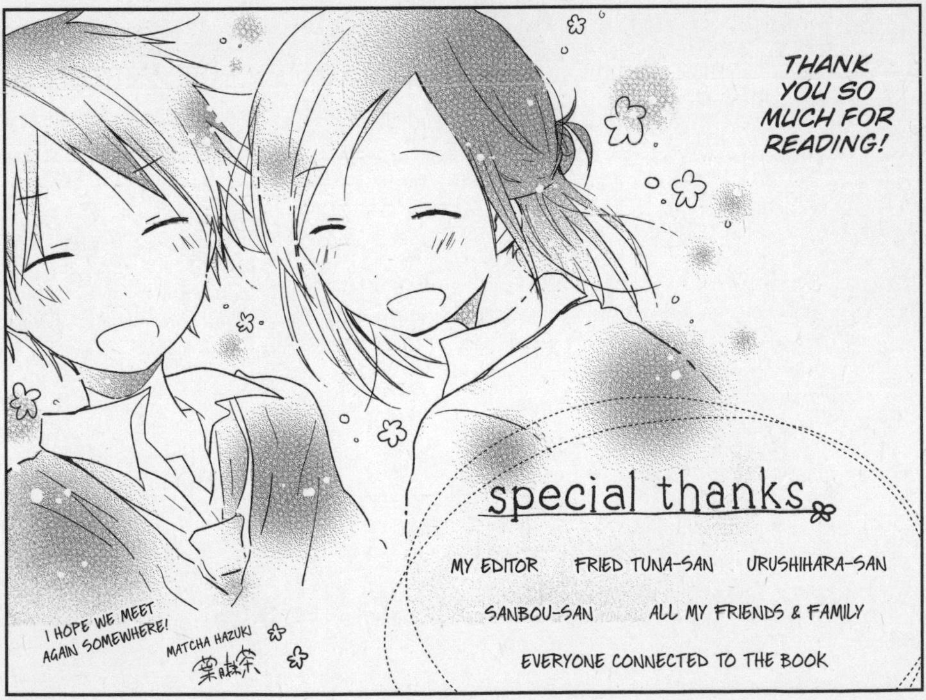
THANK YOU SO MUCH FOR READING!
special thanks
MY EDITOR FRIED TUNA-SAN URUSHIHARA-SAN
SANBOU-SAN ALL MY FRIENDS & FAMILY
EVERYONE CONNECTED TO THE BOOK
I HOPE WE MEET AGAIN SOMEWHERE!
MATCHA HAZUKI

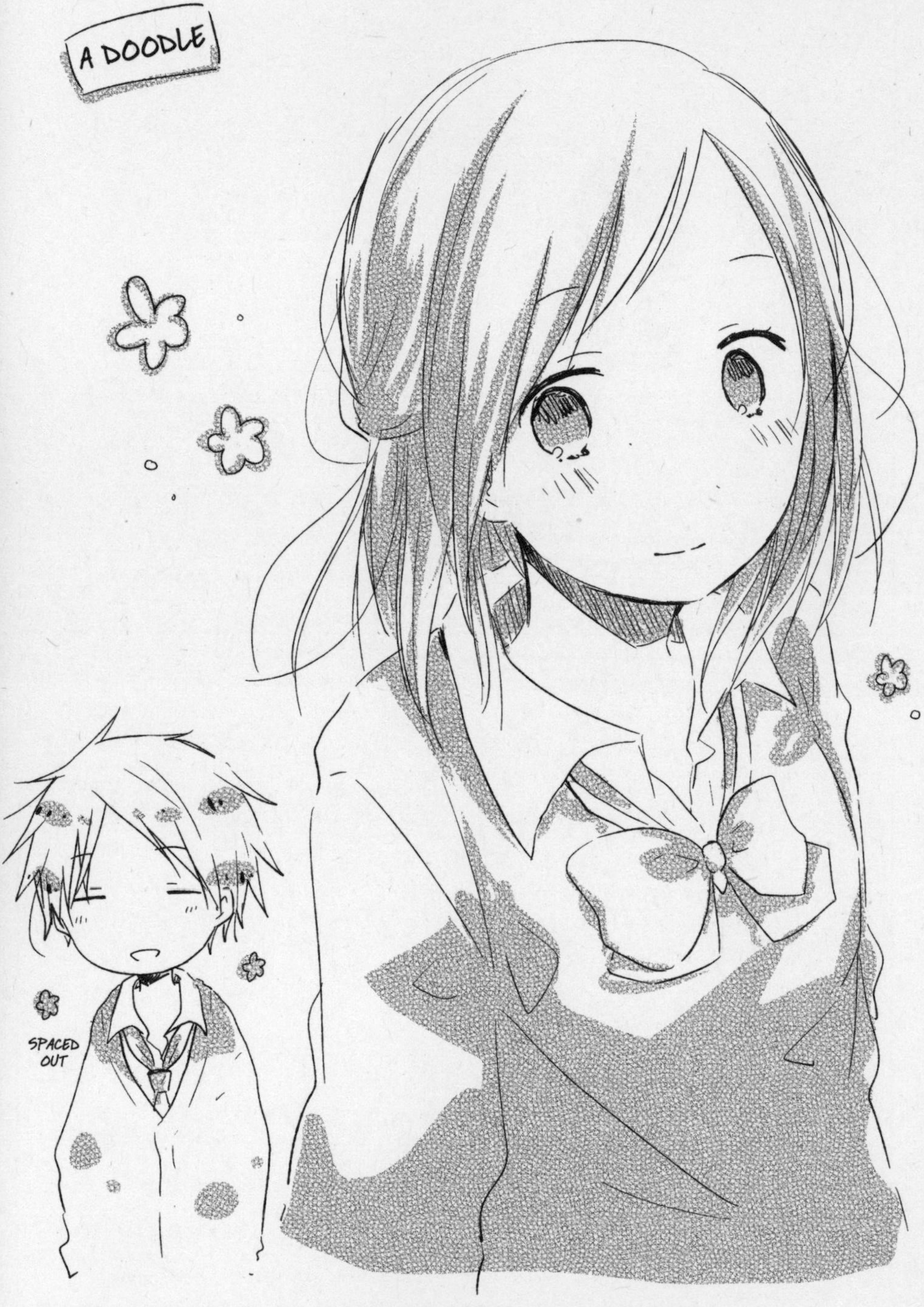
A DOODLE
SPACED OUT

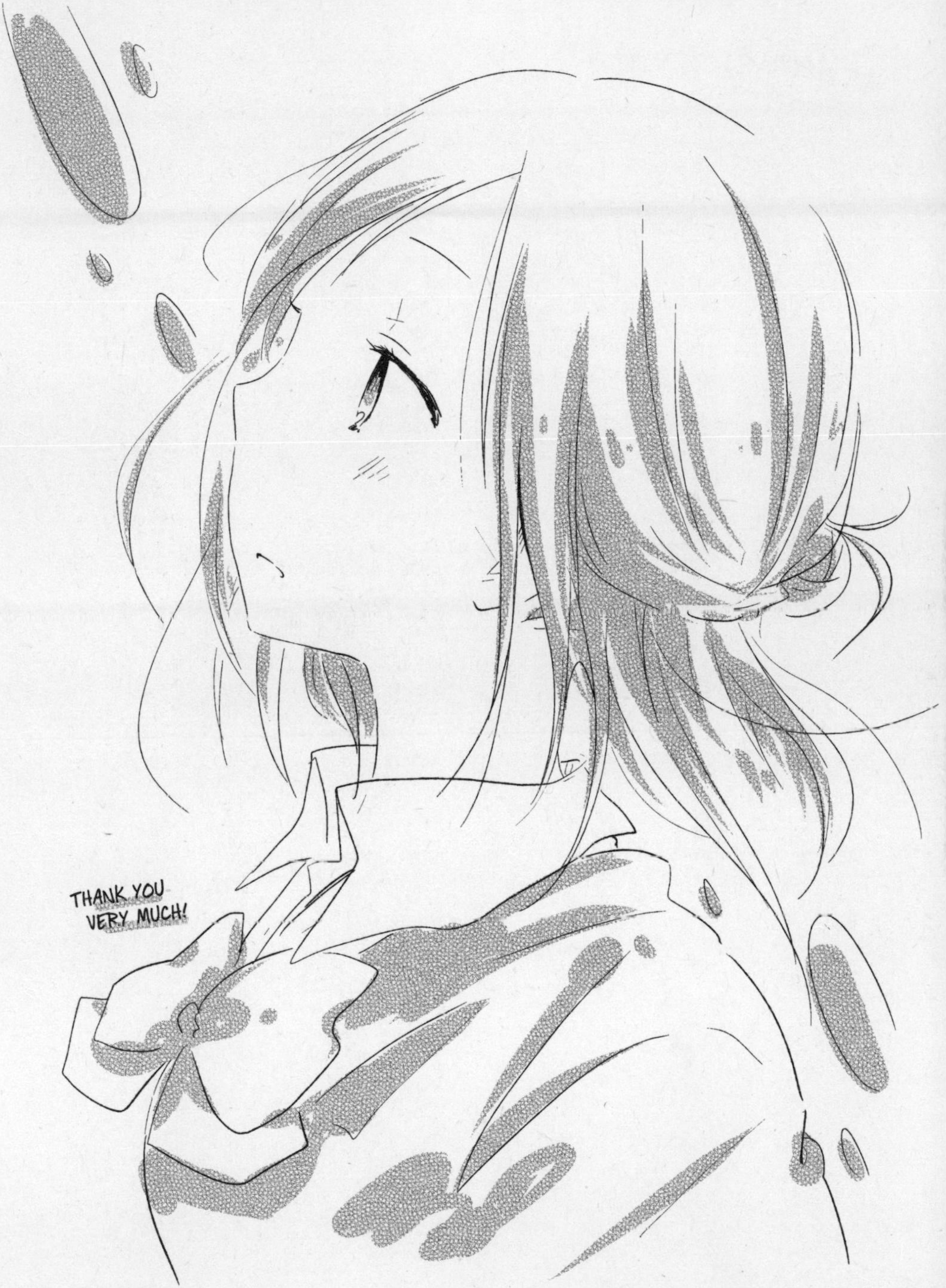
THANK YOU VERY MUCH!

TRANSLATION NOTES

COMMON HONORIFICS
no honorific: Indicates familiarity or closeness; if used without permission or reason, addressing someone in this manner would constitute an insult.
-san: The Japanese equivalent of Mr./Mrs./Miss. If a situation calls for politeness, this is the fail-safe honorific.
-kun: Used most often when referring to boys, this indicates affection or familiarity. Occasionally used by older men among their peers, but it may also be used by anyone referring to a person of lower standing.
-chan: An affectionate honorific indicating familiarity used mostly in reference to girls; also used in reference to cute persons or animals of either gender.
-sensei: A respectful term for teachers, artists, or high-level professionals.

nee: Japanese equivalent to "older sis."

nii: Japanese equivalent to "older bro."

PAGE 7
In the centipede race, single-file groups race each other with their ankles all tied together and their hands on the shoulders or back of the person in front of them (like a three-legged race, but not side-by-side).

PAGE 8
Bread-eating races are a common event on sports days in Japan. Bread is hung by string from an overhead line, and participants are required to run up to the bread, bite it off of the string, and finish a race without dropping the bread from their mouths. The type of bread used most commonly for these races is *anpan*, which is a bun filled with red bean paste.

A mock cavalry battle is a game typically played with four players on each team, three of whom are on the ground hoisting up a fourth player, who is the "rider" atop them. Each player wears a bandana, and if the rider gets their bandana snatched by a player of an opposing team, their team is eliminated.

ONE
WEEK
FRIENDS

ONE WEEK FRIENDS 7

MATCHA HAZUKI

Translation/Adaptation: Amanda Haley

Lettering: Bianca Pistillo

ONE WEEK FRIENDS, Volume 7 ©2015 Matcha Hazuki/ SQUARE ENIX CO., LTD. First published in Japan in 2015 by SQUARE ENIX CO., LTD. English translation rights arranged with SQUARE ENIX CO., LTD. and Yen Press, LLC through Tuttle-Mori Agency, Inc.

English translation © 2019 by SQUARE ENIX CO., LTD.

Yen Press
1290 Avenue of the Americas
New York, NY 10104

Visit us at yenpress.com
facebook.com/yenpress
twitter.com/yenpress
yenpress.tumblr.com
instagram.com/yenpress

First Yen Press Edition: June 2019

Yen Press is an imprint of Yen Press, LLC.
The Yen Press name and logo are trademarks of
Yen Press, LLC.

The publisher is not responsible for websites (or their content) that are not owned by the publisher.

Library of Congress Control Number: 2017954140

ISBNs: 978-0-316-44753-9 (paperback)
       978-0-316-44754-6 (ebook)

10 9 8 7 6 5 4 3 2 1

WOR

Printed in the United States of America